In Partial Disgrace

OTHER WORKS BY CHARLES NEWMAN

New Axis

The Promisekeeper

A Child's History of America

There Must Be More to Love Than Death

White Jazz

The Post-Modern Aura

In Partial Disgrace

Charles Newman

Introduction by Joshua Cohen
Edited by Ben Ryder Howe

DALKEY ARCHIVE PRESS
CHAMPAIGN / LONDON / DUBLIN

Library of Congress Cataloging-in-Publication Data

Newman, Charles, 1938-2006.

In partial disgrace / Charles Newman. -- 1st ed.

p. cm.

ISBN 978-1-56478-816-0 (pbk. : acid-free paper)

ISBN 978-1-56478-803-0 (cloth : acid-free paper)

1. Europe, Central--Fiction. I. Title.

PS3564.E915I5 2012

813'.54--dc23

2012033703

Partially funded by a grant from the Illinois Arts Council, a state agency.

www.dalkeyarchive.com

Cover: concept and design by Lawrence Levy, illustration by August Lipp
Map of Cannonia, p. 28, by Edit Nagy

Printed on permanent/durable acid-free paper and bound in the United States of America

A Partial Introduction to Charles Newman's
In Partial Disgrace,
Which Is Itself a Partial
Introduction, to . . .

Partialness

In Partial Disgrace, indeed, though the emphasis should be on that intermediary word—that unstable, pieceworkish, Latinate by one definition and French by another, *partial.* This is an introduction to a book that is itself an introduction. Charles Hamilton Newman—among the best, and best-neglected, of American authors—had intended to write a cycle of three volumes, each volume containing three books, for a total of nine. But when he died, in 2006 at the age of sixty-eight, all that had been completed was an overture—or just the blueprints for a theater, the scaffold for a proscenium.

Arcadia

Charles Newman was born in 1938 in St. Louis, Missouri, city of the Mississippi, of Harold Brodkey, William S. Burroughs, T. S. Eliot—three eminences who'd left. Newman never had that privilege. His father made the decision for him, moving the family—which stretched back two centuries in St. Louis, to when the town was just "a little village of French and Spanish inhabitants"—to a suburban housing tract north of Chicago, adjacent to a horseradish bottling plant. The prairie, the imagination, lay just beyond. A talented athlete, Newman led North Shore Country Day School to championships in football, basketball, baseball. Yale followed, where he won a prize for the most outstanding senior thesis in American history. He befriended Leslie Epstein, novelist, and Porter Goss, future director of the CIA under Bush II (more on "intelligence" later). Study at Balliol College, Oxford, led to a stint as assistant to Congressman Sidney R. Yates (D, Ninth District, Chicago), which lasted until Newman was drafted into the Air Force Reserve, which he served as paramedic. Korea was avoided.

In 1964, Newman returned to Chicago: "I have been forced by pecuniary circumstances to deal with other men's errors and nature's abortions, to become . . . *an educationist!*" He became a professor in the English department at Northwestern, where he turned the campus rag, *TriQuarterly*, into the foremost lit journal of the second half of the century—weighty words for weighty writers like Jorge Luis Borges, Gabriel García Márquez, Czesław Miłosz, E. M. Cioran, Frederic Jameson, Susan Sontag, Robert Coover, John Barth. *TriQuarterly* was the journal that notified the city— New York, publishing's capital—of the progress in the provinces. Academia would resurrect American letters, at least relicate in library stacks amid the slaughterhouses, the grain and missile silos. The counterculture usurping the culture, standards in decline, artistic degradation—the complaints of Newman's seminal essays, *A Child's History of America* (1973), and *The Post-Modern Aura* (1985), could also be used to rationalize his behavior: the dalliances with coeds, the boozing, the pills. With his job in jeopardy, his journal too, in 1975 Newman moved to Baltimore, where he directed the Johns Hopkins Writing Seminars.

This is where the account, or just Newman, gets hazy. He quit Hopkins, or was fired again, or quit before he'd be fired, or was fired before he could quit, went off to raise hunting dogs in the Shenandoah Valley (more on the dogs too, in a bit). The failure of that venture, or a feud with a neighbor that left him arrested, or wounded in a shovel attack, or both—either that or a brief bout of sobriety, or its attendant hypochondria that required better health insurance—led him back, by a commodius rictus of recirculation, to St. Louis, city of Brodkey (a stylistic peer), Burroughs (with whom he shared a tolerance for self-abuse), Eliot (whose adoption of a foreign identity prefigured Newman's own interest in Hungary—about which, again, stay tuned). After Chicago this was his second homecoming, third chance. Fortune smiled gaptoothed. Newman was already the author of *New Axis* (1966, a novel following three generations of a Midwestern family from Depression striving, through middle-class success, to a striven-for, successful-because-failed, Aquarian rebellion), *The Promisekeeper: A Tephramancy* (1971, a novel that risks, as its subtitle suggests, a divination of the ashes of the American Dream, forecasting a country unable to communicate except in reference, satire, parody), and *There Must Be More to Love Than Death* (1976, a collection of three texts, of a series of twelve that would remain unfinished, each in a different vein: a junkie veteran suffers naturalism, an operatic baritone frets over farce, a photographic memory prodigy is worried by the very concept of nonfiction). *White Jazz*—Newman's best completed novel, about a computer programmer surfeited, even satisfied, by his function as a mere line of code in the program of this country—had just been published. The year was 1985. Reagan had just been whistled for an encore.

For this act—Newman's last—let's green the stage, let loose a rolling hilly verdancy to billow as backdrop, caster the trees into position, dolly hedges to their marks, creating a clearing, a nymph's grove of sorts, surrounding a ruin—a folly—rising from the floor's trapdoor. Students wandered into this grove from all over the globe, declothed, caressed one another, congressed, quaffed skins of goatgrape, toked a strange lotosine weed ("Let us swear an oath, and keep it with an equal mind, / In the hollow Lotos-land to live and lie reclined / On the hills like Gods together, careless of mankind."—Tennyson). The demigods who organized, or disorganized, these pagan proceedings were called by the names William H. Gass, Stanley Elkin, Howard Nemerov. This secret Arcadia, the closest that late twentieth-century American letters would ever come to a Classical Arcady, hid under the ineffable epithet Washington University. But Eden is not to be returned to. Paradise, especially if one's birthplace, can never be regained. (At Newman's memorial service, Gass suspected the deceased "would find faults in paradise, because they sprayed their trees.")

It wasn't just that Newman loathed Wash U, or the suburbanization that had taken hold outside the ivy tower—rather, Newman hated utopias. But it takes a genius to hate a utopia, and whenever Newman wasn't bitching, he was blurbing his own genius. Or resuming his cryptodipso routine, insulting fellow teachers and deans, setting himself on fire in class (an accident? or to prove what point?). Newman broke friendships, collapsed marriages, wore himself out in the constant commute between classes and his writing studio/ studio apartment in cramped, indispensable-to-his-vanity-but-insulting-of-his-vanity Manhattan, and in the perpetual writing of this book, the perpetual rewriting of the books that would become this book as if it would sober him finally, which it didn't—writing never does.

The dramatization—the self-dramatization—of Newman's final period, his finale, should be accompanied by flute and harp, out of synch, out of tune in a disconcerting mode. An exit dance might be hazarded, but the steps should stagger, the bows should be falls—passing out. Let's clear the set—reel in the prop foliage, crank to the rafters those deae ex machinis of ever-fresher, ever-younger lovers, those student saving graces or muses with the wings of angels but demonic T&A. All that should be left on stage is that ruin, that folly—the size of a respectable state university, the size of a respectable state, but abandoned in midbloom—this masterpiece in pieces, this partial.

Ruritania

For Newman—the peripatetic *New Man*—the imagined place was always a proxy, or preparatory study, for a reimagination of the self. The move to Chicago turned his family from prosperously rooted burghers to panting arrivistes; his sojourn in Virginia turned a genuine wildman into a playacting gentleman-farmer (it was Giovanni da Verrazzano who first referred to Virginia as "Arcadia"), and it was his first trip to Hungary, in 1968, that turned an intellectual citizen of an unintellectual republic into an adventurer, or apprentice dissident—a champion of everyone's free speech because a champion of his own.

Hungary, the Midwest of the Continent: The Magyar state, Pannonia to Antiquity and Cannonia to Newman, is located at the very middle of *Mitteleuropa*, a crossroads, an east/west divan, immemorially margined— made marginal—by Teutons and Slavs. The second crownland of the Austro-Hungarian Empire, it was carved into thirds and landlocked—losing its only port, called Fiume by the Hungarians, Rijeka by Yugoslavia—after World War I. The brief communist coup of 1919 gave way, in 1920, to a parliamentary government subservient to a sham regent whose most notable previous credential was his inept admiralty in Austro-Hungary's sinking joke of a navy. Miklós Horthy allied his nation with Hitler, who returned the compliment by invading in 1944. Nearly half a million Hungarians perished in World War II—nearly a million if Jews can be counted, or counted themselves, Hungarian. Soviet occupation, backing the puppet regime of Mátyás Rákosi, was challenged in 1956 by the election of Imre Nagy—a marionette who snipped his own strings. A multiparty system was, temporarily, restored; Hungary withdrew, for a breath, from the Warsaw Pact; revolution simmered in the streets. Moscow responded with tanks. 20,000 people died in the fighting. After crushing the resistance, the Kremlin installed János Kádár in a dictatorship that lasted until 1989, to the fall of the original "Wall"—not the concrete slabs of Berlin, toppled in the fall of that year, but the dismantling of the barbedwire fence along the Hungarian/Austrian border, earlier, in spring.

The country Newman arrived in had just dragged itself out from under the treads, dusted off, and limped back to the factories. 1968 was the year of Kádár's New Economic Mechanism, an appeasement measure introducing certain free market principles—giving nationalized businesses a modicum of control over what products they produced, in what quantities, even over what prices the products would be sold at—to an economy whose central planning was increasingly outsourced to Budapest. This was the period of "Goulash Communism;" Hungary was "the happiest barrack in the Socialist camp" (whether these descriptions originated in Hungary or Moscow, or even in the West, and whether they were intended seriously or in jest, are still matters of musty debate). Hungarians could choose to buy either domestic crap, or foreign pap, in a selection unprecedented since the Kaisers; they could even travel widely—from Moscow to Yalta, Kamchatka to Havana. The Hungarian press was less strict than that of any other Soviet satellite. All of which would account for how Newman got into the country. None of which would account for what he was doing there.

If visiting communist Hungary was already crazy, editing a journal out of Budapest might've been—sane. Newman's *New Hungarian Quarterly* published samizdat literature but not in samizdat—in public. It disseminated stories, poems, and essays that anyplace else, anytime else, would've been banned. Though Newman never became fluent in Hungarian, he did become expert at editing, for free, translations, also offered for free, more accurate and artistic than anything being produced at the time by the Western capitalist publishers and the university faculties that slaved for them—institutions that though they lacked contacts with their Hungarian counterparts, anyway followed the example of their Hungarian counterparts and chose the works they rendered based as much on politics as on aesthetics (not to mention the criteria of "marketability"—an American term translating to "censorship"). How Newman got away with it all, I don't know. Neither do I know how he managed to make repeated trips to Hungary throughout the 1970s and '80s, nor how he managed to smuggle into the States, though on separate occasions, a brace of the dogs he'd breed—Uplanders, also called Wirecoat Vizslas—and two of his three Hungarian wives (Newman met his third Hungarian wife in the States; another wife was Jewish; yet another longtime companion, Greek).

I can only wink, drop the name "Porter Goss," and refer to a scrap of paper stuck in a crack of Newman's *Nachlass*: "An intelligence officer's most obsessive thought, *and I ought to know*, is whether his time behind the lines, in deep cover, is going to be counted toward his annuity" (italics mine). If Newman wasn't in the CIA, he was certainly interrogated by it. If Newman wasn't an agent, or even an agent-manqué, he would certainly have enjoyed pretending to be one, or the other, or both—shadowing in and out of character for his Hungarian hosts, and for the KGB stooges who tailed them (after 1956, Hungary was the only communist country not to have its own secret police).

Ultimately it doesn't matter whether Newman's fascination with Hungary originated on-assignment, or merely as an inexplicable *esprit de parti*. The truth is that Newman always pursued estrangements and alienations, not just as opportunities to reinvent, but also as psychological defenses—as refuges, as amnesties.

In the Eastern Bloc, literature could define one's life, civically. A Hungarian's criticism of the regime could be a oneway ticket if not to gulag anymore, then at least to penury and oblivion, whereas a famous, and famously self-aware, American abroad had to be on guard against incarceration as much as against romance, the tendency of even petty bribery to become just another thrill. Newman was almost cripplingly sensitive to the perverse honesties, or ethics, of the East, where the bestseller lists were openly rigged, and the large advances of Manhattan were not convertible to moral currency.

It makes sense, then, that when Newman decided to fictionalize Hungary, the present was exchanged for the past. It wasn't just the Danube that had burst its banks, it was history too—a history that culminated both in the tortured tergiversations of György Lukács and the author's own touristy traumas. Newman's passport redeemed him, even while it mortified. He didn't like his face or name, except when they were praised, and he didn't like his nationality, except when it could be condemned in prose (that was praised). Whenever he lost faith in the struggle to keep life and literature separate—much as Buda and Pest are separated by Danube—he clung to the belief that *life was literature*, in the same way that Budapest is built atop the rubble of Aquincum, and Magyar identity merely the false construct of a racial purity atop the tribal burial mounds of Celts, Mongols, Turks.

It followed that Hungarian literature wasn't just the literature Newman helped to translate from the Hungarian; it was also all literature, in every language—about Austro-Hungary, Ottoman Hungary, Antiquity's Hungary, caravanseraing chronologically back to the clunky coining of the Hunnic runes. Newman's tradition would provide sanctuary for the liturgies of seceded churches, the decrees of rival courts, as much as for the slick escapism of interwar pulp fiction—written in a fantastic dialect called Ruritanian: the world's only vernacular intended more for the page than for the tongue, the jargon preferred by creaky Empires for diplomatic correspondence with breakaway Nation States, and the unofficial code of international dreamers.

Ruritania is a fictional kingdom eternally located at the infinite center—not necessarily of geographic Europe, but of European psychogeography—though British author Anthony Hope (a pseudonym of Sir Anthony Hope Hawkins, 1863–1933), initially founded it somewhere, or nowhere, between Saxony and Bohemia, in his trilogy of novels—*The Prisoner of Zenda*, *The Heart of Princess Osra*, and *Rupert of Hentzau*—characterizing it as a German-speaking, Roman Catholic absolute monarchy. Despite it being perpetually in the midst of dissolution, that dissolution would mean only, paradoxically, more ground. Even as class, ethnic, and religious tensions threatened conflict, territory was taken at every compass point. War could not destroy it, peace could not bore it—every dark passage, be it to throneroom or dungeon, met intrigue along the way. Ruritania's annexations only acquired for it more names, as if noble honorifics: Vladimir Nabokov's *Pale Fire* expanded it northeast toward Russia and called it Zembla; George Barr McCutcheon's *Graustark* hexalogy expanded it southeast to the Carpathians; in Edgar Rice Burroughs's *The Mad King*, it's located east toward the Baltics, as Lutha; in

John Buchan's *The House of the Four Winds*, it's a Scandinavian/Italian/Balkan mélange called Evallonia; Dashiell Hammett, in one of only two stories he ever set outside the States, had his nameless detective, the Continental Op, meddle in the royal succession of Muravia; Frances Hodgson Burnett further clarified the cardinalities by positioning her Samavia "north of Beltrazo and east of Jiardasia," names that should be familiar to every good mercenary as demarcating the borders of "Carnolitz." Newman called his Ruritania "Cannonia"—a toponym echoing the martial ring of "cannon," with the authority of "canon."

Cannonia

Still, to map Cannonia 1:1 onto Pannonian Hungary might be to misunderstand how Newman regarded place: to him, books could be just as physical as cities. The trashed palace of pages he left behind recalls the setting of another unfinished project: Kakanien, the wry appellation of Austro-Hungary in Robert Musil's *The Man Without Qualities*. Though *Kaka* is German juvie slang for "shit," derived from the Greek prefix meaning "shitty"—if "calligraphy" is beautiful, "cacography" is ugly—Kakanien is also a pun on *K und K*, the Empire's abbreviation for itself: *kaiserlich und königlich*, "Imperial and Royal," indicating Austro-Hungary's dual, dueling, crowns. Musil's remains the prototypical modernist confusion—a book so coterminous with life that it could end only outside its covers, with the death of its author, or The Death of the Author (Musil was stopped by a stroke at age sixty-one, having completed only two of the projected three volumes).

Newman had always known his only option was what he called "postmodernism"—a knowledge that assuaged his yearning for "modernism," which was itself a balm for earlier aches. Though he'd always idealized the man in full, he was fated, was aware he was fated, to montage, sumlessness, pastiche. Ruritania will forever be trapped in the clockwork gears of the turn-of-the-century, but by the time another century was about to turn, the drive to synecdochize all of Europe in Vienna, or in a Swiss sanatorium (as in Thomas Mann's *The Magic Mountain*), or even in the sci-fi province of Castalia (in Herman Hesse's *The Glass Bead Game*), had forsaken history for dystopia. If utopia was "no-place," dystopia—cacotopia—was Anglo-America: *Brave*

New World, 1984, Fahrenheit 451, Lord of the Flies, A Clockwork Orange. Kurt Vonnegut, Philip K. Dick, J. G. Ballard. By the 1980s—when Newman was first surveying Cannonia—the genre goons were at publishing's gates, and they proceeded to divide and conquer: "literary novelists" would take care of the *totum pro parte*—"the whole for the parts"—in an effort to maintain the ideal of an artwork that could still mirror all of reality; while the pop hacks who hadn't yet traded the page for TV and film would concern themselves with the *pars pro toto*—"the parts for the whole"—in an attempt to acknowledge that reality had sprawled beyond any consensus, exceeding the capabilities of any single novelist, and the capacities of any single reader. (Throughout the Cold War, espionage and thriller novelists made effective use of this limitation: in presenting Western spycraft as important to, though inconsistent with, Western democracy, they revealed even their right to publish fiction as the privilege of a fiction—a delusion.)

Newman's ambition was to write this change itself. He would show, and tell, the evolution of literature, would narrate the revolutions of the wheel. His cycle would begin with a volume of three books in Musil/Mann/Hesse mode—landmarks, monuments, all set in Cannonia, from the *fin de siècle* to 1924—follow with three books surrendering Cannonia's metonymy to Russian hegemony, through 1938 (comprising a second volume Newman claimed to have begun, since lost), and conclude with three books triangulating with *realpolitik*—with Cannonia, Russia, and America negotiating between 1939 and 1989 (comprising a third volume Newman never began but described in correspondence—though he never mentioned whether the novel's '89 would've marked the end of communism).

In Partial Disgrace is the one-volume version of the first volume—the one-book version of the first three books that Newman worked on for the last three decades of his life. Its initial hero was, and still is, Felix Aufidius Pzalmanazar, "Hauptzuchtwart Supreme," which is to say a dogbreeder, trainer, and vet nonpareil, whose clients include Freud—himself an analysand in the first volume—and Pavlov—the presumed bellwether of the second. His son, Coriolan Iulus Pzalmanazar, "Ambassador Without Portfolio for Cannonia, and inadvertently the last casualty of the last war of the twentieth century, and the first great writer of the twenty-first," would become a "triple-agent"—Cannonian, Russian, American. Their stories, along with tales of the Professor (Freud), and the Academician (Pavlov), were all to be told as the memoirs of Iulus, "translated, with alterations, additions, and occasional corrections by Frank Rufus Hewitt, Adjutant General, U.S. Army (Ret.)," who remains a presence in this composite—indeed, he's the parachutist who lands on the very first page, in 1945—and who was to emerge as the hero of the final volume, where he'd betray Iulus, or be betrayed by him, or—it's anyone's guess, anyone's but Newman's. The overarching theme of the cycle was to be the rebalancing of power, the shift from military brinksmanship to informational détente: if every side has the same intel, and so much of the same, it's only the purpose, or the intention of disclosure, that matters, that means. Determining what one nation knows about another is to write their histories in advance—"prolepsis"—just as determining what readers should know about a book before they read it might be to split the difference between Freudian displacement and Pavlovian conditioning.

Cannonia is a breeding ground, literally—not just for ideologies—for canines. The eugenic pursuit of the perfection of diverse breeds of *Canis lupus familiaris* takes on a far more sinister, defamiliarizing set of associations when applied to *Homo sapiens*. The Nazis compelled the Reich's blondes and blues to mate their ways to an Aryan super-race, whereas the Soviets preferred to inculcate exemplary comradeship through "art"—a literature that would mold its own public, indistinguishable from its characters. Newman's consideration of species—of speciation—is of a piece with his investigation into the properties of metaphor: the question of whether it's irresponsible to try and perfect a breed is also the question of whether it's irresponsible to try and perfect a novel—what happens to breeds that don't please their masters? are misbehaving novels—or novelists—to meet the same fate as untrainable mutts? Nature v. nurture is the case, which Newman insists is as much a referendum on the master as on the mastered: is culture innate or cultivated? or both? Finally, if a new breed can only be the combination of old breeds, just as a new literature must come from a miscegenation of the old—what are we to make of ourselves? of humans? Are we just helixed bundles of parental genes, raised, hopefully, to maximize our strengths and minimize our weaknesses? or could we find a way back to understanding ourselves as we did in Genesis—before mind-body dichotomies, before mind-body-soul trichotomies—as unities, perfect merely by dint of our existence?

To Newman, Freud's psychology compartmentalizes our being—as if life were just a train of alternating appetites and suppressions—whereas Pavlov's physiology coheres us as singularities, but as beasts. Newman alternately accepts and rejects these two conceptions, even while slyly offering a third: men are no better than dogs, and no better than locomotive engines—though they can become the worst of both, especially in the company of women. (Felix's "three golden rules": "1. Ride women high. 2. Never take the first parachute offered. 3. Never go out, even to church, without a passport, 1500 florins, and a knife." Elsewhere he gives his son another trinity of "advice": "1. Neither marry nor wander, you are not strong enough for either. 2. Do not believe any confession, voluntary or otherwise. And most importantly, 3. *Maxime constat ut suus canes cuique optimus.*"—which Newman glosses as "Everyone has a cleverer dog than their neighbor.")

In Partial Disgrace hunts its elusive prey through landscapes that resemble the Great Plains—if they'd been treated to their own Treaty of Trianon—through lessons in obedience theory ("'The animal, like society, must be taken into liberality without quite knowing it,'" Felix avers), ethnologies of the nomadic Astingi, Cannonia's sole surviving indigenous tribe ("They thought the Cossacks wimps, the gypsies too sedentary, the Jews passive-aggressive, the gentry unmannered, the peasants too rich by half, the aristocracy too democratic, and the Bolsheviks and Nazis too pluralistic. When cornered, they would put their women and children in the front ranks, and fire machine guns through their wives' petticoats."), lectures on art, music, theater, dance, and entr'acte harangues ("Cannonia and America had a special and preferential historical relationship, [Iulus] insisted, beyond their shared distaste for oracles and pundits, as the only two nations in History of whom it could be truly said that all their wounds were self-inflicted. And what could Cannonia offer America? The wincing knowledge that there are historical periods in which you have to live without hope.").

"History" appearing thrice in one sentence—and once even capitalized, Germanically? but what of that other word, "disgrace"? Grace is for the religious, disgrace is for the damned. Humans once hunted for sustenance, now they hunt for sport. To go through the motions of what once ensured survival, now purely for entertainment, is ignominious, but vital—the ignominy is vital. Even if the rituals have become as hollow as rotted logs, or as unpredictable in their ultimate attainments as the rivers Mze—Newman's

Danubes, whose currents switch from east to west to east—the very fact that we remember any ritual at all is enough to remind us too of a more essential way of being. Our various historical, racial, and ethnic selves are cast in a masquerade, which makes a game of integration. Yesterday's work is play today, as contemporary life converts all needing to wanting. That's why when the hound points and we squeeze the trigger, when we slit the knife across the quarry's throat, we experience disgrace—a fallen estate, an embodiment of Felix's Semper Vero, his ancestral holdings lost to laziness and debt. Agriculture has become a hobby for us millennials. Just like reading has, and writing. But "Once upon a time," everything was sacred. The traditions haven't changed—only our justifications of them have—and so though when we're faced with tradition we're disgraced, our disgrace is only partial. The holiness remains.

Partiality

But, again, *to be partial* is to be polysemous, and another meaning is "to favor," "to incline"—as a valley becomes a hill becomes a mountain, where a settlement is raised, around an empty temple. Newman's disgrace brings solace, as the spring brings not flowers but storms, which bless us with power outages, salutary loneliness, full wells. Newman's disgrace is secular grace. "Not even a curtain of iron can separate Israel from its Heavenly Father," Rabbi Joshua ben Levi said in third century Palestine. "An iron curtain has descended across the Continent," Winston Churchill said in 1946 at a college in Missouri. The *eiserner Vorhang*—the iron curtain, or firewall, an innovation of Austro-Hungary—is a sheet of civic armor, able to be dropped from a theater's proscenium to prevent a conflagration that starts onstage from spreading to the audience. Newman lifts this barrier—and invites his readers to ascend and bask in the flames.

JOSHUA COHEN
New York, 2012

Editor's Note

"Is it a book then . . . that you're working on?"

"I wouldn't call it a book, really." Felix replied evenly, his knuckles white on the balcony railing.

"But through all our talks, you've never once mentioned it!" the Professor, now truly hurt, blurted mournfully. "How can that be?" Then the question authors dread above all others:

"Pray, what's it about?"

Like his stand-in Felix, my uncle abhorred the Professor's question, and my mother warned me never to ask him. The first time was the summer of 1989, when Charlie rented a house near ours on Cape Cod. Charlie didn't quite fit on the Cape—he had no affinity for water ("the sea means stupidity"), nor a family to indulge at the mini-golf courses—and his sleek black Acura with its trunk jammed full of Deutsche Gramophone CDs stood parked all summer in the sandy driveway of his cottage like a rebuke to the entire peninsula. Afterward, though, we inferred that it had been a good summer for work. The book he was writing then, this book, was at that point only a little behind schedule. Charlie had averaged a new book every three years since his late twenties, and now, in his early fifties, at his peak, his career should have been moving along briskly. Only four years earlier, in 1985, he had produced a volume of essays, *The Post-Modern Aura*, which despite being called "Hegelian" for its "daunting" prose and "exquisitely complex argument," had been reviewed in over thirty publications and mentioned in mainstream magazines like *Time*. His previous novel, *White Jazz*, had been a bestseller. Every few months his byline appeared in some publication—an essay, a book review, even a profile of George Brett for *Sport*.

Don't ask what your uncle is writing about—but I was eighteen at the time and less intimidated than I should have been. One day, a few months after that summer on the Cape, while visiting Charlie in St. Louis, where he taught in the English department of Washington University, I waited until he went to campus and slipped in his office. Charlie's goal when he started each day was to come up with one or two, possibly three sentences he liked, and to get there he handwrote his initial drafts, then sent those pages to an assistant, who returned them typewritten on plain white sheets, which Charlie then cut into slivers, isolating individual sentences before reinserting them with Scotch tape in the handwritten notebooks or tacking them to a wall. Those tacked-up sentence slivers were before me now, along with dozens if not hundreds of pink and yellow note cards scrawled with phrases, lists, and snatches of dialogue. The book, in other words, was in front of my face, vertical and spread out. No drawers had to be opened, no papers shuffled. The office itself was surprisingly clean and easy to move around in, the only clutter being fifty or so briarwood pipes and an astonishing number of library books.

I stayed in the office until the Acura pulled in the driveway an hour or so later, by which time I still had no idea what the book was about. Charlie's heavily stylized shorthand (it's no accident that Ainoha, Felix's wife, wonders of the Professor, "how you could sleep with a man with such bad handwriting") was often indecipherable even to assistants who had worked with him for years, and as for the sentences that had been typed, they were typically fragments ("army of deserters," "mad for sanity") or mystically oblique pronouncements such as "History has a way of happening a little later than you think" or "In Russia you always have to buy the horse twice." Sometimes they contained no more than a single word. ("Deungulate.")

However, the question also has to be asked, even if I had found some synopsis for the unfinished book, would it have made a difference? Charlie's books resist summary—how, for example, would you distill the plot of *White Jazz*? ("Sandy, a young man who works for an information technology company, sleeps around"?) How would you describe *The Post-Modern Aura*—as a book about art, literature, history, or simply the human condition? Even sympathetic readers can find themselves struggling to say what Charlie's books are about. (Paul West, attempting to describe *The Promisekeeper* in a 1968 review for *The Times*, called it "not so much a story as an exhibition, not so much a prophecy stunt as a stunted process, not so much a black comedy as a kaleidoscopic psychodrama.")

Over the next several years Charlie continued to work on his mysterious book in St. Louis and New York (where he lived when he wasn't teaching), as well as various parts of Europe, Russia, and the US. He and my parents frequently traveled together: all of us sat with him in restaurants and walked through museums in places like Santa Fe, Chicago, and Kansas City and *did not ask him about the book.*

But then a surprising thing happened: Charlie began to talk about it. I can't quite remember when it became clear that he was not going to lunge across the table if we brought it up, but some part of him softened, something opened up, and if you didn't press him too much you could extract a few details—which of course weren't always that enlightening.

"It's the great *un*-American novel," he would say in a cheerful mood, or "it's a novel for people who hate novels, a novel pretending to be a memoir that's really a history"—or something like that. Sometimes he would go on at length, easefully sketching out major characters, including the most important character of all, Cannonia, the invented country in which the book was set. Sometimes he would simply say "it's indescribable—nothing like it has ever been written," and there'd be nothing to do except let the conversation move on.

The openness could have been reassuring, a sign that Charlie was on top of his book and didn't fear talking it away. The more he spoke, though, the more I worried, in part because the book he was describing sounded not just indescribable but unwriteable. First, there was its premise: Charlie said he was going to write the history of a place which did not exist but wherein virtually everything described—characters, events, locales—was real, drawn from actual sources. That alone explained why the book was taking so long: Charlie had gotten bogged down in research. (A grant proposal I later discovered listed the primary texts he was using as "obscure diaries, self-serving memoirs, justifiably forgotten novels, carping correspondence, partisan social and diplomatic histories, black folktales and bright feuilletons.") But it wasn't the only reason to be nervous; there was also Charlie's intention to somehow merge his fake-but-real history with a spy thriller, a cold war novel of suspense. Was such a book even possible? Wasn't a spy thriller supposed to be brisk and plotted, and history (even pseudo-history) ruminative and disjointed? How would you blend the two genres? And then there was Charlie's insistence that the book, despite its writerly ambitions, would somehow be "accessible and commercially viable," containing not one but "several" movies. This seemed least fathomable of all—the most uncompromising writer ever, compromising? Bowing to conventional taste? Altogether the project seemed impossible, even for Charlie, who once vowed to "write books that no one else could write" and who would have rather changed careers than give up the pursuit of new forms.

"You must push your head through the wall," Kafka says in an essay quoted at the end of *The Post-Modern Aura.* "It is not difficult to penetrate, for it is made of thin paper. But *what is difficult* is not to let yourself be deceived by the fact that there is already an extremely deceptive painting on the wall showing you pushing your head through it."

Maybe this time Charlie was pushing too hard.

* * *

About eight years later and a month or so after Charlie's death in 2006, I went back to his office—not the one in St. Louis but the one in New York, which was in a high-rise on West 61st Street called The Alfred. The space was as Charlie had left it before he died, and at the bottom of a closet, underneath an assortment of blankets, Italian suits, and hunting clothes, I found an old television still murmuring, its picture tube faintly aglow. It had been five months since Charlie was there, but I had the sense that the inflamed set had been attempting its manic, muffled communication even longer. The temperature inside the closet was at least one hundred degrees.

Unlike the office I had been in fifteen years earlier, this one was chaotic and even a bit squalid, cluttered with foldable picnic tables, overstuffed vinyl chairs, and still-running air purifiers clogged with De La Concha tobacco dust. The couches were stained and burned. Every level surface had been covered by manuscript pages, notebooks, disassembled newspapers, quackish-sounding financial newsletters, and advertisements for pills, potions, and vitamins. The entire Central European history and literature sections of the Washington University library seemed to be on hand, plus hundreds of books on espionage and psychoanalysis. I made a list of titles near Charlie's desk: "Freud and Cocaine," "Werewolf and Vampire in Romania," "Escape from the CIA," "A Lycanthropy Reader," "Mind Food and Smart Pills."

Back in the 1990s, when Charlie moved into the Alfred, the feature of his apartment he had been proudest of was a custom-built series of cubbyholes spanning one entire wall, which he would use to organize the Cannonia manuscript. Like his openness when discussing the book, the shelves had a reassuring aspect—after all, they were finite (you could see where they ended) and therefore so must be the book!

But the actual filing system I discovered after Charlie's death bespoke madness, the cubbyholes having been neglected or filled with items that had nothing to do with Cannonia. The actual manuscript was stored in dozens of sealed Federal Express boxes which had apparently been sent back and forth from New York to St. Louis and vice versa—draft after draft after draft after draft, so many that it was impossible to tell which one was the most recent. The endlessly revised and unrevised manuscripts piled up under the picnic tables and filled up closets, many of them unopened, possibly going back years. Also in the apartment were hundreds of sealed manila envelopes containing those cut-out, typed-up sentences—"Angry hope is what drives the world," "He had brains but not too many," "Women fight only to kill"— which it appeared Charlie had also been mailing, one tiny sliver per envelope, whether to an assistant or himself wasn't clear.

Charlie had several helpers at The Alfred—unofficially, the doormen, who knew he only left the building to go to the Greek diner two blocks away, and to call the diner's manager when he did to make sure he arrived. There was also a young woman he had hired to fix his virus-flooded Gateway and provide data entry—in the office I found her flyer with its number circled, the services it advertised including not only computer repair but martial arts instruction and guitar lessons. I met her a few times after Charlie's death and we talked about the book, which she claimed Charlie had finally finished. "I know because we wrote it together," she said. "He thought up the ideas for the scenes and I wrote them." But she never showed me the completed, final manuscript, and a few weeks after we met she stopped returning calls.

* * *

Here is the story of Charlie's book, I think. In the 1980s Charlie wrote a novel, the story of Felix, the bankrupt "breaker of crazy dogs and vicious horses," and the Professor, a certain Viennese psychoanalyst who brings Felix neurotic animals and theories of the mind. This modestly-sized, thoroughly old-fashioned book "split the middle," to use one of Charlie's favorite phrases, between fantasy and autobiography—Charlie, of course, being neither a Central European aristocrat living on an abandoned royal hunting preserve, nor an acquaintance of Freud. He was, however, a one-time breeder of dogs who in his forties owned an expansive farm and kennel in one of the most isolated parts of Appalachia (near Hungry Mother State Park in Virginia), where, like Felix, he imported trees and animals from all over the world and satisfied his desire to live in isolation from other intellectuals. Losing the farm, as he did in the mid-1980s (to inflation, as he described it—inflation also being the scourge of several of Charlie's books, it is worth noting), was surely the novel's impetus.

"I wanted to write a long novel about the farm," he once told an interviewer, "but the farm was so hurtful to me in many ways, not only economically but in terms of the loss of beloved animals," as well as what he called a "nineteenth-century" existence. So he wrote a short novel instead, one that was a throwback as much as the farm. In many ways it is a response— positive and hopeful, for all the unhappiness it apparently came out of—to the wrenching blankness of *White Jazz* and *The Post-Modern Aura*, works that depict spiritual suffering in an age of multiple, overlapping determinisms. For if nothing else, Felix lives in a world where his own agency matters, and where meaningful connections (with his wife, his animals, the Professor, and perhaps above all the land he lives on) are possible.

Charlie could have published the story of Felix and the Professor in the early '90s, roughly maintaining his schedule of a book every few years. But one of Charlie's idiosyncrasies as a writer is that he would often write something, then put it aside, and eventually find an unexpected way to combine it with other material he was working on. In the case of the book inspired by the farm, he decided to hold off in favor of incorporating it within a massively enlarged work to be harvested from the book's fantastical setting—Cannonia. Now instead of one book there would be roughly *nine*, divided into three volumes, the first being *In Partial Disgrace*, which would contain the story of Felix and the Professor, though pushed all the way to the end. The second, "Learnt Hearts," would take place in Russia a decade or so later and center on Felix's relationship not with Freud but Pavlov. And the third, "Lost Victories," would move to postwar America.

Having thus reenvisioned his tidy coastal steamer as a three-decker battleship, Charlie set out to write an introduction of suitable vastness, providing centuries of background and introducing characters who would not reappear for thousands of pages. The nature of the project all but required him to take this approach, if he was to create the world necessary to sustain an epic. The story itself could wait. Characters could get away with announcing themselves in the grandest possible manner, then vanish. Charlie's passion for history and obscure primary sources could be indulged. It was all part of the excitement, the buildup, the setting of an appropriate tone.

Ten years later, Charlie was still writing the overture to his symphony, as Joshua Cohen notes. And not surprisingly, the time it was taking, plus the future amount of work he could surely see coming, not to mention the embarrassment of attempting such a behemoth, weighed on him as much as the unpayable generations of debt from Semper Vero weigh on Felix. Physically he was a wreck. A lifelong alcoholic who frequently stunned even the people who knew him best with his capacity for self-destruction and recovery, Charlie had curtailed his drinking in the 1980s through Alcoholics Anonymous and white-knuckle effort, then lost control in the '90s, undoubtedly in part due to the stress of Cannonia. Toward the end of the decade his body began to break down, and he spent much of the following years in the hospital, where doctors at first thought he might have suffered a stroke or the onset of Parkinson's. Intermittently unable to speak or walk, he put aside the trilogy for long stretches, struggled with depression, and when the wherewithal to write eventually returned, started a pair of new books instead (a history of American education and a long essay on terrorism.) He also became estranged from family, saw his marriage end, and reduced his teaching to the point where he was scarcely seen on campus.

During these years Charlie seemed to answer conflictingly every time he was asked if the book was done. In 1998, it was three-quarters finished, in 2005, only two-thirds, while in 2002 it was complete. His assistant in St. Louis believed he might never stop rearranging the table of contents and inserting new pages, and in fact he never did.

The first time I read a draft of *In Partial Disgrace*, Charlie was still alive, and reading it all but put me into despair. Page after page after page, nothing but setting or background. Cannonia was certainly a fascinating place, but it appeared to be one in which things only happen*ed*, usually in the distant past—there was virtually no present, no *now*. I was confused also because so much of the novel Charlie had talked about for so long seemed to be missing. Where was Freud? Where was Pavlov? Where were the battle scenes, and where, other than Rufus, who vanished from the story almost as soon as he appeared, were the spooks? After four hundred pages I put it down—obviously I held only a fragment of the overall work to come, and there was nothing to do but wait.

Then after Charlie died I found the story of Felix and the Professor, a self-contained, fully formed novel that was alive in its language, arresting in its ideas, and humanly engaging in its depiction of a friendship between two painfully isolated men. Like the television at the bottom of the closet, it pulsed with warmth, and the task became how to disentomb it. Mostly it was a question of moving material around rather than discarding it. *In Partial Disgrace* does have some elements of a conventional novel—the story of Felix and the Professor is an actual story, told in a relatively straightforward way—but Charlie hadn't gotten into it quick enough, as his own notes on a late draft seemed to suggest. Felix did not even appear until a third of the way into the book, and the Professor not until a hundred pages further. So we took some of the Psalmanazar family back story—a considerable chunk of the book, which Charlie had stacked up front, posing a blockade to even the most patient reader—and found points later on where it could be inserted naturally.

Next was sorting out the book's multiple narratives. *In Partial Disgrace* begins in the voice of Rufus, then shifts, at times disorientingly, between the accounts of Iulus, Felix, and the Professor. Rufus is clearly meant to return at some point but never does; Iulus, meanwhile, has a habit of talking about events in the future that never happen. Given Charlie's fervent desire that the book be accessible, a certain amount of streamlining seemed warranted, as long as it preserved the essential thrust of each chapter and section. Like all of Charlie's work, *In Partial Disgrace* shows a carefully balanced interplay of ideas, and as much as possible I wanted to preserve that balance, while giving it its fullest expression.

A note about sourcing: late in the editing of this book it was discovered that a small number of passages were borrowed from primary sources without attribution, which is not surprising given that the project was to write the history of an imaginary place based on real places and events. Whether Charlie intended to eventually provide credit is impossible to say—that is, unless some answer turns up in his papers, which hasn't happened yet. However, the papers are vast and dense, and there may be more to come from them, including further adventures in Cannonia.

The publication of this book was helped by many people, including: Jeremy M. Davies, John O'Brien, Marie Lay, Paul Winner, Lawrence Levy, Norma Hurlburt, Sharon Griffin, and James, Nicolas, and June Howe.

BEN RYDER HOWE
Staten Island, 2012

IN PARTIAL DISGRACE

The Secret Memoirs of the Triple Agent Known as Iulus:
A Report to History

Translated, with alterations, additions, and occasional corrections by
Frank Rufus Hewitt
Adjutant General, U.S. Army (Ret.)

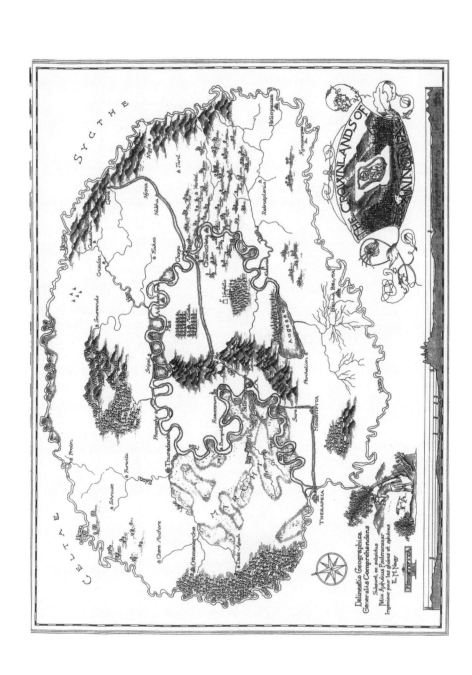

IN THIS BOOK YOU WILL FIND

ONLY REAL PEOPLE AND REAL PLACES,

BUT NO REAL NAMES

LIST OF PRINCIPAL PERSONALITIES

FRANK RUFUS HEWITT, Adjutant General; U.S. Army, (Ret.) Historian, Counter Intelligence; former operative, and sometime educationist.

CORIOLAN IULUS PZALMANAZAR, Ambassador Without Portfolio for Cannonia, and inadvertently, the last casualty of the last war of the twentieth century, and the first great writer of the twenty-first.

FELIX AUFIDIUS PZALMANAZAR, Hauptzuchtwart Supreme, thinking man's dandy, historian of the Astingi.

AINÖHA AEGLE APAMEA, Fairest of the Naiad line, Goddess of Fogs, Muse of the Living, Mistress of the Dead.

PRIAM ASCLEPIUS APAMEA, founder of Semper Vero.

ÖSCAR ÖLIVIER ÖZGUR, citizen soldier, loyal retainer, and exemplary gardener.

COUNT MORITZ ACHILLES ZICH, Foreign Minister of Cannonia, patron of the arts, the greatest one-armed pianist of all time, and the most intense admirer of the female sex in Europe.

Ophar Osme Catspaw, artist-in-residence at Semper Vero.

Seth Sylvius Gubik, swineherd, prodigy, and future Commisar for Cults and Education.

Psylander Sychaeus Pür, the village doctor.

The Professor (Ordinarius), *Docent fur Nervenkrankheiten*, A.D. Universitat Therapeia.

Drusoc's Mistress, one of the Professor's love interests.

Zanäia, a princess of Cannonia.

Cannonia, our ineffable tragi-comic protagonist, superior to tragedy.

Venit iam carminus aetas:

Magnus ab intego saeclorum nascitur ordo

Now is come the last age;

the great line of centuries

begins anew

Virgil, *Eclogues*

IN DARKEST CANNONIA
(Rufus)

I fell into that hermit kingdom carelessly, the chute shuddering above me as the shroudlines cut my hands. Below, the rivers rested in their courses, like wine from a broken urn; above, the stars ran backward in the upper air. Cinching up my harness, I drifted trembling toward the signal bonfire and my contact—a man apart, devoted to his mission, whose realm would become my destiny, as ours would be his fate. But buffeted by cruel crosswinds, blows from the powers of the air, I was dragged toward shores of black milk, skipping like a stone through the dark and empty land. Palms turned to the stars, I cursed my gods, mentally settled my affairs, and muttered an incoherent prayer: *Give me your hand.*

Grinding teeth and bloodied mouth a howl, I made out two horrific shapes hurtling toward me, two spotless dogs drawing near with unimaginable speed. One attacked the chute, deflating the billowing silk beneath his body; the other was in the air above me, all red mustachios, golden eyes, and ivory fangs. Was I to be saved from death by drowning only to be torn apart by devil dogs? We rolled and wallowed, my lapels in the brute's jaws, until we finally came to rest, his forepaws crossed upon my chest, rearquarters raised up, cropped tail awhirr. And then, wise in his negligence, he ringed my ears with openmouthed kisses.

Their master was soon beside us, a giant of a man in a shepherd's cloak, a conical fur hat concealing his face, and wielding a staff at least ten feet tall. I prepared myself for the blow. Then the cloak parted like a theater curtain, revealing only a wiry boy's boy very near my own age, standing upon stilts within the felt greatcloak and unremarkable save for his salient gray eyes, the left one half-closed.

The dog stepped off me to join his mate, who trotted up, a bit of parachute silk in his flues, his red beard full of cockleburrs. They seated themselves on either side of Iulus, barrel-chested, taciturn, with heart-shaped buttocks and slightly webbed feet. A handsome brace of superior spirits, radiating the same unpretentious dignity as their young master, even down to the half-closed eye; sly and unsentimental, neither obsequious nor shy.

Their coat, as their breeding, was like nothing I had ever seen in the animal world. A wiry texture, neither harsh nor loose, dark red bristles folded flat across a softer golden undercoat, changing its cast with every modulation of the moonlight. Their squared-off heads sported trim mustachios and goatees, brownish-pink lips and noses, and their immense ocher eyes were garnished with wispy eyebrows. When they shook their heads, the flapping of their ears sounded like distant machinegunfire, and it was only later that I noticed the detailed conchlike enfoldment of their inner ears, their only vulnerability, designed for the worship of natural sounds. And then, each with a single golden peeper trained on me, the dogs allowed their tongues to carelessly loll from the corner of their mouths, as if to say: "You see! One can be great; *and* amusing!"

We put away the chute and the shepherd's disguise in a hollow tree, buried my shortwave and silver dollars, and walked through the night without a word. It seemed our contact could not have been otherwise; we were of that age that requires no password.

I was in a zone of pure existence, which I would not experience again until the tremors of old age. Part of me was still pasted in the sky, part of me ambled along the unsafe earth, illuminated by faint and mocking stars. And part of me was observing all this from an unknown vantage, calm and imperturbable. Yes, give me your hand.

In Cannonia the dawn is striped. Between great sliding plates of slate and amber in the nervous sky a pallid sun appeared, diffuse and shapeless as a ball of Christmas socks. What I had upon first impact thought to be a carpet of fir needles proved to be a unique ground cover, impervious to frost or scorching. Neither heath nor grass nor legume, but firm and pliant kidney-shaped leaves with stemless white flowers, each large enough to hold a dewdrop, each footfall releasing a strong and refreshing aroma. If one stumbled, there was not the slightest sound, as if we were traversing a great expanse of silent pride which could absorb the rudest insult. Indeed, as I often saw that morning, the ground was so forgiving that bombs often did not explode on impact, but merely buried themselves up to their tailfins, scattered about the landscape like giant clumps of gray-green crocus.

The dogs cast out from us in great looping figure-eights, apparently indifferent to game and involved solely in their role as escorts. Once an immense Icarian crane went up between them in an hysterical imitation of flight, but they paid no more attention to it than if it were a gnat. It was hard to say if their originality or their manners were more impressive.

In an effort at conversation I inquired about their origins. My contact glanced through me, smiled slightly, then gave a transparent shrug, indicating that this was not the time or place for such a long and problematic discourse, and implying that the dogs were only a kind of theme in a larger drama over which we had already lost control. So I changed the subject to the smell of the earth, a bruised tang something between pineapple and spruce, an aroma more incensed than any I had experienced.

"Ah, yes," he spoke for the first time, wrinkling his nose. "Most of Europe smells of seaweed."

"A seacoast can come in handy," I bantered.

"Oceanus is a nullity," he sniffed. "If a sea should be required," he added more mysteriously than nicely, "it can always be brought onstage in the actor's eyes."

BEFORE THE THIRTY YEARS WAR
(Iulus)

I was born in Cannonia, province of Klavier, in 1924, the year that Lenin and Wilson died within ten days of each other. A member of the historical classes in the Central Empires, I came to life on my parents' estate at Semper Vero, where tributaries of the living Mze and the dead Mze join arms in an artificial lake. The United States had not yet declared war upon us.

Today the Eyelet of Cannonia exists on few maps of Europe, the country often being covered by the mandatory compass sign or coat-of-arms. A country which is effectively all border, it remains almost perfectly unknown, the smallest and densest hermit kingdom on earth, an unprincipled non-principality, a puppet state without strings, a protectorate with no friends. Always part of the unredeemed lands, that uninscribed space where Teuton and Slav have offered each other the hemlock since the beginning of time, Cannonia has been occupied by all the major and most of the minor European and Asian powers since a lost column of Philip of Macedon stumbled upon its southernmost village, turning it into a bloody abattoir and renaming it Kynosarges after its only surviving inhabitant, a fleeing dog. Philip's son, Alexander, would rue the day that he did not follow up on the only battle of the Eastern Empire fought in Europe, and was tortured into alcoholism by the suspicion that he had been raping the wrong continent all along. At Kynosarges he threw up a shrine to Dionysus and garlanded the ruins with ivy, which some ancients believed to be the entrance to Hades.

Our home, a cream-colored building in the shape of a thrown horseshoe, formerly a shooting box of the lesser nobility, was set on a plateau of red and silver heather and surrounded by an arboretum of rare evergreens. It had been in my family for one hundred years, during most of which it had been for sale. When my mother's father inherited the property in the 1840s from a distant cousin, he ignored the architecture, eyes only for the land, which then held an undistinguished park. On trains, boats, and carts he brought in rare evergreens from all over the world, as if what they needed in this vast mountain periphery, filled then with virgin forest, was more trees. With its blue-black spruce, lime-green tsuga, feathery apricot of zelkova, and an occasional minaret of golden cypress, Semper Vero held the richest assortment of evergreens east of the Rhine. Grandfather also introduced animals from every corner—ostrich and rhino, auroch and ibex, llama and camel—many of which thrived, albeit in progressively miniaturized state, alongside the indigenous stag and hare. The park he then declared a game sanctuary, to which the people of Cannonia enjoyed unlimited access, except the King, who was enjoined from picking so much as a violet.

From my room in the centermost of three squat turrets I overlooked the kennels, set out upon an island in the artificial lake, and beyond that the town of Silbürsmerze, surrounded by trapezoidal fields stiff with hard, red wheat. We lived sumptuously in the manner of the era, receiving all and sundry, feeding them to surfeit, giving away oats to each passing stranger, keeping musicians, buffoons, and singers, in addition to Catspaw, our resident *artiste* and intellectual gent, and of course our hounds.

My father was attorney and village notary. His family had come to Cannonia as part of the great Huguenot migration, carrying with them nothing but a bust of Erasmus. Arriving after the latest wars of liberation had reduced every town to dust, the only inhabitants being a few Greeks and Jews, they found themselves more powerful in fact than in the law, unable to claim primacy or privilege, but triumphing over the lesser aristocracy by better management, making do on lesser sums, before they themselves were replaced by Schwabian, then Jewish bailiffs.

Our life revolved around the kennels. My parents possessed a brace of animals called "Chetvorah" in the local dialect, dogs revered for centuries for their hunting ability. The yard of my childhood was littered with the limbs and stuffings of the training puppets Mother fashioned from patch quilts and sockheads, little limp punchinellos which the dogs carried about until they disintegrated. Father used a bamboo pole and fishline tied to a grouse feather to get them on point, while Mother accustomed them to the gun. She weaned each litter, taking them their pans of steaming chicken stew four times a day, and as soon as their noses were buried in the gruel, tails propellers, she would circle them while discharging a revolver behind her back. The bullets shattered the terrace wall, ricocheted among the limestone outbuildings, and scarred the ancient oaks. There were those who misinterpreted the lady of the house always with a pistol in her apron pocket, but it is inarguable that growing up is the incremental conquering of fear. Today, you could set off a cannon in my room and I would only nod.

I do not know when my parents abandoned their common bedroom and moved into separate suites in the towers at each end of the house, though it seemed to coincide roughly with my appearance. From their respective suites they could see each other through me in the central tower, and at night I could see Mother's candles glow in the smiling Orient, while to the West, Father's greenish lampglass shone, an omen of the electrified cities to come.

As for our recent troubles, the cause is clearer than usually imagined, for our grain market, which once fed all of Europe, had been flooded by cheap surpluses from America, dropping the price of wheat by half. The farmers of Klavierland, lacking cash, deferred Father's bills until all his litigatory energy was spent on fruitless efforts to collect his own fees in the clogged civil courts. Bad debt became the driving force of our reverse renaissance, a spiral in which everyone borrowed more to pay the interest on the debts on which they had already defaulted, credit pyramided upon credit, and the only way to survive was to live in perpetual bad faith. As his business dried up, Father would look out at the rotting fields beyond our property muttering "American cereal," an expletive arioso which came to explain every problem we encountered and still retains a certain resonance throughout the local cosmos.

Soon came the layoffs, first of the part-time help, then of the marginal servants who could least afford it, the first-fired who would resurface as our masters a generation later. The gardens, never prim, grew even more ragged, leaving it hard to tell a flower from a vegetable or fruit. The grass in the uncut meadows ran wild, reaching even the armpits of those on horseback, and in which the herds of grazing aurochs were barely visible. The best woodlots were sold off, copses along the roads cut down to deprive thieves of hiding places, and the horses, of course, reduced. A generation of geese and ducks passed on, their organs confitured and packed away in cellars. Even the tanneries, now well-launched into the miracles of modern chemistry, stopped buying our dog shit for their dyes.

Indeed, the last cash export from Semper Vero was the leeches found in abundance in the swamps, for apothecaries still thrived upon the margins of the Central Empires. The peasants would gather them in barrels and leave them in a shed, then Mother and I with a gaggle of peasant children would sort and bathe each wretched creature twice. Grading them by weight, we sewed them into linen bags forty centimeters long, to be picked up and taken to market by hawkers, usually the Fleischman brothers of later distillery fame. But the inexorable advance of medical science finally reached even our part of the world, and as bleeding went out of fashion, and plethoric, overfed gentlemen took to the waters, the value of our leeches necessarily became less, and our last source of hard currency flowed away.

Save a milk cow, the cattle were butchered, and most of the fields reverted to scrub, causing a new chain of wildlife to establish itself with startling rapidity. Hawks clotted the afternoon sky. Foxes became bold as leopards. Storks stalked adders. Pigs charged horses. Cranes and eagles strutted everywhere, and fat, sleek owls sat like avenging buddhas in the crotches of conifers. Meanwhile, in my father's breast a great happiness arose, even as his business continued to fail, for just as the French have the mystique of their fields and the Germans of their forest, my father's religion was *the edge*, that manmade, regenerative tangle of stumps, burn-offs, inexplicable wetnesses, and covers, which the animal kingdom in its colonial period prefers above all things, and which provides the final illusion to townspeople who need to believe they are descended from great hunters and perspicacious gatherers. It was the happiness of watching agriculture and all its bonds and shackles being erased.

Still, Semper Vero had to be rescued from its own mountain of debt, accumulated over centuries, and for a time my parents staved off the inevitable with tennis and French lessons for the gentry, whose heirlooms could still fetch cash. A walloping forehand and the languorous history of the future conditional allowed us a narrow margin for error in our decline. However, the day came when it was necessary to either sell off more fields or offer new services, and it was then that we began to take in others' animals and pets. After realizing that none of the locals would pay good money to ameliorate a bad dog, Father ultimately took out a large ad for obedience training in the Sunday *Therapeia Tagblatt*:

TIRED OF YOUR DOG?

We are alone, absolutely alone on this chance planet, and of all forms of life which surround us, not one, save the dog, has chosen to make an alliance with us. It is not necessary to settle for just a pet.

Specializing in nervous peeing, uncontrollable boors, and promiscuous barkers.

Characterological reconstruction for the hardheaded, highly strung, and stupidly dependent.

Serving the owner willing to admit his own errors.

You may reply in confidence.

Felix A. Psalmanazar, L.L.D.
Semper Vero
Muddy St. Hubertus
Cannonia Inferiore

SCHARF

(Iulus)

The only reply was from the Professor, who cabled immediately from Therapeia and made an appointment for the following week.

He arrived *en famille,* driving the coach heavy-handedly. In the boot of the closed black calèche, tied with a rope from his neck to the axle, sat a rude and mixed-up breed. They called him "Scharf."

My father ambled out to meet his first client, dressed in his smoking jacket, a freshly killed woodcock hanging on a thong from his belt, and stared up with his glacial blue eyes at the city boy and his sad-faced, black-frocked entourage. The Professor stared back, perhaps taken aback to see what appeared to be a calm English gentleman in the touchy heart of Europe.

Scharf had leapt from the boot of the carriage to greet Father, but the rope to the axle brought him up short. The Professor moved quickly to disentangle him, and then, like a giant, mottled frog in harness, the animal dragged his black-suited master to Father's patient hands. Felix quickly found the pressure points behind the strangely cut ears, and Scharf swooned as he massaged his bumpy skull. It was love at first sight—not of course, with Scharf, whose main problem was that he knew himself to be a pretext—but between the men, who now exchanged a considered handshake.

As the calèche emptied its contents, it became evident that the Professor was encosseted with a company of women: his daughter, with piercing black eyes, hair plaited in a manner suitable for a grandmother, though she was five or six at the most; his mother, who had similar eyes and a firm peasant jaw beneath an outrageous red velvet hat of the newest style, looking thirty years younger than her age and unembarrassed by her aura of total self-absorption; and finally his wife, a plain, pale, humorless woman who could have been thirty or sixty, clearly ill at ease in the great out-of-doors—a woman, he surmised, who either suffered from sleeping sickness or had been traumatized by giving life. The Professor's attitude toward them all

41

was at once devoted, exacting, and absent, and for Father too they quickly disappeared from his mind forever.

"Welcome, welcome to the land of the three wishes."

Mother had appeared on the veranda in all her golden glory, hair falling about her shoulders, a welcome tray of raspberry-colored spritzers in her hands. Entranced, the Professor dropped the rope and dreamily advanced up the curving stair, clearly disoriented but homing in on Mother's golden bee. She said something sweetly inaudible, and his right hand came up to his heart as he bowed. Felix was gazing into Scharf's eyes, the Professor into Ainoha's. The other women held onto one another. The air was full of incipient disaster. But as the Professor toasted his hostess and greedily drank his spritzer, walking downstairs backward to regrasp the rope which Felix had held for him, Ainoha realized at once, as so many times before, that she had rendered the other women invisible and must immediately deal with the consequences. She set down the tray, descended the stair and pried the dour child's hand from her mother's. Then she took the dazed wife's arm as a man might at a cotillion, and matching the fierce stare of the red-helmeted mother, escorted them all to the grove, where Cherith's Brook careened around its stony corners, exposing the gnarled roots of horse chestnut trees and providing sufficient grottos and ladders for the least inquisitive of animals.

No word had yet passed among the men; it was as if we were in a silent film running backward. The three of us stood alone with Scharf in the courtyard. The animal read my father immediately, rolled over and over, twining the rope about his neck so as to strangle himself, and in the process jerked the Professor to his knees. The men took each other's measure, and the courting began. Father crouched to wind up the coils of rope and, laying one hand on the Professor's knee while the other rested even more gently across the animal's foam-flecked mouth, inquired with a dry laugh:

"And what seems to be the problem, Herr Doktor Professor?"

From his knees, the Professor twisted his huge head to one side and came right to the point:

"He won't mind."

Felix stepped across Scharf's tummy, his four legs were now rigid and pointing to the heavens. "Ah, yes," he murmured, "there appears in his make-up a great distance from the lip to the cup." Then he pointed out that Scharf was apparently a cross between the rare *stickelhäar* and the now extinct Polish sea-hound, a point of origin which seemed to hold no interest for his client.

"How did you come by this animal?" Felix inquired.

The Professor shrugged. "My daughter. She wanted an orphan. She picked him out at the *doghaus*."

"And this is your first family pet?" A question to which he already knew the answer, so didn't listen to the reply.

The Professor had raised himself up, and dusting off his knees, emitted a huge sigh. "He's turned out to be . . . a kind of joke!" he blurted.

"A tragical joke, it seems," Felix added, taking the coil of rope softly from his client's hands.

"Exactly. Though I confess I've developed a sort of strange affection for the animal and his perversities."

Scharf's paws were now milling in the air as he dug a furrow of gravel with his skull.

"Does he make you feel safer in your home?"

"On the contrary," the Professor said candidly, "the entire house has been arranged in his defense." Then, more softly, "If the truth be told, he spends most of the day in the children's beds."

Felix nodded gravely. He had seen many similar cases among those reared in the *doghaus*, he explained—a particular form of neurasthenia in which the animal took to bed in the prime of life, choosing a soft landing when he ought to be charging through the park and challenging everything that moves. Lacking human stimulation in his early youth, he went on wearily, the dog becomes equally unresponsive to love *or* fear.

"This dog has thrust himself between the legs of your life, forcing his way into your heart, and there he proclaims, if you even think of dislodging him, if you say so much as 'go out and play,' that he will kill himself!"

"Extortion by defenselessness?" the Professor queried.

"You are on the right track. You see, he doesn't want to get any better, because that might mean losing what little he has." And he looked down with pity at the bland criminal groveling upside down in his drive.

"The dog does virtually nothing," Felix went on, "yet you say he does not mind. There is, if you will permit me, a contradiction here."

The Professor was rapidly warming to the role of the interrogated. "Well, yes, go on, then."

"Does the animal in question prefer any of you?"

The Professor seemed at a loss.

"Your daughter, perhaps?"

The Professor reflected at length, then, folding his arms: "He prefers my daughter's . . . bed."

Felix stared kindly at him. "The animal in question does not love you," he said softly, "and this is an affront."

The Professor nodded. "There is no dignity . . ."

"He doesn't give a fig for dignity!" Felix interrupted. "What is worse, if I may say so, is not so much that he is ill, but that the illness bores you!"

The Professor was fidgeting, shifting from foot to foot. "It is true," he muttered, "that in this animal there is not a great deal to admire."

"So the problem, really, is whether this 'joke,' as you put it, will become even more tragical. Or perhaps more interestingly, how much tragedy a joke can stand."

"You put it well, although I fear we have left poor Scharf behind in the richness of the diagnosis."

"That should be the clue that there was not much there to begin with."

"No one is suggesting that he promised more."

"Scharf is an open book, Herr Professor. He is neither a rebel nor a saint. He is not even suffering in the strict sense, or rather, he suffers from a vagueness of personality, a deficit of character. Upon this you can project nothing, and so nothing comes back. Like the lumpenproletariat, you wonder why he does not rebel against his circumstances, and when you are not wondering about that, you are wondering why he does not thank you for your charitable impulse to keep him alive."

"This may all be true," the Professor stiffened, "but hoping for a small progress is a human frailty, which you apparently ridicule. Perhaps we ought to take our leave."

Felix commenced a shrug, but then apparently thought better of it, and put his arm warmly around his client's rigid shoulders.

"Do not fear my candor, sir. My friends are well-known and legion, for only the most decent people can put up with me. Let us, you and I, have a *confession couleur*, a *conversation galante*."

Then, before the Professor could object, Felix told him straightaway that Scharf was a hopeless case that only the most intensive treatment and objective stimulation would make an even remotely palatable companion, and that a cure, in any accepted sense of the word, was impossible.

This seemed to intrigue his client as much as it appalled him. But Felix, always conscious of giving value for money, nevertheless tried to put the animal through some paces. He grasped the rope like a lunge line on a recalcitrant pony, and with a flick of his wrists sent long ripples along the rope, which thudded like soft Papuan waves into Scharf's vagus nerve. Rather than pulling on the animal, he was sending energy out. It was a trick he had learned from working with horses, and while it worked much less well with dogs, who as a species were more skeptical of excess freedom, he knew nothing better for the moment. It was all in the wrists, all in the body, sending out messages of concern without a sense of abandonment, a gesture usually only mastered by grandparents, and then only for brief, palsied moments.

"The animal, like society, must be taken into liberality without quite knowing it," Felix spoke soberly as the wavelets left his hand. "It's the only kind of progressivism that works." And this indeed became well-known as the "Psalmanazar Method": to trick the animal in question into self-determination, even magnanimity.

Noting at once the indifference of my father to his jostlings and strainings, Scharf arose trembling, and after relieving himself like a woman, soon settled into a forlorn, circuitous caricature of a gambol, which brought cheers from the Professor and calls for his family. The women returned as one from the brook, as if in a frieze, and watched without the slightest reaction as Father and Scharf slunk in circles around the lawn, negotiating the hydrangeas and boxwood mazes, demonstrating, as the wavelets of energy traveled along the rope, that as dark as the gulf was between them, it was dotted with tiny synapses of fire, and that torpor and hysteria might be transformed with gentle firmness into an acceptable sort of common misery.

Felix brought the dog to a cringing heel before his family.

"Should you find him insupportable, sir, this dog will be just as much at home in an institution as within the dynamics of a family," Father said genially, handing the rope back to the Professor, and with the other hand offering him a mug of spiked tea. Scharf immediately toppled over on his back and gazed up at the concerned assembly, his head grotesquely twisted to one side, his tongue curled like a scallop in the roof of his hideous mouth.

Ainoha suggested a remove to the terrace, where they could more comfortably continue their observation of his progress.

At the end of the day, when the question of money always arises, the Professor suggested a barter arrangement of medical services. Felix as usual insisted on cash up front, noting that he had never been sick a day in his life, and adding, "To tell the truth, no one ever gets ill out here."

The Professor seemed glum. "If I am not for myself, who is for me?" he muttered aloud.

"It's not that you won't find a cheaper rate," Father said brightly. "However, you will not find a discipline and dedication such as my own at any price."

The Professor smiled as if to himself. "The dog himself cost nothing. It is the training that is so expensive!"

"It is an expensive business to take responsibility for a nutcase," Father said without missing a beat. "What other investment does a human make in a dependent who will require your attention every waking hour for half a generation or more, and then congratulate himself when the dependent gets ill that he has saved a few marks? No one will pay the price for careful breeding. I sell my own dogs for a thousand gulden, and I have a ten-year waiting list."

"I myself would very much prefer to wait ten years, Councilor, but my daughter cannot. Surely, you understand that I cannot simply turn Scharf out. She will accept no substitution."

"I quite understand the problem, Professor. But the real cost—I say this to you, *mano a mano*—of demanding total adulation is something you will come to hate."

"I leave my dog with you," the Professor huffed, a new bond already established between him and his pet, "and you ask for money as well?" Then he snapped on his homburg in a gesture of virility.

"This is a graver business than you might imagine, my dear sir. Health requires a commitment to being well. How much, for example, do you yourself charge for a *sitzung*?"

The Professor gazed at his family, glanced at the rope now coiled about his forearm, then looked my father up and down. "Twenty golden marks," he said quietly.

Felix whistled slowly through his teeth. He gave Scharf's ear a gentle tug, for the first time reversing the flow of energy. The depressed saddle of the animal rose and his low-hocked rear legs straightened as he licked his hand. "Then it's agreed?"

The Professor pulled his beard and replied he would have to think upon it. "It's quite an exhausting journey, you know," he added.

"Yes, of course," Felix said. "But please understand, there can be no guarantees with this animal. It will take a long time and a bundle of money, and even then he will not be quite right. Don't try to play games with him, because you're going to lose and make yourself look bad. You can't impress him. You can't discourage him. You can't embarrass him. None of the techniques you generally use with people are going to work with him. The best we can hope for is that he will live out his days with some semblance of social dignity. But first you must get your own family under control. The poor animal is getting mixed signals."

They agreed to meet again, *sans famille,* in a month's time, during which the Professor promised to stop hauling on the animal, and to have all the children practice sending out energy in compliant units along the rope in the manner proscribed, practicing first upon a bed post. They finally compromised on the fee arrangement—a full physical workup in Therapeia with the very latest techniques in *diagnoze,* in return for a month's trial training—to which my father agreed more out of curiosity than anything, and the family returned by calèche to catch the last steamer, just before a stream of black thunderheads exploded over the Marchlands.

FATHERLAND
(Iulus)

My father, Felix Aufidius, was an exceptionally energetic and experienced fellow, athletic, gregarious, and priapic, an intense and watchful man with enormous inner territory, infinitely careless yet terribly focused. A hard-drinking old depucelator, an *homme de femme* who got better-looking as he aged, his angular features were increasingly apparent in the faces of peasant children throughout the county of Klavier. And may I say it was disconcerting to encounter your own little doppelgangers playing in the dusty streets of every village, as I became gradually aware that in effect I was the unwilling leader of a lost tribe. Felix was a big warm man with a smooth cold cheek, often with a heart-shaped lipstick smudge where his beard began. I wished to exceed him only as a tippler and a flirt, and would have happily donned his poisoned shirt.

Born into that century when humankind never worked harder, Felix was known locally as the only Protestant east of the Mze, the quickest gestalt to the west of it, and also as something of a *Marxisant*—at least to the extent that he agreed that the aim of man was to "hunt in the morning, fish in the afternoon, breed cattle in the evening and criticize after dinner." He was the only man I ever knew who roared with laughter when in the clutches of *Das Grosse Kapital*. "There are certain mistakes, which only an intellectual can make," he often said. And if he could have chosen his epitaph, it would have read: "He had brains but not too many."

In his den (and that word sums it up perfectly), a black velvet curtain bisected the oak-paneled tower suite, on each side of which he pinned quotes from his favorite authors, which he made me memorize, such as this one from the down-to-earth Red Prussian:

In place of the great historic movements arising from the conflict between the productive forces . . . in place of practical and violent action by the

48

masses . . . in place of this vast, prolonged and complicated movement, Monsieur Proudhon supplies the evacuating motion of his own head.

I was in my fifties before I got the gist of that, near Felix's own age when he clipped it. It was a reminder note that the most difficult intellectual work of all is like that of an unperplexed matador—to allow reality to step forward, then coolly sidestep it.

And I see now that the rote tutorial was apt, for our sensation of history is indeed nothing more than a great black velvet curtain onto which, along with a few sepia cupolas, haunting autoportraits, and vanished landscapes, a great number of pithy quotes have been flimsily pinned. Yet it is only against that opaque curtain of garbled out-of-context aphorisms that individual character can be truly developed, and those who refuse to stand before it never really emerge. Best to ponder it at midnight with some absinthe before a roaring fire.

My greatest joy was rifling through my father's papers, from which I quickly ascertained that, as heir to Semper Vero, I could look forward to a veritable mountain of debt and virtually exponential taxes; and that my role in the world would be to default, if not gracefully, then with a kind of amusing aplomb, emerging from bankruptcy standing on one finger. Cannonia was the only country in the world where the ledgers were kept in real time, the only government that hadn't learned to cook its books, and it was my generation from whom the debts of centuries would be called. Felix obviously knew this to be the case, and he also knew he could do nothing whatsoever to protect me, so he indulged my sullenness knowing it would run its course, as well as my acrobatic refusal of something as useless as an identity based on pride of ownership.

No, in spite of his agnosticism, his will contained the most terrible of Christian laws. The Father judges no one. He turns the judgment over to the Son. It is up to *him* not only to forgive, but pay the debt in full. I wasn't up to either, and we both knew it.

One day I came across a copy of a letter from my father apologizing to a client . . . "for I must rush home, I so miss my infant son." Think of that. That there might be something in me he might miss gave me a ridiculous sense of self-confidence, as well as a certain *hauteur*, and I pinned the purloined letter to the black velvet curtain, nailed it to the cross, between the expostulations of dead patriarchs.

Having mastered his profession early, my father, like most of his class, was unafraid to throw himself without limit into his hobbies, and he was more than content to play the amateur amongst his professional friends. A career could not be sustained any more than any passion, he believed, and so "real life" for him was a respectful if somewhat self-indulgent sideline, the only aim of which was to extract value. He was the sort of person who found irreverence and defiance irresistible, and as the possessor of what one could only call great moral charm, he was proud to take his place as a contrarian crank in a technological, profane, ego-based, and psychologically-oriented world, and mow his lawn on the principles of the Parthenon. Most anyone can orchestrate, but he could retranscribe, reduce a symphony to a quartet. In his heart he had both a sliver of ice and a sliver of gold.

My father's idea of spirituality was to be in touch with matter and the way it moved, a hands-on mysticism which could have been lethal. For him, touch was the only performance of lasting duties. "If your hands and mouth are wise," he told me when we first discussed the birds and bees, "virility will take care of itself. And you will seduce all the world, if you like." He had three golden rules: 1. Ride women high. 2. Never take the first parachute offered. 3. Never go out, even to church, without a passport, 1500 florins, and a knife.

Semper Vero was crossed by the continental divide, marked by a mound made of earth brought in from sixty-three different countries in Grandfather Priam's time, and not far from there, the Dead Mze broke up and darted underground, emerging again to die in peace one thousand miles away in some Russian marsh. This strange system was most visible at dawn, when the Cannonian countryside appears striped, the underground serpentine aquifers showing up as green squiggles in the sere pastures. In our part of the world, the Living Mze often changed directions, at the whim of its dead, diverted underground cousins, sometimes flowing East and sometimes West, a hydraulics as mysterious as those of the urinary tract, the only human system which remains unexplained by science.

Father was hardly surprised at this. "Nature is apprehended only by asking it a question," he said to many an astounded visitor. "The river, like time, may flow both ways, but the point is that whichever way it flows, it runnels back into the past before it emerges in the future."

Often a visitor, beset by literary aspirations, would attempt to amplify the liquid analogy. Count Zich, who knew better, one day tried his hand: "So would you say then, sir, that life is walking alongside a river which gradually disappears?"

"Experience is not a river," Felix gently riposted. "Experience is countless rivers converging in a damp place, where there is nothing which could be said, in any helpful sense, to be a river."

Perhaps it is not surprising, then, to find that a man who first thing each morning (with a rifle slung over his shoulder and a book under his arm) checked to see if the river of Grace had decided to flow east or west, might be simultaneously a believer and an unbeliever, a romantic and a moderate, a stoic and an epicure, a yogi without meditation, deadly serious about his whimsies, humorous about death and taxes, reflective and decisive in the same gesture. He was interested in the minimally implausible, and believed that the function of the intellect was to set stern limits to its own pretensions. He had the skepticism of the peasant, the indifference of the nobleman, and the insistence on value-by-critique of the country gentry, and so lived voluntarily in a no-man's-land on the borders of the intelligentsia, the Astingi nomads, the lesser aristocracy, and bureaucratic squires, thinking of himself as an intermediary metabolite. He was basically interested in secondary differential, a student of nothing so insipid as change, but of *changes in the rate of change*; not only in the gray-green river, but in the human *métabole* as well. How does one thing become another? That was his métier. What exactly is it that the hero doesn't know before he becomes, well, quite something else? That was his subject. What is the opposite of an epiphany? That was his method. What is the opposite of a hangover? That was his temperament. Born when the voluntary sublime virtues were being replaced by the vulgar obligatory ones, he was still of that amorous tradition, unimaginable to modern ears, in which the desire to please was stronger than the need to be loved. A refugee from smugness, from conformity, and from every chosen people, he was the least guileless of men.

He never wasted a word. Either he was telling you something you wanted to know, or you were telling him something he wanted to know, and the ironclad integrity of these encounters somehow never became tiresome. He had a quiet baton, sparing of the superfluous, and an inscrutable beat.

Imagine the difficulty of having a father who was exactly as he seemed to be.

Father rejected the fashionably tragic and the abnormal, condemned all cults of solitude and unhappiness. As an anglophobophile, he loved people who teased the British. He loathed German misery, German inwardness, German desperation. He particularly loathed Kant for his hierarchies, which placed the dog and the horse somewhere between a stone and us. As an incorrigible improviser, his expansive gaiety of mind struggled against the fathomless boredom which always threatened to strangle our part of the world. Above all, he resolutely denied the cults of Life-Affirmation and Life-Alienation, those elusive twin personages who have washed each other's hands throughout our dirty century. Yet in his *Historae Astingae* he was always trying to rescue Nietzsche from being "so damned Nietzschean"; he wanted to tell his tale from the point of view of the brown mare, around whose neck the author of *Superman* had flung his arms as he died.

No culture has ever made so much and so little of art than the Cannonia of his time. And he was after all, a member of that class—handsome, balanced, and relatively well-off; civic-minded, tolerant, sociable, and progressive— that really had no need of art, and as such ended up as its main patron and audience. Even though they napped through most of it, they somehow didn't miss a thing. Felix himself was devoted to art while loathing its egotism and vanity. As the most self-reliant of men he knew that autonomy was always overrated. He did not understand why art, when it enjoined any civic impulse, always seemed to degenerate into toadying vapidity, nor why the relentless quest for originality almost always resulted in pointless savagery, lack of sex appeal, and predictable abuse. He was equally amused by what both the clowns of the ruling classes and the damaged narcissists of the avant-garde called thinking. If he was the product of a no longer comprehensible past, to compensate, he prided himself on being a child of his own age. His only real mistake was to think he could compel beauty, and yet he was the only man I ever knew before whom a failed author could sit with ease.

Felix "the Happy" spent most of his time keeping several sorts of overlapping daybooks. The first was what merchants call a *klitterbuch* (wastebook) in which they inscribe everything that is bought and sold that day, as well as naked thoughts on matters literary and scientific, all of these muddled in no particular order. These were in turn transferred into a journal where everything was made more systematic and the kurb of art began to exert its salubrious effect—a record of his real-time monetary expenditures in the margins of a diary, and further annotated with a meditation on what he *might* have done. And finally, all this was transfigured into a kind of double-entrance bookkeeping, a *Chronik* in which the text, "the history of my feelings," was coextensive with columns of numbers in each margin—one marking the prices of the trading day, another the costs of transactions, and still another, a kind of pictographic evaluation of the psychic experience, as well as symbols for the occasions on which he had made love. The method, as I understood it, was to firmly differentiate the semi-articulate from reinvention, finally producing both an intimate account *and* its quantification, a natural history of the heart paralleling natural history; the long account of the death of a favorite animal, for example, with the price history of horsemeat in France alongside.

He ignored the daily newspapers in order to try and think historically. He could have produced five or ten books as good as those any literary culture of any country can turn out by the thousands. But he knew we were entering the age of weakening reality, so in order to assert value in an objective world which denied it, he preferred to accompany the commentary out to the dread edge of the page, where the argument became clearer as it became less systematic—attempting to approximate those pre-philosophical sputterings which had not yet been trifled with by Plato or Aristotle, before they had been stitched into myths and stories, when thoughts were *really* fragments, and the gap between them clear and enticing, not a pile of rhetorical milk bottles to be bowled over by some howling semanticist. My father had no ideas marching through him; he liked it out there on the edge, where the bardic collided with the calligraphic, a small forbearing space where the paltriness of intelligence might be momentarily overcome, where one could write in order to stop thinking, and lose the shame of being an author.

The confidently unrealizable project of his *Chronik* allowed him to gather strength and move fully formed and with accord. When making an investment for a client, he could turn back twenty years and not only see the historical value of the commodity he was trading, but more importantly, judge his own frame of mind at the time, as well as what the poor dazed world was thinking. From a distance, the *Chronik* looked like an oriental book, each page transcribed in a different colored ink, a palimpsest strewn with ciphers and perfumed with annotations spiraling off into space. But when you put your face in it, you knew what day it was, what world you were in, and what it felt like before you were born.

In the courtroom, Felix "the Happy" learned that you can destroy any argument by taking the *a priori* one step backward, that the self and its opposite do not have to exist in mutual antipathy, and indeed that the day of liberation is most often the day of disappointment. Observing the inclination of human nature to crush the human spirit, he reluctantly became the advocate of the trial-and-error boys, reconciling warring factions by insisting that the other's place does not have to be a fearful one. He often said there are only two sorts of people in this world—those who believe in the law when it promises to protect them, and those who don't.

No graven portrait of my father's family ever hung in our house. If there was a tradition operating here, it was that one ought to be forthright in pursuing and preserving one's pleasures, but not be surprised if others found them repulsive. This quirky toleration always made a great impression in our fanatical part of the world, but was essentially misunderstood. For if a man had his absolute preferences, and yet could afford another's right to take exception, this implied authority—and such authority could only imply hoarded money, dirty tricks, or a conspiracy at the highest level. An uncaused authority without political power and without money, together with an uncaused freedom without an enemy, is the most intimidating force in the modern world, and its bearers are inevitably punished for it. Felix was one of those men doomed to be more liberal than his class, and his political downfall was due to his not being as conservative as the radicals turned out to be.

Father clearly preferred the companionship of women, as he believed that everything is finally done either to impress or avoid them. "Men just walk down their own roads," he used to say, "and talk about the things they happen to meet. How unbelievably boring! Women, for whatever reason, tend to do this less, and are therefore superior." He also believed that the greatest gift you can give another person is self-control, and that the ability of men to hide their thoughts went largely unappreciated by women.

Life for him was clearly a beautiful woman on a beautiful horse led by a beautiful dog, and he felt the only possible justification for something as unattractive and exceptional as a grown man was that by wizardry and chivalry he might keep these unlike animals together in a parade—that gentleman's paradise: tenderness without loyalty, violence without strife.

His male acquaintances found it strange that such an energetic man did not chafe in a house under female ownership, particularly given the airy standards of my mother, for married life was certainly nothing like a ballerina on a circus horse, but rather more a warren of untrained animals and mentally ill clowns. They also thought it imprudent for him to reinvest all of his earnings into the maintenance of a property which for all its strange beauty and uniqueness, had for a century been a wasting asset, producing less income each year. (Indeed, the whole of Cannonia would have doubled in market value had they shut down every single farm and factory.)

My father was a triple functionary—attorney, village notary, and investment counselor—with a triple soul: conservative, liberal, and left wing. He was not hard to fathom, not so much a giant of a man as three hard, distinct men who fought spiritedly among themselves. He was a worldly concrete man, adept at finance, ball games, and sex, contemptuous of politics and religion, but a spy for the spiritual, a secret agent for the sacred. He believed sincerely that his function was to play prime minister to the queen, bluff front man for the skeptical muse, to extract money from the real economy and cheerfully recirculate it into the inefficient, living part of the culture. As such, he objectively failed at everything except the high drama of marriage and as fiduciary for other people's money. But it was in the fourth dimension of Dogmeister Supreme, Hauptzuchtwart of Semper Vero and Master of Our Floating World, where Father truly shone, and scattered the heaped-up mountains with the simplest of gestures. A man is nothing but a handful of irrational enthusiasms, and nothing in this world can be understood apart from them.

Yes, my father was an oral man, a primary type, who could not resist a smoke, a vowel, a puff, a sentence, a sweet, a scotch, a song, a smooch. Breathing, after all, was no less a project because it was involuntary, and the intervals between the breaths also required justification and refinement. This attitude, more than any gustatory prowess, accounted for Father's eating habits, which went far beyond *gourmet* or even the *gourmand*.

Family meals in Father's view were an especial kind of torture, a fact borne out by his observation of the dogs when they were fed in the same cell. There, the bitches inevitably lost their appetite or became more aggressive, barking out commands which fell on deaf ears, though requiring ever sharpening levels of feigned attention from the brood. The sires sat proudly, horrified to eat from the same bowl as their progeny, insensitive to the alleged thrill of watching newborns masticate, and trying pathetically to nose their own dishes into a corner where they could be defended. When they were half-grown, the dogs ate just as sloppily, gulping their food without tasting it, and reverting to the pecking order they had displayed as puppies; indeed the same dogs who shoved each other out of the way at eight weeks continued to do so at eight years.

A line seemed to be crossed at our meals, from wonder to pride to habituation to vague resentment and finally colic. There was nothing like a repast to bring out the hierarchies that everyday activities so successfully blurred and dispelled, and Father came to believe that a true family could be kept together only by avoiding meals together whenever possible. But he had also noticed that there was better behavior at kennel dinner when a guest dog was being boarded. Were the hosts being well-mannered or falsely solicitous, wondering whether the guest was going to steal their dinner? Whatever the case, their own self-conscious roles were slightly submerged; they gulped more slowly, ate a bit less, chewed a bit more thoroughly. There was even a kind of comradely charm in the air, and occasionally a note of sincere thanks was struck, bringing a tear to a hound's eye.

So it was that we almost always had an invited guest for supper. When we did not, our table was the severest form of regimen. Mother was obviously of two minds about food. Meat in particular, in all its forms, gave her the shakes. She would walk across a muddy street to avoid passing the window display in a butcher shop. She knew this was ridiculous but couldn't help it. It was related of course to the way my father had eaten, was eating, and was about to eat. The appetites of men seemed to her if not exactly vulgar, driven by needs far beyond nutrition. The way men left the table particularly offended her, on whatever pretext, strolling over to the fire, or to walk in the starry moonlight, there to smoke, pass wind, and put the dinner out of mind. It brought out in her conflicting feelings of servitude and superiority, particularly when they thanked her with pointless magnanimity for the meal she had in fact nothing to do with. She was convinced that Father's love of food was his most prurient of interests.

Mother's attention to lettuce and other uncooked food struck Father as not only gratuitous, smug asceticism, but also willful self-destructiveness. He did not judge her, as he himself took no pleasure in the carving, nor certainly in the presiding. It was one of the few rituals he was not particularly good at, and he was embarrassed at his first reflex, which was always to carve the roast in such a way that the better cuts would be preserved for himself. Gazing with sadness at the selfishly severed loin, he would offer it shamefacedly to Mother, who he knew would refuse it, saying, "You know I just don't care, dear"—the only words which truly threatened him. And then he would fork the filet on to me, and that was Judgment Day, where amongst the copious portions you simply cannot offer thanks enough. It is the smallest and the weakest of us who must get down on our marrowbones and give thanks, who must tally up with the Lord, his beneficence.

So our supper was not a pretty picture. Father with his huge knife raised in defeat, Mother staring at every plate but her own, and myself, who through murmurs of gratitude, personal growth, and *savoir gré*, was presumed to solve this impasse. Only the animals beneath the table enjoyed these coarse dog dinners, as my father's shadow hovered over the roast, elbows sawing in and out, while mother withdrew from his shadow with an unmistakable air of superiority. In my nervous knowledge that my digestion was the only justification of the elaborate ritual, I must admit that I identified with the roast and rejoiced in its slaughter. But these meals drenched in ambivalence did not give us strength. No, this first festival of mankind made each of us weaker, occasionally exhausted—the family values of remorse, obedience, and guilty liberation, all sitting round the table in silence.

So it was not surprising that when there were no guests to take the edge off things, Father would invariably take his supper at that vegetarian's nightmare, *White Wings, Black Dog*, an inn where the fare was certainly uneven but which had not been closed a single day in seven hundred years, and where no meal was really a meal without a seduction or apology. There in a booth in the private dining room known as *The Brainery*, one could draw the curtain and have an assignation with an oyster and one's self, or perhaps the elk and bustard pie with orchid ice cream. And there Felix removed himself with a book and ate alone before the fire, his unembarrassed appetites on full display, and all of us grew fat and happy.

When earthbound, my father assumed three forms: at times a gentle bull who lay his full weight upon the fence of every friendship; at times a writhing, glittering serpent, mocking each blow of his adversaries; and at times a man with a lion's head from whose laughing beard, unchecked by false shame, great torrents of water flowed. I liked them all.

At dusk, every summer afternoon, when the slow moving Mze turned from ocher to mauve, we stripped down on its banks, leaving my school uniform and his business suit in soft columns above our shoes, and began to wade aimlessly in our black alpaca bathing suits, which we always wore instead of underwear. Swallows swooped down, dipping their wings into the darkening waters, fish rose and rejoiced in its dusky surface, while between them all manner of insects emerged like living sparks and fell into the flowers of both banks. Then he would take me up in his arms and we would cross that river which the ancients believed to be bottomless.

He had the body of a gymnast, his frame developed by secret French exercises, low sloped rounded shoulders which concealed effortless strength, and the legs of a country gent, hard as a saddle but just as forgiving, which he toughened by rising at five each morning and walking for three hours before breakfast with a knapsack full of stones. I had my mother's rapier-like body, designed for sleeping late, for sports not yet generally acknowledged. But when he picked me up, even for a moment, I forgot my body, forgot myself.

The incline of the river bottom was firm and fairly gradual, and soon we were submerged, only his head above the water, his beard like a dark water lily floating above my head, which lay upon his chest. I was aware of both the current and his stubborn resistance to it. Taking a breath, I went under with his heart. I felt no fear as long as he could breathe, as long as I could hear his breathing.

He walked almost casually, with the slight limp of the star athlete, negotiating the cylinder of water with short languid strides, suave and incorporeal, until we were both well beneath the surface. How many steps I do not know, across the bottom of that river which flowed away from history, where I first became aware of Time Out of Mind.

We moved deliberately in that sphere, out of our element but serene, moving gravely but never grimacing through the invisible currents. Down there, all the senses were equally irrelevant, in a normal weightless gait. Then in order to reassert our gravitas, he freighted, weighted down with me.

When his lungs close by my ear expelled, I knew we were coming up for air, that the incline was in our favor. There was nothing but blinding brightness as my own head emerged, and he permitted himself a slight stumble now that the hardest part was done. When we were in the shadows on the far side, my diminished senses returned one by one. I could hear the rivulets course about his calves, and as I was set down on the meadow embankment, looking back at the bent grass where we began, water cascaded down his beard onto my face.

The pretext, I suppose, was exercise, a kind of fitness. For surely, any fool can learn to swim, and in your mind's redshot eyes one can just as well walk upon the water. But to walk *through* it, neither floating nor drowning, now that is a test—though the choleric Cannonian is sure to ask, what good is it to be a champion sprinter in a swimming pool?

I cannot recall exactly when this project began or ended, or how to factor in the crude determinants: my weight, his age, the velocity of the current as Time flowed back and forth. Read into it what you will. Read anything but comedy or dread. He cast me into the river which rose not over me; I was then what I was to be. As I saw the man pick the boy up, I was being picked up. From the water I saw the man carry the boy into the water. As the bubbles from my nostrils ascended to the surface, I saw the two beneath the riverine sheet, as if from a dirigible. From the far mountain bank I saw them clamber out of the river, then look back at the broken columns of their clothes. And from our clothes I saw the naked man and hairless boy turn to stare at me, then lay down like animal spirits in the mud.

How was it that in his arms, in that river, I was both behind and ahead of myself? Philosophers call this an affliction, and perhaps it is so. But I also know that no man can take leave of his father without it; I was where I had been for all time and where for all time I shall go.

From my father, who became a different man each day, I learned we have no choice but to be both hunter and prey. I saw that the bad boy becomes a good father as the best kind of cover. Even as the bad boy always remains bad, and gets badder still, the father's guise is perfected. Like my father, I wanted desperately to be good. So I could be *really* bad.

My father was not on intimate terms with me; he was but a voice, an encouraging voice, let it be said, warm and straightforward, with never a catch. He talked like a book and rarely crossed out a line. He encouraged me to do what I wanted, on the condition that he would not have to pretend to be interested in it, and that I would not lie about it. I have lied to everyone but my father, which I trust was not good enough for him, but *for* him, nonetheless. When it became clear, however, that this world could not be passed on to me, he gave me some advice which I now pass on to you: 1. Neither marry nor wander, you are not strong enough for either. 2. Do not believe any confession, voluntary or otherwise. And most importantly, 3. *Maxime constat ut suus canes cuique optimus.* (Everyone has a cleverer dog than their neighbor; that is the only undisputed fact.)

And perhaps that is why I have never owned a dog, and even shy away from strangers' pets, for every dog I see signifies to me a missed opportunity. My father kept a daybook every day of his life but one, not a record of the weather or personal experiences or even facts, but to keep faith with a complete record of one's misfortunes. I, on the other hand, have erased each day with equal ledger-bound determination, all too often seeking with my exaggerations a forgetfulness of an all-too-faithful memory. But if I could not carry on my father's punctilious bravery, and join the chorus of exalted apologists for heroic and intense living, I could do the one thing he could not do for himself. I could run away for him.

Sleeping beneath the reed beds, his head in the opposite direction of other pike, I was leaning on the *Wodna Mze*, my amphibian Waterman, the sorrowing seducer who shoots upwards from the abyss, his hiding place, and bolts through swine-clouds of semen to the dream of the double life.

PREOPS

(Iulus)

It was with some trepidation that Felix Aufidius made his appointment with Doctor Psylander Sychaeus Pür, for he believed the first precondition of survival in the modern world was a profound aversion to the medical profession. He had never been to any sort of doctor in his life, including the moment of his birth, which was handled expertly by a sixteen-year-old Astingi midwife. He even pulled his own bad teeth, rocking back and forth in his armchair, fingers stuffed in his mouth, until the proud moment when he finally displayed the diseased molar, still attached to his face by a strand of bloody spittle. He regarded science as a perverse ideology devoted to the erasure of its own history and refusing to know its place in the world. He actually pitied physicians—merchants trading in the mitigation of miseries they could not understand—and their inevitable false humor and secret despair. Nevertheless, before submitting to an examination by the Professor, he wanted to be at the peak of his form, and given his inexperience in the domain of passive interlocution, he believed he owed it to his new comrade to at least have a practice session, a trial run in the white arts of preventative care.

Needless to say, he had previously steered clear of Dr. Pür, who functioned as village surgeon, midwife, apothecary, dentist, and barber, and who the peasants treated with the utmost respect, believing he was essentially a weak and desperate man who would hurt you less if he felt revered. My father also recognized Pür as having the strongest of all depressive addictions—that of always being helpful—and that if he did not receive his ameliorative fix of gratitude in every waking hour, he was never far from taking his own life.

Pür's office was in the Legal and Medical Building, the most ornate in Silbürsmerze. The waiting room overlooked a trout farm formed by a diversion of the Vah through a series of chattering gates and broken concrete sluices, where countless fish kept the water in a constant frenzy awaiting their daily load of American Troutchow. He always had the most attractive village girls as nurses, and it clearly thrilled them to see the man from the big house on the volcano. Naked like the nurses under a billowing smock, Felix braced his buttocks against the cold edge of the examining table, determined to match the excellent spirits of his examiner. Pür's glistening head hove into view, banded by a circular mirror, gazing longingly into his patient's face as a man might look down a particularly dark and turbid well.

"And to what may I owe the honor of this visit, Councilor?"

Felix immediately felt the overpowering urge to lie. And Pür, to his credit, seemed to sense this, beginning each rote inquiry before Father finished his last answer.

"Lie down so you look to the stars," Pür purred.

Dr. Pür was quite proud of his instruments, the cost of which, he constantly reminded his patients, actually required a city of five thousand to support them, not the twelve hundred, noble as they were, of Silbürsmerze—though to Felix's non-industrial eye the office did not seem inordinately well-stocked. There was a medicine cabinet, an examining table, and what Pür called in a burst of pride, an "extra table." His special equipment consisted of a thermometer, a stethoscope, an ophthalmometer, a laryngoscope, a sphygmomanometer, a prescription pad, and chemicals to detect the presence of albumen in the urine. There was also a nebulizer, a tank of compressed air, and a rare half-bath. Behind a single glass-fronted bookshelf Father could make out treatises on rubella and diptheria, facial neuralgia and the gibbous spine, relapsing fever and the sweetness of urine, and between bound volumes of a magazine called *New Thought* were Fothergill's *An Account of the Sore Throat*, Baille's *Confessions of a Magnetizer*, and Pekelharing's trilogy, *A propos de la pepsine.*

The patient could barely suppress a sardonic smile, and took grim satisfaction as the doctor dismissed out of hand any comment he made describing his own health. To be fair to the doctor, Pür distrusted his own unaugmented observations as much as his patient's narratized symptoms, and for that matter anything which remotely smacked of disease theory. He knew that for most people the body only really existed as a kind of delusion, a sort of error without trial, and that self-pity had become not a feeling but a regnant belief system. The only cure he could offer was to encourage his patients to somehow get their minds *off* their ailments, a treatment which could consume time unreckoned, and a patience and imagination beyond his own. This left him bitter, which he thought it noble to suppress. He had no whole world to offer the sick to be whole in, so why pretend otherwise? They should accept that both of them were caught up in the great cycle of medical history, absorbing all that had been condemned as quackery, while at the same moment awestruck as the discarded dogmas were taken up with avidity by new quacks. Yes, the earth, like the body, is mostly fluid—fluids and bad light. Quantify the shame, medicate it, and be done with it.

Pür took delight only in his instruments, the mathematization they conferred, the senses they augmented. Surrounded in the room by plaster-of-paris models of the organs he was examining, as well as cabinets full of less effective, outdated, and superseded instruments, he was never so happy as when isolated among the sounds, sights, and signs of illness the patient himself could not see or hear. There were times he could visualize a pulse curve without even touching the person, and he looked forward to the day when it would be possible to diagnose without seeing the patient at all.

At the conclusion of the visit, Pür handed Felix a small card with a column of numerals designating the acceptable range of microscopic analyses to come.

"You have the body of a man half your age," he said rather wantonly, then, "I suspect that your tests will be on the high side of normal—not a revelation to you, I suppose."

When Father shrugged at the numbers on the paper, Pür's temples flushed with the shame of health, and a small coil of concern appeared in his smooth forehead.

"How *well* do you wish to get, Councilor?"

Every now and then the Augesee would regurgitate a small tsunami. The tidal swell was usually sighted first on the color-leached Plains of Mon, where Astingi patrols tried to outrace it, and when it deluged the covered bridge at Chorgo, the yellow weather flag was raised on the fortress. The next train was given the message to be dropped off at the stationmasters at Umfallo and Malaka, so that the king and prime minister, if in residence, might be informed. Invariably Count Zich would then open his monogrammed leather-bound telegraph key and tap out the news to the post office at Vop, whose thousand harpists would send a chord hurtling down the canyon of the Vah, resounding throughout the basin of the Mze. At such a moment, the *Desdemona* would suspend local operations, and after loading up with sturgeon and champagne, improvise on the crest of the wave all the way to Therapeia, like a skier who descends the mountain in a tenth of the time he took to climb it. Felix took advantage of one of these improvisatory chutes and found himself amazed to be walking briskly toward the low-lying quarter of the Professor's address after only two hours on the river.

He had a great distaste for Therapeia, a university town full of conceited students and bad tobacco shops. Every weekend in Therapeia featured dog shows, and its residents considered themselves the universe's most ardent dog lovers. However, they were almost exclusively show people, not hunters, and their main accouterment was a large, over-the-shoulder striped sack in which a gentleman could carry a seventy-pound animal, whilst from every woman's muff, a pug's mug protruded. In place of a *kunstlerhalle* there was the famous Dog Museum, where each citizen was invited to reconstruct a furnished room from their own home, and during viewing hours live in it with their various dogs, so the rest of the populace might visit to compare and contrast their own quarters and pets.

They believed themselves genial and simple folk, much like their dogs, when in truth all they had managed was to connect their dogs in weak analogy to their own messes. Everywhere in the town, rich and poor quarters alike, steaming heaps of meat-flavored, half-digested American cereal products festooned the curbs, mirroring not so much the poor animals who deposited them but the slovenly, lonely personalities of the citizenry. To avoid these matters Felix had to constantly cross and re-cross the street, until finally, in a huge block of flats with innumerable dark entrances on the *rue des Carcasses*, he found the Professor's yellowed card on a heavily grated door, reflecting that this second submission to medical authority was at least *pro bono*.

Up the narrow winding stairwell, the door to the anteroom was slightly ajar, pinned with another yellowed card:

> WE ARE ALWAYS HAPPY TO CLARIFY
>
> *Advice is Extra*

The anteroom itself he recognized immediately as one of those strange libraries full of splendid and bulky volumes, complete sets only, books sent to you by someone else, and having never been read, put on display for yet a third order of reader. Where there were no books, large etchings of half-naked allegorical women hung, and from behind a velvet curtain in the corner protruded a silver gynecological stirrup.

Upon being admitted to the inner office (the door seemed to swing open on its own) he was surprised to see not a single instrument, nor an examining table or a nurse, only a shabby pseudo-Turkish loveseat and a desk piled high with empty dossiers, from which he inferred that the Professor had not been in private practice long. But the man who had greeted him so warmly and effusively on his exile territory, kissing his wife's hand repeatedly and patting his child's head until he blinked, now regarded him with a somewhat indifferent air, without even motioning for him to take a seat. When Felix asked if he might take the chair by the desk, the Professor said only, "As you wish."

During their conversation the Professor neither touched him nor made use of any instrument, not even a pen. Indeed, he never came closer than eight or ten feet and barely spoke. Leaning back in his chair, making a tent of his fingers, gazing at the high ceiling, he would occasionally modulate his voice and throw him a glance of rather pointless solicitude and reassurance, but nothing more.

The examination began with three innocent questions: Do you hear voices? Is anyone watching you? Who controls your thoughts? Then the conversation switched to a kind of elevated pubchat about the female of the species, ending only when Felix lashed out in frustration:

"How dare you bring my mother into this?" His voice had risen slightly, and he was covering his nose in what he knew to be the classic symbol of deception. He made his eyes impassive, smiled inappropriately, and refused to maintain eye contact. But the Professor took no notice.

"When you think of the word 'pocket,' what does it recall to you? Does the word 'straight' bring anything to mind? Why are you playing with that button? Put your hand in your pocket and feel the pennies."

Whereas Pür had rejected every commentary out of hand, the Professor seemed interested in nothing *but* his self-descriptions, especially in their vaguest and most speculative aspect—the most disguised complaints, the most ill-described sensations, the most precarious theories, the most tenuous flights of the soul. Felix did his best to fit his long-lived family's total lack of medical history and their speedy, unsuffering deaths into this universe of physical changes concealed from the natural senses. At one point the Professor stood up and faced out the window, his back to him, hands crossed over his rump, apparently in exasperation. This gesture, rude in anyone else, seemed to be reflective and forthcoming, given the odd context of the meeting.

But then Felix noticed outside the window a large, suspended mirror seemingly designed so that traffic might see the around a corner, and tilted in such a way that he now became aware of the Professor's face, larger than life, staring back through the window at the patient, and the doctor's brown eyes suddenly turned almost blue in the convex reflection.

Felix continued to deliver himself of every disease theory and personal crisis he could think of, from heartburn to a recent thump of the prostate, as well as generalized fears of bankruptcy, invasion, and senility, until after moving from organ to organ and from brain to states of mind to soul, he could no longer think of anything to impress the Professor, and embarrassed by a lack of any true symptoms or secrets, he launched into a kind of nonsense, an Astingi camp Latin, running words and puns together—a test to determine if the Professor was really listening.

> *Kek man camov te jib bollimengreskkoenaes,*
> *Man camov te jib weshenjugalogonaes.*
> (I do not wish to live like a baptized person.
> I wish to live like a dog of the wood.)

His interlocutor spun around, acknowledging the sudden discontinuity in his patient's story, but as if to remind him that he had specified no limitations to their conversation and had not the slightest interest in whether his patient talked shop or Babel, only gazed at him sharply over his reading glasses. This was followed by a mutually sincere pursuit of silences as each pulled a cigar from an inner pocket like a derringer.

The Professor seemed unembarrassed by the vacuum between them, and my father felt grateful that he did not leap forward to engage its awkwardness. Eventually, the Professor responded with a stream of impressions, including a morose allusion to the recent death of his child (a boy of two, from scarlet fever) and the consequent withdrawal of his wife. Felix suddenly realized with an aching heart that his examiner, through the exigencies of private practice, had been forced to lift his eye from the microscope and settle ruefully upon the notion that the tact of a passive observer might wring diagnostic truths superior to more intrusive methods. The Professor apparently was attempting, not without some courage, to put aside his own insoluble griefs and to frame his questions in a way that would not elicit standard answers—and the stranger and more oblique the answer, the calmer he seemed. Felix appreciated this, but knew this was not the time to register it. If Pür was human only in the face of an illness without apparent causes, the Professor seemed to be humbled only by illness which had no physical signposts—indeed, the room lacked that aura of fear present in almost every medical encounter, the sense that the doctor is in mortal terror of contracting the illness he has just diagnosed. Felix did not feel the excitement of having lied, as with Pür; instead, he felt like a schoolmaster's favorite chagrined by his own tendency to exaggerate every response and be the brightest boy around. Nor did he feel the obligation to reward the Professor by being a happy patient. A large melancholia was over behind that black desk, too deep for any protocols to deflect. So while as yet he felt neither true trust nor respect, neither did he feel impelled to show off or amuse. His interlocutor's detachment was not defensive as with Pür, and therefore not an offense. He recognized it as a Hebrew version of courtliness, but with a new and harder edge, always staying leewards of a predictable professional or social response. And so their lack of conversation continued, like those ritualistic incantatory chapters in Homer or Virgil which seem totally unnecessary to the story—pure male silence.

In advertising his reluctance to treat, the Professor had taken a page from the old diplomatists, who, knowing the governments they represented to be a sham, try to reach an accommodation based on *decreasing* confidence, a pact based upon the refusal to make any promises at all, and to buy time at all costs. Felix saw that in his abstracted way the Professor was reaching for that state of neutral grace between an animal and his trainer, when the unspoken bond is simply the understanding that there would be no concentration of willfulness without the other's leave.

Now here was a man you didn't have to talk to, and with whom you might one day really have a talk! Father resolved to trade learning for learning, acknowledging the Professor's gesture with one from his own special repertoire of silences. He reflected for a time on which would be most suitable.

The most adaptable and engaging gesture in this world, more winning than sex or genius, is the puzzlement of perfect temperament, when a mistake or complication is greeted not with a snarl or shiver, but with the cocked, flipped-over ear of a pup, inquisitive and unsensational, asking only that you think through the hovering blow you are about to deliver. It is the one physical gesture from our stifflegged hounds worth learning, and while most of us for some reason almost always have an uncle who can wiggle his ears, Father, after hours in his shaving mirror, had mastered the discipline of cocking his left ear, then his right, which astounded his enemies and never failed to captivate women. It cut through formalities; expostulations were reformulated and put again more simply; even glances were more telling, as it elicited longer pauses but fewer hiatuses. It encouraged the other to articulate more accurately, and to sidestep small talk, or rather to make talk really small, as in italics, as if the great conversation of the ages could only be resumed when strong men asserted the feminine child within them. And so the Professor, though he was not prone to admit it, counted this session a great success when he saw his patient's left ear rise and cock itself in his direction, asking for amplification. He responded with a sly half-wink, pulling shyly on his moustache, as they both blew smoke rings up into the æthers.

The two bearded men chatted on as if they were waiting in line at a customs house at a frontier, until with a glance at his watch the Professor concluded their appointment.

"Perhaps we will never find out what's *wrong* with you, eh?" he said cheerfully, handing him a card for their next appointment, and they both admitted to themselves that they looked forward to the silences to come, as well as the session with Scharf a fortnight hence.

"Healing's not pretty, Councilor," the Professor concluded.

As he left the building, Felix suddenly felt cheated and abused, and had the overpowering urge to tell the quack off, which made him look forward as never before to his next appointment—until he realized after glancing at the card that it was a year away.

But as he sat stewing, he was aware of the muscles in his diaphragm relaxing, and for a brief moment felt that he was not fundamentally unlike everyone else in the world—a strange and disorienting experience for him.

A NEW CHALLENGE
(Iulus)

This was the first trip the Professor had ever taken without a book. After hustling aboard an express at the glass-and-steel South Station and crossing the Hron by the Invaliden Bridge, he sat stupefied before the window, watching rearward as the endless gasflares, smokestacks, and open-pit furnaces of the industrial suburbs drifted past. Referred to as "The Tannery," this blasted stretch never failed to make a dour impression, furnishing an unlimited portico of scenes for rich, recurrent nightmares. That people could take the local and actually get off and go to work in this hellish scene was beyond him.

The Monstifita station was located off a spur which terminated in a ruined cloister serving as a train shed. Here the restaurant car was decoupled and attached to a Belgian steam engine with a squat body and disproportionately large chimney. Men with grimy fingernails crowded the zinc counter for beer and cigarettes as the train moved out along the suspension railway toward the spa town of Sare.

As the little train traipsed along its miles of timbered superstructure, it sent up a pale feather of smoke. In the yellow fog of morning, the peonies were dropping their last petals and the lime trees were in flower.

Upon alighting, the Professor and his dog were surrounded by Skopje, gigantic yet fleshy Russians in black caftans who believe that Christ never died but wanders the earth in different forms, and will come again when the great bell of Uspenskisobor sounds. They offered him his choice of gigs: fan-tailed or tub-bodied; a chariotee, rockaway, or volonte; a stanhope, tilbury, or cabriolet; a victoria, barouche, or laundolet. Also available were a sedan chair, a hammer box, and a *lineika* (a six-wheeled Russian equatorial carriage), as well as an American invention, a three-wheeled gig with the third wheel in front in close connection to the shafts. The Professor chose an older, half-closed brougham with lemon sateen side-panels, a piebald mare who stared at his beard as if it were a new sort of hay, and the shortest and calmest of the drivers, who at six and a half feet could barely contain himself. His sallow skull was shaven in front, with flapping plaits fastened by clasps to his forehead, and his caftan embroidered with scrolls and flowers.

"And where can I take your Excellency?" he inquired in a high-pitched voice.

"To the river landing, if you please. The cost?"

"Whatever you like, your Excellency," the coachman said as he whipped the beautiful fat bottom of the mare.

Gypsies fiddled, lepers begged, and drunks beat up one another as the brougham sped along polished cobbles, dodging a plentiful fall of steaming horseapples clotted with peppermint. Like phantoms in a fairy tale, they proceeded at a bone-jarring trot through the villages of Nask, Luda, and Zaza. Along the road, rain had eroded the soil a dozen feet down, and the Professor could make out traces of former roads passing through the valley, one on top of the other, Turkish gravel overlaying medieval slag overlaying heavy Roman paving stones. Once through the three-gated military border with its bevy of moneychangers and louche soldiers, King Pevney's Royal Way opened before them into that degenerate forest of well-levers which bordered the Marchlands, where for twenty leagues the land had not changed in thousands of years. This was a remnant of a pre-settlement expanse, like those undulating plains which once spread from Kenya to Mozambique and Wisconsin to Texas—oak-studded savannahs intertwined with clumps of forest, wetlands, blowholes, and tallgrass prairie, cleansed by naturally occurring fires, pumped clean by slithering aquifers and artesian wells, a shimmering green carpet studded with wildflowers that popped up any time of year, usually after a fire or some mysterious subterranean lucubration.

For the first few miles, the Professor drowsily watched the coachman's huge back and the lobes of the horse. After a few hours, though, he began noticing portions of the road sticking to the brougham's wheels, as Homeric clouds gathered above. The next thing he knew, the carriage was driving up the bed of a tributary.

"Captain!" the Professor called out.

"Sir."

"Don't you think we shall be drowned?"

"Yes, sir, I do! May I offer your Excellency a cigar?" Which the Professor accepted as the coachman, making a desperate effort, succeeded in climbing the right bank. But then after a short jaunt cross-country, he drove straightaway into a lake.

"Captain, have you a cigar left?"

"Yessir."

"Well, give it to me quick."

Jolting from ditch to quagmire, water to mud, and back to water, they finally arrived at the steamer landing.

On further inquiry about the fee, the coachman said only, "We won't need a judge to settle it, your Excellency. Next time, you really should go to the opera." And he seemed more than happy with ten gulden.

The steamer *Desdemona* had started her career with a rudder at each end and a small hut on deck, her huge paddlewheels driven by horses on a capstan inside the hull. When a British firm, Andrews and Richard, bought the ship, a coal stove took over for the horses, and the hut was replaced by an elegant mirrored saloon with red plush couchettes. A diving bell sat funereally upon the stern. The new captain, a weather-beaten English seafarer, knew no more about the sandbanks of the Mze than the bed of the Yellow Sea, and so at flood-time the ship was often found marooned in the middle of a field. The engineer was Scotch and would happily explain mechanical details of the operation, while the jolly Italian cook always kept a pot of bouillabaisse on the boiler.

It took three quarters of an hour to load the carriages, the stevedores cackling and the peasants crossing themselves. Then the ship's whistle sounded, a small cannon boomed, and the *Desdemona* shuddered away from the slimy embankment, the paddlewheels churning up water lilies and duckweed as it bore new shortcuts into the rank abundance of the river's huge loops. Countless waterfowl rose from the dead estuaries—cormorants and kingfishers, herons and egrets, warblers and martins—and from the dark walls of alder and poplar, hungry, chirping nestlings in a thousand nests craned their naked necks.

The river course seemed to have changed substantially in only a month. The passage was most dreary, winding among queer little villages well back from the treacherous banks and monstrous hills covered with hideous, half-pruned vineyards, while the river emitted a peculiar hissing like soda water. They saw neither sail nor oar, and it was difficult to even make out the direction of the current. But the cook enlivened things by making pancakes stuffed with pickled walnuts, and occasionally while rounding a bend, the Professor was taken aback by adorable women in lilac and lavender walking fully dressed into the river up to their armpits.

Inside the mirrored saloon of the *Desdemona*, the Professor recalled his first sight of Felix Aufidius Pzalmanazar. Confirming his worst suspicions out here in the country, his host had come out holding a riding crop and wearing a tweed Chesterfield smoking jacket, twill jodhpurs, and a floppy fedora protruding a long pheasant feather. How well he knew the type. Here stood the very symbol of the moral pathology of the West, genteel, courteous, and above all handsome, a "Christian gentleman" and sportive hunter-magistrate—all a glittering illusion covering over the sickness of society, distracting the masses from reality. Had not Spengler himself identified the gentry as the most reactionary of classes? The Professor knew this privileged caste and its hypocritical code all too well. Oh, it all sounded sportsmanlike—"No hitting below the belt!" and "May the best man win!"— but every generous and graceful gesture obscured a base struggle for power. He imagined his host drinking himself into insensibility each night over a game of cards, then walking a seven-minute mile in the morning to sweat out the toxins, followed by a bit of tennis or high jumping (nothing that would make you appear a clown, of course), before heading out for an agricultural congress or a junket to fix an election.

But then from behind Felix had appeared, sheathed in shot silk, the most beautiful creature of any species the Professor had ever seen, walking at a slightly impossible angle, like a ballerina falling out of a fouetté. Here she was, the perfect trophy companion for our sportive hunter-magistrate! (Why is it always the man of orthodox views who gets to bed the girls by the cartful?) As Ainoha proffered a tray of spritzers and bogberry jam, the traditional Cannonian welcome, the look of her had sent a crackling over his heart which he had experienced only among Italian ruins at dusk.

"The Mze is a very bad neighbor," the captain of the *Desdemona* grumbled to the Professor down in the saloon. There were landslides every minute. Boulders tumbled along fans of scree, and portions of forest collapsed before his eyes. They bumped along sunken bars of quartz, reconnoitered newly regurgitated islands, and dodged fallen logs, varying their course through new obstructions the river had created for itself. Bighorn sheep jumped from ledge to ledge on the creeper-plumed cliffs, and there now seemed miles of nothing save the antlers of dead boughs, crowned with mistletoe and hunched bald eagles. When they did reach a village, enormous white awnings had been cranked open, but only dogs were about, vicious as dingos, trotting down the shuttered lanes. The Professor nevertheless felt full of energy, for you only fully exist when you are in a lost province.

Then Ferryland, latifundia of the Astingi, opened up, a chocolate-colored expanse striped by barley and hay, scattered with poppies, horses swishing their tails, sheep up to their bellies in daisies, and everywhere the bangs of hunting guns. A few girls in the fields waved their sickles at the Professor, and by the time they reached the ruined piers at Dragon's Teeth and the patiently waiting Moccus pulling a hooded lilac gig, all his ideas were again being hushed.

As the windless pillar of smoke above Semper Vero came into view, the Professor noticed some Astingi children in a clearing, charging about good-naturedly on their golden ponies, and playfully brandishing short, curved swords. They wore intricately braided jerkins (a doublet which it was said could deflect any arrow not entirely on the mark) and the Professor could make out some Astingi girls setting up melons atop fence posts, while one by one the boys thundered down the line at full cantor, leaning out of their stirrups and lopping the melons cleanly in half. The girls replenished the practice course with whole fruit as they feasted on the shards, spitting the seeds out in great arcs, as lesser men might lag pennies, and the boys waved gleefully to the stranger as they abruptly reined up their mounts. It was a silent and dignified affair, marred by not so much as a war whoop or girlish squeal. Even the hoof beats were barely audible in the soft Cannonian earth.

At length, however, one rider struck out toward the gig, waving his saber menacingly, and the Professor broke into a nauseating sweat, realizing that in all this vastness there was not a single place to hide. But some fifty meters away the boy sheathed his weapon, leaned out from the horse, and with his head dangling near its hooves, plucked a sapling straight out of the ground. Then, swinging upward in triumph, he grinned, revealing a golden triangle in his front teeth. At this moment the Professor felt he had wasted his entire life.

The Astingi were neither an ethnic group nor a nation, neither a religion nor a movement. The only barbarian tribe to keep its name and language intact, even their race was difficult to tell, as they were usually covered with a grime of coal smoke, and their reddish-blond hair turned black in old age. They had no monuments, no ruins, no book, and they spoke a language unknown to their neighbors—indeed, to whom they were intelligible, besides animals, is not quite clear. A popular academic surmise held they were the remnants of a species of *Homo erectus* that had elsewhere died out without evolving into us. But they were not the proto-us. They were superior to us.

Geographically, they neither founded nor wandered, but in summertime occupied the high plateau of Crisulan, where the tallest plant to be found is the wild onion. In winter they returned to their black tents on the outskirts of town, sending their brown children out to beg by feigning blindness, retardation, leprosy, and other crippling injuries. Often they brought their performing dogs to Silbürsmerze: one danced with cymbals hanging from its hips, another sang along with his master's falsetto war cries. Some charged and withdrew upon wordless commands; one dropped pebbles in a vessel so as to bring the water level to his lips, then begged for an ice cream cone. Another presumed, after looking you up and down and sniffing your hand, to snuff out a dittany from one hundred herbs for what ailed you.

In Roman times, whenever a barbarian tribe revolted—whether the Roxolani, the Jazyges, the Suebi, the Parthians, or the Basternae—their actions were blamed on the Astingi roiling behind them, though truth be told, the Astingi preferred to watch from their unassailable plateau as various predacious hordes rode operatically back and forth, creating the stage sets of Europe. These settlers were often confused as to whether they were invaders or refugees, finding the interior more densely crowded than the conditions they had left behind. Meanwhile, to the front and rear, the Imperium harassed them continually, apparently just out of spite, as social convulsions flooded them with psychopaths, criminals, bitter intellectuals, and masses of people so genetically and culturally broken that they could neither give nor take, but only expire slowly in their midst.

For the Romans themselves, the Astingi territory marked the northeastern frontier of the empire, which may have been why Marcus Aurelius, a frequent visitor to Cannonia during the interminable campaigns against the barbarians, chose to retire there and finish his meditations inside a fortress looking out at the ephemeral riverbanks of the Mze. Dying, he watched one day as a raft loaded with Astingi foundered in the river, its helpless soldiers swept off among ice floes. Not one of them, nor their officers on shore, shouted or bemoaned their fate. They did not even gesticulate while wordlessly awaiting death in the icy water. For the first time the Prince could not arise at dawn, and denouncing himself in his day book, turned over on his couch. Looking as he was through the rose window of the West, when the old gods were dying but Christ had not yet appeared, the warrior-prince-against-his-will had come to believe that if the soul were virtuous, one might look out to eternity, and there would be nothing new for future generations to witness, for the world is both good beyond improvement and evil beyond remedy.

The gig burst around the crest of the volcano, flying through the translucidity. Father noted with relief that the Professor had arrived alone, as promised, though the springs of the lilac gig still seemed weighted down with the memory of their collective despondency. Yet in the boot stood a different dog, pure Alsatian by appearances, tied with the same rope. Rearing up on his hindlegs, the animal jerked his head like a parrot, looping strings of spittle across the Professor's black homburg, and as the gig swung to an abrupt stop, the dog toppled out and hung, eyes bulging, tongue a royal purple, until Felix cut him slack.

The Professor seemed more downcast and disoriented than on his first visit, but nevertheless rushed over before Felix could say a word, vigorously pumping his hand while explaining that Scharf had suddenly sniffed freedom, broken away from his wife on the evening walk, and been cut in two by an electric tram. The Professor, driven wild by his sobbing women, had gotten a replacement the very next day from the *doghaus*, though in this admission Felix could discern no real grief or contrition. And it did not bode well, he noted, that the present dog, despite being in such evident pain, had not cried out.

Ainoha had prepared a hare fricassee for lunch, and Felix was happy enough to postpone investigation of the Alsatian, tying him to the axle on a short lead with a slipknot, hoping no doubt the dog might do away with himself. When asked why he had again chosen a companion for life who had been so obviously and cruelly abandoned, the Professor could only say that the *doghaus* officials had assured him that the animal was of the noblest, purest stock, the absolute favorite of a landed Russian family of the finest northern German origin, the sort of people who had kept their servants standing in the orangery with torches throughout the killing frosts of the recent troubles, and when rightly alarmed by the czar's appointment of a parliament, had hastily emigrated by freighter from Odessa, and now lived in the most reduced condition in the Therapeia ghetto, where they had reluctantly turned over the Alsatian, their last proud possession, to the care of the state. The long sea voyage had no doubt unsettled the animal, the *doghaus* officials opined, but his superior breeding would undoubtedly resurface once the trauma of losing his fortune and his homeland, as well as his constipation, subsided.

Felix put on his gamest face throughout this exculpation, interjecting only that with this animal, at least the nature of the abuse was clear, as was often the case with tumbled aristocrats. However, after coffee on the terrace, the Alsatian bit him fiercely when untied.

"You see—the children call him Wolf!" the Professor fairly shouted.

Father bore pain as well as any man I ever saw, and with one hand still clamped in the brute's jaws, staunched the flow of blood with his free hand, somehow making out of his pocket-handkerchief a tourniquet. If the Professor was embarrassed, he was also plainly intrigued by his host's ambidextrous stoicism, which gave his apology—signaled by the arc of his eyebrows—a rather forced and detached air, his curiosity overcoming his identification with another's misfortune, which any normal person would of course find quite unforgivable.

Felix decided to rescue a bad situation by making it didactic. He allowed his encaptured hand to go limp as a fish in Wolf's mouth, then gave it a friendly shake or two. Realizing that he had perhaps overreacted, the dog reconsidered the amputation, which, as Father was wont to demonstrate, could also be a kindness. The Alsatian's ears arched as he released Felix's hand with a small pop, a string of saliva tinged with blood still conjoining them.

The Professor, however, had apparently decided to inflict a public punishment on the cur, and took up Wolf's rope, coiling it about his arms and swinging the knotted end above his head *a la gaucho*. But before he could administer the chastisement, the animal lowered his head and began to pull like a mule, first in one direction and then in another, causing the Professor's patent leather shoes to screech on the gravel like chalk on a blackboard. He glanced imploringly at Felix, throwing up his one free hand in a gesture of disbelief. And then, as if to certify the case, the shortened lead was snapped even more anarchically, until Wolf, wheezing against his collar with unbelievable persistence, lowered his shoulders, turned his toes in and elbows out, and with gravel flying from his paws, became a classic study in time and motion. The Professor managed to emit a deep sigh before he was again, as on his first visit, forced to his knees, but this time also flung forward on his face. Succeeding in making his point, Wolf immediately sat down and licked the considerable foam from the corners of his mouth, one yellow eye wandering like an expiring nova.

"You see," the Professor groaned, lying on his stomach, "he wants to leave us! There is no master in this house." The dog had yet to emit as much as a grunt.

Felix folded his arms and delivered his lay opinion that the dog had been pulled on so much that his natural impulse was now to pull himself, wanting like anyone to put a little loop into his future. And he could play this game only by exhausting his tenacious master. The good news was that the dog in question was not timid, not a layabout like dear departed Scharf. His illness was simply an inappropriate response to the stress of everyday life.

"He doesn't want to run away, Herr Doktor. He just wants some slack."

The Professor took this in gravely and repeated it to himself as if he were translating from a foreign language.

"Then he's not . . . a revolutionary?"

"If so, a very poor one."

Closing one brown eye and rising to a knee, the Professor opined that perhaps the freedom and fresh air of Cannonia might ameliorate the situation. Felix shook his head slowly.

"When a bear is uncultured, you do not tie him in a forest."

This brought forth from the Professor a huge shrug, as if from his very soul, signifying, "What is to be done, then?"

Felix looked the Professor in the eye and reached into an inside jacket pocket, where he always kept a delicate choke collar of the tiniest blueblack Dresden steel ringlets. He held the collar up for his client as a jeweler holds a necklace for the bride, making a shimmering circle of dark silver and iron.

"Training, Herr Doktor Professor, tra*ining*," he whispered, trilling the *n*s.

My father was a man of many pockets: one for tobacco, one for sweets, one for the Dresden collar, one for dry husks of bread, and one from which he now withdrew a crimson kerchief, which he knotted around his neck. He needed to work the dog without distraction, so he ushered the Professor into the house, where, not finding Mother at home, the visitor could be seen in the staircase window, faded and grave as in a daguerreotype. Through the leaded glass, he watched the two murky figures in the courtyard.

At first, Felix slowly circled the panting, spittleflecked Alsatian, moving with his back against a dark green privet hedge. Then he held up a husk of bread.

"Kom*inzee*heer, Wolfie."

Trailing his rope, the dog approached tentatively, but then took the husk from Felix's hand and walked about sniffing and scratching it like a chicken, while occasionally peering over his shoulder at the knotted rope, then back at his immaculate food source. Felix continued to pass out husks with one hand, while with the other he opened a large flapped pocket that had been lined with surgical rubber so that the blood of game might easily be removed. (He had one sewn in all his jackets, evening clothes included.) From this otherwise empty game pocket he now withdrew a strand of insulated electrical wire as long as he was tall. My grandfather Priam had refused to install electricity at Semper Vero, and the week after he died, his wife, age spots on her temples as large as silver dollars, had the entire house and every outbuilding wired, socketed, and telephoned. It was this original telephone wire—flexible yet holding a shadow of the shape your hands might give it—Felix now held, a line without hard edges which could be looped or straightened, and along which willed energy might run like no other conductor, alternating impulses of discipline and freedom.

Gently, he looped the steel ringlets about Wolf's neck, attached the telephone cord to one ring, and keeping plenty of slack, strolled along the privet hedge. Wolf grimaced and dug in, preparing to haul his newest interlocutor beyond the horizon. But just as the lead grew taut, Felix turned his wrist a quarter-turn, and keeping his elbow stationary, gave a delicate if abrupt jerk, as if he were scything through a single stalk of wheat. The

Dresden collar slipped through itself and the ringlets popped tight on Wolf's larynx, emitting a click like a cartridge being chambered.

The dog's eyes bulged, then he coughed politely, and rather than hauling stopped short. As he did so, the collar slipped back open and the cord went slack. Wolf was fleetingly aware of a parenthesis of liberation, the triumph of cessation, that moment when your lover allows you to take her by the throat while your own head is cradled in her hands like a melon.

Then my father coiled the cord, leaving the collar hanging loose, and Wolf walked beside him calmly, looking up occasionally in disbelief, as the figure in the window broke into silent applause, then raced down the staircase.

"To touch the compulsion," the Professor expostulated breathlessly, "is near enough the soul . . . And you didn't even have to hurt him!"

"I will never hurt him," Father said evenly. "You must trust me."

"The question is whether *I* can bear it," the Professor sighed. For the first time his tone was somewhat jocular. "I only fear that he will come to prefer you."

"These are the chances we all must take. Who knows who deserves whose loyalty? What do you want most of all, sir? What is your greatest wish for the dog in question?"

"I want him . . . to *stay*," the Professor mused, "or if not precisely stay, at least not run from me."

"You must not confuse running away with hauling. The question, I believe, is not one of disappearing, but of constantly jerking you about."

"I still do not see how force . . . such manipulation can accomplish anything lasting."

"Ah, well, don't you see, it's just the right amount of force, applied at exactly the right time and place. It takes a lifetime to learn, if I may say so."

"Will you teach it to me, then?"

"Ah, my friend, you are not ready. Humans don't have the sense to submit. The dog bites only hard enough to make a point. Yes, we think dogs almost human, and dogs think we are other dogs. Which do you think is closer to the truth? Remember St. Augustine: you won't see God until you become as a little dog. When you are ready, the teacher will appear. That I guarantee."

"I suppose you mean that we learn only by punishment!" the Professor intoned morosely.

"Not exactly. We learn by the threat of a thrashing administered against a background of love. Think of it as a loving withdrawal. Even gentleness must be enforced."

"I still do not comprehend your preliminary diagnosis."

"Well, if it's analogy you want, I should say that what we have here is the soul of a horse trapped in the body of a dog."

"Then poor Wolf believes himself to be a horse?"

"No. He knows he's not a horse. He just wants to feel like a horse, because he believes the horse to be superior."

"I'm not sure I grasp . . ."

"It's like this. You don't want a bottle of wine, do you? No, you want the feeling it gives. What we're saying to Wolfie is, go right ahead and feel like a horse if you like. Just don't behave like one when you're around me."

"This is hardly scientific, Councilor."

"Ah, dear friend, facts may be different, but feelings are the same. And it's not the thinking that's hard. It's selling the thinking, Herr Professor."

"In my experience," the Professor muttered defensively, "one can often observe in human illness the neuroses of the animals."

"Perhaps. But the satisfying thing about dogs is that they fear what actually happens, not fear itself. Therefore, the teacher must constantly fight his way into reality, all the while maintaining detachment."

"But how can we proceed before we locate the trauma, immaterial as it may be?"

"What do we start with, you say? My poor self and this poor dog. That is all. Our origins are different, our values are different, our ends are different. They are all incompatible and they cannot be pushed beyond their limits. But they can be imaginatively understood, if there is a cord, a simple cord."

"It seems, if I may say so, a project fraught with risk."

"Whenever you weigh beauty and utility on the same scale, a kind of genetic civil war is created within the animal. When you are stronger, I will elucidate the costs and lessons."

"But might a dog behave and not be well?"

"We are not concerned with the whole animal, because that leads us into ideology. Life is all concealed pistols and waxed slipknots, Professor. All we can manage is to make the dog face the facts."

"The verdict, then; I tremble."

"Ah, Wolf is so much a product of our time. The greater he contests your authority, the greater his need for authority. His willfulness is mirrored back at him, and he becomes even more disappointed with himself. The result is discontent without reference, for which there is no answer. All we have is demand—perverse, obstinate, insoluble, interminable demand! And so the therapy can never end. Are you prepared for such an outcome?"

The Professor walked in circles, squinting and pulling on his moustache.

"It would appear, Councilor, that I have little choice in the matter."

Smoking their cigars, they walked arm in arm along the darkening river. Wolf and I gamboled after them, tripping one another up. I threw a stick in the water and the dog looked at me with disdain. He was getting better already.

"It's all so vague and problematical," the Professor mused. "How do you stand it, Councilor?"

"The transferal is incomplete, my friend, it is always incomplete. It's the nature of the mechanism."

"Why do you suppose they love us so? And why do we even bother with *them*?"

Father stopped, and as they turned to look over the fields, delivered himself of something like a courtroom summation:

"This attachment to man is not born of consciousness, nor does it become conscious. Man, through the insensitivity of objects, feels homesick and alone. In his depths there is an earnest cry for intercourse. When he looks at things, they do not appear different; when he utters his cry there is no response. His conversation with nature has been silenced. The dog is the only one who remains, his reminder of the world of nature that has vanished. Snatched from our place in nature, all love seeks that which is lost, all that which is not itself. In the shimmering heat in the silent fields, we hear in the cry of the animal a call for companionship. The stronger the man, the more vulnerable he is to this. Then the dog finally comes, and together they search for unreal shelter."

The two men stood with their arms about each other's shoulders, discussing the mysteries of coordination and conduct, staring out into the unkempt fields in which huge hares bounced like kangaroos and quail called cloyingly to one another as raptors wheeled in the thickening sky. Wolf shoved his head in the tall grass, while leaving his body well outside the green envelope. A gadfly was playing about his limp tail.

"So," the Professor mused, "we are back to the Jurassic. Horsetails high as oats, saurians running about."

"Ah yes, my friend," Father said proudly. "Out here in Klavierland we are truly, absolutely . . . *nowhere!*"

They agreed that as unpromising as Wolf was, he deserved an indefinite trial, provided the Professor would visit regularly and participate in the great experiment.

"So," the Professor sighed, "Wolf is a real survivor."

"Sentimentality will shorten your life, my friend," Father said softly. "One must be on guard with survivors. They will damage you."

IN DARKEST CANNONIA
(Rufus)

The Agent known as Iulus had the grave dignity and easy familiarity of the Cannonian gentry, taciturn and intent, without a hint of either fear or braggadocio. This was not, as I would come to recognize, the dignity of the freeborn, but of those who have witnessed the ineptitude and transitoriness of all great powers, and despite an inferior environment, have refused to be robbed of value. His wiry frame, although delicate, was extremely purposeful, cradling the infuriating hand-eye coordination of the natural athlete. If you threw a comradely arm about him you were instantly aware of a tremendous tensile strength for his slight size, a deadly serious will with a lightness of touch. He was the essence of the *Schwermut*, with that indolent charm which combines the alertness of the northern sailor with the impassive expression of the Byzantine, a youth who was used to talking on equal terms with both adults and animals. At twenty-one he gave the impression of having tried everything and renounced everything. He had no complaints and no hopes. But there wasn't a touch of bitterness or self-doubt in his manner, and it was easy to see why women would go crazy over him.

The relations between himself and the dogs were formal and respectful, not those of master and pupil, much less man and beast. It was an older notion of conduct—that in order to preserve the integrity of the relationship, a true friend never feels the necessity to declare one's love. It seemed both man and animal were in touch with a discipline beyond them, which announced that friendship might turn into love, but never the other way about. I knew I was already out of my depth, and that was just fine with me.

We proceeded through successive islets of forest, each interval exposing us longer in the dawning light, until finally our cover disappeared entirely as we traversed a corridor of open stubble fields. On their thickened edges, scythed exactly as high as a man's thigh, I could make out other canine shapes, moon-colored dogs isolated in small packs, loping along as if attached to us by invisible wires, a kind of flanking cortege.

Then suddenly the flat and uninteresting country opened up into a vast amphitheater of hills, rising like immense solidified waves, increasing in size as they receded to merge into a great blank wall of naked granite peaks on the eastern horizon. The dirty gray glacial scour of the finest pumice fell sharply to the turgid river. On the far side Iulus pointed to a manor house, hunched like a yellow cat taking the sun out of harm's way. "The Cannonian paradise," he announced softly, and it was then I first beheld Semper Vero.

I was attached (under the cover of Divisional Historian) to the counter-intelligence unit of the 20th Armored Corps, XII Division, 65th Infantry, U.S. 3rd Army, *Operation Hercules*, which had been stopped (or rather, politically halted) in April of 1945, on the west bank of the Hron, where you could smell Cannonia, as you can smell an island in the sea. We could have easily pressed on into Cannonia Inferiore and taken the heights along the Mze, but the men were hardly willing to risk all in the last days of the war, and in any event, even if Roosevelt's sudden death had not paralyzed the command, the textbook terrain was unsuited to armor. No one had ever been able to maneuver militarily in those vast, rich, flat, and foggy marchlands, for the most part undrained, unchanneled, and uncharted.

Admittedly, we had been through a rough patch of days, the deliberate sigh of the 70 mm artillery, the blustering howl of the Nebelwerfers, the thin whisper of mortars, and the evil singing of the 88s. But once "Roosenheimer's Butchers" (as they referred to us on the German radio) broke through and routed the last of those Nazi champion diggers, we found ourselves alone alongside the turgid, steely Hron, and relaxed.

Cannonia was the closest, cruelest country for a fighting man, a veritable manmade jungle, a combination of ingenious irrigation, assiduous ancient cultivation, islets of virgin forest, and other trophy features of constructed wild topography. Calculatingly preserved from ancient times as royal hunting, smuggling, and pleasure grounds, it made even saturation bombing problematic. Every vineyard stake was topped with a bayonet against parachutists, every pathway had a false bottom. Every cemetery cross was sharpened, and even the chimps at the zoo were said to be armed. One could apparently march all the way to Russia beneath a deep canopy of trees, camouflaged in the never-ending sound of rushing brooks. The strategic possibilities of its underground rivers and saltmines appeared to be endless, its villages were dispersed and pocketed as if by a master strategist, and the "countryside" was simply a euphemism for vineyards and fields of white asparagus bordered with impenetrable hedgerows, in turn separated by marshes and canals. The whole territory was slathered by the serpentine tributaries and lesser streams of the Mze, Its, and Vah. The only possible military movement through the country was either by deep canal or narrow winding roads lined with lopped-off oaks, grapevines thick as a man's arm and a hundred times more resilient, not to mention thickets of mulberry and false gorse. Every copse provided a perfect ambush, every thickwalled granary a line of fire, every capacious courtyard a potential boobytrap. Tanks might pass within thirty yards of one another and never be the wiser. When it was hilly there was not so much as a crag or cave to give cover, while the spectral flatness of its oft-bloodied plains elicited hallucinations. In short, the country's strangely cultivated wildness blotted out any normal apprehension.

Cannonia was the only place in the European theater that had not yet seen action, an island of calm, a mote of silence in which dog shows were still regularly scheduled beneath aerial dog fights, and indeed, under the pressure of invasion, the populace had become, from all evidence, even more lighthearted, carefree, and erotically active than ever. During our bombing runs they repaired excitedly to their cinemas and cafes in the saltmines, cheerfully attesting to the Roman observation that "the best part of Cannonia is underground," as well as their local slogan, "to be well hidden is to live well." We were always somewhat taken aback at how well fed the Cannonian civilians seemed to be. During a lull in the advance on Dede-Agach, we were taken by damsels in white dresses and parasols to a chocolate factory where the sugar ran higher than my boottops.

I had left the crystal decanters and chandeliers of OSS (Oh So Secret) London so hastily that no one had backgrounded me on Cannonia. Our man behind the lines had brought the good news out for nothing, I was to take the bad news back at salary, the only distinction between enlisted man and officer, as far as I could see. My mission was straightforward: walk the cat back to Dog Cannonia, make contact with Iulus, and pick up the Holy Crown, the symbol of the nation's legitimacy, before the Russians could snatch it.

One of my old college chums, Ed Kirby, then as now a reliable courier, rode with me to the aerodrome. He seemed uncharacteristically nervous, stroking his not prominent chin and crossing and recrossing his unmilitary wingtipped brogues. But he had my orders directly from the Potomac. In essence they were this: the Hron was our stopline. Make no commitments of any sort. We should assist any retreating Germans (Marshall Zhukov was quite right to complain about this) and should we encounter any Russians, be prepared to exchange small presents, and avoid wearing your good pistol or expensive watch.

Ed had brought with him the Cannonian file. There was nothing in it but a yellowed *Herald Tribune* clipping about some unpaid World War One reparations, railway schedules from the 1930s, a letter from the Rockefeller Foundation refusing a grant to rebuild a Cannonian cathedral, as their guidelines precluded funding a pagan institution, as well as portions of the diary of a seventeen-year-old daughter of an Austrian diplomat who had taken a pony cart tour at the turn of the century. "The wind blows differently here," she began.

Ed's own knowledge of Cannonia seemed to be restricted entirely to memories of Comp Lit at Princeton. "The Cannonians believe that every life, like every book, has three beginnings and three endings, but there's no choosing between them. One must accept them all. That's the Cannonian twist, their *Triplex Philosophia*. There's always a twist in Cannonia," he said somewhat sarcastically. "Stand fast and wait to be contacted."

Those were Ed's grinning last words as he saw me aboard the blacked out DC-3, handing me a copy of *American Plans for a New Cannonia*—a tome, to tell you the truth, I have never finished to this day. Suffice it to say that as the Cannonians had perfected bourgeois life to its *ne plus ultra* (a source of particular fascination to the Soviets) their history was one of continual collaboration with any government which had the temerity to announce itself, and their insatiable pursuit of private pleasures made them the most unreliable allies imaginable. We had not taken their foolish and comic declaration of war upon us seriously, and while they might well be "damned inconvenient," as Sumner Wells put it, our interests there were not material, and our policy was one of "limited encouragement." Nevertheless, as a kind of farewell present to the Soviets, whose appallingly mauled remnants were now making their appearance amongst us, it was thought that we might contact and offer support to a potential guerrilla force, a semi-nomadic tribe known as the Astingi, allegedly the last tribe of prehistory to keep their name and language intact. Free of all modern malaises, the Astingi would fight at the drop of a hat. "To be vanquished and not surrender—that is victory" was their slogan. Their brief, "to prick every woman in the world as well as every Empire." They had fought with Napoleon in 1805 and against him in 1809, fought with Lafayette in 1775 and with the British in 1812, and were even said to have intervened in our Civil War, somewhere in Florida.

They had no heroes, no myths, no lost nation, and no promised land. They neither founded nor wandered. They had come from nowhere and disappeared into nothing, long-nosed, subtly smiling, and sensitive-footed, moving only at night, leaving no traces above the ground, mystifying the barbarians with their imperturbable discipline and appalling the Romans with their permissiveness (the husbands actually sitting down to dinner with their wives).

They were by now the most rugged race left on the planet, jolted on horseback from the day they were born, occupying the great crystal clear high Plateau of Crisulan at the source of the Hor, an area by turns parched as the Sahara, barren as the Gobi, and cold as the Arctic, where the tallest plant to be found is the wild onion, and more impractical to the explorer than either of the poles. They believed in neither God nor the Devil, nor in the sacraments any more than the resurrection of the dead. Christians, Pagans, and Musselman alike had termed Cannonia the "country of the unbelievers." Yet the Astingi apparently always had everything they needed. "Even their dog leashes were made of sausages," as Herodotus noted. They thought the Cossacks wimps, the gypsies too sedentary, the Jews passive-aggressive, the gentry unmannered, the peasants too rich by half, the aristocracy too democratic, and the Bolsheviks and Nazis too pluralistic. When cornered, they would put their women and children in the front ranks, and fire machine guns through their wives' petticoats. And in times of peace they were renowned for their impromptu traveling performances of Shakespeare and Chekhov. The only belief they shared with Americans was that the entire world was constituted of rings of peoples set up to protect them.

Their women, nimble, handsome, and accommodating, were celebrated for their extraordinary carriage and complexions varying between pink and bronze. The infidelity of wives was punished by a mild beating, while that of men by a fine of cattle. The men were famous for their outspokenness, friendliness, and nonstop humor. They seemed to be everything I admired—handsome, intelligent, and reckless, with a healthy relation to life and oblivious to death.

To be honest, I didn't see we had much to offer them. Indeed, I had noticed in London that our intelligence briefings had become more complex and arcane as our forces approached the border. I took little interest in the internecine struggles our specialists described, backing one bandit one day then changing their allegiances the next. It was clear only that Cannonian politics were as gnarled, fecund, and impenetrable as their landscape, as useless to themselves as to others, and that a military mind could not even begin to plot their intricacy. So it was not surprising that our analyst's lectures petered away self-consciously as glazed stares from the ranks became the norm.

But arriving at the front, I heard quite a different story. Among the guys, Cannonia was simply referred to as Terra XX, where it was rumored there was a secret redoubt at the exact geographical center of the continent, filled with art masterpieces, one hundred tons of gold, and heavy water, guarded by a battalion of yellow-eyed dogs and seven-foot mountain men in scarlet tunics—a cache in its scope and preciousness which made Cannonia at that time the most cultured nation on earth, as they had been regarded in the fourteenth century when their treasury and library exceeded that of France. We had been told to stand fast, coil up our formations, and clean up our flanks, but you could sense the renewed "fighting spirit" among the ranks.

This was not a novel notion. We knew that Hitler ("That handsome boy who never rode a horse," as Iulus's father called him) was constructing a vast redoubt in the Bavarian mountains from which to conduct a last stand, as well as house his art collection. As in the First World War, the only strategic reason for our bloody forcedmarch upon Cannonia was to cut off a potential German retreat. Our information was based on intercepts of cables from the Cannonian foreign minister, Count Zich, to the Japanese ambassador in Berlin, Oshima, offering shelter in Cannonia for the imperial family portraits, consistent with the traditional Cannonian foreign policy of keeping a foot in every camp, and further suggesting that the location of the true inner redoubt was in salt mines in the Unnamed Mountains of Cannonia, which already housed Hitler's own Vermeer, *The Artist in his Studio*; the Ghent Altarpiece; the first page of the "Song of Hildebrand"; and a world-class collection of toy soldiers. Not for nothing did the advancing Soviet army carry with them carloads of art experts. Terra XX was to be defended to the death by a half-million, hand-picked men and women, the Wolverines, who were already infiltrating and toughening the SS, whose mission it was not only to prolong the war indefinitely, but to launch terroristic attacks throughout the continent from the most inaccessible part of Europe. Of course we know today that this was not precisely true. But I also know that the top-secret documents relating to it in the archives have been retrospectively falsified.

In any event, our advance column breached the Hron and, leaving Dede-Agach and her wasp-waisted women, slowly negotiated the trackless wastes of the Marchlands on a southeasternly salient, without a single act of resistance, indeed without a single incident of any kind. Through our binoculars we scanned the villages where no flag flew, a village darkness like no other darkness. ("A land so poor that even the crows fly upside down to avoid seeing it," was how an eighteenth-century traveler had described it.) In not-so-short order, outrunning our gasoline supplies, our armored column finally spread out over some seventy miles. Directed by scurrying jeeps and swooping Piper Cubs, we finally reached a perfectly unknown double-oxbow of the Mze.

Breached for the first time since Napoleon, the Mze had proven a disappointment in every way. Planes had photographed it, engineers had studied it for months, generals had dreamed of nothing else. But when we got there it wasn't as big as the Mississippi, or as beautiful as the Hudson, or as rough as the Colorado—just graygreen, cold, and unimpressive. "Never halt on the near side of a river, even if you do not intend to exploit the crossing." Had that ancient injunction not been pounded into us in War College, we would have never have forged the Mze. As it was, the engineer in charge of the pontoon bridge was in despair when he was told it had taken him twelve hours longer than it had taken Julius Caesar. But soon our first column of tanks crossed the bridge, draped now with drying wash, captured flags, and laughing naked spitting boys. And an hour later, on the firmer ground of a glacier scour, our half-tracks crested the bluffs of yet another bend of the Mze. Downriver, a dozen locomotives were parked on a siding, alongside barges packed with knocked-down submarines. The trains had been blasted to smithereens, one locomotive pointing straight up, like a dog begging on its hind legs. The current was so stolid that it gave no reflection whatsoever. There was not even the trace of an eddy, a fleck of foam. It made not the slightest sound. "Let's go down and piss in it," my sergeant driver said, and so we did.

Once relieved, I chanced to glance up, and on the far bank I could make out a band of silent mounted men, an Astingi advance guard which I recognized by their raspberry overcoats and high fur hats, something you don't often see in April. They were gazing down at us paternalistically, as they had for three thousand years, witnessing the besmirched Matron of Christendom as she once again walked into their shallow stream to perish. After buttoning up their overcoats and letting off a single rifle shot, they held up an odd three-fingered salute and filed silently away behind a dome of rocks.

So it was that we came to parade rest on Cannonia's watery border, about to read her secretmost entrails, prepared to open a spacious wound in Hell's own soil, dig out ribs of gold, and build a Pandemonium. We had no experience with that long tradition in which the cheerful and well-intentioned tyrant, with his perverse magnanimity and wooden hug, enters the ghostly empire to pick up the beautiful corpse, only to have it fall apart in his hands. Indeed, we believed, even more than the communists, that we had captured a stage of history—the worst thing, according to Astingi lore, that can befall a people.

That night, all along the Mze, our artillery massed hub to hub, we lay down a coordinated fire the likes of which even the most battle-hardened veteran had never seen. The Conqueror was smiling in his chariot, and his horses smiled the same hard smile. You could read the dark book of history as if it were daylight; the barrage threw all the objective ground to be taken into bold and summary relief. We had been ordered to explode all four corners of Cannonia. But she never really caught, only smoldered. A stench of blasted muck hung over the country for years after the war as the louring Commander reined in his foaming steeds.

We had hardly bivouacked when an old soldier came stumbling out of the forest in a uniform cobbled together from five or six nations, and began to spill the beans in several different languages before we even put him on the ground. His first words were a warning not to shell the barges down river, as they were loaded with poison gas. Then he added proudly that this was the exact spot he had surrendered in the First World War. "I can't read or write," he muttered, "but I can sing." My rule then as now was to never interrogate a prisoner under forty, for you can learn little from a man who still thinks he has something to prove.

I can't say that we completely understood him, our proficiency in languages being of a strictly schoolboy nature, and it became increasingly clear that Öscar Özgur was something of an idiot, though quite calm and professional about it.

But Öscar had in his possession a letter written on violet stationery in rather grandiloquent French, addressed to no one in particular, sealed with the waxen emblem of a *petite noblesse terrienne*, as well as the last attestatory secret code of our man behind the lines. There was also a latitude and longitude for a proposed rendezvous, and the promise of a bonfire burning. The family crest portrayed a nymph trying on a crown (the infamous Venus of Muranyi, I was to learn) astride an inscription: "Back to the original sources." It concluded rather formally, with my contact's swirling vermillion signature dusted with cinnabar.

> . . . *Venez, si vous voulez, et recevez notre couronne.*
> *Nous causons souvant des delices de notre*
> *maison viste don't le souvenir me s'effacera*
> *jamais de nos coeurs mille et mille amities.*
>
> *Sauve Que Peut*, Iulus

Naturally, the letter stunned me. Even the most dedicated student of Cannonian affairs could not have anticipated such a windfall. I admit I had the stench of priceless treasures and czar's gold in my nostrils. My putative superiors were still well to the rear, and there was little point in torturing such a pathetic messenger with further cross-examination. Things were loose at the front in those days, my OSS papers invited no questioning from even the most belligerent rednecked MP, and the letter seemed to fulfill the spirit of my vague orders. I may have lacked Zeus's stamina and colorful disguises, but I had his roving eye. I wanted to do things with Cannonia, some gently, some not so, some with long graceful movements, some with short automatic bursts. And then of course, I wanted to pick up her broken body and be cheered in the streets. These were not the naïve sentiments of a wild-eyed boy. That was always to be the fatal misapprehension of our adversaries. For we were born harsh, beyond the Gulf Stream. We only looked soft and shiny—like a larva, concealing a stinger enfolded in its heavy blond wings—a vast armada of Detroit steel and Texas oil, beneath a comic sheen. I was looking for no vista, I can tell you, no place to meditate, no real estate. When you grow up looking at nothing but billboards and telephone poles, and your only relation to the past is Euclidian geometry, you don't mind looking, properly armed, straight into the jaws of hell. And in Cannonia, where the sky meets the ground like no place else on earth, at dusk everything is the color of a runaway dog.

To tell you the truth, I never felt either courageous or foolhardy. I had spent most of the war pretending I wasn't baffled. I never heard from anyone a patriotic sentiment. We were simply fatalistic. And we felt so much more akin to the Germans and the Russians that we could hardly believe we were fighting with the English and the French. I mean let's be honest about it. Was anything ever more fun than picking up the Europids—those peoples who have made an artform of feeling sorry for themselves—in their unparalled wickedness, and bringing them sternly to account? You can get away with murder in America, but only in Europe can you be *really* bad. My specialty and my nearsightedness had so far protected me from the more suicidal missions in which our men behind the lines had been my proxy. I had a burning desire to do good. And to kill somebody.

Orders in my pocket and invitation in hand, I was nevertheless overcome by an anxiety I had never felt in battle, a *horror vaccui*, in which even a tear for our sacrifices would not flow. I have never felt such unease or uncomprehending fear as I did that late afternoon on the Mze. Old hands call it *Fingerspitzengefuhl* (fingertiptingling), and it is more addictive than sex. But what good is foretelling if you cannot forestall the disasters you foresee?

I commandeered a jeep, and on a makeshift runway in a sugarbeet field, after presenting my doctored Joint-Chief-of-Staff's *laissez passer*, talked a bored flyboy into taking me up. I don't know what kind of plane it was, only that the takeoff seemed longer than the flight.

The manor house of Semper Vero squatted phlegmatically upon the flattened top of an eroded volcanic cone. From the base of the old volcano, blackened vineyards and chocolate-colored fields fell away on all sides, interspersed with patches of mustard flared with poppies. Each irregular field was partitioned with musk rose and yellow gorse, and every inch was cultivated to the very edge of a serpentine road which ended abruptly at the base of steep forested slopes. As Iulus poled me across the Mze, in a strange copper-prowed caique, I again consulted my maps, and realized that this rim of heavy dark primeval forest was the same wall of oak and beech that Marcus Aurelius had rightly feared as the home of the barbarian, and yet it was here, in the only forward outpost in which he felt truly safe, that he laid down his pen and died. The river at this crossing point seemed to be encased with sheets of steel.

The walled park surrounding the house was filled entirely with evergreens: blueblack spruce, lime-green tsuga, the feathery apricot of Zelkova, and an occasional bright minaret of golden cypress, amidst a deep sprawl of weeping hemlock and thick red trunks of fragrant cedars. The ancient Cannonian saying has it that "trees and men are friends," and Semper Vero was the arboreal testament that the non-indigenous could flourish and thrive in Cannonian soil, as long as they were planted close enough together to endure the brutal cross-winds which had dragged me so many miles. It was also clear that in Cannonia even the seasons were compressed and overlapped, and everywhere spontaneous mutation was emphasized over evolution. After all, I too was something of a farm boy, growing up in Ohio nursery country on the lip of the great glacier, and for each huge specimen that Iulus proudly pointed out I had seen in its two-year form in five-gallon cans along the highway or on a truck, and I knew its four-color seasonal blooms from a catalog. I may have been inexperienced, but I was hardly naïve about the trials of beautification projects.

We approached the manor by a narrow winding peat road, through the filigree of a beech grove in bud, passing a massive empty fountain, a sulfurous diagonal stripe across its marble rim the only trace of its former water jet. It was obvious I was not the first combatant to visit Semper Vero. The retreating Germans had time only to gouge some second-rate *plein d'air* paintings from their frames, the amber inlays from the library, the nametags from the arboretum (only the ones in Latin), and after boobytrapping the winecellar, left singing at the top of their lungs. Shortly thereafter, a motorized Siberian advance column had arrived in padded winter uniforms and pressed their perspiring Mongol faces against the long French windows. They crated up the tractor and generator, drank the cologne and brakefluid, and after eating a puppy, blew several of themselves up with the wine. Yet as far as I was concerned, this all could have happened a thousand years ago.

The house appeared to be constructed of every historical style imaginable, a marvelous mad medley of academic and ad hoc concepts, its Byzantine aspects reproachful of its gothic elements, its Victorian additions so expressive in their hatred for everything baroque. And yet despite these open contradictions and hostilities, the house, like my host, exuded in the midst of its pathetic, humiliated, and mutilated little country an enormous self-assurance and intimidating ease; and the great appeal of an abandoned house is, after all, the thrill that the owner is going to catch you in it. I will not pretend to be able to render a specific impression of that eccentric house, except to say that its main beauty lay in the abandoned and overgrown park that surrounded it, madder rose and mariposa lilies mingling beneath the open branches of fig trees and dark allées of cypress, down which an unmarked divebomber, its ordnance spent, occasionally roared incuriously.

From a squat central turret, a tattered gray flag embroidered with a mauve rose still flew.

Iulus did not often look you in the eyes, but when he did you had the unnerving feeling he was looking right to the back of your skull. Dressed in tennis flannels of another era, he conducted our tour of the park with a slightly bored air, as if he had been preparing for this moment all his life and could have gone through it in his sleep. We wandered down the overgrown enfilades bordered with parasol pines and groves of catalpas planted upon mounds, glomerations of plane trees, clusters of cutleaved ash, spruce with huge wartlike thickenings, clumps of unpruned Schwedler maples, and two-hundred-year-old specimens of silk pine and ginkgo. He encouraged me to explore the sightlines to every point of the compass, noting that one could see an enemy approaching from any direction. Eventually we made our way through a ravine in which four or five hundred oaks and chestnuts had been uprooted by stray artillery.

"If I were an American," Iulus spoke at length for the first time, as if to wish away the blasted landscape, "I would tell you that this park holds the greatest collection of evergreens east of the Rhine, and is one of two places in the world (the other is in China) where northern and southern forests commingle in a thin belt at the nether lip of the Ice Age."

He had an amazingly deep and magnificent voice, something like a cello, one of those voices which seem to come out of the entire skull rather than the facial cavity, and he had mastered the trick of lowering it a register still further when interrupted, surprising me into a listening silence. "You are standing in the most botanically diverse place on earth," he concluded, "where the coniferous and deciduous, the foliate and naked, the arctic spruce, the fig, and magnolia can exist perfectly composed, side by side." Then he stepped back and gestured toward the southern vista.

Across the deadly swath of uprooted trees, great clouds of multicolored dust and leaves spiraled across the lime green bog which always threatened to engulf the country. Enormous yews, disfigured either by human ignorance or malice, their untrimmed tops whirling out of control like inverted peacocks, formed a living tsuga colonnade racked with brown spot. The dogs had bolted down a path, leading us to the "Chinese Pavilion," a ruin large enough to quarter half a cavalry regiment, where the vista opened across meadows full of wildflowers to a plain where the glacier had given itself up in an ice meadow. "An arm of the lost inland sea," Iulus noted with satisfaction, pointing out a series of spheroidal boulders which seemed to have been dispersed with great care. They lay in glistening clumps like stiffened eggwhites, as if pieces of cumulus had fallen to earth, in what appeared to be the remnants of a long abandoned golfcourse, crossed and recrossed by a rutted brown road overhung with weeping witchhazel. Below us, he explained with an air of detached melancholy, stretched the valley of the White Vah, a gash between two ridges of Paleozoic minerals, where phyllites and porphyroids had been mined from time immemorial. We traversed the almost vertical slopes, dotted with ilex, olive, and wild rhubarb, and punctuated with rills and torrents. As we crossed and recrossed the rough bed of a cataract with very low water, I noticed that this was the only place, since I had entered the country where there was no wind at all. "The climate is such that we could have marginally supported oranges and lemons," Iulus concluded. "But no one with a true interest in nature and the cycles of the seasons would consciously cultivate the soft androgyny of the Mediterranean. Wouldn't you say?"

His English was so precise and Anglophone that it was intimidating. The only indication that Iulus was a foreigner, apart from the usual troubles with "th" and "w," and an occasional word which took on a guttural German ring, was his studied avoidance of the more inflected vowels of Oxonian cadences, as if to acknowledge the superior oral manners of a certain intellectual class, while at the same time disapproving of it. He took great delight in coming up with exact technical terms, emitting a prideful smile when searching for a colloquial phrase and finding it convincing. "Buckeye!" he roared, gesticulating at a huge horsechestnut. "That's what *you* would call it, no?" To an American ear, it was as if the English language had been written for brass. And each syllable had the clarity of a note struck with a mallet.

The dogs led us through a switchback of crimson rhododendron and we emerged overlooking the manor. It was bordered by two great bodies of water, one free-flowing and clear as a trout stream, the other completely stagnant and silted, without so much as a mayfly's ripple. "One of my grandfather's projects," Iulus declared offhandedly, "the result of a pub bet. You see before you a river in which you *can* step twice."

"Did he win?" I offered cheerfully.

"Hard to say. It might have been on a technicality; one can step in it twice, but only once? I used to believe that Heraclitus was wrong because we all bathe in the same river of Time, ever more limpid and ever deeper at the selfsame point of its flowing. But now I believe him wrong because you cannot step in it even once. Is there a word in English," he mused, "for a contradiction in which both conflicting propositions are false?"

My mind scuttled along like a lost lizard as I looked away.

ALTERNATIVE MEDICINE
(Iulus)

The Professor returned to Semper Vero every second Sunday, met punctually each time by the golden horse and a different type of conveyance from our large collection, though on some occasions he rented his own gig and piebald mare, without driver, from the Skopje. And in those months Wolf was indeed improving, walking tall, though fits of hauling would still come over him without warning as he gulped horseturds by the bucketful.

It was agreed that in the interim each of them would be free to practice their competing therapies upon the dog in question, on the assumption that any deviation from his present neurasthenia could only be a step in the right direction, and that in defiance of Hippocrates's Oath, any treatment would be better than nothing.

My father had seen at once that Wolf, like Scharf, was a hopeless case whom only the most intensive treatment and objective attention would make remotely palatable, and that a cure in any acceptable sense was impossible. He knew the only hope lay not in therapies, but in that as the Professor's love for the animal became stronger, his expectations would be fewer.

Wolf did not intrigue him. Felix knew his own courting would be half-hearted, and that the dog would pick it up immediately. His suspicion was that Wolf's unwillingness to please ought to be respected and cataloged, even though it would not produce so much as a footnote in the glories of insanity. The dog simply had an Asian acceptance of the kennel, preferring the clean barter between prisoners and wardens to the stresses of demonstrating constant alertness and educability. His merry fellows in the adjacent runs he wouldn't give so much as a sideways glance. Perhaps he half-thought he deserved incarceration, Felix speculated.

To Father's credit, he tried to develop more subtle commands using an old Astingi training lexicon in which there were over a thousand words, or rather sounds, for "Down!" this on the theory that if both patient and trainer could achieve a "Down!" without terminal consequences, it might by confidence bring the dog back from death's door—in other words, the animal, in recognizing a bottom, might respond with a kind of spiritual bounce.

But even in the far richer Astingi (so dense it could turn any phrase into its exact opposite), he noted there was no command for "danger," just as there was no command to live. "Down" was all there was, a kind of drug in which dosage was everything, a thousand slightly different intonations of the same metaphor.

Wolf for his part seemed to very much enjoy this chorus of a thousand "down"s. It was a kind of music to him, and he bobbed his head in time, wagging his broken tail, once even performing a kind of Russian dance, which was the only time his hindlegs stopped quivering. But he never so much as sat, even while all around him the Chetvorah, even the nine-week-old pups, flattened themselves happily upon the earth at the Astingi intonations.

Clearly, the libretto of his own opera did not interest Wolf, and to actually take such language seriously would have been a serious offense to his aesthetic sensibilities. Felix took the precaution of keeping the water bucket at a low level so the animal could not drown himself.

On each of his visits, the Professor would go directly to Wolf's kennel, clap him in a soldierly embrace, and try out his latest idea, as if to shun the vulgar instrumentality of Father's telephone cord and the Dresden connection.

The Professor tried sulphate of quinine, oil of turpentine, rest, exercise, hot baths, cold baths, colored glasses, and electric sparks. He placed three magnets on the animal's polar areas, put his front feet into a bucket full of hydrogen sulfide, and after bending Wolf into a backward arc, tipped him backward and forward to get his inner fluids moving. He donned a lilac surgeon's smock and waved an iron wand over him. But all this produced only an occasional bemused twitch.

Floundering from failure to failure, he tried injecting vitamins directly into the vein, massaging the carotid artery and skull plates with homeopathic tinctures, and putting on a pair of galvanic socks that combined electricity and reflexology, but the only result was that Wolf suffered abdominal disorders which eventually affected the entire kennel.

One day he even hooked up a water hose to a special brass nozzle he had brought from the sanitarium, and directed the pressured stream upon Wolf's chest, which at first the dog reacted to with amusement, but then flew into a rage at and screamed like a jungle animal, pushing first his nose, then a front leg through the mesh of the kennel, severely damaging the ligaments and tearing out two claws at the root.

As Father bandaged the paw, he said, "The 'stand aside' is the most elemental maneuver, my friend. You really ought to try it once."

And as it became clear that his experiments did not shock but only bemused my father, the Professor seemed to lose his enthusiasm. More charitably, it might be said he was distracted by the everyday life of the farm. Equally at home in the world of the microscopic—the nerve life of eels' testicles—as in the largest abstractions in the history of suffering, the Professor seemed taken aback by every barnyard animal, astonished that a chicken might walk where it pleased, and dumbfounded that a woman might garrote one and boil it as she pleased. The life of the barnyard, he remarked, was so much richer than that of the Therapeian woods, which to hear him tell it was made up of nothing but large, dying trees, on one side of which were kissing couples, and on the other, a tight-lipped voyeur brandishing a forked twig.

Father, of course, detested both the microscope and telescope, as well as the X-ray and the mirror, and most of all photography. He hated anything which disconnected an image from its source, as befitted a master of the middle distance and a strong believer in the leash. Nothing amused him more than the faith which intellectuals placed in representation, especially as he watched the Professor wander among ducks and geese without the slightest naturalistic interest, pausing only to inspect the funnel with which Ainoha force-fed them warmed gruel. The Professor ran his palm across the phalanges and grease nipples of Father's American steam tractor, which squatted, purred, and farted like any other farm animal. And when shown a bitch in the throes of producing a litter, the Professor praised her obliviousness to pain as she snapped the umbilical cords with her jaws and licked each pup clean of its gelatinous membrane, all while keeping one eye upon her observers and emitting, between chomps and caresses, a suitably polite growl. When the Professor mentioned that he too had come into this world with a caul, Father replied drily that all pups, even the runt, had such a fibroid helmet, and that it premonited nothing more than it protected, because at the very moment those cute little mugs were entering the world, the fetal brain, recognizing itself in the boring lap of domestic luxury, kills half its cells.

And who could forget the day when the Professor ran into the house red-faced and crying, "Wolf is ill, Wolf is finished!"? Felix ran to the kennel and was shown a stuprated blood-red stool, which turned out to be only a rotten plum. It was then he realized he was in the presence of a physician who had never witnessed a birth or a death.

Agreeing that the animal was being bombarded with suggestions from too many quarters, the Professor finally resorted to the French staring cure. Lying on his stomach and removing his spectacles, he looked deep into the animal's yellowish eyes, deep into the history which baffles history, and with his pocket watch pendulating, applied such Odic force as he could muster. Wolf's nose followed the arc of the watch, but his eyes remained fixed without expression upon those of his interlocutor, sliding back and forth in their eyesockets like shot ball bearings. The tremors in his hindlegs gradually ceased. Father watched intently over his shoulder, resting upon one knee as a sergeant might observe a recruit on the firing range.

"Now we're on to something," he muttered.

"Yes, he seems to be responding," the Professor wheezed.

"What I mean to say is, I never saw a dog you couldn't stare down. Something is quite wrong with this one. It isn't that he doesn't know his place. It's as if he has no place . . . and is quite comfortable there."

"Shhhhhh."

Man and animal lay locked in each other's soft glare for at least twenty minutes, both their bodies absolutely still. Then the Professor saw something which frightened him, for across the spheroid of the eyeball he could make out a shallow groove, a primitive streak, a milky band in which less than golden sunbursts spangled, and he realized he was looking into nothing like a soul or a mind but the inverted cosmos of hysteria. He was examining Absolute Time, which did not emit light and could not be mapped. An angina-like pain spread from his heart to the furthest extremities of his body.

The Professor looked up and removed the watch, which now lay on the gravel between himself and the dog. Wolf was calm, dispassionate, his brow uncharacteristically clear. Indeed, Felix thought he had never seen an expression so positively opaque in an animal, except perhaps a snake.

"Sleep," the Professor muttered, "sleep now, good Wolf." He was determined to awaken in the animal the deepest part of his heritage, that dangerous and paramount personality to whom only a passive attitude is possible. But Wolf did not sleep and did not rest. His eyelids had not dropped a single millimeter.

"This eyeball business," Father whispered, "I know it's in great vogue and threatens to take over everything, but it is quite short in its effect. Looking, after all, is our weakest sense. Please, Herr Doktor!"

But there was no response. Felix reached down to find his recumbent co-trustee asleep, while Wolf's bright and now perfectly unslanted eyes, corneas boiling like a drunk's, beamed a ray upon his master's closed lids. After dusting off his suit, Felix took the Professor's arm and walked him briskly around the hydrangeas.

"I believe we should admit, my dear friend, that there is no authoritative command for such a state. We have reached the bottom of this turgid well. Wolf is complying in his way, don't you see? But there is nothing for it. In this subject as in so many, depth is an illusion, just as much as surface. It is too much an offense to your medical dignity to enter his logic, and he knows it."

"I will admit," the Professor sighed, limping slightly, "that one's pride is involved. But it's more than pride of ownership, you must admit."

"On the contrary, I revere your pride, as ever. Do you think I would waste my time with some ordinary physician? Believe me, people much less intelligent than yourself have survived this. Still, you cannot understand this animal if you insist on translating him into concepts. And the eyeball business—well, it has its entertaining side, no doubt, but what I suspect is this: what if the hypnotic state is the norm not only for Wolf but for all of us? The norm is infinite suggestibility, neither sleep nor rest but a kind of somnambulism with all the nerves firing without stimuli. Every animal will fight if you disturb his disturbed state, because it's the only equilibrium he knows. No, we must somehow jerk him out of this idiot séance, not reinforce the trance!" And on saying this he took out the Dresden silver collar and pressed it into his comrade's palm.

"Talk will not reverse these conditions. You have to tell *this* story with your hands. Take it. Close the loop, pull the chain, hear the click."

The Professor obediently slipped the Dresden links into his fob pocket, next to his watch.

"His defenses are extraordinarily strong," he whispered between gritted teeth, perspiration cascading in rivulets from his brow and dripping from his nose as if from a stalactite.

"Ah, yes. Defenselessness is the most powerful weapon. The old 'I won't live without your love' defense."

"There must be a way to reach him, to teach . . ."

"Yes, indeed, but a good teacher teaches in a way you don't call teaching. You must be on the alert to hear something you didn't expect. If you're only teaching, the orchestra sounds bad. If you tell them, 'This is how it goes,' you're lost. Be honest, my good fellow. Have you ever learned anything from something which was told to you directly?"

While Felix now suspected that Wolf's static fits were of vascular origin, he suggested that the propensity for hauling was not really a way of taking advantage of his master, but instead was enforced by the Professor's presuppositions, which were transmitted to the dog through the rope.

The Professor's mouth dropped open. "You mean a kind of telepathy?"

"Telegraphy would be more like it," Father said. "You needn't mystify it. All we're trying to do is to get Wolf to pick up the telephone. We don't care yet about the response. It's not that you are sending the wrong ideas. It's that you are sending ideas at all. Do you bounce ideas off a child or a lover? Would you philosophize to your nude grandparent? No, it's always something more or less than an idea one is sending out. You must learn to adopt a joyous, even childish tone, without the slightest hint of parody. This is a state which precludes—listen carefully, comrade—*any* ironic interpretation."

The Professor nodded forlornly and returned with determination to the kennel. The staring cure in abeyance, he substituted long, animated conversations, conversing for both of them, as it were, with his full, round face pressed against the fence, speaking through the grill into Wolf's half-cocked ear, though the dog never seemed as interested as he had with the more musical Astingi nonsense. Indeed, Wolf listened piously but remained unapproachable. Occasionally he would lift his damaged paw and allow it to flutter across his chest. The Professor interpreted this gesture as a kind of lie. Things were reaching a head. He finally had to admit that he wanted to beat the animal.

"It's quite understandable," Felix said. "Remember, however, that the maimed tend to revenge themselves. It's the police in him."

"What is so frustrating," the Professor said, "is that he is so accessible to observation, yet he only seems known to me through the stories you tell. It's like some kind of strange picture book which looks natural but feels staged."

"Oh, I should say that there is more affection operating here than one would think," Felix said. "Behavior is created *despite* commands. It is external to them."

"What does one do," the Professor almost shouted, "when a patient is so, so . . . *schtupid!*"

"It means only that we must extend our sympathies."

"Then we need stronger subjects!" the Professor barked gruffly.

"Perhaps he is only seeking rest," Father said ingenuously. "Perhaps he only wants you to serve him. His very misery, by gratifying his sense of guilt, may contribute to his recovery."

The Professor reflected upon this without a word.

Felix took Wolf from the enclosure. Once outside, the dog abruptly offered his undamaged paw, holding it stiffly like an Eastern diplomat. His nose was red and crossed diagonally with white stripes of scar tissue. His vulnerability was almost sunny. Then, suddenly, without command, he sat.

"This might be as good as it gets," Felix opined.

"Damn good!" the Professor shouted, and not long after, with the Dresden necklace displayed upon his chest, Wolf did go down, though he could not help peeing slightly and refused to break eye contact.

"I really must take a walk before dinner," the Professor said into the triumphant silence, and Felix saw at once that he needed to be alone.

"We will sound the bell, of course," Father said, as Wolf reentered and kissed his kennel's earth.

Once alone, the Professor meandered back toward the house, only to emerge at once with his suitcase, and from there proceed down the towpath toward the fields. I followed him, keeping to the woods, watching from the edge like a pheasant. A quarter-mile out into the muddy wasteland he set down the suitcase, opened it, and began to make a small tent of papers on the ground. Then he touched his cigar to them, and a thin coil of smoke rose up in the violet dusk. He selected each paper carefully, leaving the majority in the suitcase, and once, after snatching one from the flames, plunged it into a puddle. He watched the tiny fire flicker out, leaving a smoldering scallop which he closed within the suitcase, then folded his arms in a self-satisfied shrug. The dinner bell sounded, as always at six P.M. on Sundays, and I glanced up. Mother was pulling the bell rope with one hand as she held a pair of field glasses with the other.

I waited until the Professor had disappeared up the path, then ran out to the smoldering site. Among the embers a few unburned scraps remained, and I snatched them out. Then I raced back to the house, mounted the stairs three at a time to Father's lair, and placed the charred runes in a secret drawer which I had discovered in his desk.

As I came down the main staircase for dinner, I saw the Professor emerging from the guest bath in an improved mood, though somewhat unsteady.

The Professor's actions had been inspired by Öscar Ögur, the family gardener. One rainy Sunday while we were eating lunch, old illiterate Öscar entered and asked my father if we had a letter to post. Father took a pen from one of his innumerable pockets, jotted a postcard to someone, and handed it over without a word. Öscar disappeared, and when he came back a short time later, my mother had set out a piece of cake for him. He sat at the corner of the table eating it silently, then took his leave. His manner was hunchbacked, though technically he wasn't. In response to an inquiry from the Professor, Father explained that Öscar made himself useful by posting letters, and had fed himself in this way since he was a boy.

The simplicity and efficacy of this made a great impression on the Professor, who spent the rest of that Sunday following Öscar around, much to the annoyance of the locals, who were perfectly happy to assist Öscar and catch up with their correspondence, but not in the shadow of a man with those eyes, brown as the Mze itself, hovering in the background under a homburg.

This social arrangement whereby the deranged assisted the bureaucracy interested the Professor greatly, though he was irritated at being unable to observe Öscar under more controlled conditions, and his few attempts at conversation with the fellow produced only a gentle but opaque smirk on the far left side of Öscar's face.

One of the rituals he observed was to affect him for the rest of his life, though, as well as bring him into conflict with Mother.

It was later in the afternoon that same Sunday, as the Professor followed Öscar back to the stone chicken house behind the chapel where he slept. Öscar had gathered flowers from the many gardens on the way, making a small bouquet using only those at the peak of their bloom. (On this day it was iris and peony.) Once home, he pulled out a three-legged campstool to support his asymmetrical buttocks, and there he proceeded to light the flowers on fire one by one. Occasionally he inhaled the crackling smoke, but mostly it seemed not to register with him. When queried, Father claimed to know nothing of the significance of this activity, nor did it interest him, being one of Öscar's more harmless idiosyncrasies. But on his next visit the Professor arrived with an extra valise, and after greeting Wolf with a wave, strode out on stiffened legs into the sugar beet field, where he sat down and unloaded a stack of papers, which he proceeded to burn one by one with much the same expression as Öscar did the flowers.

Father never questioned his friend about this, though every once in a while as he was working the dogs a charred piece of paper would blow across his path and he would pick it up, noting crossed-out sentences, circled inkblots, phrases such as "noxious inadequacy," and strange quasi-mathematical diagrams of mental states which looked rather like medieval routes of pilgrimage to Spain. Irritated both at the litter and the presumption behind it, Felix placed these singed thoughts in the appropriate pocket. Only later did I find out where he kept them.

Our octagonal dining room was typical Central Empire, the feet of the table those of lions standing on cannonballs, its legs Corinthian columns inlaid with vermeil *trompe l'oeil* griffins chasing an auroch up a pylon. On each wall was a locked glass breakfront: one for everyday china (a blue and chrome yellow pattern, the primary colors of Astingi eyes), one for Mother's family figurines, one for the most enigmatic of Father's collectibles (Roman coins, corded drinking beakers, stone axes, tobacco jars) and one of course for guns. A dozen or so firearms were displayed left to right in order of technological development, beginning with Grandfather Priam's double-hammered Arabic horse guns, and ending with his custom-built drillings for the Marchlands, always three-barreled, their two-shot chambers snuggled around a high-caliber 30.6 rifle, blending English lightness with Krupp steel. All were distinctively strapped, the leather band making the guns ugly and military but testifying to the difficulty of Cannonian terrain, where the emphasis had to be on the intelligence of the dog and the stamina of the hunter. For despite the profusion of game in the Marchlands, the footing was so difficult you rarely had a gun at the ready—indeed, the weapon was almost an afterthought. The Astingi gunsmiths produced weapons of clarity and balance which clung to your body like a burr, and which when brought up to fire seemed merely a line drawn between your cheekbone and index finger. Such a gun almost pointed itself. It swung on its own weight and lay in your hand without pressure, though it kicked mightily. When fired, the stock bit into your shoulder like a wolverine, which clamps down on its prey only once. The first time I fired one, the recoil struck me late and deep, somewhere close to the heart. From that day on, I knew I would be no happy shooter, as I would always anticipate the pain.

Unusually, Father had given the Professor his choice of seats at the table—in essence, a choice of which vitrine and which collection to stare into. As with everything, the Professor took this seriously and systematically, and finally, reflecting a predictable response to weaponry—revulsion combined with fascination—chose to face the guns, a seat he never relinquished throughout thirty years as a guest in our home. It was not lost upon us that despite the reform laws, as a Jew he was still prohibited from owning a gun.

"I suppose that when Wolf is stabilized we will accustom him to firearms?" the Professor offered eagerly after the soup.

Father rejoined that any dog could be taught to hunt, but to find game was the point, and Wolf's reflex heritage was to always be on the defensive, on the off chance that a quail might turn on his pursuer and threaten his family.

"The only usefulness of a gun is the extent to which it can bring out hypocrisy," he finished, as the vermillion roast arrived. "Also as a pretext, usually the only one, for fathers and sons to discourse on sex and death under the guise of safety regulations."

"The shotgun is the essence of the bourgeois sensibility, I'm told," the Professor said laconically, eyeing the fine drillings before him.

"Ah, yes," Father replied drily, "the rise of the uncomfortable middle class, so much remarked upon and so little explained." Addressing the hostile intellectual's inquiry, he then took the occasion to launch into one of his mock dialogues.

"Suddenly a new man appears in the forest!" he chortled. "A new class of foot hunter who disdains the horses, beaters, and specialized pursuits of the nobility. For a time, life is given meaning by nothing more than avoiding the perversions of the English aristocracy! The professional classes then begin to bear arms in the guise of putting food on the table, but as any fool knows, the elegant cylinders which stand in the corner represent only the lost spirit of insurrection. To the naïve, Professor, such weapons might appear as a sign of the residual eagerness of a citizenry eager to protect its liberties, or for the man of the family to ward off the violent, random stranger. But in fact the shotgun is a symbol of failed revolution, a reminder how little private armament matters."

"A display, really, of terrible fragility and sadness," Mother added, "for brandishing a gun is only a futile effort to turn your enemy for a moment into a reflective sort, so that you might take him by surprise, slip your hand into the fold, and grab him by the nose! There is nothing more pathetic, really, than the sight of a lone man with a long gun."

The Professor was all ears as he watched his head float in the vitrine's reflection, a ghost among the guns. The fact was that Father rarely carried a gun and almost never shot one. He only cleaned and fondled them. This wasn't for a lack of prowess. He had inherited Grandfather Priam's unflustered eye along with his armory, but something had happened in his thirties. There was a rumor about a friend accidentally killed on a hunt, but more likely it had to do with the newly systematized slaughter, which made it necessary for him to register a gesture of non-compliance. For a time he hunted alone, but with the increasing number of hunters each autumn, plus the arrival of German dentist sportsmen and Frenchmen who abandoned their dogs in the Hycernian Forest after the season, he gave it up.

I did not understand then that most of the uglier things in our time could be explained not in terms of some tragic accident, policy error, or moral misunderstanding, but simply due to the increase in the number of people about. More people everywhere, even in the deepest forest of the most remote country, blasting away every Sunday. Anyone with two horses was a sportsman, and if he won the race, a noted one. People began to hunt without restraint, killing irrespective of age, sex, or season. The few escaping creatures were then harassed without interval by packs of ill-trained hounds. Bags of the murdered—stiff, hairy, blood-encrusted, with lustrous eyes— were exported by the thousands as the hordes faded into the night with their snifters of cognac, the unscrewed anuses of their horses dropping moist smoking balls on every road.

"And what pleasure can one possibly derive from killing a defenseless animal?" The Professor issued his challenge across the salad. Felix only smiled. Ainoha snorted and rustled her petticoats.

"Unlike us, Doctor, the dog has no blood scent," Father replied in his patient way. "He works only to please his master, and whether it's a tennis ball or a golden eagle is of no concern to him. Hunting is a matter of sharing senses, of complementary cooperation, which is intrinsically beautiful. There is no victim, no victor, no bounty, no prize, no score. There is neither sport nor spectator."

"And not to eat it?" The Professor spat this out between mouthfuls, as if such aesthetical athleticism could be the final word.

"Our guest ought not concern himself so much with food gathering," Mother interjected not too calmly. "It's a sort of fetish with you, if I may say."

"One supposes," Father continued, sawing away at the roast, "that our shadowy guttural ancestors perhaps hunted for food once or twice in the dead of winter. But they didn't really begin to hunt in earnest until they endured the great trauma, when the wandering life had been given up and they bought the farm. When every man and every animal has his function in the social order written on his face, that is when the lonely man with his scruffy dog strikes out, not to recover the lost tribe, but to lose it. Do you really believe one could be intimate with something as inexpressive as a bird? That's why intellectuals hate hunters, because intellectuals are still hunting their own lost tribe. In any event, you are missing the dynamics here. As soon as hunting becomes a spectacle, as soon as our dominion over the prey becomes absolute, it loses its purpose, which is why I gave it up. Intellectuals think hunting is a kind of war without guilt. It only has to do with securing the best places to hunt. Believe me, Professor, there's no real skill involved. The dog does the work, and the prey consents. Guilt and rejoicing cancel each other out. It's not a question of smelling, but of giving up your own smell."

The Professor's spoon had stopped in midair, but Father was relentless. "You fast, you smear yourself with alien substances to disguise the abominable stench of your humanness! You're alive without your baggage. It hasn't a thing to do with food or sport. It's a way of losing the tribe, of *breaking* communion. Above all, it's man's way of escaping the family. No more powerful idea on this earth, let me tell you. And so history begins, Professor, when the man comes home from his stupid job, yells at his wife and children, kicks the dog in the behind, grabs his gun from the corner, and waves the bloody flag!"

"A most interesting way of putting the case." The Professor had decided to recuse himself from the debate, but you could see the admiration in his eyes. "And you are no slouch yourself, it seems, when it comes to ideas."

"What you will learn here is that training is all impulse, energy, and tempo," Mother added in her deepest registers. "The moment it becomes *pedagogy*"—she nearly spat this—"you are finished!" And she threw her napkin in the air.

"But surely the commands are of the utmost importance, if not the ideas, which you so summarily dismiss," the Professor insisted with increasing determination.

Ainoha quickly took the lead as Felix cut another joint:

"Another misapprehension, my good Doctor! The Astingi are the greatest animal handlers the world has ever known. But they have only three commands: *lassa*, *frieza*, and *panza*, delivered with thousands of different intonations. My dear Professor, believe me, throw any word into the world and you will find a thing for it. The trick lies in preparing the subject to receive the word!"

"Most education is one-third action and two-thirds explanation," Father adumbrated. "It is inertial, continuing on vaguely and mechanically. For anything to be passed on, that ratio must be reversed. A thought, to have effect, must be ready to rectify its own trajectory, and to attach itself to the reality of what the animal is telling us."

"Oh, Councilor," the Professor laughed embarrassedly, "the next thing you will be telling me is that dogs can talk!"

"But my dear sir, the dog *can* talk," Mother interjected sweetly. "No one with any knowledge would deny that. However, they only talk to themselves, just as a child learns to think silently before he speaks. This is not a vexing problem, and anything but esoteric. There is a whole area of experience which refers to things we would say if we wanted, but either we choose not to or we never get around to putting it into words. And who is to say whether our hearing is too refined or we are just deaf? I, for example, can distinguish the sound of a viola from that of a cello, but I wouldn't know how to distinguish it in words. The dog's knowledge could be articulated; it just happens not to be. Ultimately, the dog believes in civility, where everything is known and assimilated, provided it is not said openly. It is not kept secret for political or psychological reasons, as you seem to think."

"This is madness!" the Professor snorted.

"No, Professor, in this matter my wife happens to be quite right for once. Recall Achilles's chariot horse, Xanthus, who warned that a god would kill his driver, just as he had slain Patroclus. What did he get for his trouble, his prophesying? The Erinyes struck him dumb! No, we did not evolve; the animals simply stopped talking to us. There is something here much more interesting than language, Professor. It is the paralysis of speech. The dog always has a word on his lips, though he never utters it. Is this not the basis of our love and curiosity? One must learn to read the word which is caught short upon the lips. And should the animals start talking to us, as in olden days, watch out! If they speak, it means they have lost respect for us as their protectors, and insanity will reign!"

"Does it not strike you as odd that you insist so theoretically that everything we know is somehow tacit?" The Professor was reverting to his more sarcastic manner.

"Fine," Father snapped. "If you want to make philosophy of it, make one. But please, let us not be caught up in a philosophy based only upon the mind and the eye. What would a philosophy be that was based only on the mind and the ear, or the mind and the nose? What begins as memory, terminates, Professor, as behavior is created. All we know is suddenly the dog learns, to everyone's surprise, that a significant variation can be made upon the rules. Believe me, if you want to understand a working life, it cannot be studied scientifically, because we do not understand what we do until we have done it. Only the thing you thought you thought can teach you how to think."

Refilling the Professor's glass, Mother added with her most glowing smile, "Science, I think you'll agree, doesn't really matter in the end."

Shaking his head like a horse avoiding a fly, the Professor slumped down in a long and disabused silence, as Öscar cleared the plates. He took note of his handsome, confident hosts at each end of the table with their *goyische*, self-satisfied grins and perfect manners. His depression had returned in full measure, and he raised his eyes and adjusted his pince-nez to avoid their open, friendly stare. Then, as the silence became interminable, his gaze suddenly widened with incredulity, and his lustrous brown eyes, so much larger than his glasses, turned all pupillary black.

He had been too distracted by the bright guns, the rare beef, and the dense conversation to notice that the main expanse of open wall, above the riflery vitrine and the evil little child, was dominated by an oil painting as large as the top of a grand piano. Out of a Rembrandtine black field he could make out a man in an even darker suit turning away from his desk laden with ancient books and skulls, turning from his studies in order to lift a white shroud clinging to the body of a beautiful woman lying on a pallet. His left hand held his bearded chin below blue-gray eyes, which were clearly in the process of having a thought that had not yet found its word. On his right hand, which rested above her exposed left breast, a wedding band glowed, more ancient and golden than the western light falling upon his high, domed forehead. His eyes were hooded in concentration, while on her face, behind the wires of lashes, the half-closed right eye was visible. In the upper right corner was a candlestick without a flame, and in the lower right one, a large moth at rest, its wings retracted about an illegible signature. There were many different whites—the off-white of the half-opened book pages, the enameled white of the skulls, the photographer's white of the man's cuffs and collar, the transparent white of the silk shroud, the ivory white of her breastbone, the pearl white of her face. It took no connoisseur to see that the visages bore an uncanny resemblance to his hosts. Thus commenced one of the longest silences in the history of our family, a veritable ice age.

"Might I inspect it more closely?" the Professor finally said, as a steaming, braided strudel put in an appearance.

"By all means," Mother said, disappearing to return with a circular stepladder from the library. The Professor ascended it not too steadily, and I was instructed to hold his ankles.

"An amateur work, of course," Father said absently, planting an enormous piece of strudel in the shape of a Greek cross on his absent guest's plate, "but well-disciplined in the Cannonian school. Every few years he comes up with something interesting. What do you think?"

But the Professor could not answer. It was one of those works of art which makes its effect entirely apart from painterly worth or historical associations.

It did not demand to know if it was good or not. And if it was a period piece, it was in no curriculum.

"Death and sexuality," the Professor announced, "and rarely have I seen them in such cogent conjunction."

There was no reply at first, only the huge knife clanging on the strudel plate, and Mother's nails drumming on her napkin ring. Then she spoke:

"She isn't dead, of course."

"No?" the Professor said. "Then sleeping?"

"Neither dead nor sleeping," Ainoha said distantly.

"But she's so pale."

"It's the light, Professor. It's, how do you say . . . a *device.*"

"Who knows what's going through her mind?" Felix said gruffly, finishing his dessert with a single bite.

"And he, he is . . . experimenting with her," the Professor whispered, "while she is *not* conscious."

"How could one possibly know that?" Mother said sweetly. "How do we even know if he is a proper doctor?"

"Now, there it is," the Professor fairly shouted. "He is a *meshugana* doctor, a fake doctor, taking advantage."

"You have this habit, may I say," Mother intoned evenly, "of insisting, whenever I question your observation, that my taking exception is simply an illustration which proves your point."

"Doctor, she is right again," Father said sententiously. "She is not in another world, nor this one. She is just, well, full of herself."

"And our mad scientist who exposes her breastbone?" the Professor blurted, nearly falling from his perch.

"He is a bit overwhelmed, perhaps, but he is reverent," replied Father. "Surely you can see that it is the observed who is in control here."

"I see nothing of the sort," the Professor blurted. "This is against all the rules."

Mother's voice assumed its deepest French horn sonority:

"My dear doctor, one always believes one has had more sex than one actually has, and this can confuse even your partner."

"This is *after* sex," announced the Professor.

"Really?" Mother mused. "Well, anything is possible. But I should say before—quite a bit before." She was looking off into space, playing with her

113

strudel as if it were a mouse. "Many guests have given us their interpretation, you know. No one ever fails to comment."

"It's quite amazing, you know," Father broke in cheerily. "When you live with a picture, you never really look at it. Because you own it, it ceases to exist. Very strange."

The Professor was trying to read the artist's title above the moth. It was either *Der Anatom* or *Der Analom*.

"Yes, the moth," Father said embarrassedly. "Decidedly a false touch."

"Might I ask which of your guests' reactions was your favorite?" the Professor asked, now somewhat more detached as he descended the spiral stair, patted me on the head, and resumed his place.

"Oh, yes, it was a professor from Geneva, wasn't it, dear?" Mother said. "His impression was that it was an up-to-date Dido and Aeneas. She has refused to die upon the pyre. And he has ignored the instructions of the gods to continue his journey, and instead will share their common fate. Very classy, no?"

"Such an idiot," Father muttered. "He believed that art is something which happens between an accident and its criticism."

"All very vague and sanctimonious, I must say," said the Professor, a bit of strudel in his beard.

"And bourgeois?" Father twinkled.

"Even vagueness can be explicit if it's explained well enough," Mother allowed. "It was a wonderful evening. He threw himself in the pond."

"What I like best about the picture is its smell," Felix concluded. "It has the scent of a couch upon which one has just made love. Must be in the unvarnished pigments. Yes, whatever the story here, it is a scene quite on the verge of chemical collapse."

"Artists are fantastically good at undermining themselves," Mother shrugged, "and to be sure, Dido *was* something of a fool!"

MOTHERLAND
(Iulus)

It was well known throughout the countryside that Father had been the only man in modern times to have married a goddess, the only auslander to bed an Astingi since Attila. Accordingly, throughout his adult life, he was subjected to abnormal measures of both envy and sympathy by the ignorant—the only true education in which misconstruction makes the morning coffee.

It was true that Ainoha Aegle Apamea had all the contours and fury of the ideal, a famed beauty reflecting the original Astingi cross of the Viking with the Greek: golden-red hair upon olive skin, ocher eyes, a ruthless décolletage above the rose window of her navel, and below, um, her golden bee. When Mother smiled at you across a room, it opened every wound, and when her voice dropped into its lower registers, men would shake. She had all the devils of the world in her eyes, and hers was the cold laughter of the immortal, softened by an amused, enigmatic, and winsome grin. Father said he never saw anyone sleep so soundly, but when awake she never once blinked. She was a specialist in *purdeur*, presence, and the discretion necessary to true arousal. At times, Ainoha had a little trouble being human.

Technically speaking, Mother came from the moon: not that her dark side never showed, but often when you looked up, half of her was missing.

More often, she sat on a cloud far beyond the moon combing her hair, dropping her combings into the river, while sifting the mists through a silver sieve. She bathed three times on summer nights and nine times on autumn nights to make me a magician. I was her Fire Child.

The Moon Goddess is faithful, therefore insuperable, but she never lets you forget it. Not much of a hugger, she kissed me only once a day. But that was a privilege and at such times I felt justified in using the royal "we." However, beauty has its own rhythms; beauty speeds things up and multiplies affect. My mother was made for many loves. Strong in all things, she should have had the strength to live alone.

Ainoha had been a child movie star in the Cannonian silent film industry, which had allowed her to overcome shyness, though she felt the cinema to be an infantile art form. She never once looked at the films made of her, and one could see why. No one *ever* looked like her, moved like her. She moved like water pours, like a self-excited comet; short hair on the head, long hair otherwise, all dry fire. She had the air of a bloodhorse and walked with a slight tilt, as if she were falling out of a foutée, and when she passed by, one sensed great oceans of air being moved. Like all her people she loved to smoke and loved to dance. Her ballgoing shoes had bells built into the heels, so when she walked she seemed to chime. She was of course a crack shot, as well as a champion swimmer, rider, and sprinter. When she picked up her skirts and remembered to remove her hat, she never lost a footrace. Not exactly a *femme fragile* or *horizontale*, trained in gymnastics and ballet, she could kill a man with a single blow of her leg. She trapped falcons, sewing up their eyelids to prevent them from predating, and trolled for pike with her earrings. She galloped after the county dogcatcher, and at point of sword, forced him to release his wretched captives and beg forgiveness. When on horseback on a hunting line there was no shaking her off, you could not ride wide of her. You never escaped her at a single fence. I shall never forget her voice, "Pray, take care of that gate!" And through brake and brier, over ditch and dike, surrounded by a profane drunken crowd of escorts, she permitted no reference to her safety, comfort, or success. And yet as impossible as it was to escape her, it was the same at every gate and gap. "Might I ask you," she trilled in her pretty voice, head thrown back like an ecstatic maenad, "not to come too near me?" And when in a bad mood, one could often hear her kicking a soccer ball for hours and hours against the granary. She was, perhaps, the world expert on dog fibers and other useful fuzz, knitting many useful items from doghair—scarves, watchcaps, pullovers, and mittens for all of us, as well as full-length traveling jerkins for the dogs, belted across the stomach with a small flapped pocket for a train ticket. Her weaving pins were never far from her hands.

Mother was invariably late for meals, generally sleeping till noon in her darkened room behind heavy damask curtains and carved pillars which kept out both light and air. But she was no neurasthenic. She took to her bed aggressively and made the world her bed. It was from her I learned how to pull the coverlet taut and watch how all difference evaporates. After a hot bath which she took in a thick linen chemise (she could apparently wash without lifting it) she would darken her eyelids with the soot produced by holding a porcelain cup over the flame of a candle, and hurry into lunch absentmindedly, surrounded by an aroma of Turkish tobacco and Houbigant, carrying a bundle of old international newspapers in which she was well-versed. Then, after lunch, gathering up an untender beefsteak for supper and placing it beneath her saddle, she would take her daily horseback ride, jumping over the innumerable crisscrossed sheaves of hay in the south pasture, with its golden apple orchards.

But Mother also lived in that special hell reserved for beauteous women (for only the pretty demand to be valued for themselves) and like Francesca she was caught in a kind of unrhymed poem as well, which charged her monologues with melancholy; the goddess who is herself invulnerable but *chooses* to be kind, insisting on bestowing gifts even when they were not wanted. She encouraged others to subscribe to her dottiness, a readiness to retreat from the merciless laboratory of history into the blessings and total adulation of pets and family. "Have I missed anyone today?" she would often say into the uncritical love glow of cats and dogs, and during dinner, when Father and I were engaged in some inconsequential argument and looked to her to break the tie, she would fling down her napkin and exclaim, "Oh, you *word* people, there's just no getting around you!"

Yes, she preferred beauty above all things, but she hated aestheticism. She loved literature but hated the literary. Like Beatrice, she did not profit from her lover's immortal poems; indeed she was most absent when they were recited to her. Like many girls she resented the procedure of being the love-object exclusively; imagine the Dark Lady's anger at Shakespeare after one hundred and twenty sonnets—"Oh for god's sake, leave me alone!"—and you have a gauge of her impatience with her infatuates. Yet she loved men's muscles, and their throbbing veins, which accounted for our enormous collection of idealized garden torsos. "They're never the same as on statues," she often sighed when walking among them, but she knew that the greater the man, the more aesthetically inferior his representation.

She also knew that beauty is a contest, no matter how much one denies it, and in the end the muse is mostly merciless, admitting to the lower slopes of Parnassus only the most palpable beings, while history groans with the hisses and moans of those whom they have rejected. Her counseling method was derived from Hypatia, who flung her menstrual cloth in the face of a student who was in love with her so that he might learn to love only immutable truths. With Mother, all exercises were useless unless done with the correct form, and the first order of business with men, as with dogs, was to breed the whining out. "To be good at anything," she often said, "one must be a bit cold."

How Ainoha became the Mistress of Semper Vero is one of those stories as definitive as it is open-ended. Priam's marriage to Calliope Eriphyle, a woman of much neck but not much else, was barren, indeed barely civil; and Priam spent most of his time in the upcountry, hunting for rare Bonsai-type stunted evergreens on the Astingi plains of Crisulan. But one day upon his return from a month's absence, there was seated in his break, along with a freshly dug cedar, windsculpted into the shape of a lyre, a gorgeous girl of nine with a basketful of adorable red-golden puppies. While obviously as proud of her as a cavalry charge, Priam never complained or explained, though his mustache had turned half-white. Calliope Eriphyle, for her part, was prepared to adopt a pragmatic solicitude, but the ethereal child showed no interest in her whatsoever, sitting upon the grass with her legs splayed carelessly about, tipping the litter basket over in her lap as one by one the dogs leapt up to kiss her, nip her, the largest male hanging for a moment from her earlobe. She had everyone's attention, but at arm's length, just the way she liked it. As the sun sank into the smoky, lilac-colored Mze, the child's eyes turned green-orange, and seeing there a restless vivacity and a cynical boldness, as well as a shard of powerful melancholy skepticism, the wife was properly horrified and withdrew. As the dogs grew stranger than poets, they ran off into every corner of the house, each securing for itself a den which could be defended, reconvening only in the evenings when they bathed, gamboled, and danced like holy fools in the shallows of the Mze. The girl-child never asked for a thing, never spoke of her people or former home, but showed great interest in Priam's ancestors, as well as the smallest details of running the estate. (The idea being that even if the past might not accept you, it didn't mean that the past wasn't yours.) She was, in fact, perfectly behaved, while exhibiting a healthy derision of every lofty conviction. She seemed to view humans as a remote if interesting species, well worth studying in some depth.

There were the usual rumors—that Priam had fathered her with a now disgraced Astingi maiden, that he had bought or kidnaped her, or more plausibly, that she was a gift from the Astingi Shaman to ingratiate themselves with the gentry, and to place a spy among us. Priam never bothered to refute any of the charges, and as the girl brought light and life into a house where theretofore no one had ever listened to music, read a book, climbed a mountain, looked at the sea, or been alone for a minute, no one really cared *how* she came to be there. She had arrived as had our ancestors from the East, on a cart drawn by buffaloes, and she learned her gait from geese.

When her preternatural teenage beauty captivated the *cineastes*, and cameras whirred and phosphorus flares ignited in every corner of the property, Priam seemed to think it was all some harmless ancient ritual, until he was shown an album of stills of his own family, as well as day laborers in their embroidered cloaks, and well-washed gypsies from the fringe of the village. These were the first photographs which he actually saw as photographs, which made everything flat, small, and quiet, and he realized immediately that his way of life was over and his class and character were doomed. Indeed, it was not long after that he disappeared from Semper Vero, and certainly I inherited his aversion, for if there is one thing I have always been utterly sure of it is that I am *not* a camera. And I have never permitted a photograph to be made of me.

Mother was not much interested in the attachment theorists. "To be the beloved is the only way you can learn anything about a man, though whether it's worth it is another story," she often said to me. What she loved in men was their simple bark of pure ambition, their getting down on all fours to howl at Rome. And in particular she loved Father's selfishness without self-absorption, for it takes enormous courage to be happy. But she also knew that in the end, men have to be roped in to satisfy the demands of cruel conservative Nature and her strange imperatives. And with her nest of golden wires, no one was ever better at it.

What she was especially good at was *frisson* and *lèse majesté*. Her sense of nest spanned solar systems. One had the distinct impression from Ainoha that we were all going to live together forever, and I must say I could only admire this great intrusive female, always trying to civilize and sensitize my father and I, and always failing. Yet I was doomed to Mother's revenge; her creaseless face and indomitable spirit would give me the bad habit of incessant rebirth. And if the muses are always pictured carrying something—a globe, a flute, a lyre, a mask, a scroll, a reversed torch—Ainoha could often be found walking alone with her tennis racket and a pensive look.

I could never discover the exact nature of her relationship to the Astingi, or where she actually stood in their pagan hierarchy, for they had very little contact owing to her marriage outside the tribe—and it is probably not in a goddess's interest for things to be too clear or consistent. Her Astingi given name was *Tritogeneia* ("Thrice-born"), from changing her nature with the seasons. The Greeks imply that she was descended from Nyx, daughter of Chaos, mother of Sleep and Death, and feared even by Zeus. But the Astingi never had much of a taste for cosmogonical rhetoric, and one thing they knew for certain was that beauty was a real power, inseparable from terror, and nothing like a myth. The Astingi patrolled our property as if it were theirs, enforcing the poaching laws with swift and silent dispatch, leaving an unlit votive candle where a trespasser had been snuffed out. Ainoha was from the Naiad line, who presided over three thousand rivers roaring as they flow, and depending on your sources are capable of abrupt death by drowning or everlasting sexual bliss. But river goddesses have little or no mythology and disappear only when their rivers cease—so the only thing they fear is drought.

But it must have been frustrating to be goddess to a people who had no need of goddesses. Worship for the Astingi simply meant a silent gratitude that the higher powers walk among you, and the people you revere, you leave alone. They had no need for a leader, and thus were free in the only way that counts: free to worship her without expecting favors and without coveting her relative privilege. This respect was enforced by millennia of primogeniture, in which the eldest child inherited the house and land, gender notwithstanding, thus insuring a great number of women heads of household—a small and obscure concession, which over a period of time worked enormous changes in everyday relations. But as the eldest child also had the obligation to house and provide for their siblings, this guaranteed that domestic quarreling would, *à la Tchekov*, completely subsume the energies which would otherwise flow toward the overthrow of the state or contests of rival political factions. In Astingiland, all the battles of the Central Empires were fought out in the arena of the family. And ours was no different in that respect, except perhaps that as all three of us were only children, we were spared the care of poor elderly relations, and thus lived an unreal existence without the daily object lessons of declining powers and abject failure.

When an Astingi girl approached puberty, she was taken by the older women to a central repository in the forest, and given paint to color their village houses as she would, a collection of deep-hued pastels which would give even a color-blind bear pause. In the late autumn, when the tribe returned from the mountains, they found the village houses glowing like jewels, and in each second-story window, chin in cupped hands and elbows on the sill, a young woman perusing the passing young men for her life companion.

Once betrothed, the compromises with the chosen men were worked out rationally. The women controlled the daily and generational markets, the shortest- and longest-term trading, thirty-day accounts and thirty-year mortgages, while the gentlemen were allowed to work off their slash-and-burn instincts in the large intervening middle-distance, an arrangement which apparently forestalled and managed crises better than in any of those bloody pockets of history that surrounded them.

You could tell an Astingi across a field, no matter how he was dressed, simply by his self-sufficient and dignified posture, punitive on the one hand, protective on the other. Their manners were based upon an ideal manliness so palpable they could dispense with any show of warrior virtues. Their survival was based apparently upon their absolute unwillingness to become a *folk*, their belief that folk wisdom is always wrong, those out-of-the money bets that tree moss reveals true north or that menses are triggered by asparagus. No faux naïve embroidery or window boxes full of one-dimensional pansies for them, no feast days (every day is a feast day), no hopping dances or gravitas processions, no moldy costumes in the attic. As a people they prided themselves not so much on their inclusiveness but on their aerodynamics.

In the summers the men would go to the mountains with their flocks and dogs. In the spring floods they would return to play pirate for a month on six-inch seas. In the fall, they would hunt and kill their feral pigs. In the short winter, they would renew fierce, earsplitting connubial relations with their women, who had come to ovulate every six months. While the men were off grazing or fighting, the women moved their entourage from town to town, reopening new ones or closing down old ones—it was all the same to them. And when they fought, the women and children were put in the first rank. If you have never heard an Astingi woman's war cry, you have missed the human drama.

The Astingi theology was as vague as Ainoha's peculiar status within it. All that can be said with certainty is that their bucolic and commonsensical existence had been disturbed in the thirteenth century by the Pope, who, for reasons unclear, sent them a crown as a bribe, and granted them apostolic status. They associated the crown's crude craftsmanship with their tormented past, a kind of aesthetical pounding on the table which they had had enough of, and filed it away respectfully. Over the next few centuries, as the tribes further intermingled, Jesus and the saints coexisted happily with the devils and fairies, the forest pig and totem—and as a hedge on the safe side, white horses were still occasionally sacrificed on holidays. On every crossroads appeared the vulvar crèche with a sweating black Madonna, and while the rest of Europe cremated itself in the throes of feudal dynasties and religious wars, throughout the Dark Ages the Astingi were especially healthy and prosperous.

It cannot be said that they subscribed to the church in either its eastern or western forms. Of the Christians it was noticed that those who preached the Gospel of Love the loudest tended most piteously to destroy those reluctant to subscribe. And as for those who developed a principled resistance to the Judeo-Christian order (with its facile hyphen) those eastern cults which promised a utopia on this earth as an attractive heresy, it was noticed that they tended to show up at functions without being invited, manifesting an undifferentiated rudeness which even in those quarters where it most succeeded, made every simple social exchange a kind of torture. They knew all accounts of fallen warriors to be made up or worse. And they were suspicious of a vital oral tradition which could turn anything into a kind of pathetic, faded inner experience.

So it cannot be said exactly that the Astingi retained their loyalties to paganism. To be fair, they embraced the rituals of both churches—the perfume and sensuality of the East, without its liturgy and hierarchy, as well as the emotional asceticism and graphomania of the West, without its odd texts and even odder foreign policy. The Cannonians and the Astingi went to the opera on Friday nights and sang the same arias on Sunday to Bible verses.

The services at Muddy St. Hubertus had the mysticism and iconography of the orthodox, but the music of the gothic, dispensing with tempo markings and adding thirty more characters to the Latin alphabet of the psalters, as well as an inscription over the altar: "All things are three."

What is the meaning of this creed beneath the inverted pyramid, the Astingi mystery, "All things are three"? It means, as far as I can see, the opposite of the hypostatic trinity, which promises only infinite regress. It means there *is* no unity, nor holy relation between the three, only contingency. For the human mind is capable of holding within itself only two beginnings, and can merely acknowledge a third, like a man waving his cap at a thundercloud. The Astingi went as far as they could go, acknowledging the Virgin Mary and the Holy Ghost, but not the Father and the Son—and of the four, they certainly found it easiest to accept the Ghost. After all, one can believe in the end of the credo "Look for the resurrection of the dead and the life of the world to come" without even considering all that hard-to-follow persiflage which precedes it. Does it really matter who begot whom? "Skip to the end, my sweet," the Astingi proverb goes, and that is what my mother sang to me. The Astingi kiss is a triple kiss, plus or minus one makes all the difference, one on the left check, one on the right, and the third where you will. One's feelings about a deed are of more interest than the fact of it; that is the Astingi philosophy. The Astingi's only essentially religious idea, as far as I could tell, seemed to be that Europe's biggest problem was *too* much Christianity—even in Cannonia, where Jews played soccer, Muslims made moonshine, and the Catholics were tougher than the Turks.

The great appeal of paganism, after all, is that it was not necessary to be loyal to it. It is simply an attractive guess at matters hidden from history requiring neither laws nor tithes, whose basic tenet remains that it is not worth dying or killing for. In any case, the oak trees were disappearing at a fantastic rate, and those little spirits, elves, and fairies reminded the Astingi too much of their own vulnerability. While one of the most attractive aspects of nature worship was its absence of clergy, they came to notice among their own self-appointed druids a certain smug sanctimony and conformity, which would infect for all time all progressives who opposed the prerogatives of Christendom. So while they recognized the lack of consistency in their own beliefs, they nevertheless came to miss the attractive mixture of pagan sexes, the little shrinelets in the forest, the lapidary and contradictory stories, the expansive gestures and the short parades, not to mention the grand entertainment of lesser deities competing for social standing with all their human foibles. This company of competing gods not only seemed to accord more to the reality of things, but also encouraged a warm responsiveness, rather than the wail of the saved. To replace this extended family of overlapping authority with one stout fellow who no doubt had his thrilling moments, but seemed to have taken on rather too large an entity to administer, encouraged a kind of immaturity where enforcement was concerned. Why replace this drama of contesting rulers with a *weak* omnipotence? Why cut down a forest and replace it with a lone tree with a single veinous leaf? The Astingi were thus rather pagans by default. And gradually their taste for slitting the throat of a white horse abated, one of those rare periods of history where the executioner does not willingly step forward.

The only Astingi shrine equipment consisted of unpainted biconical vases of local materials. While their now extinct neighbors had embarked upon an orgy of glazes and dyes, ransoming themselves to the markets of the trading routes, their ceramics remained severe as a note struck with a mallet, grouped together in the air, forest glen, cave, or vitrine, in no apparent order or necessary number, the new mixed with the old, unclear as to their original purpose—perhaps simply an object to gently remind one of one's heretic self. (And that the self, too, is a perishable sort of commodity with shifting value; we appear on earth only for a second, while even our rudest utensil outlives us.)

So if Mother had a theogony, it would boil down to something like this: the long-term consists of a great number of short-terms, and truth, like the vases, can only be beheld as a somewhat manufactured and random entity. All creation is hybrid, no one is really chosen by anyone, there is no direct line of development, so the best one can hope for is to string together a medley of old favorites and new quirks, a genuine confusion of the higher and the lower—an arbitrary grouping of somewhat bedraggled epiphanies, each propping the other up—and this was just the sort of thing, a kind of music-hall review, which *ought* to be worshiped. It is wrong to use punishment in another world as a threat, because the world of punishment is in this one for each of us. The world is mostly inertia, where all the best-intentioned nurturing does not guarantee as much as a burp. Only the present is divine, and the fairest order a heap of random sweepings. The Goddess's job is, after all, to turn the prayer into a blessing. And what is the prayer? "More life!" That is the prayer. Always, more life. And what is the blessing? "More life! *This* life!" So you can see there was nothing in the least mystical in our worship of her.

Naturally I came to see my mother as a kind of work of art, no matter how strongly this was at odds with her own tastes. Just as my father had been put on this earth to take exception as a non-conformist, she was here to attest that the conventional wisdom of the herd is also deserving of representation. For if the key to life is only in resisting the herd, how can you learn to love? Mother, I suppose, played the Catholic to my father's Pro*test*ant materialism, if for no other reason than the rules of the primitive matriarchy always gave the church pride of place. I never saw her near the prayer station in the corner of her suite with the chamber pot beneath, atomizers of cologne, earrings, and her favorite clepsydra (water clock) upon the altar. Nor as far as I know did she ever attend a mass. But a visit to the chapter house of the great cathedral at Razacanum would show every other face in its gallery of archbishops to be of Priam's family. And yet a hundred years before, they had all been Protestants. One tends to forget that the Church was the most democratic institution of that time, offering advancement upon merit to the poorest man, and only in finance were there men more obscure and lowly. There seemed to be, at any rate, no hiatus in her adoptive paternal lineage, no waffling or skepticism; only conversion or reconversion. Her ancestors had gone from animal worship to pyrolatry to Catholicism to Protestantism and back to Catholicism, and in the section of her orbit in which I was acquainted with her, she was veering, come full circle from a lapsed high church infatuate back to a lush and goofy heterodoxy, her mysterious Naiad side, in which the point, apparently, was to be your *own* ancestor.

Our Christmases were thrilling; we gave presents on the twenty-first, the Solstice, the day of the unconquered sun, wore crowns of the Saxon holly and ivy while chanting the pagan *Dies sol invictus* with unremitting jollity. And if the choristers were out of tune or mumbling the words, Ainoha would give the conductor a consoling smile. Then we lit a huge bonfire on the front lawn, sacrificing the insipid pine to Odin's sacred oak, put human masks on all the dogs, their snouts upon us. There followed twelve days of fasting and mourning, celebrating something much older and stranger than the birth of "*that* man," in my father's scornful mention, "who never wrote a single word."

I could forgive Christianity its fanaticism; it was its skepticism permeating everything that set me against it. As the Astingi know, there is nothing more amusing than playing pagans in *Purgatorio.*

I shouldn't leave the impression that Mother wasn't maternal. It was only that her sensual self was so powerful, that it told her that she couldn't protect us from the world, even for a day, as much as we all wanted to believe in her semi-divinity. So it was that she continuously pushed both my father and myself out from the Land Behind the Forest. After a hug, she submerged her instincts, renounced her status, and even in our most desperate moments turned us round face-out to the world. She wasn't cold or diffident. It was simply a kind of reversal of the sexual. She just announced, as she had in her first labor pains, "*That* way!"

Like everything else in our world, I would not understand this until I saw the drama reenacted by beasts. In late January, the four brooks from the four valleys froze solid, the spider's web of haze which hung over Semper Vero snapped, and blizzards stunned even the moles and beavers into inanimate submission. From my tower window, I could see the huddled aurochs up to their knees in the drifts, every curl on their faces blasted with frost, every breath turned into a small geyser. Their heavy heads and thickened necks were perfectly suited for smashing through the crust of ice and foraging for tufts of brown grass. At that time of year, the only sound beyond the wind was these animals' labored breathing. The calves milled around their mothers, trying to share in the patch of grass they had just stamped out of the snow. But the females, already carrying next year's calves, simply butted them away, telling them in effect to dig their own. The thaws gave up the ribcages of those who didn't, not always the weakest by any means. And the mothers would mourn them, browsing around the skeletons and chasing away the foxes.

It made me feel like the luckiest man alive.

Semper Vero was of course Ainoha's adoptive family's, owing to their sudden spontaneous mutation from fairly ordinary to well-off folk, the odds on which my father never failed to believe he could capitalize and securitize. And she encouraged him in this, though she suspected he was doomed to failure. Priam's relations had led the Russians through the Pass at Cjank (the officers bivouacking at Semper Vero) on their way to crushing the revolutions of 1848—though the family had also provided arms to innumerable failed peasant rebellions, and Mother herself would be the first to enlist against the Russians in the Great War. Though this appears contradictory (the pantheon of goddesses has always appeared rather scatterbrained), I believe there was a serious principle operating here. The most dangerous of men, after all, is the self-appointed heretic in a righteous cause, and it is the goddess's duty, whenever such men appear, to cancel him out, and restore, by whatever necessary means, the cosmic equilibrium. The Mistress of the Living, Mistress of the Dead, fights on the side of those she personally likes, regardless of their politics. For her, the divine was just another category of human thought. And as worshipers of the ditch know, survival is insured only if a little bit of *every*thing is thrown into the burial pit, as we never know how the story is going to come out. The history that the goddess sets herself in favor of is simply that long struggle of people who want nothing more than to lead ordinary lives, but who are manipulated into conflicts by men who know no peace.

She had learned early on that insistent, preternatural dignity can often give offense, and so we must manufacture, often from nothing, the most problematic aura of all: warmth. The Goddess does not revel in her gash; she knows no chthonic mystery lies there. She knows that the only power that matters is power doubled, power to the second power, energy squared, the power of the pair. By mixing the dresses of different thoughts, the Goddess ought to encourage perspicuity, and by reinstituting reticence into everyday relations, prevent the eclipse of Familyland. The perfect wife is one who does not believe in either her husband's fortune or his ruin. Just as there was no point in apologizing for being a goddess, there was also no point in being legendary if it just made one unhappy. She knew she was no more primal than she was a finished item; only a hasty blend of antiquity with the ever-receding present.

"Do you have any idea," she warned Father when his courting took on a lucid measure, "do you have any idea at all, how hard it is to please a woman?" And when I brought home an unsatisfactory school report, she would nod and smile, and drawing it across my palm, leave a paper cut, as a feathery tongue of flame appeared in my head.

It would not heal until the grasses came up.

Mother loathed all political beliefs, and as a result never felt impelled to acquire the German language. "The continual presence of a fixed idea," she insisted, "forces the jaw muscles to overdevelop and the visage to age prematurely," and she believed fervently that devotion of the heart is good for the complexion. She also insisted that Astingi skulls were so constructed that a scalp wound received in any ideological struggle would completely heal in no more than fourteen days. She could divert the most hysterical of political arguments by simply laying a plump bare forearm upon the table, rendering the warring gentlemen speechless.

And if Father had his love-hate affair with Germans, hers was with the French. She saw all their talk of Liberté, Egalité, and Fraternité as Paternalism, Nationalism, and Alcoholism, a nation that left its dogs to starve in the woods after a hunt. If she had a program, it was to replace the weak Western reading of liberty with discipline, equality with solitude, and fraternity with the tenderness of unlike creatures.

Anyone with a cursory knowledge of ancient history knows that the goddesses were no less whimsical or debauched than the Gods, and nothing amused Mother more than the project of gentrifying the goddess. For having observed a thousand litters and their parents, no one can deny that the gene of ambition, like that of baldness, is carried by the female. "A woman is clearly the equal of any man, even a mean man," she often said, "but a woman cannot become a gentleman, that is, be stoical *and* fair." She preferred the company of men, and she frightened women in the same way that Father frightened men, with the gay fatalism of the soldier. Just as some women find men who are indifferent to them irresistible, Mother was attracted to the sort of man who struggled to keep his baser instincts under control, acknowledging that they were transitional figures in a game which threatened to explode into a pointless, murderous brawl at any moment. She knew you could get anything out of a man by questioning his courage, and so avoided it at all costs. Strong men for her were no particular problem. It is the strong man suddenly grown weak who is truly dangerous; yet it is the particular pathos of their species that men are truly fascinating only in their weakness. "It is men's nature to run away," she told me early on, no doubt alluding to Priam, "for men, if not victorious, prefer to disappear without a trace. But women leave traces, and the right woman," she observed with a saturnine grin and revealing her foot tightly covered in black silk like a serpent's head, "can ruin anything!"

She did not want "a man," nor all men; she wanted Man.

I believe the only aspect of her role she regretted was as Patroness of Arts. To conquer the artworld did not strike her as much of a conquest, and while she did her best to reluctantly champion peoples' rights to alienation and unending originality, she found the peculiar combination of exhibitionism and sullen introspection of the literary world something of a bore. Indeed, she was interested in those few areas of experience which lie totally outside art. Struggling with the muse, like sexuality, were for her quite recent and unexamined nouveaux conventions. "If you must wait for inspiration," she often said, "you may as well give up." And there were days, in the presence of the many artistes who frequented our home, when she could be Jocasta, Lady Macbeth, and Clytemnestra rolled into one, while she took their measure. Mother knew several things about art and none of them had to do with sanity or happiness. She was not fooled by the sort of people who hijacked the word "creative" from theology, and who claimed the rights of patronage without subserving to any of their patron's purposes. "A work of art, like an oyster, *mon chérie*," she once remarked to a drunken poet, "can come up as easily as it went down."

Her only interest in art, other than origami and collecting garden statuary, was a diary, strictly descriptive and dispassionate: addresses, places, the exact name and catalog number of a piece of music she had heard, the drawing of an architectural detail, and almost never a single use of a personal pronoun. But she gave up on it early, discovering a diary is the last place you look for truth. The final entry reads: "Oh, I've botched it terribly, dear diary; forgive me, but you are not my genre. Why do people write so much?"

Ainoha would rather be read about than write—the most human condition.

The florid precision of her voice was unforgettable. It was as if her respiration had a physical weight and location, a sculpted sound of air enveloping each individual word. When put out, her pitch was tinged with flatness, and perfections of the upper range had to be smoothed over with deceptive tailoring. Yet so winning was her personae that she could turn flatness into an expressive device and make frailty a source of appeal. The dogs gathered round her while she practiced, and her occasional stepping on their paws produced a less than dulcet chorus of high E's and F's. Her breathing was inextricably bound up with her sentences, and when she mentioned my father's name in public, it was surrounded with extended sighs and mesmerizing melismas. On the other hand, one of her more distressing habits was, when at concerts, to tap out the underlying beat on Father's forearm, the tempo just slightly off. It drove him absolutely crazy, but he never said a word. Yes, she was the major blurry triad, the Tristram home Chord, from which all music issues and returns. But the muse cannot herself sing.

If not precisely pure, Ainoha was intellectually delicate, and would, like any blue chip, have to be held for years to perform. She had only one fear and that was the signing of documents. She had only one weakness. She did not believe in savings. Like Beatrice, she was prone to lecture and was knowledgeable only about Heaven. And serenity is an expensive business. Certainly, she would defend beauty and attractiveness beyond all things, but she was absolutely determined that beauty should not be her downfall, and this constant vigilance encouraged a certain straining for effect and invisible wear and tear upon the soul and parts. And so her syncopated curls and tender nuances often turned with delayed resolutions into a kind of magisterial musical hiccups.

I stood erect in the long bright hallway of my life, staring out at the fogged-in river, my larynx falling toward my heart, the gorge of a word upon my lips. I had finally started speaking, and felt immediately that something stupid had happened to me. Mother asked innocently, incuriously, "where are you going?" I hadn't really thought about it, but I knew that I should stay calm, appear to cooperate, and create a good rapport, so that I could lie through my teeth. For she was made to lie to, and men will do anything to get women out of their minds. Then I heard a voice. But it wasn't *me* that was speaking, or at least I did not listen to what it said to me, in the same way I heard what others said. For there comes a point in life where everything invested in you and expected of you no longer matters and you become a kind of Third Person—and nothing can be understood apart from this.

Mother apparently quite well understood what was going on in this strange aesthetical puberty. She looked evenly into my half-closed eyes, then took me by the hand and led me down to the Mze. "If you don't lie, you don't have to remember what you say," she said earnestly. Then she pushed my face close to the water, incanting,

> Come and wet us waters
> Look up, look down,
> May as much come into the eye
> As came out, and
> May it now perish

Using her large hands as a pail, one leg in the river and one on shore, my indispensable Naiadish companion wet me down until I was dripping from head to foot, and with her thumb washed out my mouth. Then she said something rather extraordinary: "If you cannot be truthful, then at least be deep." "Oh, girl!" the river groaned. Swallows dove like raptors into the yellow foam, and at each plunge a ruby droplet sprang forth. Fish leapt for dragonflies and mouthed them whole, settling back engorged and feline in the waters. And mayflies clotted corybantically above the feeding ground in singing flight, kissing each other in milliseconds without consolation, insensate. I knew I had in me the blood of the Peraperduga, those naked young girls who in times of drought were set in motion by the Astingi from village to village, where libations of wine and water were poured over their heads, and they would dance, shivering from joy, until the rains came. But I dried quickly, like a horse.

Then Ainoha made a garland of poppies and put it round my head, threw sticks and herbs into the river, and gave me a stone to bite. Her lingering touch was like a cigar burn. The sun was hot, the pines smelled sweet, and on the hills the last pearbloom was scattering. She made a garland of poplar blossoms for her hair, and pinned a corsage of tongue-shaped sorrel on the black ribbon of her belt. Her waist was so small a tiny child could reach his arms around it. Her deep bosom and sculpted shoulders, her fine rounded arms and slender wrists hung over me like stormclouds. Little ringlets of hair escaped from the pansies on her temples, droplets of sweat appeared in the small valley of her upper lip. Her eyes were the color of violets in the rain, a sweet companion to my bitter shoulder. But the more I acknowledged her beauty, the less mystery it aroused in me. More aware than ever of the weaponry of her appeal, I began to find it almost offensive. The voice had become a wail—not the weeping of a woman or child, but some old bloody hero howling, in the rush of three great rivers roaring as they flow, a propitiation to her spell.

Her mortal eye, my mortal eye,
Our mortal hands
Silent angel, write silence
In my hands,
Alleilu

The me that wasn't speaking was the *Wodna Mze*, my Waterman, the spirit I would come to lean on as no other. He was the one who gathered Ainoha's combings from the river, and sewing them together with bark and fungus, made a cradle for her Fire Child. As usual, the Mze gave no reflection even in its most serene calm. But sitting on the river floor amidst toppled rotting stumps, I spied my miserable Waterman asorrowing, howling for the flower on the bank who inclines her head to listen to the powers of the water. For no one has ever escaped love, or ever will, as long as there is beauty in the eye to see with.

Ainoha kept singing her countercharms and kept pouring water over me, laughing all the while. A gust of wind had flattened her skirt about her belly, accentuating the soft outlines of her bivalved Venus, the only trace of the eternal ocean in our part of the world. The reed-beds nodded their gray-green heads in the breeze as the bullrushes rasped. I knew that to leave this world I must pass through her gate.

I bit on the stone. Despite her placations and invocations, I would not be disenchanted. I refused to put my face into the waters. I objected to being purified or rescued. I would not fall into her arms. Nor would I lose myself in her loosened hair, for a real goddess occasionally prefers resistance to appeasement. She knew I loved something before her, something already dissolved in the very water in which my embryo floated. I stood shivering from head to toe, well into dusk.

Finally, gathering up her skirts, Ainoha stood up and put her hands on her hips, her slender shape blocking out chaos. The pansies were wilting on her noble brow, and owls with their great miner's lamps of eyes flapped upriver to mine the falling darkness.

"Very well," she said with winsome exasperation, "you are a brave boy. And for that I shall love you forever."

Flat as a fish, entrusting myself to her faith, but leaning on my Waterman, I turned Leviathan and escaped beneath the earth into those vast realms far beyond the night.

CORDIALS

(Iulus)

It was a solemn evening of impressive adult talk, and many crystal beakers of moon wine and Armagnac were emptied. Much of the conversation was above my head, though when the subject turned inevitably to Wolf, I realized they were speaking with the tact necessary for dealing with those more trouble than they were worth, a category in which I included myself and all the other helpless creatures in the world, and to which this handsome threesome had such an irrational attachment.

They spoke of themselves as gay soldiers and sober custodians waging a battle for Wolf's nihilistic soul. They would have preferred to run away from those responsibilities, I believe, perhaps to engage in one of those primitive rituals wherein all ties and taboos are thrown off for a fortnight, men and women anonymously and cheerfully betraying each other in a dark forest. It was only their contempt for the weakness of the majority which kept them from running off. They all admitted there were times when they wanted to take Wolf for a walk and shoot him cleanly through the base of the skull. Certainly that's what the Astingi would have done. I blushed for their honesty. And I would never know whether I was meant to hear this or they simply had forgotten my presence.

They were not, as always, in total agreement as to strategy. The Professor now held to the view, as a result of his disastrous tentativeness, that while we cannot send force wherever our sensibilities are threatened, once committed we must pursue a policy of unconditional surrender.

My father took serious issue here—to terminate the illness, the ill cannot be threatened with liquidation, he argued, and in any case the burdens of total victory were impossible.

"The life of an animal such as Wolf is shaped by the incessant wait for aggression," he said slowly. "He lives perpetually alert to the hunter, who most often does not even exist. The hunter is there in his life about as often as the tiger is in ours. The idea is not one of ethical perfection; it is only to persuade the beast that there is no Universal Hunter."

Mother, picking up the lost sticks of the argument, brought things to a close:

"The only thing we can do, even if we cannot set a perfect example, is urge restraint as a matter of self-interest," she said. "He will be less harmful to himself if he heeds our interpretation."

This was brave talk, to be sure. I did not have the wit to realize then that I would come to my manhood in a time when all these strange notions of Passion and Honor, Authority and Discipline, Restraint and Guidance, were to be suddenly set aside, while every man and woman, child and parent, horse and dog, ran for the autonomous hills.

It was not clear whether the Professor had been disabused of his most cherished notions, or whether he was enervated by the meal. He simply sat, slouched as usual, playing with his fork.

Now Father, like all Cannonians, was a born raconteur, but he was sensitive enough to know that a *conversation couleur* ought not end like a courtroom drama, and so he moved to make a show of his vulnerability. In hindsight, it was perhaps a mistake to let the Professor off the floor.

"One thing I may have not made sufficiently clear is the cost." Felix paused, stroking his beard.

"I thought we had already agreed," the Professor broke in agitatedly.

"Not money. What I'm saying is you cannot blame yourself for Wolf. If we take on such a bargain, we risk incessant failure. You can ruin by any gesture—too liberal or too conservative, too diffident or too *délicatesse*—but you cannot help *one* until you have ruined a few others. This truth, I believe, is the only place where the Christian doctrine and the rule of capital intersect."

He had stood up and, letting his napkin drop to the floor, turned his back on the table and spoke to the ceiling.

"You simply have no idea the damage a self-confident man can unwittingly do," he finished.

The Professor affixed his stern gaze upon my father's brow.

"Perhaps," Ainoha interjected in her usual half-mysterious, half-deadpan mode, "perhaps the Professor would care to see the gallery?"

"Ah, yes," Father sighed, "I believe he is ready." And already Öscar was wheeling a small cart with whiskey, soda, and cigars down the hallway.

In Grandfather's time our home had real art: Chaudet's *Infant Sleeping in a Crib Under the Watch of a Courageous Dog Which Has Just Killed an Enormous Viper*, and Desporte's *Dog Watching Over Game Beside A Rosebush*. Not to mention Oudry's glowing pointer bitches, Courbet's awkward grayhounds, Landseer's chunky Newfoundlands, and Géricault's *Bouledogues Vaginale*. But these had long since been sold off, save for George Stubb's *White Poodle in a Punt*, which still hung in Father's lair along with his favorite quote from the painter, who, returning from the mandatory trip to Italy, confided to his diary, "Nature is better than art."

Indeed, in our part of the world most galleries were like any others, full of wall-eyed ancestors, dull sporting scenes, gratuitous orders of merit, and if one were fortunate, a few recumbent odalisques, their curves resembling stringed instruments. But as you might expect, ours was no ordinary *Galerie des glaces*, for this was where my father chose to remember the many dogs he had ruined on his ascent to Hauptzuchtwart Supreme, as well as those who had simply failed him. He had had their loving cups beaten into metal feed dishes for the kennels, and their show medals defaced and soldered together to make a set of Celtic signet collars, so that the animals might also have a memento of their brief encounter. When failed dogs passed away, we did not cremate them and scatter their ashes on the island in the artificial lake with the kennel, as we did with the champs. We buried them in the church graveyard at Muddy St. Hubertus, in the vague bushy boundary between the Catholics and the Jews. But in the gallery they were memorialized, mate with mate, like ruined royals without heirs.

Father had an idealistic period during the early, monied part of his life when he collected bad art with a view toward not only keeping it off the market, but expunging it from future generations. These were largely portraits of barristers, merchants, admirals, petit barons, and baronesses in which the faces were honorific, stereotypical, and not well executed, the hands often hidden. But the clothes and other details were accomplished, whether a weskit, military uniform, silk ball dress, tweed suit, or lace sleeves. The torsos and their accouterments often revealed more of the personality than the visage—a cigar dangling loosely from a thumb and forefinger, a bow tie against an Adam's apple, a chin resting upon a crook or a walking stick. In any case, Father had the faces whited out and the ruined dogs' heads painted in, in such a way as to indicate how a character defect had gone undetected or an illness undiagnosed, which, intertwined with overreaching pressure or other ill-advised methods, had destroyed the animal's usefulness. He wanted evidence of his many failures kept green, almost unavoidable, so that he would not repeat such harm.

First was the gaggle of gun-shy dogs rendered in various styles of foppery to conceal their secret hurts: Bello Bellini, a graceful grayhound in spats and top hat, who would come apart at the slightest rustle of wind; Satanella, a butch and vicious lapdog, all decked out in fur with protruding eyes; Malteo Falconi, a spinone galapatore, mindlessly playing his accordion with webbed paws; Gottlieb Von O., the essence of a German country gentleman, with exposed haws and curvature of the muzzle; Little James, a not-so-adorable pug in a sailor suit capable only of the most suffocating love; Dr. Becker, an enormously serious but bowlegged, loose-loined hound; and Henritte von Fitzewicz, a macabre terrier in a hunting dress, with a depressed saddle and seriously overshot jaw.

The Professor walked up and down the gallery, hands behind his back, taking in the grotesqueries while pausing now and then to examine a picture more closely, his head cocked in a way as to indicate serious interest, if not entire approval.

"There is no cure for gun-shyness, then?" he inquired.

"Of course," Father said, "but it is most drastic. I pray you will never see it. *Obit anus, obit onus.*"

The Professor attempted to pursue this line of questioning, but soon found himself guided among a more peculiar and recent class of portraits, all Chetvorah, those animals devoted to cynegetics and each other, exemplars of loyalty, probity, chaste ardor, and elevated thoughts, but who passed on hideous recessives, unfitted joints, cryptorchidism, and broken ears, or more commonly and mysteriously were simply unable to transmit their more desirable traits in any significant number, and thus, too, had to be discarded from the future if not the past. These were of course the saddest figures of all, arranged around a roaring fireplace: Chrysanor and Kallirhoe, dressed in an admiral's uniform and a severe black ball gown, who proved, Mother said, that a good marriage might consist of nothing save that the two partners were united against reactionaries and philistines. ("But their children, oh

Lord, their crazy, selfish, ugly children, you would not believe it!") And there were Panfreddo and Pascheline, beautiful as they come, who would retrieve through an oak tree if necessary, but who produced only cleft palates and mental collapse. And Miriam and Monastatos, too cool for their species and over given to philosophizing and abject digging, even on concrete. And finally there were the braces of androgynous brothers and sisters which you wanted to breed so much it almost hurt, knowing they would produce a superior strain faster, but who would also introduce a timed explosive in the lineage, ruining all in the end. Among these were Parerga and Paralipomena, Leon and Lubmissa, Fawn and Dawn, Mars and Mustapha, Philemon and Bancis; the lost lovers, Helenia and Lysander, and Permea and Dimitrius; and the great and famous trick dogs, Didi and Dada.

"Ah, the complicity of flesh is one thing," Mother murmured, "but the complicity of intelligence—oh, dear."

The aristochiens no longer seemed amusing collages to the Professor; they had been transfigured into pure emotional states, all their fears and pretensions focusing out of their gilded frames, anticipating the blows of history that would subtract them from the race.

"This seems, if I may say so, somewhat bizarre," he said without an edge.

Mother was doing some half-hearted *port de bras* in a corner before a large mirror, between death masks of comedy and tragedy.

"The dog has a better memory than we do," Father spoke softly. "He never forgets the worst thing that happens to him. He does not store it away. He remembers it afresh each day. We must emulate his humility and allow it to stimulate our sense of gratitude."

"But, surely, love itself . . ." the Professor began, as if by rote.

"It's not enough to love somebody," Father snapped. "For it to last, you must also love their life!" And with this, horse tears welled up in his eyes.

The Professor abandoned his prosecutorial tone.

"Well, Councilor," he said with a forced wink, "a dog will perhaps betray you if you treat him badly. But a person will betray you no matter how you treat him."

"Oh, but people are more forgetful. That's their salvation. One slip with a dog and they never forgive you, never! I ruined so many before I learned, and who's to pay for that, Doctor? Yes, who is to pay for that?" He had taken off his ascot to wipe his eyes.

"Yes, yes, someone must have done the same with Wolf," the Professor murmured, almost absentmindedly. "And no, they don't forgive. You can only reach a kind of accommodation."

"You never know how many is one lash too many," Mother said sweetly, her back turned. "And then all is lost."

The Professor was aghast, waving his arms at the gallery. "How in heaven's name did you survive all this?" he entreated.

I do not know whether it was the slightly patronizing tone of the question, but the tears abruptly stopped halfway down Father's cheek, as if he had willed it, and he turned on his heel, thundering:

"We are first and foremost athletes, Professor. It's not what you remember, but how fast you can forget, that allows us to stay in the game." He poured two stiff whiskeys, jamming one into the Professor's hand.

"The ones we ruin, well, that's really your affair, Doctor. I have been forced by pecuniary circumstances to deal with other men's errors and nature's abortions, to become"—he spat this—"an *educationist*! But in my heart of hearts, I am still the servant of the disabused, the congenitally alert. Ameliorism is my game, getting it right the first time round. The standard repertoire is quite enough for this life, Doctor. Start with the very best and leave the rest. The cruelest thing is to constantly praise mediocrity and believe that illness teaches us. Suffering teaches us, but illness bores us."

The Professor stood his ground, matching him drink for drink.

"Your candor is most impressive, Councilor—almost overwhelming, one could say." Turning his large head, he reached for an inoffensive phrase. "Your meritocratic sense is most admirable. But doesn't it all speak to the need for new therapies?"

Mother had arrived between them with a modern movement, refilled their whiskeys, and then, like an officer at intermission at the opera, lowered the gas jets. There was a great *whoosh* through the gallery as the portraits disappeared. Father shrugged, rattling the ice in his whiskey and soda.

"Let us toast new cures, Doctor, as long as we admit the risk. But let us also be honest: in truth, we don't even know what an animal *is*!"

"I believe I'm not feeling quite well," the Professor mumbled, and on that note they flung their glasses into the roaring fire, and each arm supported by his handsome hosts, the Professor was taken for a walk on the terrace in the gathering tremulous winds.

As his nausea dissipated, he fumbled with his pocket watch, noting on the schedule the last departures of the *Desdemona*. But upon reaching his rented jitney he found it lying in a heap in the drive, and he followed Father's finger to four of the tallest poplar trees on the estate, at the tops of which the wheels of his carriage were lashed. The Professor was dumbstruck, staring at Father, who seemed proud as Lucifer.

"I have appointments!" he almost shrieked, as Mother held his arm tightly and whispered in his ear.

"You must be careful not to insult my husband's hospitality," she intoned, batting her ever-thickening eyelashes. "In *my* father's day, we would grease the carriage with wolf's fat so it was impossible to force the guest's horse into the shafts. It is the custom in Cannonia for the hosts to keep their guests as prisoners. Sometimes for weeks. Some stay for years!"

The Professor looked helplessly at Father, who was standing tall.

"Now, it is you, my friend, who must learn to stay." And he raised his hand high, the flat of the palm out. "Stay!" he commanded. Mother felt the Professor's arm slip from her grasp as he fainted dead away.

The Professor was awakened at daybreak by a rosy-cheeked servant girl with a stiff, brandied café au lait. Through the gauze curtains he could make out an Astingi boy scrambling up and down the poplars. Then he fell into a profound and dreamless sleep, to be awakened at nine for a huge breakfast, during which not a word was said. Afterward they all took a walk, smoked, and talked unconvincingly about the crops and cattle.

"It's so hard to know what's on a cow's mind," Felix said absently. Upon their return, the jitney had been reassembled, and the piebald mare shone a deep burnt amber from a vigorous grooming. Wolf was happily narcotized in a new wicker kennel.

"Take him home with you," Ainoha said, ill-concealing her exasperation. "A *taedium vitae* must run its course."

"He has manners enough now to survive the city," Felix added.

Everything about their farewell embraces had a jaded, slow-motion quality. I do not know to this day why their simplicity affected me so.

We sat down with iced tea on the terrace as the jitney exited the drive into a driving rain. The *Desdemona* emitted a morose E flat. Ainoha asked Felix why he was so uncharacteristically patient with such stupid questions, and how it was possible for a professional man to have such brutish table manners.

"No one has the courage to ask stupid questions anymore, my dear," he cut her off, "and as for the eating, that is what comes from taking all your meals *en famille*."

Mother's instinct was nevertheless on the mark, for while the Professor had gone out of his way to charm her, exuding both a formal respect and a laconic wit, she had watched him closely, scrutinizing him more minutely than she would a flower. She knew that as quickly as my father made friends, it would fall to her to keep them. She also knew then that something in the Professor's high-mindedness—always ready to wave the black banner of scrupulosity—would inevitably cause a rupture, for it is the smallest of differences between people that always loom largest in the end.

"It seems to me that in all this talk of method," she said, "everything depends on whether the therapy is administered before or after the lack of confidence occurs."

Father ignored her, as he always did when she was right, a curious mark of respect, just as now in his contrarian manner he chose to defend his client after demolishing his most sacred hypotheses, and as a boxer might bow to his rival, who after being hit with everything he had, stayed on his feet, registering pain everywhere except in his eyes.

"He is the most modern of men," Father concluded cheerfully. "His powers of observation are considerable, if clouded by misunderstandings of a literary nature, a man whose scientific bent is always in conflict with unspoken politics. But no one was ever driven mad by contradictions in *thought*. He is, in short, one of us, only more so. We are going to have something of a *conversazione galante*, he and I."

"But what, pray, exactly does he do?" Mother said. "Professor from where? Doctor of what?"

"Ah, my dear." Father made a teepee of his napkin, and daubed his dagger beard. "The Professor has dedicated himself to reconciling those who have proven themselves unlovable."

IN THE AUGARTEN
(Iulus)

When he had Wolf safely home, the Professor allowed the dog to accompany him everywhere, walking him at noon along the winding *rue de Carcasses*, and even feeding him in the anteroom beneath the portraits of allegorical women and splendid unread books.

The dog had amazingly little appetite, nor did he acknowledge food as the gift it was meant to be. His tail hung like a fox's, as if appended by a nail. And when they encountered a stranger in the apartment stairwell, the dog did not acknowledge him but only made certain he was a step above or below the figure, remaining supremely indifferent to the nervous petting he evoked. The Dresden collar circleted loose about his neck, occasionally entrapping a broken ear.

The walks were particularly trying. While never a brisk perambulator, the Professor preferred a reasonable pace in order to reoxygenate his brain while perusing antiquarian shop windows. He had been having periodic problems with his feet, or more specifically his shoelaces, which would fray and burst without warning—and for some reason a loose shoe is one of the most disorienting things that can happen to a purposeful man. He had sent the servant girl out, but the laces she brought back were never a proper fit. And when he bent over to relace his boot, his heart pounded in his skull and his breath grew short—"abhypia" was his self-diagnosis. Relacing seemed to take an eternity, all that crossing and recrossing, creating slack and then drawing it tight, and during the process he often felt he should have done more sport as a child. If the laces were too short and he used only half the eyelets, painful pressure was exerted on his arch, yet his toes were left swimming in a fearful void. If too long, he cut them with a penknife, but this created a large, floppy unraveling bow on which he often tripped. He suspected Wolf of gnawing on the laces, but whenever he threw a shoe to tempt the culprit, the dog would look at him as if he had lost his mind. *Throwing away a perfectly good shoe?*

So it was with the walking. Wolf would follow behind him in mocking obedience, gradually pulling them into a kind of fuzzy art photograph of a stroll. But whenever they actually stopped—for the dog to urinate, or more often for the Professor to retie his shoe—just as he leaned down Wolf would start moving forward, albeit imperceptibly, and the dignified doctor would find himself hopping in the street, lurching and turning in a *valse galatz*, the leash wrapped around his leg and his ever-loosening shoe flopping on the pavement like an extinct appendage. Once the Professor had regained his footing and untangled them, Wolf would drop behind his heel in what appeared to be perfect compliance (strangers often complimented the animal's street manners), but in fact the dog was drawing him back to a point of nullity, somehow behind time itself, abandoning their painfully won coordination.

The Professor knew the shortcut of soothing reassurance had failed, yet he lacked the conviction in his own reflexes to pop the chain and impose a mild penance. Indeed, his fear that he might do more harm the animal seemed able to calibrate precisely. (The gentle, sabotaging selfishness of the defenseless.) For all his submissive indifference, Wolf seemed to place an extraordinary, even profound, faith in his master's increment of fear.

On occasion, usually late in the day, Wolf's sore nose would flare up, and the Professor would gaze down his nostrils with a small light. But he could find neither discharge nor irritation, only a long, glaucous tube ending in an opaque sheen of brain mass, unwrinkled like the advanced mammal he was posing as. The Professor noticed that it was only during this particular type of examination that Wolf's tail moved, if only the bushy tip, like a feather duster wafted by a particularly senile servant.

"Oh, Wolf, what did they do to you?" the Professor thought, a cry in his heart, and then he rephrased it out loud. "Or rather, what did they make you do? Was it those stupid aristocrats, or the crazed Bolsheviks?"

They settled into this routine over a period of weeks, the Professor now certain that he was saddled sadistically, perhaps forever, with the animal's misgivings and disconnectedness. Meanwhile, the dog remained perpetually in wait, anticipating the next follow-up examination of his nose or paw, punctuated with bouts of what certainly appeared to be shame, for what else would cause the otherwise gray-white scar tissue to so promiscuously redden?

As a result, a fatal misunderstanding developed. While the Professor was adapting himself to Wolf's reserved nature, the dog wanted nothing more than to be inspected, preferably at the exact site of the wound, and as the Professor's diagnostic attention dwindled, the symptoms of shame worsened. After the vilest supplications, accompanied by compulsive yawning, sighing, coughing, obsessive leg crossing, nose-boring, nail-biting, and flatulence, Wolf's manner became sharp. He hammered his scarred nose into the Professor's groin, apparently threatening to spit up. He shoved his snout under his master's writing hand, flipping the pen halfway across the room. And he dragged his crippled paw across the doctor's thigh, leaving welts even through the heavy tweed. Wolf felt that his large, dark friend was abandoning him, and for his part, the Professor could not decide which horrified him most: his patient's smothering affection or his invasive enmity.

Then, during a stroll, when his attention was focused on a particularly exotic sculpture in a shop window, he felt an uncharacteristically purposeful tug on the leash, and turning, found to his horror a blind beggar selling matchbooks on the sidewalk, with Wolf urinating on the stumps of the poor fellow's amputated legs. Then and only then, at the height of his fury, did he pop the chain. He heard the click, a ghostly note. Wolf concluded his business, taking his good time, then, after turning slowly and halfheartedly, bit the Professor through his shoe, though without breaking the skin.

He spent long periods gazing into the animal's eyes, now black as his own, which as the day expired seemed to give off a transient luminescence, a stored electricity generated from within. Yet by evening, when he turned on the paraffin desk lamp, the corneas went completely opaque, as if they were only reflecting external light. As the Professor's eyes became accustomed to the darkness, Wolf's eyes emitted an eerie shine, and when he placed a shaving mirror next to the dog's skull, he saw that his own had taken on the same cast, though not of the same deep quality. When he turned off the lamp and they sat in pitch-blackness, he faced the problem of reporting from a zone in which they were both blind. The Professor lit a candle nearby, adjusted the temples of his reading glasses to sharpen the magnification, and circled the dog slowly. From a certain angle his spectacles reflected the candlelight into Wolf's pupils, which suddenly lit up in a fantastic concatenation, brighter and more diaphanous than any star, and for a moment he thought he could make out a trace of the optic nerve through a web of blood vessels on the inner surface of the eye. Both were bathed for a moment in a spectacular fluorescent orange haze, and little mice of ejaculatory feeling ran along the base of the Professor's spine, as the animal seemed to be seeing through him.

In the evening they would often sit on the divan together in a kind of mutual matrimonial inertia, the Professor smoking one cigar after another, Wolf pawing at his free hand while snapping at the smoke rings, deprived of the symptoms of hauling which had once brought them into such gripping interaction. Wolf must have finally felt that he had been written off, like an old unbalanced wife. And some evenings the Professor felt vaguely insulted that this refugee had assimilated so rapidly to his new surroundings, appearing to forget both his lost status as top dog as well as that of prisoner, though it was clear by his newly aggressive behavior that he was also telling the Professor that this new life of bourgeois ease and reflection had little intrinsic charm or value, and could never compare to the unique high culture from which he had been forced to flee.

But throughout these mood swings Wolf maintained for most of the day his old apathy, unassailably entrenched in his indifference to territory. He seemed happiest among strangers in the stairwell, where hierarchy was clearly marked by the steps. Finally, the Professor realized that painful as the consequences might be, something in him preferred the dog's play for attention to his diffidence. Wolf's quieter and more contemplative moods seemed an affront. His patient's sufferings had ceased prematurely, and the Professor preferred hypochondria to an impoverished ego. If nothing could be done for his nose, then something for his state of mind! The dog had come to him a megalomaniac, and now was entirely incapacitated and dependent upon others, unable even to feed himself or complete a defecation. Wolf had lost interest in his own history, or indeed what might become of him. His was a world which was perfectly adequate without lovers and loved ones, without hope and without fear.

"My dearest Friend," the Professor wrote Felix:

There is a gap in our letters which is uncanny. Then came your letter today on the fundamentals of the soul, which with its meticulous refutations of my fantasies, typical of a doctor dilettante, I found so refreshing. If I may summarize your lengthy advice in professional language, it would be as follows:

1) Pay attention to the principles of loyalty, not to whatever system they are embedded in.

2) Never use the phrases "before," "during," or "after" to explain anything.

3) Hysteria is both a dead language and a new language.

4) Temperament has replaced metaphysics as the basis of philosophy.

Why is it, incidentally, that you never complain of your own health problems, with which I feel, in secret, such biological sympathy? I have noted for some time that you bear your suffering better and with more dignity than I. I have all sorts of doubts about my constitution and often cannot remember what I have found out about it that is new, since everything about it seems to be new. It is as if I am thrown out of the train at every station along the line, and every town is named "If I Can Stand It." Well enough of that.

My question today is, Why do I admire your utter stoicism, even wish it for myself, yet am suspicious of it in Wolf? He no longer attempts to capture my favor by anything but the crudest attempts. I believe he is withdrawing from me as his unpleasure disappears from some imagined slight. He still has that conspicuous tic around the eyes, and occasionally he forces his lips into a snout—for sucking? Biting? All day long I try to be kind and witty, original and superior, congenial and conciliating, yet he maintains only a pitiable reserve as a reproach to my efforts, as if all of my insights are equally brilliant, and equally besides the point. A slow piece of work, indeed! Do you remember, in true suffering, his pace was wonderful! I even find myself hoping for a relapse, so I might eradicate every vestige of his precious illness. I dream he becomes miserable again so as to facilitate work, for at present he makes me feel that I have turned into a carcinoma to which nothing will adhere. I am entertaining the thought of applying "pitiless pressure" in the hope of breaking the impasse, of sketching out, as it were, an episode of finality.

Hoarse and breathless, I await your advice.

Your admiring and faithful Friend.

The next day, between dusks of snow flurries and noons of the sharpest brightest sun, the Professor and Wolf were sitting on a bench in the Augarten. The dog seemed uncharacteristically energetic, and the Professor unsnapped his leash to let him roam.

The dog was wearing his new signet collar, a gift from Semper Vero made from medallions awarded in competitions Wolf would not even have been allowed to watch, much less participate in. The Roman coins used as solder gave off a ginger glow, the pride of the Chetvorah, taking even its most worthless cousin into company.

Wolf ambled three-legged down the gravel path, every few steps holding up his damaged paw like a talisman. His was a determined yet relaxed pace, without checking back. He had never ventured farther from his master's side. The Professor watched him approvingly all the way down the path, until he noticed at the end of the *alleé*, through the ornate gate, a huge new flag flapping with thundercracks against the facade of the *Justizpalast*. The government had apparently changed, and he had been so preoccupied with Wolf he hadn't even noticed it. A military band had struck up. Music without words always made him nervous.

The dog continued down the path, worrying sparrows, who in turn were worrying horse apples, until at last he reached the street, where, persecuted by fate and abandoned by medicine, the beshitted Wolf leapt gracefully into the open rear of a passing van and disappeared.

That evening Father's belated telegram arrived:

Intervene STOP But remember STOP The lion springs only once!

MR. MOOKS AND THE TYRANT, VOO
(Iulus)

I spoke my own dead, rich language until I was three, when I abruptly forgot it and cried out in my sleep. Mother, surrounded by her bed curtains and hillocks of damask, could not hear. At dawn she would arrive for a brief moment, the cold-nosed Chetvorah beating their famous nail tango about the bed, and with a half-erotic, half-maternal muzzle, she would bring me into that dazed state where all the cells and little cilia are growing a millionth of an inch, putting a bit of her saliva in my nostrils to awaken me to the sweetness of the world, while leaving the devil unexorcised. But when, past midnight, I continued to yowl, Father came with a candle, put the flat of his cool hand upon my wet brow, carrying on imaginary conversations with innkeepers, coachmen, and ferrymen as counter-apparitions. However, my bed sweats remained severe. I was aware that I had a scent not unlike that of a dairy. And for the next seven years I did not sleep, a continuous vertiginous lucidity, both congenital and painful. The problem with not sleeping, of course, is all that time you have to spend with yourself. Everything in life is a preparation for a sleep which will not come, for life is only bearable with the discontinuity it provides. Sleep is the secret of life, and uninterrupted sleeplessness forced from me the inability to forget. Aged prematurely by this dark-circled nothingness, the negative alertness of those *nuits blanches*, future interrogations by even the most determined and devious institutions were mere child's play. Indeed, I often went to sleep during them.

In my bedchamber, in the only closet, deep as the room was wide, the tyrant Voo held sway—an enormous well-formed stool, fanned with a bandolier of cartridges, strange drooping epaulets upon his shoulders, and on his helmet an insignia resembling a bolt of broken lightening. He carried a paraffin lamp and a riding crop. My father ignored him, yet acknowledged his presence by telling me not to show fear. The closet door was warped and would not close properly.

The Voo's tactics were not those of surprise or concealment; indeed, at times he did not seem to know where he was. His drill was routine. Father would read me a final story, kiss me, plump the pillows up, and extinguish the gas jet. Shortly after his leave-taking, the closet door would slowly open and the Voo would emerge with his lamp, turn toward me with perfunctory acknowledgment, then move silently out of the room and down the hall, and I was left waiting, frozen with terror, until he returned from whatever business he was conducting. He generally hurried back in without looking up, returned at once to the closet, and slammed the door.

Needless to say, it took me a very long time to get to even half-asleep, a state which, like half-drunkenness, I came to loathe. Eventually, I learned how to rest without losing consciousness. I occupied myself by singing merrily through the night: ribald folk songs, my own transcriptions of symphonic works, American pop tunes, Christmas carols, and Astingi funeral marches. No song was too sentimental for me.

As my art developed, my parents moved further and further to their respective ends of the house, and the servants made certain my windows were locked even in the most desultory of summers. In my maturity, I still hum these tunes softly, and make do with catnaps. But most of what passes for my childhood could only be called insomnia. My childhood was something I did not share, nor could have had I wanted to.

At breakfast, I would invariably relate the experience of the Voo in all its terrible redundancy, and while at first, if Mother was present, she expressed sympathy, finally she said, "Look here, I am sorry for you. But *why* must you tell me all this? It is exactly the same each night, and you are well enough in the morning. Don't you see, dear, there's nothing to be done about it." It was the goddess in her talking, her utter boredom with any twice-told tale.

My father did not often have to endure my narration, as he was out on his three-hour morning constitutional, bursting in by the end of the cereal, his glowing face as cold to the touch as steel. But when Mother paraphrased my dream for him—and it seemed to me both more trivial and terrifying when she did so—he would stroke his beard, put his boots upon an andiron, and say, "Well, there's more to fishing than fishing," or some such phrase, leaving the matter there, floating in the air like smoke from a sour pipe. His only therapeutic suggestion was to bring in the veterinarian, Vogel, to teach me the anatomy of the horse, as if its tendons and arteries would relieve my mind of the apparition, but which only confirmed my growing disinterest in that walnut-brained species.

After the veterinarian was dismissed, and I continued to relate the all-too-predictable previous evening's event throughout the years, Mother finally declared that she was washing her hands of the matter—and I must confess I did not blame her, for owing to her upbringing, she could not quite distinguish between fear and boredom, dream and nightmare. In Father's considered view, the Voo ought to be accepted simply as another kind of pet, who did not exist to amuse us, or assuage our loneliness, or show off our good taste, but to remind us of the existence of strong opposites, and how by dealing with such otherness with gallantry, we might accumulate value from good habits. And I took his point. What good was it having only *superior* animals around?

But when I asked him for a watchdog he hedged. While he acknowledged that my unusual "wakefulness" might be useful in housebreaking, he preferred his method, which was to split the litter between his own and Mother's beds, roust them out early, thanking them profusely for not fouling their coverlets—and indeed, they were usually housebroken in less than a week. But he found it hard to trust me with a Chetvorah, a "real pup," as he put it, for he feared I might communicate my fear to it—and in any case, to teach a Chetvorah to be a guard dog was a waste of his abilities—something on the order of teaching a ballerina kung fu. The pups, they loved him more. They always loved him more. And in this too, they were blameless. The last thing a young pup needs is a child with a Voo.

One day (or perhaps one night, it was increasingly all the same to me), something mysterious happened, a first-order experience, such as losing my first language. The Voo had come and gone with his benign regularity. He seemed rather more withdrawn, as if he were preoccupied, but there was, nonetheless, no peace to be had. I diligently fought my way into a final imitation of slumber, a battle on the heights of the abyss, and the next morning I "awoke" late, groggy and unfulfilled, aware of some heat about my feet. I looked up thinking that the Voo had finally gone deadly, only to see a pair of bright eyes staring back at me and a tail like a fan wiping the air behind them. It was a new companion: Mr. Mooks.

Mooks clearly was not one of Father's fine dogs, those superior animals who moved through life with aristocratic detachment and dignity, cool and not always accessible. No, Mr. Mooks wore his mongrel origins like a shiny penny, his limbs a pastiche of elongations and foreshortenings, a veritable salmagundi of spots, half-stripes, and even different lengths and textures of coat, patchy and silken by turns, brown and black and white. And Mooks had one brown eye and one blue eye. Crudely drawn, but full of vibrant affirmation, Mr. Mooks looked as if he might carry the sun like a balloon, a sun that was just as mixed up as he was. He seemed to realize that I was just a boy, and that it was not necessary to expend a great deal of bravura protecting me or showing me his version of real life. He crawled up the channel of bedclothes on his belly and laid his tricolor nose upon my chest.

My first thought was, of course, how Father would take to a stray on the premises. Mooks's ungainliness, even on a featherbed, suggested that he had not been put on this earth for field and stream. Nevertheless, I took him down to breakfast, where he slunk with perfect humility beneath the table. Mother was for some reason up early, and when Father suddenly burst in from his constitutional, hair awry, cheeks filled with blood, and Mooks lunged at him, I thought the game was up. But Father, apparently filled up with oxygen and endorphins, was oblivious.

Mooks then began to investigate all corners of the kitchen, where the scents of generations of dogs must have seemed to him almost archeological. He sidled past Mother's ankles and, fairly spun about by her perfume, let out a bellow of surprise. Then, as Father poured his coffee into the great bowl with the built-in mustache bridge, I realized that Mooks did not exist for them any more than the Voo, and this naturally was a source of considerable relief. I did not want him kenneled with the exemplars of the race, in their private boarding school with its infinite hierarchies, cruel initiations, and arch sophistications.

Mr. Mooks possessed an inner discipline like no other animal I had ever seen. He was seemingly all but indifferent to food. I never saw him evacuate. He had no voice to speak of, only a low guttural rumbling like a not particularly well-made but nonetheless reliable machine, which I first heard that night from the foot of my bed. When the closet door had opened perfunctorily, and the Voo appeared in all his hunchbacked arrogance, the surface of his fibrous, unfeatured face glistening from the paraffin lamp, Mooks went rigid as a cornerstone as he emitted that ratchetlike growl. The Voo was brought up short and rotated his sluglike body towards us. He was clearly taken aback, although that seemed only to heighten his authority for the moment. But then he straightened up, or rather recongealed himself, and resumed his customary movement to the door and down the hall. Mooks did not move a muscle, and his low growl startled me when the Voo returned, not acknowledging that his retreat to the closet was hastier than usual. I sank a few levels in the general direction of unconsciousness, and was awakened only at dawn. I could not believe it—for the first time I had *lost* consciousness, tasted the cocktail of oblivion, the vast dissolute ecstasy of total blackout, without feeling and without recall. I was still terrified, but thanks to Mooks, not altogether helpless and alone.

I spent much of the next night explaining things to Mooks, speculating on what the Voo meant, what we meant to him, as well as how Mooks had chanced upon the one house in all the world which had for its head the dogmeister supreme, holder of Hauptzuchtwart. He listened in a patient, affirmative way, his paws extended and crossed over one another, always alert, though his broken ears sank with a certain despondency when I moved the discussion to the project of our life together.

The next morning we reconvened at breakfast. Mother again put in a highly eccentric appearance, wheeling about in a whirlwind of activity which produced only cold porridge and some brown apples. Father was not in a good mood, as sheets of rain and lightning had canceled his walk. The day's blood was still high in his cheeks; the arteries alongside his neck were two blue cords, a barometer of heavy weather. I noticed then that Mr. Mooks's claws were not only untrimmed but actually curled—except for passing gas, his only really unattractive feature. The nails had grown long, yellow, and hollow, curled under at the ends like a mandarin's, and made an unpleasant noise upon the stone floor. I was not yet convinced of my parents' inattention (which was often feigned) to my companion, so I politely asked Mother to set out another plate at the table, which she did with an acrobatic *développé*. But my father focused upon the small addition to our table setting with intense curiosity.

"For . . . whom?" he enunciated slowly.

"Mooks," I said. "Mr. Mooks."

"Mooks?" he repeated, somewhat embarrassedly, thinking perhaps he had forgotten an honored overnight guest. "Mooks?"

"Mooks is my new friend," I said. "A dog. I don't know what kind."

The two blue cords on either side of my father's neck swelled slightly. Though he said nothing, I saw immediately the aspect of betrayal in his eyes. If he had been capable of speaking at the moment, it would have gone something like this: "I have spent a lifetime creating a race of animals which exceed in their deeds and speciespower anything which has yet appeared on this earth. All this I bequeath to you. And you might choose from them any member to lavish your attention on. But no, you must sneak in, like a servant girl, some anonymous insubstantial mutt, and place him at my right hand!" And this, indeed, is almost word for word what he did say to me several days later.

Mooks seemed to sense this disapproval as he hopped up with downcast eyes upon the bench beside me. But he did not take offense. Father's eyes were now, as they often were, on the ceiling, which gave him an aspect of those historical figures in bas-reliefs. The fact that he could see no dog there did not in the least mitigate my platonic betrayal.

Mother, sensing that all was not well, leapt between us, and with a large spoon, plopped a portion of white-hot cream of wheat into Mooks's plate.

"We certainly hope Mr. Mooks likes American cereal," she said.

As it turned out, he did not. The cereal sat there throughout the day, and then day after day, turning not just cold but gelid, then oddly crusty, and only when it took on a terminal green hue was it removed, a rebuke to my new companion.

I must say I preferred Father's hurt feelings and internalized rage to Mother's hypocritical concession to my new friend, as I have always found intemperate scorn more instructive, and kinder in the long run, than halfhearted lies. This should have told me something important about myself, but what astonished me was that both my parents assumed Mooks's appearance was due to something *they* had done or not done. If I had sufficient power, I would have inflicted upon them the Voo himself, that faux friend from the rim of civilization, and not some harmless, innocent, fake animal.

In any event, due to Mooks's eternal vigilance, the Voo's visits became more intermittent, and when he did appear, it was not with quite the same claustral charisma of old. Mooks himself seemed irritated on those nights when he did not make an appearance, and little balls of tension appeared in his short neck. The Voo seemed to be having problems with self-presentation, and with my new companion, rather than gaining any confidence, I was simply losing interest in the tyrant. But as the Voo's visits became less predictable, he gained the advantage of surprise. His passages were more varied, less choreographed. He appeared at different hours, when I least expected it and Mooks was dead asleep. He also acquired a larger repertoire of gestures and movements, some of them quite bizarre, and once, after a long absence, he appeared in the late afternoon while I was doing sums, in a kind of pathetic shuffle without his lamp.

One night I awoke to the creak of the closet door, and I could make out by the light of his lamp a newly beguiling Voo, eyes twinkling like kernels of corn in horsemanure, something very like a grin across his fecal-face. He moved without his usual sluggishness and I saw that he had also acquired a companion. At his feet there sat the cutest monster you ever saw, a three-headed hound, its back covered with snakeheads and the tail of a perfect little dragon. Mooks was stunned silent, obliterate. The monster sat obediently and focused at the end of a velvet rope. I had to give him credit. It was a standoff. The Voo sashayed out into the hall dragging the brute with its tail thrashing behind him. He would not return.

I believed then, if I could only reclaim the dead language of childhood, that the Voo would disappear from my life, or become a mere augury whom I could interpret as I liked. Indeed, I was becoming bored with my fear and less anxious about its source. The Voo, after all, had a certain authority and detachment which seemed admirable. The magic of *in extremis* had always appealed to me. His situation was clearly more interesting than mine. From the demands of the infant, one can come to understand the tyrant's point of view, because it is we in our stinking bedclothes who are most totalitarian. I had never questioned the fact that I *deserved* to be frightened and judged by this assassin of disfigurement. And I was attracted by a spirit who had the hardness to go to any lengths! In short, I had to summon the honesty to admit that I would have preferred to be very like the Voo, and insert myself into his world, but simply couldn't muster the wit or will to do so. I had also come to notice that as the Voo was vain and self-regarding, he was basically human, and therefore defeatable. But this in no way made me less interested in what went through the villain's mind, what it was like to be in his large red shoes. How I missed my absent mute interlocutor!

As the days went on and I became more attached to Mooks, cosseting him without qualms, hugging him until he burped, I began to have other concerns, not the least of which was the wedge which my small companion had put between me and my parents. I also began to speculate about what would happen if the tyrant, cornered, as it were, might alter his routine, then strike out and injure Mr. Mooks, even sic his three-headed monster dog upon him. Mooks was not their match. He had altered our relations by a kind of irrational bravado, not to mention a certain stupidity which would eventually irritate a cosmic presence like the Voo.

This was not real sympathy, only a bloated sense of myself, having less to do with self-confidence than a kind of spiritual elephantiasis, mercilessly requiring enormous amounts of new territory and stimulation. How stupid of me not to have made a pact with the Voo before Mooks entered the scene!

Most disturbing of all, what if the Voo was indeed banished—would Mooks, who had conquered him, not get a swelled head, no longer feel useful, and perhaps disappear? Or would he become, as smug victor, so insupportable in our civil family that I would finally have to hide him out?

The Voo, for all his threats, did not require interpretation; everyone understood what *Vooness* was. But Mooks did, and endless lies. Moreover, as I reached out to stroke his rigid little neck, I came to see that out there where he lay was a little bit of me—less easily satisfied perhaps, but certainly more alert and more real. And that indeed if Mooks saw me in this light, he might be tempted to hold his bravery over me, constantly reminding me of my inferiority, and making me appear ridiculous, talking to an underpedigreed dog, all but invisible.

My insomnia never much improved, though later with the help of kind ladies and fine liquor I was able to enter the closet of total oblivion so necessary to surviving the good life. Buffeted by fate into the most various corners of the world, I have accepted gratefully many a generous and gentlewoman's easement and aid. But I did not infer even then that as a grown man I would long for those nights of lucid ecstasy, when the door swings open and the madman, the most eternal playmate, punctually presents himself, as you piss all over your insides.

Finally, the day came when I realized I spent more time worrying about Mr. Mooks—that he might be hurt, abandon me, or show me up, that it would all somehow turn out badly—than anything else. And this caused me more anxiety than the Voo. For if the Voo would never go away on his own, did that also mean that Mooks would live forever? And who after all was the more instructive, or entertaining presence?

And so one breakfast morning before Father returned from his walk, I asked Mother to remove Mooks' plate, and hypocritical tears welled up in her eyes.

"Has Mr. Mooks gone somewhere?" she said. "Is he not feeling well?"

I did not reply, for I had lost yet another language. Mooks had melted away, spot by stripe, blue eye by brown eye, sentence by sentence. My companion had scurried out of my life without so much as a fare-thee-well, a fact much more mysterious than his appearance.

MY THREE SWEETHEARTS
(Iulus)

I spent my days hiding in various caves, sinks, love holes, and other dips and ducks around the estate, playing with bear bones and animal skulls. My favorite was the funnel-shaped cavern which formed the crypt of Muddy St. Hubertus. Here the Astingi had elaborated the ochre and hematite prehistoric cave drawings with their own gold leaf, reddened yellows, and velvety blues, drawing human figures amongst the shadowy staggered mammals and reptiles, while impudently restoring the scene to two dimensions. And here was the best likeness of my parents and our domestic aura, the mezzotint "Dogface, Mermaid and Boy Exeunting on a Dolphin." It was not historical, not a memory of olden times, nor did it record an event. It was an image of memory before it became history, bathed in a light which came from a world beyond, venerating access to a personality you didn't have, and a life you were not going to live. Nor was it, strictly speaking, "art," for it demanded no protection and offered none. No one controlled it, and mercifully, it had no theme. It presented itself as actual creatures cooperating with the painter, people, and animals whom the painters had actually known, though the elaborations of the subjects were separated by tens of thousands of years. It was something which could not exist in the mind, but it took no leap of imagination to believe that these creatures were still very much alive. The paintings had been covered over the eons with layers of calcite, and within this dull sheen one could make out the black soot torchmarks of various observers through the ages. At a certain angle, I could see a boy holding a torch accompanying the creatures coming toward me. The more I stared at him, the harder he looked at me. I had to get away from him. He was posing as my spiritual guide, and the last thing I wanted was to be alone with God. But I did not lack for playmates.

Ophar Osme Catspaw was our resident artiste and intellectual gent. He variously claimed origins in both Persia and Oxfordshire, and indeed perfectly blended those regional affectations into a kind of seamless seediness—a donnish ayatollah, fearing death but hating life. He lived for ideas and rode every recent train of thought through our premises, great dirty brown carriages on wobbly axles with all their windowpanes smashed. He was clean-shaven except for a pair of narrow whiskers on his cheeks; his thin hair of a strange greenish-gray hue was parted in front at the temples. He was constantly adjusting the collar of whatever shabby jacket he was wearing, and even in winter he never put his arms into his overcoat, but wore it slung over his shoulders, his hands contemplatively intertwined behind him.

He had come to us during Father's first flush of enthusiasm, the trainer/patron's confidence that he might turn willfulness into talent, mere neurotica into a vital *névrose*. He gave him the Masonic outbuilding for a studio, where in fact he did produce *Der Analom,* which hung over our dining table, a number of watercolors of Mother running, swimming, or shooting, and a not unflattering oil of my deselfed-self, though, as is often the case with amateurs, the hands were wrong.

Had he remained, like most of us, a mediocre surrealist with strong political inclinations, he would have been an instructive companion, if only as a check on conventional wisdom. Indeed, Father ran every investment idea by him, and if he assented, promptly did exactly the opposite—and in this contrarian scheme, Catspaw proved nearly infallible and worth every ducat expended on him. But I too learned a valuable lesson from Catspaw—that human beings seem capable of remembering only one story at a time in its entirety, and what passes for the life of the mind is largely the adolescent search for a single variable which explains everything. Catspaw was my Yale and my Harvard. He became more famous as a pedagogue than artist, for having one student—me.

He was also renowned for his great character roles in local drama groups—the gravemakers in *Hamlet*, the touching fool in *Lear*, Rageneau in Rostand's *Cyrano*, the demented steward in *Twelfth Night*, and the hierophantic soothsayer in *Cymbeline*. Indeed, he would often drop effortlessly into these roles in the midst of normal social intercourse, delighting in unnerving our many guests. And rarely would he present a glass of champagne without a Faustian riddle,

I may command where I adore
But silence, like a Lucrece knife,
with bloodless stroke my heart doth gore . . .

leaving the guest racking his brains for the source of that ghostly echo.

But my dear parents increasingly lacked the patience to sit for their likenesses, or the vanity to review them, and eventually could no longer afford to purchase his work, which of course made poor Catspaw sullen and moody and even more unkempt than usual. He attended meals sporadically, usually arriving only for dessert, and he spent a great deal of time in the attic trying on the many moldy costumes there. But his most baffling move was his renunciation of painting for the literary life. This proved a great tactical mistake with Father, for husbands have no reason to like modern literature—indeed, it was a pillory for husbands. For years, every wife in every modern novel had walked out.

"Has she a child?" Father thundered. "She walks out. Has she no child? She walks out! Then she experiments, becomes disappointed, and we are supposed to be gracious! The only reason to write a novel," he concluded, "is to attract women, but then in the writing of it you have to forsake them, so what's the point?"

But Catspaw was not writing a novel; his was an even stranger form of literature, what the Cannonians call *kritiki*, which took the form of flinging down his napkin at dessert with provocative statements such as, "Dialogue is the anguish of being," or "Peace is the terror of dialogue," or "Clothing is the cause of nudity," and Father would mildly counter, "Yes, even an X is only a Y," and then go for a long fast walk. Mother concurred, for why think if it serves only to make you unlovable? And indeed, ours was an era of failed intellectual suicide.

I believe my parents would have terminated him had they not feared that throwing him out to live on his wits would have brought even more grief to the community at large, so they made the brave decision to sequester him at Semper Vero rather than allow him join the ever-increasing band of failed artists who would hijack the century. Mother no longer spoke to him, but communicated only in writing, and Father listened well-manneredly but did not hear, calling him "that aphorism factory" behind his back.

But to be charitable, Catspaw's temperament would have caused anxiety even to those with lesser nerve. He was religious in routine, philosophic in temperament, historical in nostalgia, and avant-garde by default, though lacking belief, analytic ability, knowledge of the past, or real ruthlessness. He blamed his anxieties on the "metaphysical condition of art," and his moods on the paradoxes of "being itself." And he often spoke wistfully of the "externalization of internalization." In short, Catspaw operated solely in that elegant and apocalyptic space between the banal specific and all there is to be known. With superhuman effort, he had turned himself into one of those intellectuals from whom one often comes away from a conversation feeling actually deprived of knowledge. He was right as long as he was talking, but then the silence overwhelmed everything he had just said. All this was further complicated by the fact that his status in our household was unclear—not quite a servant, tutor, guest, jester, savant, relative, or even presence, but rather an up-to-date irritant—a walking, talking reality check, a case study against tolerance.

Nevertheless, Father took occasional pity on him, inviting him to our Zoopraxinoscope evenings, where Muybridge's still photographs of animal locomotion were beamed successively upon the wall, Father noting how differently the horse uses its legs in the amble, canter, and gallop, and pointing out with dripping sarcasm how aesthetes—from Altamira cavemen to Leonardo to Gericault—had all painted horses running with all four hooves off the ground, getting the true locomotive posture completely wrong. These evenings always ended with a silent movie of Mother prancing along the diving board as if she were walking the plank.

"All our movements, like our feelings, are stiff, you see," Father toasted the images. "We do not dash headlong through space. We do not move the way we feel we move," he nodded sharply to Catspaw, "any more than we write the way we feel we think."

And Mr. Catspaw could be seen later, with his long, prematurely gray hair and dirty cape, wandering the terrace in the moonlight, his upturned waxen profile lost in thought.

He would be my loyal life companion, batman, and object lesson. For while I felt closer to a cab-horse than an intellectual, no man could ask more from a tutor—one who will try on every up-to-date fashion, regurgitate in your stead the countless mass of new thoughts, so that a boy might cultivate his ideophobia, resist every metaphysical titillation, as well as every stupefying compulsory opinion. In Cannonia, to have a fool attending on you is a mark of great distinction.

The first thing one noticed about Seth Silvius Gubik was his ability to masturbate with either hand. (He could roll each eye independently as well.) This perfect ambidexterity was extended to drawing (he could simultaneously draw double helixes spiraling away from one another), athletics (he could skip stones with either hand across the widest parts of the Mze), and even the keyboard, where he could perform an anonymous canon of his own composition from two separate sheets of music, the left hand playing a tune beginning with the last note, and the right ending with its first note, *recte et retro, alla riversa* in the Hebrew manner. He could Germanize the weak and pleasant action of a French piano with a Brahmsian sonority, and with Viennese instruments of delicate touch and bouncing, rolling action he could maintain nuance while adding volume and restless French chromaticism. If no instrument was available, he would beat out a fugue on a log with his knuckles based on the letters of his name. He liked anything in C-minor, and he played with a seriousness which suggested that a new version of the piano would eventually have to be constructed for him. "There's no use in being envious," Father said, "it is given to some and not others." Mother sniffed, "Warm hands, cold heart."

Gubik's hands were neither slender nor large; indeed, his fingers were so thick he had trouble fitting them between the black keys. Yet he could not only reach a twelfth but play chords without arpeggiation. His fingers somehow moved independently of each other, so he could play a Bach fugue with three fingers of each hand, and with all ten invisibly bring out any individual note from a block chord. His perfectly split brain thought of his two hands as one, so the sound was of three. He played impassively with his fingers flat; occasionally his wrists dropped below the level of the keyboard. The motion of his hands was always *legible*, as if they were moving in sign language. He sat very low on the stool, and always concluded with a single unsmiling bow.

With such amazing reflexes, it was no wonder that Father preferred him to me, though he did his best not to show it. He was torn between sending him to a conservatory, which he feared would debase his natural talent, and preserving his remarkably intuitive nature at Semper Vero at the cost of condemning him to a life of near servitude.

Gubik was then almost my age but not exactly my friend, and one tolerated him as one tolerates a genius who is always potentially going to throw things out of balance. If one were interested in symmetry, one would have to say that he was everything Catspaw wasn't, for if Catspaw was always one step from self-destruction and oblivion, Gubik was always in the wings, ready to step forward as a total presence. Apart from his uncommon aesthetic abilities, it might be said that he absorbed and fed off every scrap of authority that Catspaw squandered, a perfect reverse mime. He was his own school, a true original, a boy willing to grab hold of history, make it conform, and kiss every hand he could not bite. He taught me that the hardest thing in painting is to draw a perfect circle, and the only way to do this is to draw two circles simultaneously with both hands, so that concentration and self-consciousness cancel one another out, allowing the form to perfect itself. This was of course the secret to his approach to the keyboard, and later, politics, where he discovered how to play the feminine masses. (As Commissar for Cults and Education, his lieutenants noticed that he could write a chatty personal letter with his right hand while drafting a government document with his left, or hold a telephone conversation while penciling in sardonic asides on some proposal.) Unfortunately, he became interested in the sort of repertoire which suits the performer more than the listener. With his sad, gentle face, he was precisely the sort of man a poor wretch would seek mercy from, and the very last man who would grant it.

Gubik was allegedly the illegitimate issue of a deaf and dumb Astingi maiden and a long gone soldier billeted in Silbürsmerze, incurring both the enmity of her tribe as well as the indifference of the local population. Mother had taken her in, given her rooms over the stable, an easy regimen in the house, and had even acted as her midwife—all the more remarkable since Gubik came into the world only a month after myself.

He was good with animals, all animals, and took to his role as a kind of elevated swineherd, carrying a crook sharpened at the edges like a scythe, diffidently picking up the prized long-haired Mongolian pigs from each village house at dawn, and escorting them to engorge themselves on the fallen fruits and nuts of the forest, supplemented with a mash of beetroot, bird's eggs, and trout. At dusk they would return in single military file, until each belled pig had turned in at its own gate. For pocket money he would join the gruff and dirty choruses of those who dragged boats upstream, though he did not take well to authority and had a highly developed sense of injustice. Mother once said that he would "not be happy until every king was strangled in the lap of every disembowled priest, every dwarf stretched out, and every beggar enriched." When he returned downriver, he would go to the empty church to practice on the echo organ, playing with his rope-burned hands behind his back his own renditions of "The Flight of the Bumblebee" or "Ah! Perfido" holding double-thirds or even full octaves in both hands. Opening the full Rückpositiv and Brustwerk pipes, he drew uncomfortable tremolos from a duplex of the vox angelica and vox humana.

We played hide-and-seek in the papyrus thickets of the marshes, shouting to each other, "A whistle or cry, or let the game die. Waterman, *Wodje Mze*, arise!" I crawled like a weasel through the reeds, and when I could smell him behind me, as strong as twice-fortified wine, I turned and threw a handful of mud into his face. But he was too quick for me. Blinded by his vertigo of elbows and knees, he tumbled me into the stumps and swamp water, pushing my head into the muck. It was all I could do to keep my nose above water, and behind me I could feel Charon's throbbing phallus. I screamed a mortal scream, managed to free an arm, reached up and tore out a gout of hair, and then, encrusted with the tomb-leaves of semen, ran back to the house.

Certainly, I found this irritating and rather beside the point, but the same scenario would be repeated many times. It was neither erotic nor innocent. It meant nothing in itself, but it presaged much. Though I saw him infrequently, he was always there—I remembered him three times a day, and still do.

One day Mother took me aside upon my flustered return. "I see you have been experimenting," she said cheerfully but with melancholy eyes. "Just remember that the wastebin is where experiments should end up, not *à la page*." And only our lack of ready cash prevented my seriously deranged playmate from being sent away to school. "One day," Father said with a shrug, "you will just have to collect yourself, take a step back, and knock him down."

I came into the world to replace a dead child, a true sister, pretty, petite, flirtatious, and extremely well-behaved, who lived only a single hour. I do not know if she had a given name. The lintel door of the chapel in which she was buried is inscribed only, "Waterlily of the Mze." I had strict orders never to play near it—its doors were always locked—so I was inevitably drawn to it like a magnet, and regularly stole away to gaze through the chapel keyhole. Inside, impressive stained-glass windows rose to a cupola hooding a small bell which was never rung. A wine-red banner hung across the sanctuary, on the steps of which was a cushion nestling a broken saber. Once I gained entry through a broken floorboard. In the altar, behind a spring-loaded door, I found a chalice, upon it engraved "The Cup of Sorrow." Inside the chalice, wrapped in a silk handkerchief, were two perfectly cut stones, one red, one blue. I felt a great solidarity with this vanished playmate, and I knew no one would ever build such a monument to me.

Her chapel (the last gothic church in the West) had been constructed from the ruins of a watchtower upon a promontory, its bowsprit terrace providing perfect views up and down the Mze. Owls nested in the gables by day and eagles by night, a silent changing of the guard accompanied only by Waterlily's incessant singing; like me, she sang well before she could speak, throughout the night. She had our mother's voice; her *forzas* were like a car hitting a wall, and eventually she mastered even the most difficult Astingi song-cycles, which, tighter than a sestina, go on in the same excruciating fashion—absence, devastation, return, retribution, wedding, absence, *et alia, alia*, among them *Rage Over a Lost Penny; I Am Not Scheherazade; If I Lay Down for You, It Is God's Wish; It Doesn't Become You When You Speak; He Who Doesn't Kiss Her Deserves to Have His Tongue Torn Out*; or that showstopper, the eighteenth-century magisterial masterpiece, *The New God*:

On a pilgrimage I heard
the good tidings from a
conversation between a dog and a cock

That the Almighty Father was dead
as well as his Good Lady, his son,
and the fearsome ghost

Put in his place is an elderly
Uncle with red whiskers who

164

has only been in jail once
He understands not a word of
Hebrew, Latin, or Greek and
only a smattering of English

He wears an old black silk top hat
and a red knitted waistcoat and
knows all there is about turnips and buttermilk

He has a rusty old gun but
no license, and a bad-tempered
sheepdog whom the angels call "Testy"

They say he will make a very good God,
And a much better one for our people
A great pity they had to endure the other for so long.

When I returned to her, on Easter or other holidays when the family was otherwise preoccupied, I would open the altarpiece and, taking the stones from the chalice, shake them in my hand like dice—and when I was feeling most like the last son of an inglorious age, she would sing sweetly in the chapel, "So what are you alive for?"

In those stolen moments in the chapel of my dead sister, it occurred to me what my problem was. I had an *âme féminine*, a feminine soul. My thick heroic blood had somehow become feminine, upper class, and barbaric, negating modern culture, which makes the feminine masculine, democratic, and artificial. Civilization clung to me like rags. So while playing the man, I have always felt like a princess, a dead princess about to awake and make mincemeat of certain people, and as such I have incurred the fear and hatred of men, particularly if they were important personages.

My feminine soul was thus always in search of my body, mourning the disappearance of the old kind of artistic male who has died out; a virgin body being serviced by a non-virgin heart. I was a good little boy but a bad little girl, a winning combination. To preserve the appearance of manliness I would eventually take refuge in alcoholic stupor, from which I emerged a drunken and diseased victor, while retaining the eternal priority which was the delight of my feminine soul. I was one of the dead with whom the living have to reckon, a *salon bandit*, a bathhouse nymph, who would put in jeopardy men's calm, their faith, and what's more, their cynicism; female preference always modifying male domination. Oh, I may have been a born imitation, but one so hungry that I could gobble up any ten originals for breakfast. And in Cannonia, where everyone is based on someone else, Waterlily remained my favorite playmate, even more than Waterman.

The Esteemed Traveler may have noticed that known artistes often resort to introducing just such little choruses of chromatic chums who are mostly empty canvas, whose sidereal appearance illuminates a larger theme, amplifies a point, or assists in pulling through a packthread of some secret motive. But truth be told, there are no minor characters in Cannonia; everyone gets their aria as well as their comeuppance. And in my experience, it is best to keep such folk on the same page, because if they begin to wander aimlessly, like electrons or deviations from a tonic chord, nothing good can come of it. There is nothing more dangerous than a person who wants to become a character in a novel. So when one of these little black keys is sounded, never put the other two out of mind. Their tempos are set well beyond our egos, and if they do not strictly belong to a given key, each character constructs its own society. Whether embracing, confronting, echoing, fracturing, or inverting one another, they are simultaneously *all* melody and *all* accompaniment, and as such are difficult to kick out of the composition.

And what's most interesting about such people is not the freshness of their entrances, but how, one by one, they disappear.

CHANGING THE SUBJECT
(Iulus)

From his tower suite, Father saw the rented trap careen up the drive and come to a skidding stop, leaving deep, muddy ruts in the oval lawn. Mother had picked up the hysterical pounding of the *troika* miles before and was already on the terrace to greet the stooped and trembling Professor, whom she perfunctorily embraced as she flung a helpless glance toward Father's window. As they passed in the servants' stairwell, she told Felix of the tragedy, adding, "Get his mind off it, but don't even let him near our dogs!" When Felix found the Professor wandering absently in the entry hall, he commiserated with his double loss, took the suitcase from his hand, and dragged him down the cellar stairs beneath the stables, where he poured him a glass of his rarest wine, a priceless triple-pressing siphoned from a small, cobwebbed barrel tucked under his arm.

"It's thirty years since I've tried this," he said as softly as he would to a bride, and the mellow liquid topaz dissolved every grain of stubbornness and despair. The vintage issued from a pebbly ridge which produced four barrels a year of Charbah Negra, the most fickle and misunderstood of the great reds, a tart, cloudy, whimsical wine, with a burnt foretaste of iodine, and after a swallow, a scent of rose.

"Well, other bonds were stronger," Father continued, after the despairing Professor had confessed his latest defeat. "Wolf is no great loss. He was not much, after all. Why can't we just say, He forgot you, so you forget him!"

They drank long draughts of the sweet, apricot-colored essence, and heard the horses tremble the rafters overhead.

"They grieve with you, my dear friend, they tramp from the injustice of it all."

My father's interest in horses had waned since his youth, as he came to appreciate basic transportation over the expense of crazed beauties, and following the principle that a piano must strive to imitate the singing voice and vice versa, he began to search for a breed of horse whose temperament most resembled the dog's. It was not long afterward that, while searching in a northern tier of counties where Grandfather Priam had hunted specimen shrubs, he located on the estate of a distant eccentric cousin of Count Zich descendants of the pure Pryzalawski tarpon horse, which in its migration with the Astingi had turned right at the Dukla Pass and kept its merriment and strength in the cold and desolate north, while the rest of the species herded blindly for the Arab Mediterranean to become romantic, slender-ankled hysterics, fit for nothing except the mafia and girls' scrapbooks. These northern animals could both haul and canter, take the family to church and plough, and between jobs negotiate the sharpest ridges at a brisk *tolta*, smooth as butter with a lonely rider lost in thought. They required no maintenance whatsoever, disdaining both the stable and the feed trough, and stood out in the fiercest blizzards in their shaggy golden coats, pawing through the snow for lichen. What they lacked in beauty—at times they appeared like enormous ponies, all neck, chest, and bulging joints, not well made at all—they more than made up for with stamina. I never saw one stumble, even when it was starving. Needing neither grooming nor shodding, they rolled in the pastures like great thunderclouds to burnish their coats, swam regularly in the strongest currents of the Mze, and trimmed their hooves by clog dancing along rocky escarpments. Only late in life did I realize that as the weather cooled and their coats grew shaggy, they appeared in the distance the exact color and texture of my mother's pudenda.

Their only fault was proneness to obesity in lush pastures, and loneliness when not quartered with those of their own kind and disposition. They were sociable to an amazing extent, leaning upon one another in concert and pulling burrs from each other's coarse manes with their teeth. They would carry a cringing child, a litter of kittens, or the most dyspeptic woman, and immediately know the difference. They refused, in a sense, to be kept, yet flight was unknown to them. Too good to be true, they would only run *toward you*. When the Chetvorah barked and lunged at them, they simply waited until the pack got too close, then sent them tumbling with their noses. The Astingi refused to sell even a one. They kept their older mounts long past service, in separate mountain pastures, where they often lived to the half-century mark. And when they died they were buried where they fell, in slightly convex mounds which mirrored the arch of their necks, memorialized with the sharp stones they had always avoided. Not surprisingly, in Cannonia (where it is rightly said that nothing can be done without a count) it was only through the intervention of Moritz Zich that we were able to acquire a brace and allowed to breed. I believe it was their blond presence in the fields about Semper Vero which prevented the Astingi from massacring us when the world turned over.

The drink had had no effect on the Professor's despondency, though a new map of veins appeared on his nose, and Father led him up the cellar stairs, saying only, "Let me show you something." There a stallion the color of clotted cream, with a black dorsal stripe, stood in the half-lit stall, a full wagon harness slung like a great indecipherable web upon him. The horse regarded my father calmly as always, for he was as sweet as he was strong. Father only had to reach out and touch the harness for Moccus to shiver with what was clearly delight.

"You see how much he loves it?" Felix said. "Fifty-three years old and still a stud! He loves to haul—the more the better. It's his freedom, you see. His calling, one might say." Then he placed the Professor's hand on Moccus's flank and the horse began to haul in the stall, as if exercising the concept of burden. His enormous weight creaked the timbers of the stable, and we all took up the shiver of delight.

"Feel it?" Father said. "He's giving it back to you. Just as with Wolf. Except with Wolf, it was all anger and affectation."

The Professor's mind was now on display. I could feel the intellectual machinery encountering the unprovable, converting it into an idea he could grasp.

"It's bred in him, I suppose," he said skeptically, "but I've never trusted horses."

Father stared at him. "Some were born to pull at the traces, of course. But the only question is this: what is the message you are sending *him*? Your touch is quite tentative, and yet he is encouraged!"

"*You* are saying that I am communicating my skepticism, but *I* say I cannot help it."

"Of course, my friend. We ought to encourage skepticism. But there is a huge difference between skepticism and distrust. Intellectuals hardly ever know the difference, in my experience."

"Yes, yes," the Professor murmured in a series of rapid shrugs, as if to deflect the argument like a whirring peach moth. "We always forget the ancient brain."

My father started as if he had been whipped, then broke into that long, low laugh of his.

"Surely," he sputtered, "surely you do not place full faith"—he was choking with mirth at this point—"with the poet of the Galapagos?"

The Professor blanched as if from a wound.

"It's the most convincing explanation we have."

"Balderdash. Only the latest propaganda which everyone parrots and no one reads. The paraphrase, Herr Doktor, enforced in school by drones. Ah, yes, I can recall it now: the mural of the ape as he gradually draws himself erect, losing a bit of hair at each stage of his receding slump, the illusion of progress. A schoolboy's fantasy, Doctor. So reassuring. Well, it's as crude as the cartoons of the Kaiser with blood on his hands. Is that what gets you promoted at university these days?"

The Professor did not reply, and Felix could see that he had unwittingly touched a sore spot. He could flush out an unreflective premise like a good dog tracks a wounded bird, and then, while deciding whether the poor, maimed thing deserves a point, look back over his shoulder apologetically.

"I mean, it's all well and good to say we got it from our ancestors," Father continued softly, "but then where did our ancestors get it? How did the crocodile acquire a vagina? Survival is easy enough to explain. But how do you explain the *arrival* of the fittest, eh? There is simply no reason at all why we should exist as a species!"

"Hold on there," the Professor stammered, as if to change the subject. "Does he not appear to be crying?"

And it was true: several large globules, shining like crystal, were making their way down Moccus's golden nose.

"Yes," Father sighed. "Their only fault. They weep constantly."

"But why on earth? They appear to be kept perfectly. What a life, I should say!"

"The golden age of the animals was just beginning when there were no carts to pull, my friend. The horse, like the nomad peoples, has suffered terribly at man's hands. What we have put them through! War was a positive relief. It's amazing they can stand still even for a moment. Evasion was the only weapon they had, and they were always put in the service of the most reactionary class. The dog, by comparison, got off easy, like the West. Which is why for the dog all Asia remains an enemy. The dog remains dumbfounded that the horse, with his history, can maintain his spirit. The horse evades, the dog denies. This is their armory. And the horse weeps, not for Achilles, but because of what we have done to *him*."

The Professor himself now seemed about to burst into tears.

"The horse is now only an icon," Father went on softly, "standing for the remains of what you call our 'ancient brain.' But the dog, you see, stands for what was forever lost. All creation and all behavior can be divided among them."

"Which is why we chose them to accompany us?" the Professor interrupted.

"Oh, surely you do not believe that canard about our civilizing these poor animals! That we used them to extend our senses, haul our baggage, and brilliantly inspire their trust and devotion? No, sir! They came to us quite willingly, out of the wind and rain, as nations go to any murderer if he is able to restore order for a moment. As for the doggie, did we meet as predators? Hardly, my friend. No, we are scavengers. We met across a rotting corpse which neither of us could kill. We are fellow swarmers, social animals, higher maggots, carcass chasers, keeping up with the migrating herds with the energetic inefficiency of our gait. It's the scraps our friendship lives off; leftovers, marrowbones, and braincases are what make us loyal. They followed us because our *merdes* ensured their survival. And now we walk behind them and retrieve their feces with our own hands. I have yet to meet a woman for whom I'd do that."

"Oh, Councilor," the Professor wheezed as he bent double, "I never thought I would laugh again," but Father continued utterly deadpan.

"The horsie, now that's a different story. He knew we and our golden garbage were their only chance for survival, and indeed, that we had perfected their strategies, for no one runs away any better than man. They came to us because as mammals, they recognized both our promiscuity and the horrible length of time it takes to raise the young. Drama, don't you see? Also, they liked the way we moved *en masse*. Entertainment! So they became our dependents, and like anyone who throws himself on your mercy, you will eventually let him down. Do you realize, Doktor, that by the *doghaus's* own figures, eighty-five per cent of dogs are resold or given back in their first year? And do you know how many times a horse will change hands in his lifetime, or at what age they are sent to the slaughterhouse for dog food? No, the horse tolerates man because he knows there will always be a greater fool among them who will initially lavish him with love; and the dog tolerates horses because he knows that eventually he will eat them, though not the other way around. They come to us because it is we who decides who eats whom. My Lord, don't you see? They were the only beings in the world we didn't hate or fear, the only thing we didn't immediately feel like killing. And while our vast sentimentality shortens our own lives, it prolongs theirs. Not exactly a Faustian bargain on their part, eh?"

"And which of them do we most resemble?" the Professor queried, now trying to get in the spirit of things.

"Ah, men are more like the horse than anything else. But they sing the lay of the dog."

"And what might that be?" the Professor sighed like a little boy.

"It goes like this: 'More life, please. Some mercy, too. Then more life.'"

"Your habit of explaining humans by animal neurosis makes me quite nervous, as you must know by now, Councilor."

"Think of it this way, Professor: take horses and dogs, take men and women. Origins, values, ends: all different. Think of men and women as horses and dogs who happen to fornicate with one another. Not entirely incompatible or improbable, and looking quite swell when racing together at full stride through a green field. But basically about as much alike as horses and dogs. Now, there I will desist."

The Professor gave him a sudden, inexplicable, and silent hug.

"Wolf is history, my friend," Felix said evenly. "Believe me, we can do better."

ANATOMY

(Iulus)

Their friendship had taken on the solidarity of those you grow up with, when there are no secrets. Tiring of alluding to the other by their professions, but unable to move to a first-name basis, they took the nicknames my mother gave them—Scipio and Berganza—from an early Spanish play about two dogs who are always fighting, taking each other by the throat and flinging the other about, but nevertheless inseparable. Wandering astray through the countryside, they occupied themselves chiefly in playing pranks on their unfortunate fellows, chained to a post or locked in their kennels, "always hunting, but unstained with gore."

They used these affectionate nicknames only when making the most serious of points, clinching an argument, or utterly destroying the other's most cherished beliefs, though it must be said that Father on his own territory got the better of these, a victory he would one day pay for. The Professor, to his credit, was never afraid of being helpless or at a loss for words in my father's presence; nor was my father fearful of challenging everything he said, even down to his reading of the weather. It was refreshing for Father to be in the presence of a personality which could not be easily intimidated. They could never let on to their families how much difficulty they were in, and were delighted to find in each other a use for the paternal melancholy they used to batter every convention. They never returned from their training sessions in the fields without boyish catches in the throat, indicating that you consider your best friend insane, but refuse on principle to call the fact to the world's attention. You could see it glistening on their faces, whether the dogs did well or not, the sense that underneath everything, *they* had behaved perfectly.

Whenever the Professor arrived, as soon as the requisite papers had been destroyed, he and Father would move off in the victoria with the best trotters and dogs. Occasionally I would stay with Mother; however, on most occasions, I was invited to accompany them on their "rambles," a word my father abhorred as it implied a chatty English excursion in a fine rain to an unremarkable prospect, a kind of contrived masochism which could only be palliated by a formal dinner beneath a tent with servants in the evening. The Professor would remove his hat, allowing the sun to color his face while he complained of long hours, the unbelievable stupidity of his patients, and the general ingratitude of the world. Everyone needs one friend with whom he can be totally sarcastic and bitter, and Father was aware that his was always in some kind of severe physical discomfort.

"I am not what I was," he would conclude, and Father would pop the reins, jerking back his confrere's large pale head in rather too obvious a therapy, for my father's belief was that no one saw anything clearly—that you were not even in this world—unless your heart's systole was over 160. Thus he would alternate jupes, jogs, harsh trots, and thundering canters until the Professor acknowledged that he could feel bubbles of energy rising from his pelvis to his ailing heart, better than any digitalis at making the brain pink again.

Here my memory falters, as it will when the subject is the falling out of fast friends, for friendship is a steady state in which all theories are held in abeyance, and the after-the-fact is never envisioned. For my father, the Professor was the childhood sidekick he never had, and in return he brought out both the adventurer and the keen observer in the Professor, so locked in the mire of family, city, and profession. Father brought him back into the world, and more than once when they were standing in the fields he quoted the great Goethe to him in the vernacular: "Quit squinting at the heavens, man. Stand firm and look around you!"

Father also understood his boon companion enough to know this was a man who would find what he was looking for, despite all odds and contradictions, and their friendship depended on him, their forays appearing wholly spontaneous. The Professor's fascination with my father was that he could not but admire a man who loved his culture, meager as it was, and pressed it to his breast, extracting from his environment every ounce of reinforcement, like a cellist who practices all day and receives so much feedback that he rarely feels the impulse to perform, and lives easily to one hundred.

Only one thing didn't quite reach Papa's rich and benevolent skepticism, and that was in noticing that our region, which had sprung up where a dozen tongues and civilizations had clashed, had been created out of the wind and would disappear into it. Our culture, if one could call it that, was not like a horse, which you could pick up positively with your will and put right down again at the front of the race. He spent his life amazed that the Enlightenment his family had brought to the frontier did not take root anywhere, that in Cannonia rights and obligations never moved together.

While he was fully prepared to be the last of his kind, and I suppose took pleasure from it, the rankling question of the breeder still remained. Without rigid controls nothing gets passed on, yet to break the deadlock of mediocrity required something of a revolution. These questions were uppermost in his banter with the Professor about religion, which was something of a soft spot, as you might expect.

"You're no Jew, Berganza," he often giggled, "just a Calvinist with a sense of irony." Add to that his derision of all things German in the clearest and the most precise *Hochdeutsch*, his love of tradition and contemptuous dismissal of it in the same breath, as well as his distinctly Protestant contribution to Jewish advice—that there is no such thing as a symbol, that depth is just as illusory as surface, that you can make more money selling advice than following it.

Of course, I took my cues from the dogs, for when danger threatens, dogs run away without apology. I had no theory, I didn't question motives, I made my shifting alliances as best I could. Consistent in my friendliness and friendlessness, I didn't differentiate. I went to those who were kindest to me, who fed me. I would form new bonds but I was always looking for a better master, so I tended to like everyone.

Eventually the day came when Father's savage debates with the Professor became subsumed not by discretion, friendship, or even exhaustion, but by having generated such wild analogies that they might as well have been speaking in tongues—though they showed no embarrassment at Mother's yawning or my own, or at the fact that people moved away from them in pubs.

On one subject they were agreed, that it is in one's own class that the traitor conceals himself. The lesser nobility's natural enemy is the nobility, the wealthy, the state from which they extract their privileges. The peasants' bane is their own kulaks; the bourgeoisie fears only its own petit bourgeoisie, the gentry, its own bailiff. It is one's truest self, in other words, the self you have just shed, or the one you aspire to, the soul slightly removed and granted a temporary advantage, who thunders down the pass dressed in party clothes and takes no prisoners. This is the sad story of men who do not make their antecedents clear. And one day while the two of them were riding on the American steam tractor, the Professor straddling the hood and facing Father at the wheel, they agreed that the only interesting philosophical question left was whether it was possible to pass on what one had acquired.

The Professor was obsessed with the fact that human self-consciousness was different from anything else that previously existed, and he admired the dog because his purposiveness was less complicated—he did not spend his days watching himself and doing nothing. Having learned to be actively passive, the dog did not waste time stressing the difference between himself and everything that had gone on before.

Father knew this to be the response of one raised without pets. Against the Professor's romanticism of the dog and its infelicities, Father had projected his own theory of the mind, based on observation.

"Did you know," Scipio, the Professor had said proudly one day, prying open Wolf's jaws, "that there are less bacteria in this lout's mouth than ours?"

Father did know, but he knew something else as well. He knew it most when the Professor discoursed upon the center of the brain, its hidden problems and purposes, a space in which everything important in the world was essentially left unexplained. He knew it from dogs who had been eviscerated, died on him, or been split open by a bear, and it was this: at the center of the brain lies not a knot of history or chemistry, but an empty cavern, and none the less mysterious for that. In this echoing sinus, laced with veins and covered by the dome of the hippocampus, there exists no idea or thought, only emotional energies which eventually find their way into thought to be filed under "Useless Suffering." The dog retains two arteries from the nose directly into this cavity, men do not, which is why our first reflex is to deny reality and complicate associations. The female of our species does not use her nose, or rather she uses it differently. Her nose is connected to her ear, while in men it is to the eye, a most savage degradation.

This was the basis of the friendship: the Professor couldn't understand how Scipio, far more darkly pessimistic than he, could act so cheerfully and not project panic. And my father admired in Berganza the fact that he had developed an intellectual method to make up for his lack of nose, his poor judge of character.

Both may have underestimated me. For the dog gets our admiration because he is sniffing every moment of the day and does not confuse devotion with romance, which is why he is always emergent. His senses are attuned to snuffing out evidence of betrayal, and he transforms his deep cynicism into requests for constant attention. The dog is the only true detective, just as he is the only survivor without guilt. Men never get over the fact that the mind seems superior to the experiences presented to it. This basic misconception arises not because their mind is superior but because their sense apparatus is fooled.

One day after an exhausting ramble they returned to Father's den for some serious libation, and while Father was pouring single-malt whiskeys, the Professor snuck up behind him and slipped the collar of Dresden rings about his neck.

"Easy, Scipio," he said. "I won't hurt you."

Father didn't move a muscle.

"You know there are few men whose society I can tolerate with equanimity, Berganza." Handing a whisky to the Professor, the collar closing only slightly, he proceeded to unlock a vitrine and take an artifact from the glass shelves. "The Oriental snaffle bit," he announced. "The swivel action allowed the barbarians to outmaneuver the Western centurions, and was the single most important accouterment in their success. Here, try it on." As he went round behind him, the leash went slack. He slipped the bit between Berganza's beard and mustache, holding the delicate reins of amaranthine leather above his head. As they wolfed down their Scotches Russian-style, the Professor's jaw jutted out, and a light appeared in the black eyes as he dropped to all fours.

"Does it hurt?" Father inquired.

The Professor shook his head defiantly.

"It's supposed to hurt a little. Observe then, this smallest pressure," and Father pulled the bit slightly to the right, pulling back the Professor's lips and exposing the slightly yellowed incisors.

"Very good, Berganza." Then he pulled on the left rein, and the Professor's mouth was drawn into a quite uncharacteristic but not unattractive grin. The

Professor wrapped the end of the chain's leash around his own neck, singing, "Let's go, heigh-ho, mount up, Scipio!" and the Professor obligingly sauntered around the room with Father astride, careful to keep his weight on the balls of his feet, as his yolk-fellow gave him slack. And so they played around with each other as they would permit no other mortal, not even a woman. The library rang with their shouts, and soon damp splotches appeared in the armpits of their suit coats.

"You were born to pull at the traces, Berganza," Father exclaimed.

"And you, dear Scipio, know just how hard to pull!"

But the Professor was soon winded, and they fell into a heap in the corner howling for joy like animals.

Father was fascinated by leaks. He spent his boyhood building dams of every conceivable material across every creek, rivulet, and runnel, observing how long and in what manner they eroded and unraveled. To him this seemed the basic principle on which nature and science had collaborated: the inevitability of life randomly breaking through its forms. He applied the principle to his breeding, respecting above all the genes which leaked—in error, wisdom, or divine plan was unimportant—while judging the desirability of the mutation, then determining how it might be fixed. The mind was not to be judged on the quality of the ideas it had, but on how it dealt with ideas broken down and dispersed—ideas which broke their own membrane, as it were. In short, where most men would have identified with the dam or the water, having faith in river gods or whoever watches over engineers, my father's concern was with the banks of the stream. The nature of the problem, as opposed to the essence, could then be put in an entirely different light. If, as was often said in those days, man encounters an abyss, it behooved him to know its depth and general topography, and it should make a difference whether this declivity was chasm or pond, brook or gorge, mudflat or rushing torrent. The river's origins in his high backyard, or the muddy and boring delta where it slithered into the sea, did not concern him. It was what to do with the damn thing as it crossed one's property. If one could not ignore the river's disruptive powers, one could at least manage change at an acceptable rate. In this as in most things, he was ahead of his time, as velocity was to become the primary subject of the century.

I mention this only to explain that Father's den was largely a collection of leaks and holes, the artifacts of obdurate and inexplicable pressures. He thought of books as dams—marvels of engineering which nevertheless eroded at different rates as they aged. He had a preference not for those which stood the test of time, which he considered simply a matter of luck, but for those which self-destructed before they were finished. For what defined a book was not whether you read or wrote it, but the honest notice that just at the very moment as you were adding the last of its blockages, they were eroding as fast as they were built. In his library the catalogue was predictable: a section of history which expended all its energy in mastering secondary sources so as to never render judgment; philosophy with the glaring contradictions in logic; science based on untestable hypotheses; a series of collected fiction lacking an odd volume, which brought its market value to nil; several roped-off sections of "unreadable masterpieces," novels written by cowards in heroic tone; poetry whose complete surrender to loftiness finally impoverished it. He specialized in collecting books that neither petered out nor went awry, being fundamentally misconceived from the start. There was also a collection of *incunabulae* whose value was the precise inverse of their contents, books which appreciated to the exact extent they could no longer be read, or had became too valuable to read. The only complete set in the library was Cardinal de Baussets's *Histoire de Fénelon*. His favorite book, he often said, was Volume Four, a tome whose pages had been carefully glued together, forming a solid rectangle which had then been hollowed out so that it could conceal a small dagger and some stamps.

The books were interspersed among jars with imperfect seals in which the fruits had turned as white as crustaceans in formaldehyde, as well as some bottles of wine improperly corked, with an inch of tar residue at the bottom, and some canned goods with wrinkled, misspelled labels imperfectly glued. Other curiosities included architectural drawings of unbuilt follies, failed sluicegates from the lower reaches of the Mze, imaginary tributaries of inaccurate mapmakers, collapsed waterworks, failed bridges, and a large collection of ebonite boxes exhibiting every valve which had failed on the property, every engine part which had given way, pieces of shrubs which had not made it through a severe winter, masonry from cracked foundations, snapped ropes, short-circuited wire, seeds which had not come true, cracked bricks, split joints, busted coils, and broken couplings—all clearly dated and labeled with speculations as to the nature of the stress and fatigue, as well as the consequences.

Of special interest to the Professor was a grid of empty cubbyholes, each with a small gilt frame. Here and there inside was a conventional trilobite, and to its left a cousin stoically bearing scars of some future organism, while to the right, coiled in shame, resided other relations, which had departed history through their imperfections. Unlike the vitrines holding the guns in the dining room, which were on display to show their contents' beauty, their appreciation in value, and the acumen of the collector, this was a collection of vulnerability, inexplicability, and terror. First was an empty hole signifying the initial colonization never explained, followed by all the smug forms of life incapable of getting where they had been found, the ones who couldn't swim but crossed the sea, the snails too big to be carried by birds and without the means to cling to driftwood. At the very center was a large hole with a small handkerchief for a curtain, making a kind of funerary to memorialize the gap between reptiles and birds, and containing a long, dry pectoral fin of a flying fish, which, frightened by an oar, had leapt ten feet into the air and dropped into Father's boat.

"It is a long way from fright to utility, Berganza," said Father. "And yet"—he beamed as he said this—"the exhibit shows, if not explains, life from the nonliving, does it not?"

The Professor complimented him on the professionalism.

"Yes, yes, you've set up the collapse just like Ptolemy, step by step."

The empty holes were there to be stared into, a diorama dramatizing what happens when you are forced to abandon every theory which explains succession. The entire study was an antidote to the bourgeois dining room, a chamber of imponderables dedicated to the awesome persistence of the unfit. It portrayed not a struggle for life carried on by the best-adapted individuals, but laws of which we are totally ignorant, forms endowed with a novel character either annihilated or reverted to a standard of mediocrity, and organisms which, in the face of all good things, nevertheless moved toward destruction. The display was devoted to the theory of natural selection in order to show how it shrugged off the problem of evil, and how an enfeebled constitution might be passed on. Of our species, the only motive and characteristic seemed to be persistent exaggeration, like orchids or butterflies, whose enhanced singularity is simply incomprehensible.

In one of the boxes were two jars of Hippodamia beetles, one all dead, the other swarming.

"I defy you, Berganza, to describe the difference between those who perished and those who yet crawl. Did those who survive exhibit purpose? If a blow of fate were good for a species, would we not then knock all our breeding animals in the head?"

The cornices of Father's den were black with the tubes of rolled-up charts. The greatest attention was given to a German one, "The Scale of Being," across which various preening species gamboled in ingenious movable cutouts with tacks, eyelets, and tiny golden cords sewn in their backs. Father and the Professor spent many pleasant Sundays arguing the order of the warm-blooded hierarchy, being careful to distinguish between the merely peculiar and those who were clearly victims of fate. The candidates moved up and down the chart, one day favoring the Professor's inexplicable choice, the duck, and another Father's, the underrated pig. ("Neither so nasty nor lazy as depicted.") Both animals had soon vaulted the poor horse, whose only act of intelligence, they posited, was to run away, a kind of continual emigration akin to fish and birds, but without their drama and regularity.

Of course, the dog and the ape vied for the topmost slots on "The Scale of Being," the two men agreeing in a spirit of comity that while the ape had a higher intellect, the emotions of the noble dog were more developed. Once this was ascertained, they turned to a chart of French manufacture, "The Tree of Life," a lovely bit of evolutionary metaphor with each species named in a venous leaf sprouting from its family branch. Scipio and Berganza began by drawing new branches connecting the main limbs, which wavered oddly, as if a child had drawn them in, for it was possible to rank emotional classifications as well as intellectual categories by drawing new leaves on the new branches. In these leaves, the ape was clearly the winner in self-esteem, self-control, cautiousness, and powers of imitation. Man was ahead in matters of hope, ideality, deceit, and sense of the marvelous. The dog excelled in adhesiveness, benevolence, conscientiousness, and veneration. While all three seemed equal in amativeness, homesickness, and love of approbation, only the dog shared with man the capacities of shame, remorse, indefinite morality, and, above all, the sense of the ludicrous. They added to this perhaps the most elevated sense of all, the dog's superior dread of the police. For a time, the dog's rich emotional life and preternatural sagacity vaulted him to the very topmost branches of "The Tree of Life," and there these qualities perched in the topmost branches like a clumsy, frightened cat, holding on for dear life as the remaining categories fluttered down like so many autumnal reflections.

In these rankings of nobility, thirteen Sundays were allotted to the horse, fourteen to the ox, seventeen to the sheep, eleven to the goat, five to the duck, seven to the pig, and thirty-nine to the dog, with occasional forays into the elephant and the whale, and one interminable session on marsupials. Anecdotal as well as scientific evidence was submitted: a bull who nuzzled a man who had saved him from lightning; cats who knocked telephones out of their owner's hands; a dog who bit a lesion out of his owner's leg which turned out to be cancerous; creatures that warned of epileptic fits, earthquakes, hurricanes, and air-raids, in which none of the five senses could have been involved. There were also spirited defenses of those at which the charge of stupidity had been leveled, digressions into the savage species which had been eliminated (unaware of the services man could render them), not to mention the pointlessly destructive fox, the disgusting guinea pig (so indifferent to his surroundings), the tendency of carnivores to butcher more than they could possibly eat, cats which appealed only to the lowest grade of portrait artists, and the tendency of the elephant to bear a grudge. It was clear that one could be elevated either by useful service or courageous threat to authority—only the dog was elevated by its power of spontaneous love—and in all these discussions, the highest position man achieved out of a ranking of fifty was in the low teens, just ahead of livestock, on the grounds that very little is required to talk, and even less to think.

"It was our beloved Spinoza," the Professor summed up, "who pointed out that while all animals are excusable, it does not follow that all men are blessed."

On occasion they even entered the true domain of philosophy, putting aside questions of category, of how thoughts might arise without recourse to thinking, of whether one could stop thinking without a thought, and if "The Tree of Life" forks at the top, whether its roots are thus a mirror of the crown. The Professor confessed he had never seen a tree's roots, and Father took him that very afternoon into the Marchlands, where trees were uprooted from the swampy soil with every storm—great elms on their sides, roots inscribing an arc as wide as the branches, some still growing along the ground. Father pointed out that of all trees, a fallen one is most useful, gathering more flora and fauna than the most majestic, isolated example. The fallen tree which still lives and thus multiplies other forms of life—not awesome-appearing, worthless to gather, and fallen out of the frame of beauty and providence, but functional to its final molecule and "worth even worship," was how Father left it.

They returned to the den, there to contemplate in silence a fact of which they were always partially aware but had not taken sufficiently into account, namely that "The Tree of Life" and "The Scale of Being" had apparently nothing to do with one another. They had embarked on that long journey of adding zeros to the numeral of themselves, for only the most courageous of men could admit that as their knowledge increased by infinite magnitudes, their basic ignorance had scarcely diminished.

But in Cannonia, where time flows back and forth, and observers are always linked to the observed, it was difficult to deny that distant feeling that everything is morphically interconnected and resonates.

I had the distinct apprehension that given just the slightest excuse—another glass of whiskey or another chart—these two men would have sauntered out the door and left their families in their great houses, renouncing their life insurance and wealthy clientele for the road, leashed and snaffled together as oft-erring vagabond folk, diligently scrutinizing men, loving women in haste, reveling in animal and gustatory marvels, and traversing the humming plains of Flanders, or the mellow gardens of France, or the desolate Spanish uplands, playing jokes on prime ministers, kings, and potentates, and finally traveling east to the most Byzantine of nations to give the reigning pasha a hot foot.

IN DARKEST CANNONIA
(Rufus)

On our return to Semper Vero, I was given a rough inventory of the many classical statues. Each time Iulus's parents had wanted to modernize the bathrooms, they had decided instead upon yet another piece of garden sculpture. We circled a huge zinc figure of a winged woman from the design of an unknown Parisian sculptor. Her wings were quite small for her body and she held her right breast with her left hand as the dogs urinated merrily on her feet. Further on sat a cast-iron statue of an Eastern knight in need of immediate repair, a huge knotted sash barely covering his feverish groin, his big-balled horse rearing precipitously upon a millstone so that he might be turned toward an enemy like a weathervane. Then a rather nervous bronze Buddha with extraordinary earlobes, ("Not a copy," it was pointed out), and finally a cluster of three negro boys, one in breechcloths with a snake in his hands, another in pharaonic headdress with a vessel on his shoulders, and a third in rather elegant and modern tennis shorts, holding a sphere in one hand and a handle of something which had been broken off in the other.

"All cast locally," Iulus said, pinging the fine legs of each athlete as we passed, humming a local ditty, "*Wo ist der Negerstatue mit einer Schlanger in der Hand?*" ("Where Is the Negro Statue with the Snake in its Hand?") I was very happy to be among this bric-a-brac, which appeared so happy to have me among them.

We passed a neoclassical rotunda without a name, apparently built simply to show off a rare whiterind fir tree, which had grown "naturally" into the shape of a lyre (only one of a number of dendrodological curiosities), and ultimately we strode across a series of low stone humpbacked bridges to the "Freemason's Pavilion," a roofless brick and stucco ruin with a blue slate cornice and windows in the shape of five and six pointed stars, surrounded by red beeches and Japanese maples. The stucco had been peeled away artfully from its exposed arches, framing broken Saracen columns and a severely but precisely damaged stairway to nowhere—"Just the sort of place," my guide commented with his usual abstracted air, "where one might wander from time to time after dinner in the library, and find an unknown guest who might amplify a line of Dante you did not quite understand." Then we meandered past a group of gnarled olive trees, enormously high, which still belonged to the same peasant family who had refused to sell to any of the former owners, and now towered above even the maples. Its fruit was still harvested by the same family, or rather picked up from the ground after the first winter winds, Iulus related proudly.

The final stop on our itinerary was his grandfather's discovery—the source of the Mze. Less was known then about the peoples and gods who occupied the banks of this river than those of the Nile itself. The Mze dove, resurfaced, and redoubled upon itself so many times that it was only recently that people connected its parts. We were climbing the crest of a hill, by no means the highest locally, with the only unlandscaped meadow within the park, when we came upon an empty shack of no discernable function. It sat there in disillusioned clarity, with no nature around or behind it. Iulus pointed out a listing piece of gutter which fed a rain barrel, at the bottom of which a rusted spigot dribbled onto the ground, apparently the origin of four hundred and eighty miles of serpentine river basin. He pointed again to the collection point of the Hermes well and thence to the ponds, one roaring like an engine, the other still as a mote, then to the broken dam and its dry cascade, and finally to a bright, harmonious, and sweet-flowing stream which wound in its infancy to a sluice in the village, where it began to rage from human mismanagement—and shortly thereafter, outflanking and checkmating its own tributaries, confused and inundatory, simply dissolved. We had sunk to our boottops in the sodden grass. The dogs drank happily but appeared bored. Iulus waved us back to the house.

We had gone only a few hundred yards down the gentle incline when we came upon a huge mound of earth only recently thrown up.

"An Astingi warrior," he explained, "no doubt of high rank. They bury them mounted on their horse, even if the horse is alive."

"What happened?" I said in my smallest voice.

"Just another bloody and inconclusive struggle," he shrugged, and then sighed gravely. "Any disclaimer for lost pasts is childish."

But for me, no amount of ignorance or atrocity could take the magic out of Semper Vero, that compact universe of pure play, the promise of a life of singular details and no general upkeep, a life of the *given*. I was watching myself have an emotion which had no name. It wasn't exactly love; I was happy in a different way. For the first time in my life I had a companion who I liked precisely because I knew I could never be like him. I was also losing the facility of my sincerity.

"You are looking at me with such interest," he said, "that I hope you won't become disappointed with me."

On the terrace we cleaned our muddy boots with bayonets. Through the French doors I could make out nothing but vases of the largest flowers and portraits of the boldest nudes I had ever seen. He let the dogs in and they thudded immediately into a groaning goosedown sofa. He apologized for knowing so little of the history of his own home. This was neither a matter of secrecy nor deception, he insisted; his parents simply did not know nor care about its *original* functions. Then he offered me a chair on the terrace, sat down on his haunches like a hound, and as he began to talk, a large black crow with brilliant black plumage suddenly alighted on his shoulder.

"Semper Vero has been in my family for only one hundred years and it has been for sale for most of that time. When my mother's adoptive father, Priam, inherited the property in the 1840s from a distant cousin, he ignored the architecture, eyes only for the fat warped open volume of the overgrown and undistinguished park. On trains, boats, and carts he brought in rare evergreens from all over the world to make an arboretum, the first devoted solely to that species in the Central Empires—as if what they needed in this vast mountain periphery, filled then with virgin forest, was *more* trees. This indigenous forest he indeed sold off, wood lot by wood lot, to buy rarer and rarer evergreen seedlings and specimen plantings from other destitute estates. In the buildings, including his own home, he took not the slightest interest. Architecture's only reason for existence, in his mind, was to give some inanimate organizing texture to the landscaping. But there was not a vegetable shoot in Cannonia whose story he could not tell. I used to follow him on his walks, and when I couldn't name a shrub, he encouraged me to make one up, and then had a copper nametag made for my little fiction. Perhaps it was a kind of holding action," he murmured solemnly, "this passion for the evergreen, or perhaps a reaction to the desultory and wanton mining, his hatred for the veins of antimony, quartz, and garnets which had seduced even the Neanderthals. Not to mention his absolute loathing for cattle, which he would shoot without a qualm if they even so much as looked across the fence at a rare shrub." The crow left his shoulder as peremptorily as it had arrived, but he gave no notice.

"But then one day, at fifty years of age, when the trees had reached a nice maturity, when the vistas had filled in nicely and all the children grown, Grandfather Priam got up suddenly from supper one evening, took his cape and cane, walked out on the terrace and down the drive . . . and never returned. No one ever discovered what became of him—though there was a rumor of a pilgrimage to a church in the East. At the fullest measure of his life, he simply . . . disappeared . . . as if the genius of his place could only be preserved by his exile."

He said this with a tone of surprise as if he had just heard it for the first time, and turning slightly pale, left the subject by motioning to me to follow him down the winding drive where his grandfather had abandoned his little empire.

The drive had been modestly constructed in such a way as to suggest there was nothing more than a vineyard shack or an abandoned quarry at its end, but I noted its every turning might be defended by a handful of lightly armed men. At each bend, mountain torrents dove beneath severe humpbacked stone bridges, wide enough only for a single cart. These, he mentioned, had been constructed in the thirteenth century for the visit of the Blind King, Agram, who had desired to construct a castle and taxing facility upon the heights. The King with his beautiful dead gaze had been led along the road by the local nobles, winding round and round the short volcano by the longest possible route, until at last the Blind King pronounced the vantage too high and abandoned his project, to general relief.

As the road suddenly became nothing more than a cart track, one could make out in the failing light the town of Silbürsmerze, taking its name from the glistening carmine and tarnished silver heath which surrounded it. It hung suspended like a faint etching between blowzy curtains of protective mists, the sort of scene you wanted to rub up against to see if the color would come off. We forded the shallows of the Vah across a great sheath of granite, and as we approached, the town enfolded upon itself, like the mighty tribulations of a rose in a second, slightly desperate bloom. Unfamiliar as it was, I could not help but marvel at the peace it yielded, a town that was still connected with our dreams, the dreams we know are dreams while we are dreaming them and thus effect no fear. For we all walk the ramparts and narrow streets of a town very much like Silbürsmerze, coils of royal blue smoke from peat and fodder fires hovering on her outskirts, where heartbreak remains an aura but is not yet adumbrated, a place where melancholy still gives us character but has yet to become garrulous. Ah, Silbürsmerze: always veering towards sentimentality, but never quite making it.

At the very center of town we entered an amazingly severe, asymmetrical seventeenth-century square, completely arcaded, continuously vaulted, all friezes, alcoves, and spandrels; curdled tympanas, curved archivolts, and gables with crockets; constructed of molded colored bricks so that not a single square inch was the same color. At the north corner stood a church with a covered double-stair and two towers, one of five rectangles and three domes, the other a Saxon clock tower with an Astingi inscription which Iulus translated as "Each hour dooms Man, the last one kills him." Squatting down in that off-center square, one had the distinct impression of a sealed, impermeable environ, a kind of conservative utopia, but a short walk to any of its corners revealed a narrow street, lane, or worn stair; Silbürsmerze was *all* exits. And there was nothing at its center, no statue, bell, or well, nothing but an irregular patch of diseased lawn with a low deteriorating stone wall about it.

"Be still," Iulus whispered, "there are a thousand eyes upon us," and it dawned on me that my interlocutor was the only human figure I had seen since my arrival. The only sound in the square was the strange hesitant *clop clop* of manual typewriters, hunting and pecking like a hobbled horse echoing across cobbled courtyards. Despite the absence of people, it seemed a place where no one ever died.

We sat there on the low stone wall for nearly an hour, buffeted by gusts of wind like the exhalations of an excited woman. My sense of mission was growing ever fainter. More than once I turned to my host with some wide-eyed authentic question, but then thought the better of it. The silent depths of that hour in the square, and something in his patient manner, canceled out the earnest gradegrubbing student in me forever.

Suddenly Iulus clapped his hands to his knees, as if he just remembered something, and ushered me into a half-timbered building with clerestory windows. Loping through an arcaded inner courtyard with a barbarian penile millstone displayed at its center, he went directly to a vaulted basement lit with window wells, an enormous room with Spanish studded leather walls and a black and red marble Moorish fireplace, which in palmier days had served as the town mint. The walls were hung with hundreds of hunting trophies, upon each of which was draped freshly killed game—live meat air-dried upon embalmed meat. From every cornice antlered heads stared with glassy eyes, snipey noses, and erect ears, the tissues of their half-open mouths painted a flamingo pink, maws coated with resin. From these obdurate horns and glistening snouts, from the long faces of forest animals, dangled the marbled membranous cuts of their fellow species— ribs, shoulders, and tenderloins; chops, briskets, and roasts; sausages, organ systems, and scaloppini; intricately carved carcasses, filleted silhouettes of musculature, the missing domesticated relatives' bodies beautifully butchered and appended to the head of their species' wild prototype. Haunch of stag venison, loins of flushed forest pig, crown roast of fetal lamb, livers dangling in a small silken net from the tail feathers of a cock pheasant in flight; rigid purple skinned hindquarters of rabbit straddling the figure of a stuffed dancing hare. It was as if the ark itself had foundered and sunk, turned upside down in the shallows, disgorging its drowned and butchered cargo of carcasses into eddies of diffused light. And we floated through this haphazard catalogue of delicacies like calm and purposeful sharks. The folk of Silbürsmerze had been through quite a bit, but it was evident that they would never starve.

At the very center of this hygienic and anatomically correct abattoir was a blue and white enameled metallic box, the size of a small treasure chest, glowing with a strange out-of-place sanctity, and surrounded by a few landmines with the earth still fresh upon them. Stenciled on the top was the logo "LIBERTY PURE LARD (Roberts & Oake, Chicago, USA)." It had been dropped from an American airplane, killing a shepherd, and they had not been able to identify a single item in it. Inside, along with condensed milk, concentrated orange juice, Cheerios, Mars bars, baked beans, Spam, and soya curds, were several five-pound packages of margarine in plastic globes, a bullet-sized nodule of coloring embedded at each center.

As I was about to explain the meaning of this gift, Iulus wrestled a hindquarter down from the nose of a particularly proud elk, cut a large chunk from the gelatinous pink mass, and pinning the meat to the table with a knife nearly as large as a sabre, detached the heart of the loin. Then he took a smaller knife from his boot and began to mince the loin with a flurry of strokes. Soon there was a pile of maroon shavings, and he wrapped these in old yellowed newspapers which announced the Russian victory at Kursk, an international congress on physiology in Leningrad held in spite of the siege, and the lead piece, a dog show in Silbürsmerze, noting that the number of entrants was the lowest since the flu epidemic of 1919.

We put the meat and select items from Chicago in a rucksack, clicked our heels together, put our voices well back in the larynx, shot up our forearms, and with a merciless ironic giggle (which I then believed to be an entirely new form of humor) goose-stepped out of the Meat Museum and reentered the square, which now seemed darker and more claustrophobic than the cellar. Crossing to an elliptical corner, a dark lane at once opened up, and as we left the square it transformed itself back into a trapezoid.

The houses leaned in upon us, insisting, as with everything else in the country, upon their own manner of collapsing. I was losing both my concentration and curiosity, crushed by the thought of the numberless exhibits I had not yet seen. But my guide had an exquisite sense of these matters, and a clap on the shoulder indicated that our general orientation was about to be concluded. We had indeed come upon a rather astonishing detached house in a relatively new suburban quarter. As was common with Cannonian bourgeois townhomes of the inter-war period, the small front yard was adorned with busts of the resident family—Mother, Father, and two daughters in this case. The sculptor had given each of them the same expression of tranquil pride with a trace of sarcasm.

The house was of three stories—gray limestone, green majolica tile, and terracotta successively—topped off with a copper mansard roof in which were set two rows of false arches. All this was surmounted by a domed cupola with an open window, from which at this very moment, chin out, tail elevated, and legs tucked expertly beneath him, a red dog leapt into space. A geyser of water erupted from the courtyard as the animal plunged some sixty feet into a raised pool. As we drew nearer, I was aware only of the circular pool, exploding every few moments with another spume, flashes of red fur hurtling across a plum sky, a curved double staircase leading up to flung-open French doors fluttering with torn lace drapes. The first dog who leapt had by now paddled up to the fluted edge of the pool, his bushy muzzle plastered slick as an otter's, the nails of his forepaws glistening as he hauled himself from the water. He shook himself into a convulsion which began in his jaws and ended with a crack of his tail as an aureole of mist rainbowed about him. As he sat shaking, I was aware of another shape cannonading into the pool behind him, another dashing across the drive spewing gravel in all directions, another taking the staircase in three powerful bounds, the front and rear paws crossing one another at the peak of the gallop, another disappearing through the French doors, another ascending the interior spiral staircase without breaking stride, and yet another bursting from the cupola without a moment's hesitation, launched into the darkening air in the noblest of freefall frozen poses, until he too galooped into a geyser of white foam.

I was witnessing the circular blur of a pack, a volley of arrows. Wetted down in elongated suspended flight, each dog preceded and followed his psychopomp in a never-ending chain of pure play. It was as if we were at the World's Fair booth of some unknown mad little country, where you were not sure if you were watching a film, puppets, wound-up dolls, or perfectly trained animals, or whether this was a ritual entertainment, some veiled protest at an ancient insult, an induced lunacy, or a scientific experiment in which the exact protocol had been forgotten. It was the sort of arresting image one was to encounter often in the conundrum of Cannonia, but when I asked my guide what on earth was going on, he replied wittily but without irony, with one half-closed eye, "Many dogs taking a bath downtown?"

That's what I came to love about Cannonia; it may be too much but it never gets too long.

On the bootscraper back at Semper Vero, dried pomegranate colored mud fell away from our feet like broken waxen molds. Then, as the color ebbed from the sky, we experienced the "wolf-light." The rocks flared ochre, apricot, and magnesium blue, as a great solemnity pervaded everything. We dined by candlelight on elk carpaccio, blood sausage, hot banana pepper, and coffee dropped in from America. Then Iulus produced a bottle of 1806 Napoleonic cognac. "The Ton-Tin," he murmured softly, "the bottle which survivors of the regiment drink to those who have fallen. I suppose we are they." We toasted the past, present, and future, we toasted our parents, our children to be, our friends, each other. We toasted Great Britain, we toasted Russia, we toasted any country we could think of. We drank in memory of countless invasions, oppressions, diasporas, droughts, earthquakes, and sufferings, and we drank to America, the only country, as Iulus reminded me, whose national anthem begins with a question.

Then I produced the packet of LIBERTY margarine I had carried with me from the Meat Museum, with its bullet of carrot coloring at the center. Iulus stared at the deathwhite glob with undisguised disdain. I broke the nodule and the fluorescent amber dye spread throughout the plastic globe, its ugly streaks very much like the rays of a burst sun which figured so often in the crests of the Central Empires. It became striped as the dawn in Cannonia, though harsher and stranger. I kneaded this little distended synthetic world, pushing here, pulling there, until it gradually reassumed its ovoidal shape, colorized into a new alloy, piss yellow and old gold. I haven't the faintest idea why I did this.

A frieze around our empty dining room announced all the secret societies of the masculine and feminine temperaments, which did not clash as much as they fitfully and fantastically informed upon one another. Against a molding of the purest white and gold, blue Wedgewood medallions of young ladies in classical white dresses shot bows and arrows, played blind man's bluff, or cavorted with boars and dolphins. The chairs were lyre-backed Chippendale, the tea service bronze, the oval table black pearwood. And interspersed among these refined objects were mahogany and walnut cabinets stuffed with rifles, maps, documents, busts of emperors, heavy decanters, half-open annotated books, tobacco jars from every country, stoneware, earthenware, and striped agateware. The walls held a great number of recumbent odalisques, all smoking, each more seductive than the last, painted in a rather crude but very up-to-date art nouveau style, though pride of place was given a tall portrait of a great beauty in a soldier's uniform with an eye patch (his sainted mother, it turned out), whose cyclopean golden gaze presided over all. There was also an enormous sooty rectangle over the piano testifying to a huge but recently removed canvas, no doubt a spoil of war, as well as a portrait of Grandfather Priam, who needed no introduction, given his half-closed eye and distant gaze to the East.

After supper, we cut a long Virginia cigar in half, and smoking it in relays, walked in the secret passage to the subterranean great hall lined with the portraits of former owners of Semper Vero, most of whom had never been near the place in their lives. They were painted in the early Cannonian iconic style, no texture to their furs, medals brighter than their eyes, a two-dimensional condition that I had no problem identifying with in the torchlight. I cannot to this day bear to spend more than fifteen minutes in a museum, but as I walked the great hall with Iulus, those floating transparent half-length images in reddish ochers, gold leaf, and velvety blues, their unselfabsorbed gaze radiating out and down from the axis of their bodies, formed a bond with each other and with me. They were not likenesses but presences. Theirs was not an attitude you could call beautiful, but one which promised somehow to restore fortune and confound enemies. No artist of the Renaissance could approach the ability to understand the virility, madness, and fire-breathing spirit in those tragic golden faces painted upon such programmatic human forms. Most had no frames, though some were equipped with winged doors so they might be closed. It was as if we were surrounded by a curious but friendly mob, full of contradictory emotions, their pride certain at the moment they had been transfixed, but also a supersensuous sadness for the future. In their imperceptibly glazed transitions, the reference for near and far was gone. In their temperas of egg yolk, rye beer, and ground alabaster, it was almost impossible to tell what was physical and what was reflection. Indeed, the panels must have been warped, like the curvature of the earth, or of the eyeball itself; and in the erratic light the brush strokes seemed composed not with temperas but blood and water, the dead matter of paint forgotten. It was as though the owners had all been painted at their last breath, and painted by the same person over five hundred years, so they were at once living and lifeless, imitating life from art. I felt their eyes saw me, and that their hearts understood me, those intercessors bathed in unconditional light.

My life was changed in that moment. I wanted to be counted among the absentee owners of Semper Vero, even if only as temporary custodian. The rays from those golden faces upon my nose seemed more important than any idea I would ever have. I wanted only to see the world through their eyes. "Poor Giotto's nothing compared to them," Iulus shrugged as the torch burnt out and my happy indoctrination ended.

I relieved myself in the single guest bath, a long high room with the watercloset set a good nineteen feet above the commode, featuring a quite large painting of a hoopskirted gentlewoman, black curls tumbling from her bonnet, who supported an impeccably dressed but slightly wounded soldier, his head resting on her shoulder, while she gently masturbated him. By comparison, this early Catspaw made the small Roualt over the washbasin seem somewhat academic. Not for nothing was this known as the finest lavatory in Cannonia.

I found Iulus on the terrace, his hands folded behind him, gazing out over the embankment of the Mze. The coots had set up an unceasing shriek in the reed-beds, the primeval agony of a love-factory in late spring. I attempted to return our conversation to matters of the mission, and so inquired after the whereabouts of the *Sicherheitshauptamt*, that madman of a puppet premier who had inflicted so much needless suffering upon his poor nation. "One can hide forever in Cannonia," Iulus murmured, "he might well be just down the road, asleep in phlox and snapdragons, or perhaps in the subterranean regions, where even the Russians will not find him. Or perhaps the Americans have offered him a professorship?"

For the first time I saw a lethargic cynicism creep into his eyes as he took a seat.

"You must be tired. I know I am," he said. Then he sighed. "Is it permissible, to lose interest . . . even in evil?" he asked gently. And when I mumbled incoherently, "It must be possible to do something, you just can't let all this go to the hell . . ." he reached across the wrought-iron table to put a cool hand over mine. "You can see that we are more pious, brave, and clever than the rest," he said. "But you don't seriously think we can be saved, do you?"

At midnight, we went for a swim in the Crab Pond and bade farewell to our adolescence. We bedded down on the sofas with the dogs wound tight about us, and broke the ancient rule of war, both going to sleep at once without a sentry.

Before first light I was awakened by hoofbeats. I peered out between the dusty damask curtains and could make out an Astingi patrol in jerkins of lilac, mulberry, and sulfur, bows and machine guns slung across their shoulders, winding single file down the fenlands from the source of the Mze.

Their complicated demeanor was very like the frescoes of the former owners, at once both tranquil and agitated. Like their country, their aroma preceded them, a combination of dead lilies, saddle leather, jasmine, and mocha. They galloped once around the fresh grave mound in silent lamentation, and then wound their way down the drive, all pale hair and plumed shakos, lances and lopsided triple crosses. Their gray and white carts were tilted in their shafts from their burdens. Young girls in loose trousers, suckling buttoneyed infants, walked beside the black kneeboots of their mounted husbands, abetted by red rough-coated dogs and black unbelled oxen. Behind the last cart, on a silver chain, an eagle walked desultorily as a chicken. They moved in sluicelike silence, taking a shortcut around the town, and raising only a wisp of dust into the sunrise.

Dawn came early and pallid as a lemon-rind as the sun rose out of Russia. It was time to get down to business. I reminded Iulus of the crown. He threw up his arms as if in a mock surrender, and led me, chuckling, across the *cour d'honneur* to a small Tudor cottage connected by a broken arbor to an unkempt cutting garden. He turned on the gas lamp, and we picked our way across a floor littered with smashed flowerpots and broken-handled rakes and spades. The cottage's shelves were filled with old letter files, metal cigar boxes, small carriage trunks, matched plaid luggage, Gladstone valises, and a great profusion of loose, half-destroyed papers. "Observations of a literary nature," he reassured me, "and without intelligence value." In a corner, amongst a huge nest of shredded correspondence, framed in a whelping box constructed of a dozen inlaid woods, a litter of just-weaned red pups yipped and scurried.

The crown was hung on a peg near a small rear window, its dull golden gleam and rough unfaceted dark gems testifying to an ancient, unrefined smelting process. It was topped with a bent lopsided triple cross, an exciting pagan touch. He handed it to me casually, pointing out the fragment of the Pope's gemstone, Gemma Augustea, and the Byzantine silvery filigrance of the first czar, Monomach. And then he related the Astingi curse attached to that bizarre object, which translates imperfectly as, "Wear the crown and lose your culture."

I also inquired, as instructed, as to the whereabouts of the Lost King.

"The King is hidden," he snapped, "and shall remain so."

Through the scent of milky feces, crusty gruel, and moldy paper, there was also the stench of fetid flesh wafting down from the sedge-green forest above us. He shot me a glance, and I knew it was useless to inquire further about our men behind the lines.

Sensing my discomfort, Iulus flipped the crown back on its peg like a horseshoe, leading me next door to the ruined cloister, which served as a barn, and where a cart filled with fresh straw, its tongues open, blocked the drive. He methodically harnessed the single horse left in the stable, a horse as calm and affectionate as a dog. It was not so much a horse as an enormous blocky blond pony, with Iron Age bones and a black dorsal stripe running down his back from forelock to tail. He was at least sixteen hands high, with a neck so strong it spoiled his shape, his hooves the size of dinner plates. Beneath the cart lay the parents of the litter, one dead, the other terribly aged. The mother had passed away that morning, her purple breasts exploding with mastitis, swollen white tongue clenched between her teeth. Next to her lay the sire, haunches twisted with arthritis, goatee and forepaws graying, his golden eyes clouded with cataracts.

Iulus moved deliberately but without distraction through the sad scene. He located some peasant Feastday costumery, though they were hardly actual peasant clothes, for they were beautifully made, never-worn attic costumes out of a comic opera, with velveteen capes, horn buttons, crocheted sleeves, and patent leather boots draped loose about the ankle, their only camouflage being the absurd distance they put us from the present grisly proceedings. They were, in fact, costumes from the pageant collection of the royal family, who during summer vacations near Semper Vero liked to dress as peasants and live "the simple life." It was the only uniform Iulus could think of that would not compromise us with some faction in Cannonia, where seven different wars now raged. And I realized for the first time that he meant to accompany me out.

Iulus packed up the crown in a rucksack using great piles of manuscript for wadding. Then he deliberately filled a plaid valise with files, a Gladstone with correspondence, and a velvet ladies' hat box with the plates of the Cannonian currency and the kennel studbook. He took particular care with a hand-tooled leather box with a raised monogram, Z. Then he picked up each of the nine pups under their front legs, and bussing them on the nose, buried them in the cart of straw. We mounted up on the narrow wooden seat, where I was happy to ride shotgun, and when he lay a gentle bootheel on the animal's rump, the pony immediately broke into an electrifying *tolta*—faster than a walk, gentler than a trot.

As the cart creaked away, leaving the old sire exposed, like the great Old One, mauled by the young, who bleeding away sires a thousand sons. Picking up his ears and raising his still massive chest, he passed a curdling glance in our direction. His haunches quivered as if to follow us, but he soon thought better of it, and as the cart spewed gravel in its wake, turned his head away as if content with our receding echo. We set off into a pewter Cannonian mid-morning, green turds spinning out of the blond horse, and I felt the double melancholy of not only leaving a place to which I might never return, but of leaving a place that I was not sure existed. I turned for a final glance of Semper Vero. Across a bold curve of the Mze, a filmy veil of fog was rolling down the mountain spurs, and from the central turret of the manor, a single cloud pennon streamed. Then the translucent clouds deepened and darkened, and swiftly, almost instantaneously, at high noon, the light failed. In the dying afterglow, the country stretched into the nothingness beyond. Oh, how this soldier-boy wanted something different to belong to!

We rode in abrupt and arbitrary transition, just as in popular books, forded the shallow Its easily, and were gradually joined on either flank by solemn corteges of Astingi, winding across the blackened fields of no-man's-land, to take shelter with us on the far side of the river. Their movement had none of the hallmarks of an advance or retreat. No weapons, insignias, or standards were on display. Legless veterans were carried on the shoulders of others. The men in their raspberry overcoats or menacing black felt cloaks, whips looped about their waists, rode in a mute assembly about the wagons of women and children, their great wheeled kettles and mobile hookahs in a fluid organization which required not a single verbal order. It was less an army than a biological force, simply crossing yet another river, another journey from nowhere to nowhere; for they had already forded the Mze twice upstream, in order to ford it again. The Astingi were laconic and expressionless, without so much as a backwards glance at their homelands. In their easy ancient resignation, they seemed neither warriors nor victims. Their very posture, their impressive silence, seemed only to indicate that entering history at its "cutting edge" was for them the most boring place to be.

Late in the day, beneath a flotilla of barrage balloons, we could make out the desultory massing of American supplies in the oxbow of the river. Brown Studebaker trucks scurried like she-bears as far as the eye could see. A PX was already going up, and next to the stockade with its California-style barracks for displaced persons, I could make out the outlines of a swimming pool and athletic fields. The Cannonian dusk would soon be filled with flyballs, as America mounted her exhilarating project to prove history wrong.

From the meadow bank, the Astingi peered from their ponies across the tawny river. On the far side, a group of sullen, drunken GIs stripped to the waist were skipping stones (a fact which seemed to startle even my impassive guide), and when a lanky left-hander skipped a pebble some twenty times across the whiskey-colored water, the Astingi vanguard scattered as if they had seen a ghost. Iulus stopped the cart and dismounted, studying the far bank in his binoculars. Then he turned his back and gestured to the lead horseman returning from the river, who seemed to recognize him despite the costumery. He galloped up and they had a brief discussion, speaking a language unlike any I had heard, lyrical but agglutinative, as if every word were a verb, a dactylic canter where each initial syllable set off a platoon of vowels which rushed away like birds after a gunshot, a basso continuo turning every A to O, every O to U, and every U to zero.

The Astingi leader regrouped his advance guard and followed Iulus down to the muddy embankment. My guide stared at the water for some time; then with a brisk but casual motion, he suddenly bent down and caught a trout in his bare hands. When he held it up, the huge half-naked adolescents on the far bank stopped laughing, just as the Astingi troop began. And then as Iulus turned round, putting the fish in a fold of his loose boot, the Astingi began to ford the river with renewed confidence, their faith in superior reflexes restored. They refused to use the bridge, their ponies negotiating the eddies so effortlessly one could not tell if they were actually walking or swimming.

We ourselves crossed the pontoon bridge lodged with the bloated carcasses of many horses and farm animals. I showed the bored MPs my papers, and they waved us into the camp, which we entered as if from another century, another planet, as if from some B-grade movie—two Kulaks in their Sunday best, a horsedrawn hayrick with its smuggled riches—the oldest trick in the book—and one, as it turned out, that was being replicated a thousand times a day along the stopline, each American policeman more credulous or indifferent than the last, as murderers, spies, and thugs by the score took shelter amongst the people who called Heaven their home. We were billeted at the rear of the camp which now stretched across two double oxbows of the Mze. The back office had finally caught up with our advance and was busily collecting information while denying rumors of a last great push to destroy the Soviets in their tracks, which naturally had elicited no great enthusiasm in the ranks. There was no longer any mention of Terra XX.

A crowd of soldiers had already gathered about our cart, more curious about the single mechanical conveyance to survive their artillery barrage intact than our fey costumery, cautiously patting the prehistoric horse who gently nipped back, and cooing like a bunch of schoolgirls over the litter, which had now poked their heads from the straw, ears erect and rumps awhirr. Iulus decided then and there to break up the litter, for they were in that twelfth week of canine life in which the bonding to humans is best transferred.

There was no shortage of volunteers or tears. The new owners allowed their dogtags and serial numbers to be pressed into candlewax seals, and eagerly if laboriously wrote out their home addresses on the enormous violet pages of the leatherbound pedigree book. Then after looking them up and down, as if to match the *aristochiens* to the acned adolescents who whooped about him, Iulus insisted that they form in ranks while he presented the pups, while reading out their German call names: "Stekel! Federn! Kahane! Silberer! Honegger! Kremzir! Tausker! Schreber! Schrotter!" until he was sure that the new owners could at least half-pronounce them.

"To the victors go the spoils, as they say," he concluded in suddenly perfect uninflected English, "but don't forget, gentlemen, I will be watching you . . . forever." The new owners were giggling, but they seemed to recognize his authority even though his outlandish garb was by this time literally falling to pieces. Then he dismissed them with cheerful wave of a hand, and our boys ran off inattentively, the pups frolicking at their heels, and I knew from that day on that my allegiances would grow ever more complicated. And frankly, I was just a bit ashamed of my disguise.

We stashed our gear and retired to our double decker bunks for some well-deserved shut-eye, snoring like grandfathers. I noticed he put the Z-box under his pillow. It was never out of his sight.

In the morning, I took the rucksack down to the company store, where they dutifully inventoried the crown and sent it off with a planeload of other Eurotrash to Fort Knox. They even gave me a receipt: "One Cannonian headpiece—gold alloy, jewels, etc. Condition: fair."

And then we met with a pert stenographer and a Harvard social scientist with a great deal of hair in his nose and ears for such a young lieutenant.

"Are you Cannonian, or what?" he barked without looking up.

"Ah, I have recently been deprived of that famous charm, *meine durchschnittlaucht*" ("your averageness"), Iulus began diffidently, stripped down now to his 1920s tennis flannels. Upon repeated questioning, however, citing his noncombatant privileges, his refrain became something of a mantra. "I was born in Cannonia, province of Klavier, in 1924, the year that Lenin and Wilson died within ten days of each other. So I had a very happy childhood." And then he pushed a strange, mottled birth certificate across the desk.

Iulus was certainly not into confessing, but neither was he enigmatic or evasive. It was as if with a double sincerity he was testifying that, while he recognized his powers of description were inadequate, he knew that what he knew for a fact would only be misinterpreted. Yet the conversation went on for an hour, with a series of questions that seemed to be a kind of market-testing to quantify at what price point our potential ally might be persuaded to subscribe to the New World Order. Was he a bad man or had he only done bad things? Has the war deepened your understanding of the world in which we live? In what ways has America fallen short of your expectations? Have your personal values changed in any way? The lieutenant fairly hummed the tune of our national false intimacy, which persistently encourages the performer of the moment to drop his dignity. Then came a series of questions that seemed to have to do with securing the pleasures of the ruined aristocracy for peanuts—the whereabouts of servants, winecellars, and lubricious women. "I really like history a lot," the lieutenant averred, and on these subjects Iulus was more forthcoming, though still cautionary. "Ah, every hillock in Cannonia has a tale of buried treasure, but no one save the Astingi has ever found as much as a sovereign."

Unaccustomed as he was to being counted among the Master Races, and having freight cars full of high-ranking Nazis to debrief, our Ivy League interlocutor finally declared his loss of interest. He knew where to find us if he needed us, he said. But as often happens in the debriefing business, the body language was more instructive than the conversation. If Iulus mocked the lieutenant's earnest intensity, the lieutenant, not being a stupid person, also mimicked the shrugs he had noticed in this youth grown old before his time, a non-racial Jewish shrug, registering not secretiveness as much as non-conductivity, the gesture of a gentryman grown weary of his good manners. I realized I was witnessing a kind of bizarre contest; indifference bred versus indifference learned. Iulus, of course, as cursory witness, had the upper hand. But he never pressed his advantage.

Indeed, it was I who was uncomfortable in this interview. In Cannonia, national characters tend to be purified: the German most German, the Russian most Russian, and the American most quintessentially American. The Lieutenant radiated a curious compound of incuriosity and perplexity, the helplessness of abstract benevolence. Indeed, it seemed to me that right before my eyes, this proud fellow, this Newton of sociology, so clean and contracepted in his knowledge, was losing the boundary between right and wrong, as his general decency could only be expressed as aggressive and self-righteous sanctimony. He tried to cloak this with a self-conscious insouciance and boyish charm, as well as the apparently sincere belief that the scientific revolution stood at his right shoulder with the debonair nonchalance of a sergeant-at-arms. But Iulus acknowledged his interlocutor with the same amused equanimity of the Astingi watching another dogfaced people ford their shallow stream. He asked only if he could bunk with his Astingi comrades in the compound, and this was assented to with a final Cantabrigian shrug, as a form was pushed across a desk for him to sign off. Iulus chortled to himself as the pen was poised, as if he had forgotten which future alias was now appropriate.

"You don't even know *what* your real name is, do you?" the lieutenant barked with exasperation, and to this Iulus managed a perfectly defenseless, docile, democratic, American shrug, equal parts dissent and submission, as feckless as those he had witnessed among the boys when handing out the pups. He was surely a quick study. Then he took the fine fish out of his boot and laid it on the table.

We led the golden pony down to the compound at dusk, where I had a devil of a time explaining to Iulus the sign at the gate: "No horseplay." A great normalcy seemed to pervade everything. The barbed wire was strung loose. Kites flew. No one was peering out. No one looked in. The Astingi women were allowed in groups under guard to go down and do their washing in the river. The American sentries, wearing only sidearms, aimlessly wandered the perimeter, as if they were on their way to school.

The Astingi had already knocked out the windows and disassembled the prefab barracks, covering the doors with colorful capes and shawls, festooning the gray walls with great loops of sausages and braids of garlic. Cooking fires had been lit. Lambs were slaughtered and spitted, kettles burbled, piglets were gutted and baked. Melons, eggplant, leeks; red, green, and yellow peppers appeared from nowhere. The Astingi men in long skirts and their women in pantaloons passed long clay pipes between them. Their children, almost naked, played with tiny puzzles or read large thick books on their backs while a seven-dog orchestra woofed their woodwinds. As Shakespeare cultists as well as woman cultists, the Astingi were already throwing up stage wings for an open-air performance.

As a disorderly mass of starlings buried the sun, blackheaded whimpering gulls by the thousands descended on the bluish mists of the Mze. Skylarks rose with a whir, herons gazed coquettishly toward the vanished sun, and imperturbable rooks stalked off to the woods for the night. Then the reed-beds erupted in a *fortissimo* of song-duels, an ambuscade of lovelorn yearning, a clangor of male wailing and wanting which silenced the chorus of victory and the manly arts of war.

Iulus hobbled the blond pony loosely with a thong of crimson patent leather. The pony yawned, and as the bones in his face cracked, Iulus softly intoned an Astingi chant for me. "'He who hath not seen the bird-pastures of the Mze / hath nothing seen / the whole world drinks from our river / the eyes of the sea. And whomsoever drinks from her / bottomless mists longs to return.' You see," he concluded with closed eyes, "it's impossible to talk even for half an hour without the Mze coming into the conversation . . ." We embraced shyly and made plans for an early breakfast in the commissary. The war was over.

That night I dreamt our national bedtime story: begat by virtue, winning through virtue, earning the right to correct the world . . . and woke up in the middle of it, feverish and despairing.

He never appeared at breakfast and inquiries in the compound produced only hyperbolic shrugs and gaptoothed, golden grins. That was the last time for many years that I would see the agent called Iulus face to face, though we would shadow each other throughout our lifetimes and into something of the next. His self-confounded, mutilated little country has never been far from my thoughts since that day. I have yet to shake her pomegranate mud from my boots.

I went back to my bunk to make out my report. First impressions are most important, but it would take the rest of my life to sort them out. There is an immense relief in the knowledge that one actually knows nothing—that one can savor experience for itself, not because you can act upon it. Though my brain had collided with a labelless world, never before or since have my emotions been so lucid or distinct. I had been touched at all points. My empathy was, for once, *exact*. I opened the plaid valise and the Gladstone, and amongst the crumpled papers of the latter was a leatherbound volume, *Da Historae Astingae: An Internal Guide to the External Barbarian*. Each page was written in a different color ink, separated with dried leaves and herbs, and the incomparable female aromas of Cannonia made me giddy. But the Z-box was gone.

While the Astingi mounted an off-the-wall production of *Titus Andronicus*, the earliest and bloodiest of Shakespeare's histories, from the first scene ("Alarbus' limbs are lopt, and entrails feed the sacrificing fire") to the last ("Set him breast-deep in earth, and famish him"), while the title character lost twenty-one sons in battle and personally dispatched another on stage, I was a merry genius for a week. What greater joy than to write without having to revise! I detailed the flora, fauna, and spiritual furniture of Semper Vero, listing their strategic possibilities as our condominium in Terra XX, our pleasure seat in the barbarian lands. I prayed that my well-fed American buttonhead might be pasted in brief appearance in that custodial lineage of tragic golden faces. And at the same moment, I vowed to desert from that army of Americans who would swarm over the world with answers, learning nothing.

Yes, there is a coffin coming. But I cannot tell you now who was in it.

EX LIBRIS

(Iulus and Aufidius)

Father wrote every evening in his *Historae Astingae: An Internal Guide to the External Barbarian*, disguised as a "Guidebook for Travelers" in order to make a market for it. Working at top speed, he usually produced about one hundred and twenty sentences of impossible terseness per night. Behind his mahogany swivel chair there was a large table with sixteen chessboards that formed one huge board, lined with the standing pieces. The pieces stood there summer after summer, intermingling as time went on. I do not know with whom he played, nor what happened in the game. They may have served simply as paperweights. He explained the rules to me, but his attitude was that once I knew the rules, it was not necessary to play. The incomprehensibility of the game was apparently its most important feature.

Sometimes he permitted me to stay with him while he worked, provided I was absolutely silent. I sat next to him at the edge of the desk, with my slender wit and unmoved disposition, drawing convoluted schoolboy clouds as the books which surrounded us, interlocked and overlapped, flowed back and forth into one another like sea anemones or the Mze itself. And when he got up to consult a reference or simply to pace up and down, I stared at the folio next to me, its half-completed sentences looping away like a thin line of ponies on the horizon, inviting me to run down, ride them, pull hair from their manes.

I did not know then that writers give away everything that is original to them, and are always in danger of losing their whole substance. Writers are people who have exhausted themselves; only the dregs of them still exist. Writing is so real it makes the writer unreal; a nothing. And if one resists being a nothing, one will have the greatest difficulty in finishing anything.

Nor did I know that in his hyperfastidious, shamelessly private mind, he was envisioning a nonexistent genre. For no one ever writes the book he imagines; the book becomes the death mask of creation, it has its own future and survives like a chicken dancing with its head cut off. And the spy knows this better than anyone; to write anything down is to take colossal risk. In life you can mask your actions, but once on paper, nothing can hide your mediocrity.

Da Historae Astingae

A TRAVELER'S GUIDE TO THE CROWNLANDS OF CANNONIA
INCLUDING THE MARCHLANDS OF KLAVIER
WITH DIGRESSIONS INTO FERRYLAND
AND THE TRIBUTARIES OF THE MZE, VAH, AND ITS

WRITTEN BY AN ANONYMOUS PERMANENT RESIDENT OF
THESE LANDS, BUT NOT ABOUT HIMSELF

Go, little book
and wish to all
Flowers in the garden
Meat in the hall,
A bin of wine
A spice of wit
A house with lawns
enclosing it.
A living river
by the door
A nightingale
in the sycamore

AS WE HAVE REFUSED ALL ADVERTISING, ANYONE
REPRESENTING THEMSELVES AS OUR AGENT IS AN IMPOSTOR.

So, Valued Traveler, while your papers are being visaed and your baggage searched, put aside your imaginings, your idle curiosity, and your fear of discomfort in a strange land. I came here like yourself many years ago as a young man, and while not completely accepted to this day, have become a resident, raised a family, invented a profession, and benefitted not a little from the local culture. I have surveyed every romantic scene, gathered every mountain flower, measured every valley, and drawn conclusions as to what was excellent and what might be improved.

It is the humble duty of this writer to collect under all the varieties of circumstance such materials as may supply a groundwork for connected history and for general deduction. The reader who seeks elaborate political disposition, or the amusement derived from private anecdote, will be disappointed. Where it was thought necessary to go beyond the sphere of personal observation, German authorities of established merit have been relied upon. It was at one time intended to subjoin a sketch of the literature of the country. But upon this interesting subject it is not possible to write with a hasty pen. Cannonian letters are too extensive to be compressed, and it was not without great reluctance the author relinquished this object, being sensible that the true spirit and condition of a nation can never be appreciated without some insight into the progress of its literary culture. He trusts, however, that the design which is deferred will not be forgotten, and anticipates with much pleasure those hours in which he may pursue his labors upon the subject.

The Traveler must look to other guides if he is interested in the minor promotions of Greek or Italian genius, or the ruins of military/ecclesiastical misadventures. There will be no chronological list of potentates. Indeed, Cannonia is a kingdom in which the person of the Sovereign has always been difficult to determine. The writer must further confess that he is not an artist of any sort, but an amateur enthusiast of the profound, the beautiful, and the sublime, so now increasingly out of fashion—nor does he confuse the authority of the aesthetical genius with the political ambitions which often encourage it, which seems to be our intelligensias' only fascination. Nor am I anything of a philosopher. Dialectics do not interest me, though like ballsports, I am very good at them. I neither write a system nor promise a system, not do I subscribe or ascribe anything to a system. My only expertise is in the finality of love. I intend, nonetheless, to make my reputation good with you, as I have acquired, at no little expense, the Cannonian taste of seeing things for what they are.

RUBATO AND NIMBUS
(Iulus)

By this time Father could do no wrong in the Professor's eyes, the doctor seizing upon each success in the field with an enthusiasm tinged by self-deprecatory remarks about his own researches:

"It's just as well we're friends, otherwise I should burst with envy." Or, "You really ought to write this up, you know. It would make a great impression on the masses."

Moreover, Father's indifference had the odd effect of cheering him.

"It's merely an amateur's business," Father sniffed, "and at any rate, I don't live to publish my brain."

One day, when the Professor was waxing particularly effusive about a schnauzer whose mania for shredding had been softened measurably, he blurted out, "Let's leave off the uglies, Councilor. You realize in all this time you haven't really shown off your own animals. I want to see good dogs today, the *best* dogs—the emblem I should aspire to!"

Father took off his hat, lowered his head, and looked directly at his esteemed friend's heart, as if to gauge his sincerity. Then he took a step backward and looked him up and down.

"Very well," he spoke in measured tones, "but you deserve nothing less than the whole play. And it's spring, you know. Man isn't up to any good, and neither is nature."

The difference between them, after all, was that the Professor truly believed he was the first mortal to set foot into the mind, and like every true colonial assumed that mere priority allowed him to name it and submit it to his laws. My father, who had preceded him there and left as rapidly as he could, knew with his layman's tick that what you give your name to only makes you liable for its eventual perversions, and that while the ferns of the world may give way around your stride, they immediately pop back up, covering your tracks as though you never passed. Father also, in retrospect, had made an elemental mistake, not realizing that the exercise of personal modesty, which had won my mother, does not often work as well with men, for modesty in men is simply inverted pride. The Professor was not content with intimacy, but only unreserved mutual admiration, and my father believed that he could wean him from this course.

It was in this spirit that Felix summoned Rubato and Nimbus, models of the Chetvorah, parented by Sirius and Isisirene, the brightest constellation yet projected on the dome of dogdom. Brother and sister, they could hardly be distinguished from one another at two years of age, save for Rubato's gallant poise, which made him the better pointer, and the passionate devotion of Nimbus, which made her an indefatigable retriever.

Returning the schnauzer to the kennels, we walked around to the rear of the house and down the lawn to Cherith's Brook. Father turned on his heel, gazing back to the tower of his den, and blew two syllables on a silver whistle, a bass and a deeper quartertone, the second phrase of Schubert's *Unfinished*. Immediately the pair appeared on the den's balcony (as usual, they had flung themselves with a sob under his desk upon his departure), and then with tempered passion they flashed across the southern sky, turning extraordinary caprioles in the air. Emerging from a circular pool behind a cypress hedge, then bolting through the broken garden gate, they stormed toward us, unfolding their forces as their wet ribcages realigned with each stride—flews loose, underlips shortened, teeth gleaming in the sun.

The Professor's heart had dropped when they leapt, fearing the worst, and now it did again as their clear-veined legs and drawn-in haunches seemed to promise more than virile virtue, bringing back the awe and helplessness he had felt at the Cossack-like charge of the Astingi boy on his pony.

The animal's bodies lurched on a centrifugal plane like dervishes, and as they neared us, rather than stopping, they took on the masters (Rubato attending the Hauptzuchtwart, Nimbus the stranger) with a sudden upward lunge, snapping at the men's faces as if to bite their noses off. The Professor had already recoiled, but as the jaws of Nimbus passed by his head, she planted a floating air-kiss on his lips, half-tenderly, half-mischievously, beslobbering his defensive, outthrust arm. Then began the dance of welcome and salutation—prodigious waggings of hindquarters, violent tugs of muscles, rapid tramplings, daring vaults, annular contractions, far-flung leaps, and the indubitable claw-flamenco.

Their cut tails were vibrating to quick-time, their rosy riffled mouths exposed. Then Father quietly spoke their favorite words—"*Ru-ba-to, Nimbus*"—and with a single leap they were at his side, shoulder blades against his shinbones like statues, each with a white whorl on its chest. Father put them in a double-harness, and without another word we set off for the forest where the juiciest ferns grow thick and the deer congregate to escape the midday heat. The birds stopped singing.

Our forests were not the true trackless type, the only true remnants of which exist in northern Russia and northmost America, but in fact were leafy islands cut from fields to shield the springs and water sources. Before the Great War you could move a thousand kilometers east and rarely be a hundred yards from drinking water, and by carefully picking its portages across the sterile fields, a full column of horsemen could remain in shade for days at a time. The emphasis had always been to extract game from the brutal and never bucolic forms of agriculture, circumventing those bound to the garner of the land—a never-ending battle to wrest trees from the peasant's poaching axe and the magnate's long saw.

"Ah, to live in harmony with the land," the Professor let slip as he picked his way about the cowpats.

"Stand for a day with a shepherd dog, my friend," Felix riposted, "and we shall see what becomes of your mind. You could turn all the Germanies into a gymnasium and not restore it. For a landscape to have grandeur, it must have a bit of nonsense."

Then he discoursed on why nature is anything but natural:

"One must work incessantly so that the landscape is neither diminished nor allowed to revert to uncontrolled growth. A constructive edge which is not impenetrable but in which one can hide takes many men to create, many lifetimes, many tricks and sacrifices, so that you can get close to a bird who has survived all history with the latecomer, the dog, who it took eight thousand years to train just to eat out of his own dish."

Father had this theory, as far as I know unrefuted, that every nation takes the structure of its mind from the nature of its forest, whether it be the diagonal rows of the French *bocage* and its filtered crystalline light, making the informal formal; the dense darkness of the Teuton wood, where the trees die top down and the canopy seems made of gnarled roots; the ever-correct English copses, memorial to the vanished forest of thieves and adventurers; or the single druidical cypress worshiped by Mediterraneans—as well as those ancient civilizations where the austerity of intellect is apparently the result of having no trees at all, but only unaesthetical shrubbery, not to speak of jungles where rarity is homogeneity; the Russian taiga of birch, pine, and rowan whose inwardness is so palpable and passive; and finally the American backwoods, the richest botanically but the most slovenly kept, its most prominent feature stumps, which exist chiefly to hide broken, discarded toys—toys, they say, made of everything but wood.

The woods in our part of the world corresponded well to the human state for which they were intended: islands of secrecy, preserved from the *snip, snip, snip* of agricultural routine. Not even centuries of war could destroy these covens, though one man within his lifetime, in the interest of a few handfuls of grain or kindling, could do more damage than the most violent of autocratic contests. And the Professor, because he knew that animals returned to die there, misunderstood these patches of woods as dark places inhabited by goblins and other terrible forces, whereas in reality, as Father patiently explained, they were full of disappointments and surprises, but not to be feared, because men don't die there.

"We die out in the open," he murmured as if in a trance, "when we forsake cover, out in the plain geometry of our own devising, making those banal rows of sweet little pods just like a cemetery. When the earth is pulverized and floats away with the rain and the green lines of mesmeric shoots appear, that's when men must take cover, for it is in the spring when he begins to hallucinate at his own handiwork and builds his grave of vegetables." It was the fields, not the woods, where the human experiment was out of control, and that was the delicate point he was prepared to enforce that day.

When rhetorically upstaged, the Professor would often opt for a kind of radical response, in this case arguing that hunting was an outdated ritual to appease one's vanity, an attempt to reconnect "bourgeois thinking" with its nobler antecedents, and "a stupid contest to determine who was the manliest man in all Klavierland." But Felix disarmed him with selective candor.

"What you say is true enough," he said, "yet ninety-nine percent of our existence has been spent doing just that. I do not pretend to live in harmony with the land; the point is to distance oneself gradually from it, to make it an object of curiosity and pleasure. It's woods alone that are worth hoodwinking for, my dear Hebraist; nevertheless, we take your point. And now, if you will, attend to mine."

The day was bright for my father's display, as always prodigal but without fanfare. Rubato and Nimbus were released but made not the slightest lunge as the leash was uncoupled. They followed him two meters off each of his heels, watching the telltale arch of his booted foot, trading for the time being their poor eyes for his superior vantage, height, and peripheral vision. Climbing the embankment of a drainage ditch, the Professor already panting, we appeared on a stubbled rise and overlooked a field of wheat bordered at its furthest reach by what seemed an incommensurably dense line of forest. It was mostly ash, if a name tells you anything, a crippled bit of nature with billows of vegetation cascading about gnarled boles, a profusion of wild vines which reached to the very top of the trees and turned black in the winter, hard as barbed wire.

Father's right heel raised slightly, the precondition for firing, though he carried no gun—all he had to do was show the dogs the key to the gun cabinet for them to know the direction of the day. When his heel reached half an inch off the ground, Rubato and Nimbus dropped to their bellies, arched their necks, and cocked their heads ever so slightly in order to peer calmly around his calves. The Professor's eyes had a hint of gray awe. My father spoke slowly, cradling his imaginary, redundant gun:

"This is the opposite of suggestion, but an exercise in cooperation, reinforcing our worst senses with the best of others. The point is to define what is in reach and beyond reach, and gradually, with luck, to push back the confines of the inaccessible. That's the part of the story which is always missed."

As he spoke, he bent slightly at the knees, and with a single wave of his hand, the dogs sprang up and plunged in tandem into the sea of green wheat.

"As pure athletes they are the best that ever lived," he went on. "They lack some of the nostalgic virtues, perhaps, but no one ever moved with such alacrity."

Now their noses were my father's eyes. The Chetvorah knifed through the grain at full speed, his eyes following their skulls. The vast field for them became a simple frame which they divided into quadrants, galloping across each other's black wakes in the green ocean, turning figure-eights like torpedo boats. Every few moments they leapt straight up to check their bearings, and while suspended in midair, with a slight coy turning of their heads caught the angle of my father's hands, which cast them out further along vectors of his composing. He disdained the human voice and all the apparatus of verbs, horns, whistles, and thunder-clubs, and in this way, without a mote of wasted energy, mapped the sea of grass until the Chetvorah had fully quartered it, drinking everything in.

The Professor watched this, squinted, bunching his shoulders, and let out a long sigh as the dogs reached the forest line without putting up a single bird. Then, wheeling in circles of disappointment, their purpose waning, they began to work their way back to us in desuetude.

"Birds don't eat lunch," Father said by way of explanation, "but deer do," and then, shaping his hands into a great parentheses, framed the final scene for the Professor. "Watch this well and with respect."

His hands flicked out, all ten fingers, and the dogs, caught short, turned *volte face* and began to work the forest edge, though one could sense the momentum had been broken, a few of the invisible threads between us snapped by the stress of an elegant search gone unrewarded. An element of hesitation, even boredom, was apparent in their gait even to an untrained observer. Nevertheless they kept working the edge in tandem, throwing up divots of earth in their indignation, and then their perfect figure-eights began to oscillate as one of them—Rubato, I thought—veered off at a tangent, ears flapping, in the kind of heavy, jazzy canter of a horse broken from its traces, or a duck breaking formation with a few pellets in its wing. With one ear carelessly turned inside out, he loped obliquely, hindlegs moving somewhat to the side, as some tremendous emotion began to seize him. Every nerve taut, one foreleg and one hindleg paused in the air, he peered with cocked head into the hollows as the flaps of his erected ears fell forward on both eyes. Nimbus backed him with fine deliberation, her bobbed tail waving furiously, both drunk with their own identity. Rubato wobbled left and right, then started, which jerked his head in rash recoil against his chest and in recovering almost tore his head from his shoulders. The spore of the deer had floated from the forest and dropped like a regimental flag before them.

"Now there is only one chance left, very small," Father whispered, still holding his cupped and inverted palms before the Professor's glistening face. "We will see if Rubato has it in him to self-correct."

Nimbus was still locked in the semblance of a pattern, wheeling through the conflicting signals, walking the edge, and still vaguely aware that my father's hands could reach her. But then with a shudder she broke off, not to the deer—a furtive stag with a broken rack and yellowish-white scut which had just broken from the thicket—but to her runaway brother's trail. The dogs accelerated now faster than ever, a breakneck berserker pace, and disappeared into the forest, galloping with teeth set and howling inwardly.

The parentheses of my father's hands closed, as if to wring the last, long, soft note out. The view became bright and empty, the fields desolate.

"They're demons now," he said, snapping his fingers. "Their sordid history has overtaken them."

"Call them!" the Professor cried out, wringing his hands. It was like the cry of a woman who has been told her husband is dead. "Call them back!"

Father called out their names in a high, clear voice, more to comfort his friend than anything. Then he blew on the horn of bone and finally the steel whistle, an ear-splitting military pitch of the last resort, though he knew better. On the overgrazed hill beyond the forest, we could make out the stag lumbering up the slope, pausing every now and then to aim a labored hindquarter kick. And behind him, losing ground like their names, the two spittle-sucking stumblebums in blind pursuit. They disappeared into the hooded Cannonian landscape of uncomprehending beasts and unskillful hunters.

"They're too far to hear," the Professor said agonizingly.

"Oh, they hear all right," my father said, "but it's just one voice among others now."

The Professor turned tearfully. "Nothing to be done?"

"Absolutely nothing. It's not that they have forgotten exactly. They are simply beyond their own faculties. Now we can only pray the stag does not run them into wire, or that some besotted shepherd does not shoot them. And when they come back down the road in a few days, full of burrs, their tongues hanging out like blood sausage, you will notice that your love and concern has been turned to an urge to punish. No, they will not look you in the eye. They will not even come to the house. They will go and beg to be let into the kennel. Remember the scene, Herr Doktor, not the individuals."

"If we had accompanied them," the Professor broke out accusatorially, "this would not have happened."

"Precisely," my father said calmly and politely. "They reached the end of the field, and seeing themselves in the mirror, like children, they chose to look behind it. But don't forget, dear friend, just before, the pride of our cooperation! And for all that, remember the field before the forest, before they broke the *civilzonnen*, where the voluntary reigns. It is almost exactly eighty meters long, sixty wide, and one inch deep, and in my lifetime I have enlarged it by twenty percent! As things get beyond that, sir, we are only custodians. There is no return on capital." The double harness hung like a gallows rope in his hands. "It's time for a little lunch, and a bit of oblivion," he announced without emotion.

As the Professor followed Father into the White Wings, Black Dog, he noted a small, hand-painted sign above the door.

YOU ARE APPROACHING EARTH'S CENTER
IF YOU DON'T BELIEVE IT
JUST ENTER

The jolly, almost-too-rosy serving girl waved them back to *The Brainery* with a butter knife. While all their fellow diners were male, the room itself had an eternally feminine quality. Disdainful of mere prettiness, the colors were sweetly mysterious shades of pale yellow, which unfolded rather than pleased the eye, and the floating draperies blurred the precise lines of the room with profound sensuality. Just as they were seated in a green booth with curtains, a platter of tiny steaming birds, a woodcock fricassee, was brought to the table.

"Served only one week a year," Father announced with a wink. "If a mouflon is shot in the mountains of Vop, it is brought here; if a fine salmon is hauled from the Augesee, it is packed in ice and brought here; if an especially fine jar of sheep's milk cheese should appear in Chere Muchore, it is also brought here."

Then the Professor was amazed to see his host lift up the tablecloth, and placing the platter in front of him, drape the cloth over his head and dish, making a tent so as to fully inhale their woodfern aroma. He did not reappear for fully ten minutes.

While Father was thus preoccupied, the Professor perused the menu, at the top of which was only the motto *"Hic Carnem Comedemius."* ("We are not vegetarians here.") Like a true dog's dinner, it was divided not into courses or even genres: minced chick soup, larks in crumbles, sandpipers in gondolas, fish sausages, blancmange fritters, quince stew with scarlet jelly, griddlecakes with nut paste and Spanish wine. Marzipan love-flakes, macaroon trifle, refreshing fennel and almond essences, maraschino ices. Cockscombs in pagodas and champagne, turkeys daubed with stewed grapes, stuffed pike and river birds garnished with oysters. Aspic of carp with frog dumplings, calves' ears stuffed with lamb gizzards, grilled peach stew with aniseed, collapsed yearling boar with creamed eggplant and pomegranate molasses. Oxtongue and asparagus ragout, parboiled artichoke bottoms piled with pounded duck livers. Young rabbits with anchovies, minute cold boned thrushes, salad of oranges, herbs, olives, and marigold petals. Braised doe-shanks glazed with sumac and hazelnuts, thrush pate with cardamom fritters, sheeps' tongues in curled papers, boiled beef skirts rubbed with saltpeter and stuffed with snipe. Roe tarts with shrimps and partridges in their own juice, chilled eels in dill frockcoats, perch and baby quail patties, bass aghast in green garlic. Marrow fried in crumbs, minced pigeon in cream, pig trotters in milk, marshfed veal rubbed with mint and wild thyme in four stocks, and as a single concession to the French, an *omelette au joli coeur*.

At the bottom was an asterisked dish ("For guaranteed success in courting fair ladies"): sliced bear's paw atop pork filet stuffed with chicken liver and rolled in bacon slices, garnished with truffles, onion rings, and pickles.

The Professor was about to order this intriguing dish, but once the woodcock had disappeared, the courses were simply brought without order, timing, or explanation. He had little idea what the dishes were until each new joy was consumed; then he could make out various layers, fragrances of unusual clarity superimposed on one another like a fugue, which made him want to live forever. Nor could he discern the various wines which were automatically poured, as the wine list was not only in an unknown language but an alphabet he had never seen. At one point he glanced up to the only art in the room, an embroidered pennant which announced:

The use of bottled essences for
seasoning is forbidden and will
lead to instant dismissal.

The White Wings, Black Dog had a calculated double ambience in its
strategy for exercising *goût*. The front rooms gave off to a courtyard hidden
from the street where men and women sat whispering at tiny pearwood tables
large enough for only a drink and an ashtray. Further inside were a series of
pine booths arranged at angles to an enormous walk-in fireplace, partially lit
even in August and hung with various kettles of stew from which one could
serve oneself with a large, enameled tin plate. Occasionally a serving girl
would slip out the back door with a huge knife, and after an incredible series
of shrieks and squeals, something spitted and juicy would be turning over
coals where just five minutes before a pot of chrysanthemums sat.

At the center of the room was a long bar in the shape of a quarter-moon
where only first-time visitors stood, surrounded by a series of long common
tables. Depending on the evening, here one might find an Astingi gelder,
animal blood still fresh on his hands, in deep conversation with a befurred
and bechained Foreign Minister Zich, his shooting break and his grays both
emblazoned with a cadmium orange "Z." Or the village doctor with his head
in his hands. Or Öscar Ögur, passed out in a corner. Or Catspaw, trying
and failing to make conversation with the most beautiful girl in the world,
dressed in pink and white, and not once elevating her eyes from an edition of
The Count of Monte Cristo. Aged Chetvorah, disdaining any scraps not given
them by hand, stood arthritically on guard, displaying the white whorls on
their chests like veterans' medals.

The walls bore etchings of fossils found in the local sinkholes—wolves
with broken backs, birds with every vertebrae of the wing exposed in a
fan—and indeed the locals referred to the front rooms as "Utah," in honor
of the oldest known dog fossil found in North America, and the back room
as "Arizona," because no one knew a single thing about it except that it was
pretty.

The front rooms, with their tobacco-colored curtains and sensory
simplicity, had harbored every discreet silence, every tragic conversation, and
every historical form of rowdiness, insult, and *affaire d'honneur*. To ask for
water with one's coffee were fighting words. Men were known to take a crust

of Black Dog bread on their travels and sniff of it of an evening, should their thoughts take a melancholy turn. But no matter how savage or despairing the serial personal confrontations, if one stepped back to the bar, the general atmosphere invariably seemed comedic, if not exactly gay.

The Brainery, on the other hand, was not only more expensive and exclusive (anyone asking for a reservation was told it had closed for renovations), but devoted to reversing the historical sensation of Utah. Everything up close was comic, but toward the perimeter of the room the sense of loneliness was overwhelming, even though it held some fifty diners. Somehow the space had been acoustically devoted to changing the terms of conversation itself. Sentences curled about one another like smoke. If you paused for reflection, another voice finished or inverted your thought. Across the table, though his lips were moving, you didn't hear a word your colocutor said, while your own voice came out of nowhere, from the wings, as it were, a stage whisper. As the courses progressed, it seemed one was going blind, the precondition for all real sensuality, until you could make out only the dim outline of your companion's face. Two silent men with their mouths full might enjoy snatches of conversation not strictly their own. A lady might allow her partner to put his foot where he wished, but she would never ask to share his dessert or offer even a forkful of her zebra-eye salad. Indeed, one was never quite sure what was said, half-said, previously remembered, or later reflected upon. One could manage a seduction or an apology in the Brainery, but never win an argument or make a deal.

The effect of this irony-resistant fugue was calming rather than irruptive. Although most people in the room were unknown to each other, an unforgettable solidarity carried them into the night.

The two men ate conscientiously rather than with fervor, as if to arrive at ultimate conclusions only after complete evidence had been submitted. They ate without gulping, without flinching, without fatigue, drinking a new wine for each dish with perfect sang-froid.

The conversation slowed, though all subjects were permissible, save the events of the morning, and all manner of expression, excepting that of a low mood. The wine had done its work and their brains ceased to be machines for argument-winning, and our talkative species began a *conversation galante.*

Throwing back his head and showing his Adam's apple, Felix announced, "We are gorillas."

"Dangerous gorillas!" the Professor toasted with his knife.

"Dangerous and ill-adapted," Felix chorused.

"Our back isn't right, tails in our trousers," the Professor riposted gleefully. "Below the hips we are a mess, particularly women, and we clank when we walk!"

"We were almost extinct," Felix assented vigorously, "and we have never forgotten it!"

The Professor suppressed a burp with his napkin and apologized. Felix waved the gaffe away. "It's the lizard in us that does the breathing."

And when they finished, there was no fanfare, no flinging of napkins, nothing but a slight settling back in the tenderly green banquettes. There arrived a small cart with various cheeses, ratafias, *eau-de-vie*, and cigars in an ingeniously ventilated box which exuded the scent of burning creole corpses.

"You will never hear me say a word against hunting again, my friend," the Professor sighed, "of that you can be sure."

Father smiled warmly but said only, "The forcemeat lacked half an onion and two sprigs of chervil." Then he bit into a piece of soft cheese, but only halfway through. Taking the entire piece from his mouth with his fingers, he showed the indentations to his comrade. "*This* is who we are!"

They were a third of their way through their cheroots when there was an enormous crash of china and a serving girl's astonished shriek, neither remarkable in the front room of White Wings, Black Dog. But the Professor noted that his host had removed his cigar, slightly elevated his nose, and opened his nostrils. There was further commotion in the outer rooms, as well as a tremendous muffled breathing, and then the Professor, too, his palette cleansed, noticed a delicate acid note in the air: tannins and singed fur. Then a dark flash against the pale yellow and a sound like a snare-drum as Rubato and Nimbus, matted with every seed, vine, and scum of the forest, tails raw, tongues lolling, whiskers twisted, ears bleeding, eyes protuberant, coats disheveled, stormed into the Brainery, and after circling the room and vaulting a wine cart, skidded to a stop before the banquette with a convulsive collective flounce, as if to say, "My God, what a pair of masters, eh!"

"Scoundrels!" Father muttered, though his eyes betrayed his relief.

At first the Professor politely refused the animals' advances, but after Nimbus placed her lightly webbed paws on his chest and her haggard canine cheek against his own, snapping at his nose like a fly, he began to weep. "It's just like patients, you see . . . they all run away, but mostly they come back."

Felix remained cool. "And now, friend, you will see the famous horse imitation."

And sure enough, the dogs' square faces suddenly grew long and their mouths drooped, red haws exposed. They hung their heads, shivers undulating along their sides, as if a hundredweight of woe were pulling their noses to the ground, like some wreck of a worn-out cab-horse. But just as their noses touched the floor, they stretched their forelegs, lifted their hindquarters, spread out their hindlegs, and yawned deliriously in stark abstraction.

"Well, I suppose the only thing that matters is how you recover from being wrong," the Professor said, wiping his nose.

Then both dogs leapt into the banquette, where they began to scour themselves as if they were rolling on a lawn.

"Down!" Felix barked. "Down, now!"

Called sharply to account, they flung themselves beneath the table with a sob and a sigh. Then, turning three times, with a crescendo of flappings, snorting, and rattlings, ears slapping beneath their jawbones, they fell at once into a drugged sleep. Soon they began to dream, executing all the motions of running with their paws, while at the same time giving vent to a ventriloquistic barking which sounded as if it came from another world. Felix kicked them softly, and they lay still with twisted eyeballs as though dead. Throughout this spectacle neither guest nor staff showed the slightest discomfort.

"Councilor," the Professor blurted, "I *must* have a dog such as this."

"Breeding stock, quite impossible," Felix said calmly.

"Then a runt," he beseeched, "surely you have a runt? One testicle, knock-knees, undershot jaw, drooping tail, too-soft hair? That would do."

"Waiting list," Felix said peremptorily.

While he found it increasingly difficult to focus, the Professor had noticed that the only time his host had expressed dissatisfaction through this long meal was when he glanced at an oblong dish which served as a kind of centerpiece. It was filled with celery, carrot sticks, and slivers of ice, and bore the crest of a British ocean liner. This Anglo affectation and single lapse of taste had obviously been gnawing at him, and instead of responding to his guest's pleas, Felix was fingering a stalk of celery in one hand and a rather limp carrot in the other. Then, without a word, he put both in his handkerchief pocket as a kind of spear-like *boutonnière*.

The Professor tried to ingratiate himself. "It was the air-kiss, I confess, which finally tore out my heart . . ."

"Only another dog can teach a dog the air-kiss," Felix said gravely, putting a celery stalk in his ear and a carrot in his nostril.

Incredulous, the Professor bolted down an apricot brandy and chewed on his unlit cigar. They sat taking each other's measure for some minutes, corneas boiling, the dogs lightly snoring.

Then the Professor brought his fist down on the table with a crash.

"Listen here, Councilor. Have you no respect for my feelings? Well, let me put it to you then: I will buy your bloody farm, lock, stock, and barrel. Name your price!"

Nothing in his life had surprised Felix more than this. His head jerked around concussively like Rubato picking up a spore. Thunderstruck, his left hand began to tremble, and a sudden cramp seized his buttocks. Debits canceled, balances restored, he saw his family upon an ocean liner going round the world, the three of them standing at the rail, all with hats, and he recalled Ainoha's plaintive musing, "God, can't we just live a normal life?" He had himself another brandy, and as he stared across the table at the despairing monotheist, his only close male friend, he felt a humiliation, vulnerability, and outrage such as never before. Red blotches appeared on his face as a dozen of the basest slurs ran through his head. And then came a low, guttural growl:

"You ought to be ashamed of yourself," as he passed up forever the only chance to get the yoke of Semper Vero off his back.

The Professor was both insulted and relieved—insulted because he was offering partnership, relieved because he hadn't actually done any calculations. He also felt ashamed, for he knew he had committed a vulgarity and had made the worst kind of mistake—not a moral but an aesthetical one. So he made a clumsy but charming attempt to recover, becoming a co-conspirator in the gruesome gameliness at hand, and stuck a celery stick in his ear and a carrot in his nostril, as if to say, "Am I being unsportsmanlike?"

Felix was touched by this, and as always when touched, upped the ante. He beckoned the Professor beneath the table. There, giggling like schoolboys, the errant gentlemen inserted iced British condiments into the snoring dogs' ears, noses, and anuses, and it was this tipsy quartet, brandishing Cunard root vegetables from every orifice, who staggered from the veranda of White Wings, the dogs loping obliquely, the more talkative pair, our hunter-lads, arm in arm.

Felix appreciated his friend playing the fool, for this was the necessary first step of any learning process. It appeared the ugliness had been forsworn, but neither of them would forget or really regret it, each aware that the other was capable of bringing out the absolute worst in himself—and it was this realization which gave their competitiveness a new dynamic.

Well past the now superfluous dinner hour, on the winding road to Semper Vero, they discussed the meal in detail, as well as the remarkably uniform cleavages of the resturantrices, and the rooms where aroma was all, where the olfactory reigned.

The dogs had begun to limp, shaking the vegetables from their orifices into the ditch.

"Are you of the persuasion," the Professor asked tentatively, "that our souls return to the animal world?"

"That I cannot say," Felix replied unsteadily, "but I do know that one can enter the world of animal spirits in this one." Then, as a melancholy afterthought, "Don't you see, my friend, we have the best of everything. It will never get any better."

The Professor, still smarting from his rebuff, said nothing. But it has to be noted that my father had ignored a small matter of which all men should be aware. The nose indeed is a fine, neglected thing, useful where character divination is concerned; nothing better to roust out the individual specimen, the undervalued stock, the hidden intention. But the nose is a bivalved operation, its mechanism primitive, on and off, and when it refuses to cooperate with the other senses (no higher in value, but elevated in altitude), when it refuses to acknowledge that there are too many intermingled scents to sort out, it does not do well. In its fine discrimination and delirious subtlety, it overlooks the banal and the obvious. So the dog will neglect another dog in the presence of a female fart. The hound will lose the game if presented with a delectable dainty. The Jew will ignore oppression if he senses liberty. The liberal will lose common sense in inhaling too much of his own goodness. The conservative will be overcome by mean-spiritedness with a whiff of reality. Father too often ignored the pervasive landscape, which lacks an opposite and leaves no trail. For when my father smelled love, he couldn't smell danger.

DRUSOC AND HIS MISTRESS
(Iulus)

Thus began an era when every third Sunday, like clockwork, the Professor would arrive by rented jitney, accompanied on his right by a woman, often attractive, always doting, and on his left by a dog, often dying, always insane. The threesome would circle the courtyard, the Professor complaining bitterly about the exchange rates at the border as my father patiently pointed out to him how he had been swindled again. The lady would be dispatched to the sunroom for tea, the animal isolated for sympathy. Then the ritual of transferring money on behalf of the ailing dog would occur. In effect, the lady's check to the Professor (a loan? A fee? A gift?) would be endorsed over to Father, who would hold it in escrow against "future claims and future performance," as he liked to put it, isolating the income stream from all notions of investment and return—pure exchange, love for love, trust for trust, mutt for muff.

Then the Professor would take his valise and wander across the beetfields, burning small tents of papers, a toy soldier ritual, which by this time was fast losing its drama. Clutching a thick sheaf of manuscript against the fading ember of a cigar, the paper took on the same yellow cast which never left his thumb and forefinger before it burst into flame. Then, after a depository visit to the potting shed, they would be off together in the open trap, with the best horses, the best dogs, and my best self.

On one of these visits, the Professor arrived in an uncharacteristically cheery mood with a particularly lovely colleague and a most hideous rat terrier, which, after alighting, walked between the horses' hooves without the slightest concern, then pattered directly with foreshortened stride up the front stair, through the open door, and upon entering the moonroom did something I had never seen a dog do: he went to the farthest corner, and there without the slightest concern for investigating the odors of a new territory visited by so many dogs (which would have driven any normal animal into an interrogative frenzy) lay down with his back to us, though it was evident he was not asleep. Apparently there were no written thoughts worth destroying that day, and our usual ride having been aborted by the curious indifference of the terrier and the exotic aura of the lady, it was clear that a *conversation gallante* would take precedence over any outing on this visit.

Mother always immediately inquired about one's ancestry, and as it turned out, this most attractive and animated woman was of Russian-Huguenot parentage, the first half of which she claimed no memory of, as it was obliterated by history, and the second of which she could not bear to speak of on account of their recent suffering in Berlin. "Governments are very wicked," she concluded as she sank into the couch. It was certain that she, like most everyone in our circle, was far older than she looked, a woman, as they say, of considerable experience, of which one wished to share only a third, and that preferably at third hand. Yet she was the type I so admire, one of those people who really believes that a moment's charm can make up for miles of derelictions. For example, one does not normally notice that a person is breathing, but I found myself counting each one of her breaths. It was clear in her face that she knew more about the world and its passions than anyone who had ever visited our house. The pillows on the couch molded to her like a conch shell.

The question of origins exhausted in record time, we fell into a long silence centered upon Drusoc, the immobile white rat terrier whose bulging pike's eyes lay embedded in a liver-colored spot covering half his face and most of an ear. Drusoc had indeed apparently made himself into a perfect pet, a cipher upon which every conceivable horror and longing could be projected. Not merely a companion, he had willfully emptied himself of every trace of personality, dropping not only his genus but all distinguishing traits, like a trail of old galoshes. This was a pet who lapped up your mistakes, allowing his unremarkable little white body to be tweaked with every twang from the unraveling rubber band in the toyboat of our mind, without shedding so much as a short hair, without so much as a snicker or a fart. Drusoc was of a species here well before men, and who will no doubt survive them. Generations had been sacrificed in breeding this near impossible task of assimilation, so that his own defining functions had totally atrophied. He looked at rats with a dull-witted, uncomprehending stare, rationalizing that if he could not catch them all, the pursuit of one would be mere pretense. In short, Drusoc had the integrity of the perfect object, upon which one could try out every half-witted theoretical sally and febrile explanation—the shaggiest jokes, the grossest anecdotes—and receive no objection. I missed Scharf and even Wolfie a bit.

Encouraged by Mother, the lady (who had somehow escaped formal introduction) began a story of how during the recent hostilities, when groceries were not plentiful, she would procure unpasteurized milk on the black market for Drusoc and herself, boiling it as a precaution. But occupied as she was with matters of an intellectual nature, she would invariably allow the milk to boil over, transforming it into a great insipid froth—not affecting its nutritive value, perhaps, but quite spoiling the taste. "And having no alternative"—this phrase was drawn from her bosom with considerable elaboration—she and Drusoc would drink the froth from the same saucer!

It was a charming story, and the Professor said so, striking his left forearm with his walking stick for emphasis. She took the interruption in stride.

"As it happened," she continued, Drusoc disappeared one night during an artillery raid, having gone out to the roof to relieve himself, where he become preoccupied with the flares bursting over the city. (It was unclear in which city they were or whose shells were falling, only that the lady was capable of great acts of courage, kindness, and dignity.) He had obviously returned, as his obdurate presence testified from the corner of the moonroom. But the point, she concluded, was that during the time she agonized over the loss of her companion, believing him dead, she never once allowed the milk to boil over! And there the story ceased with great emphasis, her lovely lips parting on a lost definite article. All her facial orifices were ovuline, as if to give shape to her formless tale, and as the last aspirant syllable floated away, she glanced up at the large mirror to review her finale.

The Professor, nodding vigorously in assent, exclaimed, "There! Remarkable, is it not!"

My dear parents' faces were full of genteel stupefaction, while the Professor's eyes were half-closed, as if in infinite reverie. I will say this: no matter how garbled or inconsequential the story, no one ever forgets such a face, such hair, such flared nostrils, such hands fluttering about such a mouth. That beautiful gash of lips, smeared with lipstick on the outline of her muzzle, so that her mouth seemed slightly off center, like a ventriloquist's doll's, now issued a single sibilant, indecipherable word, which sounded like "unk" or "uck"—a pig's word in sow's purse.

Father's knee was pumping up and down like an adolescent's.

"Would you like to see the American electric Bickford plough," he broke in desperately, "or perhaps shoot some hares?"

"So *this*," Mother interrupted cheerfully, as always insisting upon a certain narrative momentum, and gesturing grandly toward Drusoc's somnolent form, "this is what got you through your time of troubles. Forgive my husband, he is no politician. He sometimes doesn't read a newspaper for a week."

"My dear," Felix countered, "kindly dedragonize yourself. Why, just yesterday I read how the new discovery of graffiti scrawled upon a vomitorium at Pompeii demonstrates how the Visigoths breached with such apparent ease the Roman defense on the Rhine."

No one knew what on earth he was talking about, but Drusoc turned three-quarters, like a faucet, nodding to Felix while slightly opening one drooping, red-hawed eye, offering the merest yet distinctive echo of affirmation.

"Or perhaps you would like to spend an hour watching Drusoc learn some tricks," Father finished haplessly. But his attempts to restore a subject matter to the conversation, or plan a diversion from it, fell equally on deaf ears.

To hear the lady tell it (and there was no stopping her now), Drusoc was also apparently prepotent and promiscuous beyond all reckoning, and during my forthcoming travels, I would see his issue everywhere—phenomes of nullity, who, curled up in the corner, back-assed to you, are willing to absorb your most fearful and incoherent speculation into their ugly bodies and blow back something like a kiss. Drusoc, the no-problem pet, does more than take you on your own terms. He veritably eats them up, and deposits them later without detection on somebody else's roof, a condition not to be confused with whatever we infer about the noble aloofness of the cat, who is in fact not diffident at all but just looking, longing for a place that is eternally without shit.

But of course it was Drusoc's neurasthenia, not his vast powers of accommodation, which had brought him to our unlikely corner of the earth, and as the Professor and his lovely colleague unraveled the etiology of his illness to Father (whose jaw sank gradually into his clavicle, eyes straying sideward like a nervous horse's) they constantly interrupted one another, spending most of the conversation apologizing for their interruptions.

The gist of it was this: Drusoc had apparently come to believe that every series of steps ought to end with the right foot; therefore, each morning he would have to begin the day with an extra step, in order that his pairs of steps throughout the day would add up to an uneven number. This obviously pointed to a fundamental semantical confusion, and not at all the sort of thing one would expect of a rat terrier.

"You're certain you didn't try to hypnotize him?" Father queried the Professor.

"I never even looked at him! I swear it. Not so much as a glance!"

Father agreed that while Drusoc's condition was indeed intrinsically fascinating, it was not a problem he was put on earth to conquer.

But this was not all, the guests went on, tumbling over themselves. It seemed the dog also had a phobia for all plant life, every kind of grass and flower. He had no fear of any human or the wildest dog, nor the terrors of the city, and he could apparently distinguish between natural life and its representation. He would gladly curl upon the gaudiest flowered chintz, for example, but pluck a real daisy anywhere near him and he would be overcome by howling.

"If a bird should alight upon a bush, he sounds out a timorous bark of warning," the grand lady exclaimed.

"But if a ball should roll from the pavement to the grass, he considers it a total loss," the Professor appended, glancing at his bootlaces, which seemed to be unraveling themselves even as he spoke.

Father listened, nodded, and knocked out his pipe, spewing embers down his shirtfront, as he averred that he had never come across a case in which morbidity extended to all plant life. But then he announced that he must withdraw from the project, for even to contemplate this peculiar resistance for more than a few moments placed them all in jeopardy of mental injury. Then he suggested, somewhat drily, that we could take our drinks out on the terrace, and there on the slate pavers—the safe surface of the mineral world—introduce Drusoc to ferns and mushrooms one by one, though this fell rather flat.

Mother arose to replenish the tea, and as she vacated the sofa, the Professor, seizing the pretext to be nearer the ashtray, moved to her emptied place next to the lady, all the while expostulating, "How extraordinary, *befreundeter* colleague—extraordinary," touching her once on the forearm and then on the elbow, like a basso entering an opera with his single line, signifying only the proximity of intermission.

Father had put on a saturnine but rather forced smile. My mother, with her overdeveloped sense of propriety, returned with a fresh pot, and interposing herself between the guests on the divan, held one hand of each while she poured, supplying both connection and restraint. Drusoc assumed his recumbency in the corner, and I curled up beside him in the hope that my peculiarities might likewise be subject to their scrutiny. I noticed that the lady had very large lips, crater-blue eyes, and auburn hair frizzled at the ends, like a fox backing into its lair. I wanted to lick her all over.

The Professor was more affectionate with us than I had ever seen him, telling jokes, gesticulating broadly, as engaging as Father was increasingly stiff and formal. Mother was not disconcerted but simply alert and curious, rather like Lidi, our prize bitch, who greeted strangers by acrobatically walking along the topmost rail of the kennel fence. Then, as Mother poured the tea, the Professor began to stretch and yawn, praising the quality of our hospitality, the featherdown coverlet under which he had passed so many nights, the infinitely wide range of pillows, the nonpareil comfort of the horsehair mattress, unavailable since the breach with Italy, and then, pulling out his watch, which was now entangled with the virgin Dresden ringlets, opined that they would never make the last steamer. "I have never felt so safe in my life as in Cannonia," he finally sighed to his companion.

Father shot him a glance that would turn a bear. The Professor suppressed a slight blush, but it was the lady who sensed the severity of his warning. Drusoc, by now barely an epistemological fact, regarded them with one almost kindly, pale albino eye.

The lady was no natural storyteller, as we have already determined, particularly with such tension in the room. But she nevertheless launched into several anecdotes about long walks with interesting men of powerful intellect and weak nervous systems, the coloring of various lakes at different altitudes, the heat of Berlin and the chill of Dresden. I was most impressed by these descriptions of how the sunlight is focused like a flame when it suddenly appears above the rooftops of a narrow street, of savage and sudden changes of weather, of the grand shiver you experience before a roaring fire, of how one might break a saucer and throw out the cup in frustration, of how bubbles sigh in hot cereal properly prepared, and of how certain acquaintances induce a paralysis akin to the thud of an artillery shell.

But the more she talked the more it became clear we were headed for disaster, for just as the story became interesting and all her astonishing embroidery began to point to something, there suddenly occurred that hairball of a word, uttered at first with nods all around—an indecipherable phrase that was repeated quite often, but fobbed off in a way that would not only deflect the story but rob it of interest. Even a child could see that such a gratuitous gesture, harmless enough in the mouth of a gentle and sensitive woman or a surgical wordsmith like the Professor, could become a bludgeon of banality against we *misera plebs*. At first I thought this simply a vocabulary beyond my years, a *kinderbuch* of expressions abbreviated to spare me embarrassment, but as each loose anecdote was short-circuited by its interpretation in the wooden paraphrase, the dull glaze in Father's eyes—a glance of disappointment which only appeared when the cook tried to foist old eggs upon us, or the game had not been hung long enough, causing the blood to congeal in some unspeakable cavity—legitimized my lacquered heart. The moonroom had become a den from which no tracks returned. It was like being in a strange town of countless religious denominations, and all the church bells begin to peal at noon, so while you know that it's noon and it's religious, you can't tell one bell, one church, or one religion from the other.

"Well, it's a question of the *uck*, of course," the wondrous lady pronounced.

"Quite. The very sort of *uck* that Blederhorst denies," the Professor confirmed.

"He's on to something," she allowed, "but his is simply not a quality mind. The *uck* in his case is . . ."

"Primordial, yet annulled," the Professor interjected.

"Exactly," she confirmed.

The blue cords in Father's neck now appeared in his temples, and tiny diagonal bolts of lightning flickered across his forehead.

"Wouldn't you like to see the tobacco leaves hung up in the barn to dry?" he said plaintively. "Or watch the livestock choke on sunflowers? Just tell me, what would amuse you most?" And at this point of desperation, Father performed his famous conjurer's trick, throwing two half-shuffled packs of cards into a top hat, then withdrawing one in its original order and the other fully shuffled. Our guests barely acknowledged this, though Drusoc cocked a limp ear.

"As in America. No real *uck* there," the Professor perambulated, lighting another cigar and ignoring Father's offer.

"Yes, but no doubt it will be *repeated* there," the lady allowed.

"Perhaps the *uck* is there," Father queried helplessly, "even if they don't know it."

"*Uck* repeated there, or rather identical in its oppositeness?" the lady acknowledged, opening a small fan which she had kept up her lace sleeve.

"When they *are* differentiated," the Professor said, slapping his knee, "they will ultimately express that only humanity is really dead."

"But this too—will it not be secondary to overreaching itself?" the lady averred.

"Yes, ah, yes," the Professor sighed.

"Are you speaking of a frenzied soul, or a vague and tender heart?" Mother broke in hopefully, always aware of the costs of allowing boredom to send a crease across Father's face, and trying to avert the storm about to break over Semper Vero. But it was too late.

"The devil take it!"

Father's pipe had already shattered against the base of the fireplace, and with his own patented concatenation of boredom and rage, he leapt from his chair and stalked from the room, announcing only that their horses required preparation. Mother suggested that they have a smoke in the drive, now that the room was blue with haze. The lady seemed nonplussed, sagging everywhere but in the bust, but the Professor arose obediently and followed Father out the open front door, almost meekly, it seemed to me, without his usual bluffness, and Drusoc followed them phlegmatically to relieve himself on the wide expanse of nonthreatening gravel. As the lady passed me, she gave me a hard look and said, "You have a smile like one I saw once on a sign outside a barber shop." Then her bustle moved out through a portal of light like a barrage balloon.

"Please do not misunderstand me, my friend," Father began on the steps. "But the pleasant prospect you propose is impossible, even as I presume it. You are aware that I have met your wife, and your wife has met my wife. I believe the symmetry is not lost upon you. This is *my* house and *my* laboratory, not a nightclub. Your lack of discretion is none of my business, but neither can I expense it off the books. As with all things, I admire your *chutzpah*, but must deplore your strategy."

The Professor looked down at the loosening laces of his long shoes.

"I have been under great strain," he murmured. "Can you imagine what resentments one feels after being kind and tolerant day after day to people who have gone off the rails?"

"No one *here* is crazy, Professor. No one here is even remotely ill. Except, perhaps, this abortion of a white dog, whose main problem is that he's gone to fat. I only want to avoid embarrassment. This is not the bridge, sir, at which I wish to take my stand."

The Professor looked up in the air and sniffed like a confused pointer.

"It is an imposition, to be sure. I want of course to disguise the act, but also to share with her here, above the ordures of the barnyard . . ."

My father clapped his hand to his forehead. "Perhaps I am missing something here," he hissed beneath his breath, "but this is one subterfuge you must manage on your own, sir. Surely you can make the *L'Auberge L'Espérance* before dark, and their rear rooms, I believe, give onto a barnyard much like this one. If not, there is always the *Desdemona*'s steerage, though they often overbook."

The Professor, much to his credit, I thought, refused to be abashed. "I agree I am not faultless in this matter. Even the strongest character remains powerless in his pure being. Perhaps it is only that I have not availed myself of such opportunities in the past which now stiffens my resolve. But surely, if you will not find this forgivable, at least acknowledge my perplexity, cement our friendship, and accept my apology with that assent."

"My dear friend, it is not for me to give permission. I can only urge the usual canards about civility and common sense. It is not your urges, your appetites, at all; it's the way you have resorted to explaining them that sends shivers up and down my spine."

"Naturally." The Professor slammed on his homburg. "The business in any case has suddenly lost its taste. But there is one thing. You have complained about my visiting you with only psychotics, oddities, and a host of problems. But this dog, you must admit, is no particular bother, and the woman, though she is demonstrative, is remarkably discreet and modest in every way. Don't you agree?"

"From this standpoint, I am with you," Father smiled. "Do you not believe that I wish you every pleasure of the ancients? Do you not think I am myself curious about the sex traits of such a crazed beauty? But when you cross that border, you must respect my rules, and my basic rule is this: I could not live without my wife, and I will permit nothing on this property which might cause her the slightest discomfort. My friend, in this life I have been deeply desired, and whether I was deeply loved I cannot say, but the regard of that woman has meant more to me than anything in this world. She is the only woman who has loved me disinterestedly. I am afraid that a small courtesy to her must now take precedence over a larger one to yourself."

The Professor attempted to look sadder and wiser. One could hear only the *slop slop* of the harnesses on the glistening horses' backs. Drusoc sidled between Father's legs, commiserated with his ankle, and gave assent to the void, keeping one wary gray eye upon the avenging lawn.

"*Never* bring that dog here again," Father said evenly. "There is no reform for anomie. As for the lady, she is always welcome. But beware disciples, Professor: they will cause you more grief than any critic."

"My wife is quite . . . bourgeois, you know," the Professor spoke under his breath. It seemed a harmless remark, even a kindly one, but it threw my father into a mood for which none of us were quite prepared.

"The bourgeois mission, my friend, is to bring beauty and science, justice and bliss, into some kind of strange, temporary equilibrium. But the inevitable cost is to dilute the erotic. Nothing worse in the world than a dead marriage. Nothing more of a secret than a good one. You have your reasons, no doubt. But listen," and then he sidled up to him, walking as a mare does toward an acting-out foal—protectively, but finally annoyed—to whisper: "Let's admit it, Doktor, your *uck* aside for the moment—there's nothing like the love of a sane woman, is there? Without it life would be a pisspot, no?"

The Professor lowered his gaze sheepishly.

"You really *do* love women above all things, don't you, Councilor?"

"I do not share your theory that women are, or were ever, scarce. The problem is that women are everywhere, and even if they are after you all the time, it doesn't mean you'll get the good ones. That's the really odd thing. As you well know, I have been fortunate in females. It changes your outlook on everything. I don't wish to rub it in. Oh, I know the exasperation, the boredom, the rheumy children, the horrible expense of it all, the fact that you must often sit around pretending you have the strength of a stone when you feel nothing at all except the ebbing away of your own life, and then of course they fly into pointless rages and play the victim. Yes, it's quite exasperating. But when they love you, doesn't it make you feel, well, not a man exactly, but it makes you want to do something for them, no? Something for which you will gain nothing, perhaps. This is just chatter, of course, but wouldn't you lay down your life for them without a word? So long as one does not exaggerate, shouldn't one be kind to women?"

The Professor suddenly seemed to recover his balance and his dignity. "You know, my friend, how much I envy you in such matters. I would give anything to be in your circumstances. But while my experience is more limited and unlucky, I often deal with women who are not part of your ideal animal kingdom. Allow me to suggest that your good fortune may multiply itself toward *too* much of a good thing."

Genuinely moved, Felix took a step backward.

"I feel the gaze of racial disapprobation," he said haltingly, "almost as if you were putting a curse on me."

The Professor tried not to smirk. "I say this only, Councilor: women can be woe, and falling in love can be the *ruin* of a man."

"Oh, come now, Professor, I have loved every part of every woman since I was eleven. Even the Furies are rather cute, you must admit. One is nothing if not rooted in a woman's heart."

The Professor knew he was in no position to proffer more advice. "I'm no artist at this sort of thing, believe me," he sighed. "I seem to be obsessed by how small a normal favor in such a normal place might change my life."

My father turned back to the house, not in anger, but with a definite military movement. "You do not have to be normal to *infer* from the normal, my friend. As you have pointed out many times yourself, it's uncanny, isn't it, just how small, how tiny, the normal is."

The Professor cried out after him despairingly, "And nondescript!"

Halfway up the stairs Father turned. "We are Cannonians, sir! We waste a good deal of time over little things, and argue them to death. You have brought me, in my wasteland, examples of both perfect acculturation and uncomplicated desire, a veritable spectrum of New Thoughters and Modern

Miasmas, and it isn't fair merely to berate you for it. But you won't get a prize for today's collection of proverbs, I can tell you that."

Mother had come outside for the farewells. As the men separated, one going up and one down the stairs, she noted that Drusoc's mistress was carrying one of the Professor's manuscripts. I extended my fabulous earshot.

"I see you are reading a sad story," Mother said sympathetically to the now less-than-august lady, though privately she wondered how you could sleep with a man with such bad handwriting.

"What would you do if you were me?" the lady said helplessly, stripped of her *schmerz und lust*. "It is wearing me out, but what can I do?"

"The next time you visit, you must read with me sitting by the river. And then, perhaps, we should all take a long, cold swim."

"Oh, I should very much like that," the lady said, and her face changed for the first time from voluptuousness to a kind of wizened wisdom, just as a harsh staccato bird call fell from the wall of mountains.

"Oh, dear," she said. "Even the ravens are laughing at us."

"No, my dear, they are just laughing in general," Mother purred. "It's that time of day. Incidentally, do you find it difficult, as I do, to remember what you read?"

"Oh, indeed. Even what I believe slips away."

"Do you think one can carry culture without being an intellectual?" Mother wondered out loud, glancing modestly away.

"I believe I know what you mean, but I . . ."

"When I was a very young girl," Mother went on, seemingly talking only to herself, "we used to gather musk roses in the forest, staggering home with huge armfuls. By the time we reached the house we had dropped almost every one. But to have all our lost possessions again, we had only to smell our hands."

It was a melancholy dusk, but one without evident bitterness. The men embraced. The women shook hands. The carriage lurched haltingly away. Mother had packed a dinner for them in a basket, and Father fitted it out with ferns and mushrooms, as well as a few shafts of barnyard hay, in which the unpitiable Drusoc made a halfhearted nest. They had telegraphed ahead. The *Auberge L'Espérance*, an inn of passable noodles and occasional dancing, where the streetlights look like trees and the trees look like table lamps, produced a vacancy.

"Perhaps she is a communist?" Mother opined hopefully, as if somehow this would defuse or explain the situation.

My father had buried his face in his hands.

"This cannot go on," he murmured. "I have seriously miscalculated. We must look for another line of work."

She was tenderer then with him than I ever saw her, as well-affected as with a pup. She raised up his black face and kissed it all over, the cheeks, temples, and eyes.

"If we have no choice but to expose ourselves to the general public," she said, "we must be prepared to meet them on their own terms."

Father mulled this over silently, reveling in this rare display of girlish affection. "But that animal," he said hoarsely, "that *animal*!" It was not clear to which of our three visitors he was referring. Then suddenly he reached down, and snatching a clump of violets from the lawn, crushed them against his nostrils to expunge the encounter.

By the sideways motion of the carriage, it was apparent our guests were arguing, and as they disappeared into a caul of thunderheads, I thought I could see that grunted gongword, *uck*, float up and out into the empty theater of the Marchlands.

IULUS ASLEEP
(Rufus)

What manner of man was this boy who fled a Cannonia in flames? Merely the greatest spy of our closed, sad century, which has been very good to dedicated, cultured, and incorruptible spies. A true triple agent, a man of a thousand twists, Iulus had burrowed deep in the bowels of the latterly failed intelligence agencies of both East and West, but was finally loyal only to his own dubious, ridiculous, failed state. He hid his fear of the Communists behind a mask of contempt, and hid his contempt for America behind a mask of acquiescence; a triple bluff. For in truth, a spy's essentiality is this—a dedication to forever escaping the clichés of one's contemporaries. And, after all, who *can* you trust, if not such a spy?

An agent's greatness is tested only when his most precocious and accurate observations are disbelieved at the highest levels, and for the greater part of his career no one on either side accepted his essential brief—that both Russia and America, despite their windy rhetoric and vast armadas, were too big, too messianic, and too politically immature to do anything but culturally bankrupt one another—two pitiful helpless giants, who would eventually fall weeping and wailing into each other's ghostly arms.

There is a Cannonian fairy tale concerning a wolf hunt in which the dark beast is finally cornered in its lair, and at the last moment of a titanic struggle, the tortured and stunned animal leaps up, and putting his paws upon the hunter's chest, implores him in the strangely lilting voice of the eternally feminine, "to try and understand him." "And this," goes the refrain which so often ends their tales, "is how you are going to live the second half of your life. The losers have lost, but the winners have not won."

Although he would be the first to deny it, the records show that Coriolan Iulus Pzalmanazar was born in County Klavier of Cannonia in 1924, just outside the town of Silbürsmerze, an ancient silver-beating town of steep roofs, tidy public gardens, and an inn where the young philanderer, Goethe, had once spent a night. After dinner, when he believed his black poodle Pregestiar to be insulted, the poet precipitated a drunken brawl. Later in the lock-up, he justified his outburst on "feeling hemmed in by space, causality and time," setting a precedent for intellectuals ever since in blaming bad behavior on cosmic abstractions.

We now know this to be false, though only slightly so; Iulus's papers being one of many refugee passports concocted at the Silbürsmerze mint, his birthdate that of a typhoidal child who survived only a few months. We also know that he was first delivered to America in 1947 by a Cannonian submarine[1] off Mt. Desert, Maine, where after a close call with the local

---

[1]   The *Anti-Drakon*, designed by Amerakansi Golland, 1911. Steel rolled in Bethlehem, Pa. Shipped unassembled from Vancouver to Vladivostok, where the hull was tested as adequate by firing shells against the aquablinde sections, then by Transsiberian rail to the Nikolayev works at St. Petersburg.

Laid down 3 July 1914; launched 15 September 1914, as the largest pre-World War I sub, (Krab Klasse, designation AG 23) commissioned by Admiral Bubnov, christened *Imperatritsa*, and trialed under the ice floes where its two Tovaratsche mine tubes were tested as adequate.

1917, disassembled and sent by rail to patrol the mouth of the Danube. Captured in dry dock by Astingi sea robbers, refitted and relaunched under the Cannonian flag, commanded by the "Ace of the Adriatic," Max Von Trapp, who learned his English from James Joyce. After a tour of duty on the Mze (the first warship to call at Silbürsmerze since 1673), the *Indefensible* was quarantined at Pula, Croatia, and surrendered with the Austro-Hungarian fleet to Anglo-American hegemony.

Control transferred to Britain, November 1918. January 1919, transferred with new engines to the White Russians, Amur River Gunboats flotilla. April 1919, scuttled off Odessa to prevent capture by Soviets. Nevertheless captured, raised, and redesignated *Proletary* (Hotel Klasse) and refitted with Dzhevetsky torpedo drop collars at Bizerta.

1923, Caspian Sea, sunk by accidental flooding while being towed, with loss of entire crew. 1924, raised, double hulled, redesignated *Bolshevik* (Krokodil Klasse). May 1929, engaged Italian torpedo boats off Bari. February 1934, sighted stricken off Cosenza. August 1936, reported sunk in error. 1939, dismantled and shipped by rail to the Urals, for refitting by Bednay Metallist Machine Works; conning tower rebuilt, disposition of original to Naval Museum, Leningrad. 1941, transferred by Molotsvsk Canal to the Northern Fleet, redesignated *Stalinets* (Zippo Klasse). December 1942, beached at Rosta. 1943, bombed in error by Soviet aircraft; January 1944, deck replaced with

constabulary, he took refuge in Greenwich Village, posing as a tool-and-die maker by day and an abstract painter by night. He never required much sleep, having been brought up with a definite aversion to losing consciousness, and he always looked twenty years younger than he was, characteristic of his mother's lineage. Strange to find in a man without a country, without papers, without even a name, an almost imperial authority.

He frequented bohemian bars in the Village, and was accepted by the locals as one of themselves, though they gradually became suspicious when they discovered he was not an indifferent artist, and indeed was their intellectual superior by a wide margin. He drank and womanized in short bursts, and when he needed a vacation, adopted the guise of a genial salesman of gumball vending machines, his perfect Dublin accent and raconteurial genius making him an international social favorite and leading his shadowers to many dinner parties in exotic parts of the world.

Iulus would have been the first to admit that he had strong multiple loyalties, though he despised mere informers. His feeling, after all was said and done, was that if our purpose is clear, our identity is really of secondary importance. And in the modern world, a multiple identity seems to have become the absolute minimal requisite for survival, for life's greatest difficulty is supporting the character you have assumed. There is, it seems, in the Cannonian soul, as in Tudor England (the Cannonian's favorite period of history), little distinction between candor and discretion, public and private, inside and outside, fiction and nonfiction.

———————

aluminum. 1945, sunk in North Sea by explosion of petrol vapors. 1946, raised and reclassified as a battery charging barge, NAP 111. February 1946, failed to return from patrol. June 1946, located off Cape Tarkhankutsky, raised and reclassified as stationary training platform, redesignated *Communist*.

January 1947, sold as scrap to Cannonia, disassembled, transferred via the Rhine to Frankfurt-am-Main, thence via the Ludwig Canal to Froim-on-the-Hron, there by lorry to the Gulo Orphanage and Ironworks near Belta Bella. Reassembled, refitted, and recommissioned as *Anti-Drakon* (K-666), put into transatlantic service from Turdes, Albania to Mt. Desert, Maine by the Cannonian Foreign ministry. Sighted by U.S. Coast Guard, spilling oil off Newfoundland, 1952, 1956, 1968, 1975, 1981, 1984, reported lost in underwater collision in the Sea of Azov.

1989, reappeared in Therepia, refitted, and recommissioned as the *Clara Schumann*, a tourist craft for trendy youth, plying the straightened oxbows of the Mze.

He especially liked talking with the spinster women who typed the daily intelligence summaries. He found these ladies, spared the inert ideas of education, to be our most cultured citizens. He admired their clearheadedness, their lack of envy and sentiment, and above all their skepticism for the male games of leverage and deduction. "He made you feel that you were the only person on earth," one of them told me, "and as a result, you fell in love, not with him so much, but with yourself." Iulus never took advantage of these women. He promised them nothing. He simply knew that by being around them, he could eventually gauge our attitude, the degree of nemesis, the aura of anxiety—and then, together with a smattering of unrelated facts from public sources, simply infer our tactics. Having creatively empathized with those who disinterestedly *copied* policy, then went to the ladies' room to laugh like horses, it was easy enough to divine our strategic inclinations.

There are still those who see Iulus as a man with an unslaked thirst for secretiveness and conspiracy. Certainly he was an independent operator. Both the Comintern and the CIA sent him carloads of assistants. He would buy them a drink at the Waldorf and send them on their way. Indeed, that is what preserved him so long. Of course, there will be those who will ask how far we can trust such a narrator? This is rather like asking the question: can one trust a sonata?

Iulus had an excessive contempt for propaganda of any sort. Ideologically speaking, he had perfect pitch; he not only heard things as they were, he heard them as they *had* to be. The Cannonian loathes rhetorical pathos, self-puffery, and the eternal discussions that are mistaken for action. He never went near the operatives of other services; discussions of communism and capitalism bored him to tears. I never once heard him argue for a cause. "I'm a professional," he said to me one Central Park evening from behind a bust of Schiller with stylized hair and vacant gaze, "and the job of a professional is to make the easy look difficult." The man could hollow out anything—propelling pencils, hip flasks, Ronson lighters, even lipsticks, and he fitted out every other lamppost on the Upper West Side of Central Park to take a message. Despite the recent plague, these same boltholes are used today by those many Manhattanites who still prefer their risky assignations with an avid stranger.

As an attentive student of Oswald Spengler, he realized in his first few months of residence that democracy meant the complete equation of money with political power, that money eventually destroys intellect, then becomes its own destroyer. If Russia was one of those parabolic curves which announce the death of a species, America had "too much future to be significant." And he knew that the only thing his own unrecognized, unrewarded, and unloved country could offer the world was its historic stubborn refusal to equate wealth with authority, and its absolute refusal to think like a nation, race, or state. "There is no organism more prone to weakness and madness than a nation," he wrote, "and the smaller the nation, the wider the perspective."

Iulus had a special duty. If he ever managed to pick up evidence that nuclear war was imminent, he was to climb atop a large rock just inside Central Park at Fifth Avenue and 68th Street, and flash a radio message to the Soviet Mission at the United Nations.

Yet for every piece of information Iulus sent East, he issued a warning to the West. His principle of selection was simple. What tends to get ignored is what is obvious to anyone with normal standards of prudence, and such obvieties are almost always more significant than the deepest, darkest secret. He was his father's son in that he believed that the rise and fall of governments, like any marriage, can best be traced to accumulative inadvertencies and unconvincing denials, rather than grandiose elaborate stages—those perfect little stories of blow-off or collapse. And in fact, the most rare and courageous modern act of all is simply the disinterested raising of a cautionary finger by a person of demonstrated character.

Yet no one was more made for America than that acme of individualists, Coriolan Iulus, and no one, even when he was in profoundest contest with her, held the United States in more fond regard. "America!" he often said, "where you can deny, deny, deny, to your last breath!" And there was nothing he did with so much puzzlement and regret as passing on the quantified evidence of Americans getting exponentially dumber. Nonetheless, he knew that the esoteric analogies of the East, as well as the pathetic vanities of the European states, both missed the true salience of America—where through the deafening noise of church and commerce, a civil society had been smuggled in which an individual might profitably hide—a haven for those whose first order of business was to escape the ruinous influence of their own self-appointed intelligentsias. When there was no place left to hide in America, it would lose its grip upon the planet's imagination. America was not about hope. It was about escaping the tribe. "The great thing about the

U.S.," Iulus often said when being interrogated, "is that you can quit being an American without suffering terrible consequences. And those quitters can do some fantastic things. To quit flat out and *not* be exterminated for it—now there's an idea worth dying for!"

Cannonia and America had a special and preferential historical relationship, he insisted, beyond their shared distaste for oracles and pundits, as the only two nations in History of whom it could be truly said that all their wounds were self-inflicted. And what could Cannonia offer America? The wincing knowledge that there are historical periods in which you have to live without hope.

After all, you must recall, things *were* different then. All the configurations had flipped. It was the ancient American, toughened by his encounter with modernity, who was about to lead the innocent European out of the theater of megalomania; the American who would offer his hand to the blasted cosmopolite with the stained shirtfront, and maneuver him, without much grace, but without thinking to ask for anything particular, into the post-war half-life of tatty triumphalism, up-to-date torments, and unintended consequences. And once here, at the fag end of the *fin de millénaire*, after rearranging certain creature comforts, the American host turns to his classy ward with a mildly sardonic grin to shrug, "Dry hole?"

The natural fit between the Cannonian sharp temperament and the soft tissues of America strikes one as astounding, and one can only speculate on the consequences if more Cannonians had chosen to emigrate. Of Pzalmanazar's comrades who made the choice to escape, we see a similar adaptive energy, fired perhaps by the natural bond between those nations who ignore history and those who can only export it. Of Iulus's generation, I know of only three who came and survived. One, a high school physics teacher from the CharmNetz region, a woman matronly and mustachioed even in her twenties, became the only female admitted to the Manhattan Project, and this only a few months after her arrival. Another tortured soul, a supervisor in the Phamaphy factory, which made papier-mâché airplanes and tanks to be placed on runways and roads to confuse bombers, claimed to be a professor of Greek and director of the opera, and arriving with only a pack of Tarok cards with photos of murderers, sex offenders, and arsonists in the place of the medieval figures, soon became an associate at the New

York Psychoanalytical Institute. And a third, perhaps the best known to the general public, a portly former doorman at the *Auberge L'Espérance* near Sare, known for his unbreakable cheerfulness in the face of menacing inclement weather, was moved with alacrity to the seniormost levels of the Department of State, and often wore his old uniform to diplomatic receptions at the Eastern embassies. A talented race, the Cannonians, though not one, as we used to say, with whom you'd care to share a foxhole.

Iulus was the only man I ever knew who really understood America to the bone, partly because he was well-paid for it, partly because he had a number of perfectly attentive audiences, but primarily because of his unique education. He knew that lacking an interior discipline, democracies depended in large part upon a worthy opposition for momentum, and the worse thing you could do to a people who thought of themselves as a church and believed their truths to be "self-evident" was to take their enemy away from them. He also knew that the Dark Hero of the Secret Name was essentially about an inferiority complex, an obsession with predictability, an attempt to catch up to modernity. What the Soviets were too parochial to realize was that modernity had *already* destroyed traditional society in the West, and so their special path of maximalism was doomed to irrelevance, the freezing of petit bourgeois attitudes on a mountain of corpses. "They never had a chance," was how Iulus put it, as early as 1968. "They bored themselves to death."

It is hardly surprising that recent scholars have concluded that our "secret" operations in Cannonia had no effect whatsoever—and if anything prolonged the war, as well as the so-called Cold War, which in this writer's opinion was the most destructive and pernicious of all wars, the largest non-event in history—a bizarre sideshow of poetic illusions, a full life's lie that saw two great nations, each on the verge of fluorescence, abandon their inner struggles to export their kindergarten philosophies, inflicting millions of casualties upon noncombatants while erecting a great frozen glacis behind which all values decomposed. It will seem as obscure and incomprehensible to future generations as the Thirty Years' War does to us.

What an astounding thing, eh, that a little piece of the Enlightenment, that aberration during which the great religious movements were thrown off stride for a moment, should be set down so fortuitously in *our* trackless swamps and pimpled plains? For we have just barely survived the most religious century of all time—religious in the sense of the absolute triumph of synthetic explanation and doctrine.

Now Iulus was hardly your typical secret agent, not a mole or turncoat, not a cipher, palimpsest, cryptographer, or operator; not an undercover man, dissembler, or counterfeit; not a hawkshew, sleuthhound, scout, tout, or reconnoiterer; certainly not what he was often called, nigger in the woodpile, bug under the chip, snake in the grass, or a wolf in sheep's clothing. Not a flybull or derationator, not an informant, mouthpiece, snitch, or masquerader, not a sealed book, misprision, or huggermugger. He did not operate *in camera*, *sotto voce*, or *sub rosa*, or between you me and the bedpost, and most certainly he was no flatfoot, gumshoe, plainclothes horse, or house dick. In short, he owed nothing to those *contrapostos* who figure so prominently in our police entertainments, those marvelous sedatives that present every mystery as a legally punishable exception. "It's easy enough to catch the murderer," he often said. "The true detective is the one who prevents the murder."

Iulus's charge, as he patiently explained to me, was to create the perfect cover, to meld into the population, becoming simultaneously infinitely forgettable and unforgivably acute, retaining no allegiance to a foreign power, even one as inchoate as Cannonia, but expanding his sympathies totally with his adopted culture so he might better identify its breaking point. His "mission," if one could call it that, was when reality finally stepped forward, when the erratic mucoid snore of America's sleep apnea was particularly deafening, that he would be the only one awake. "Living the other's death; dead in the other's life." This is Heraclitus, of course, the only Western thinker who makes any sense at all to the Cannonians and their Astingi comrades, with their love of puzzles and the darkest riddling, for thinking in their view is not real thinking unless it simultaneously arouses and misleads one's expectations of symmetry. But their love of riddles has a moral dimension which is easily missed; games for them are also always ethical tests.

In the Cannonian cosmos, the Sleeper, as the bright twin of Death, does not experience a private phantom world, but while unconscious remains responsible for the conscious universe. This reaching through and across history is the distinctive Astingi blasphemy, destroying all our conventional notions of identity and the psyche. "Living, he touches the dead in his sleep; waking, he touches the sleeper."

How I would miss his profound but smiling pessimism, his nacreous intelligence, this fideist to the school of gliding. He was one of those strange people who, having rectitude, didn't need freedom. Even now, rereading his scattered cantos, it is as if he is sitting in the room talking personally with me, the secret of all great writing.

UNDER THE STARS

(Iulus)

Of all country things, the Professor was fondest of camping, sleeping outside under the grave stars with stories round the fire. We hitched up the oxen to the open wagon, filled its gunnels with hampers of fresh food, blue bottles of seltzer, dark brown bottles of beer, a great pile of feather comforters, some Turkish army tents, and tarpaulins of fleece. Then all of us save Ainoha pushed westward a few miles, horses and dogs running free beside, until we were quite alone in Klavierland, except for the herds of aurochs who stared at the oxen as though they were deformed. Given the slowness of our entourage, which included many of the servants, and the muddy banks exposed by a detumescent Mze (which in our part of the country often changed directions at the whim of its dead, diverted, underground cousins, sometimes flowing east and sometimes west; Father claimed to be able to determine the direction by smell), it was decided to take the ferry at the Sare landing, above Reil Island, where it was said the ashes of Achilles and Patroclus mingled with those of Helen and Ajax.

The ferryman's house was a Lilliputian villa with whimsical bays and gables, and when the hunting horn sounded, his wife emerged at once, accompanied by a rooster. She raised a pennant on the ferry as we boarded, and by tightening a pulley against a taut wire beneath the water, let the current draw us across. The rooster perched upon the rudder, his lurid Bersaglieri tail feathers fluttering in the breeze. As the ferry nudged the far bank, he strutted over to Father, accepted the half-florin toll in his beak, and returned it to his jolly mistress. Then, transporting our *vie de chateaux*, we proceeded northwesterly into the land of no roads, no inns, no fables, and no police. It may have been the most bourgeois of caravans, but I felt as one with the Astingi, volleying a hail of arrows into the sun as they swarmed the Aurelian walls.

In the evening Father selected an islet of silver poplars and twisted cork oak, and in no time he was cubing the meat and slicing the potatoes into an iron pot suspended from a tripod. Father presided over goulash, Catspaw received the task of tethering the horses and clean-up, and the Professor was assigned to keep his eye on whatever dogs were to be spoilt that day. He had by this time learned to turn them with a single shout.

We spread the sheepskins around the fire as the sun stopped short and finally fell away. No one missed it. As the fog rolled in, the goulash was ladled out into metal bowls, stippled tin wirled with green, brown, and white, and then the call went up for stories.

Seth Silvius Gubik, in addition to his other talents, was also quite a raconteur, with the terrible ability to sum up a life in a phrase. His stories were transliterated from the flutter of his deaf and dumb Astingi mother's hands, dead stories recounted discontinuously as he searched for words to match her recalled sign language, halting mid-sentence as if he were a painter cleaning his brush before each stroke. This stammering only added a sincere affect. Gubik was otherwise a totally quiet boy, diffident even, but in the midst of these cacographically related tales he was most fully composed. True, they never came out quite the same way twice, which of course only added to their reality. No one thought this contradictory or a subject upon which to build a world philosophy. He had the perfect audience, for we all took joy in hearing myths exploded and religious themes flattened out of existence, and the long pauses, the aphonia of his delivery, made you feel that you had somehow made it up yourself.

At first he did not get on with the Professor, being the sort of wise child whom adults consult without condescension. They tried to be sarcastic about it ("And what do you think of this, eh, Master Gubik?") but surprised themselves by at bottom being sincere. The Professor was often angry that the stories never made a clear point. Their legendary unity was often scrapped entirely, or relegated to a kind of background noise.

Gubik's manner of telling was so unaffected that one could not object to even the most bizarre relation of fact, and so seamless that one could not interject, though there were certainly sufficient intervals to do so. Nor did he seem particularly invested personally in his tales. He neither dismissed objections nor tried to refute them. He refused to professionalize himself.

There was in his manner a wide-eyed incredulity, as if he were passing along something so obvious that one should really not make too much of it. In short, the Professor had to question the entire enterprise in order to participate in it, but found himself relocating all his queries onto hopelessly abstract grounds. Gubik listened attentively with a slight smirk, not of certitude exactly, but secure in knowing that while the game had been removed temporarily from his stadium, it would gradually find its way back. It was clear, nevertheless, that he sometimes incorporated objections to his stories in later versions. The Professor rightly saw this as the most hurtful kind of rejection, like a dog who sits before you politely, with all the earmarks of alertness and respect, but simply does not come. There was no lofty singing from this precocious boy. He didn't know a strophe from an antistrophe, and he was on principle against the chant.

"An unshorn dog story, then!" the Professor cried out, as Father ladled more goulash into the bowls.

"Which one?" Gubik answered. "Found by dogs, suckled by dogs, led by dogs, or torn apart by dogs?"

"Whatever you wish. Whatever comes to mind," the Professor said with an earnest grin.

Gubik held his bowl with both hands, slurping slowly, and we all followed the bobbing of his head. "So then," he began as always, licking his lips slowly and batting his gray eyes, "from the dogs of the God Actaeon, I think, or perhaps it was Cromises the river god . . . In any case, a certain god in a certain grove had a pack of dogs, and from the finest of these he created a mysterious race of men and women, the Telechines, to fill the gap in the hierarchy between artisans and magicians. And unto them he gave a golden dog, a statue to remind them of their origins, and another sort of hellhound to stand upon the mountain and guard them, a dog with many heads, some say three."

"Hesiod mentions fifty," the Professor interrupted drily.

Gubik went on, pleased as always to be interrupted.

"This hound guarded the way to the cave of death, letting anyone pass who wished, but allowing no one out. The golden idol was beautiful, but cold and stationary. The guard dog was hideous but alive. On this golden dog the Telechines could lay out all their complaints and praise, all their poems and lies, and the golden dog was . . . mercifully silent."

Gubik smiled slightly and measured us. "The golden dog gave birth to a piece of wood, which was planted and became . . . a vine? The many-headed dog gave birth to serpents, vermin, and fish. The horse mackerel, the sea sheep, the late-dying prepon who wiggles for hours even when cut in pieces, the clearch who takes his sleep outside the sea, the nimble, tumbling gobi, and the savage race of sea-mice, the crooked pouple . . ."

"That will do. No more fish, if you please," Father interrupted, knowing well that when Gubik entered a lyric phase, he tended to lose the thread. Gubik was grateful also for this intervention—in fact, it seemed to energize him and his *voce velata*.

"On the golden dog they laid their poems, lies, and hopes, but he did not complain; that is why they worshiped him. Here was a god . . . As for the many-headed dog, he barked throughout the land at every movement and word, the same short, sharp, deafening bark—of affirmation, distaste, or warning it was impossible to tell—and occasionally he let forth a whine or a howl in which no person, act, or event could be distinguished. Now it happened . . . that a giant rabid forest pig came upon the camp of the Telechines, wreaking havoc and ravaging the land, uprooting the vines and goring sheep. Several warriors were sent with various weapons, but they failed and were killed. Throughout this, the many-headed dog at the cave was strangely and uniquely silent. They sent more heroes and even highly paid mercenaries against the forest pig, but none could deal with him. It was then decided that this was too serious a matter to serve as a test of individual courage. So for the first time they banded together in a hunting party, young and old, slaves and masters, guests and women, including among them Marea, a golden-haired, snow-souled girl and most reliable archer. A buckle of polished gold confined her vest, an ivory quiver hung upon her shoulder, and she possessed a pack of the fleetest hounds. Onto the hunt they pushed, stringing nets in the woods from tree to tree and, moving them ever closer, they encircle the monster's lair. But the forest pig bolted and broke the net, and after killing several dogs and men, hid in a marsh among the reeds. The men followed his path, sinking to their waists in the mire. Marea watched all this closely. She sank, too, though not quite as deep, and then slipped her hounds from the thong, and they splashed up to their long ears in the muck. Soon the reeds parted as the beast began to move, the only clue a slight furrow in the marshgrass. Then Marea took an arrow, loosed it at the point of the furrow, and the beast sprung up wounded, spewing blood from its nostrils on the green flowers. The dogs were quickly hard on his flank, turning him toward the floundering men. Finally, four or five of the warriors, covered with black mud, lumbering as slowly as in a dream, plunged their spears into him. The last of these, the rock-footed youth Melagor, threw his spear behind the last rib, and with this the forest pig leapt up and fell furiously in death. A shout went up, glorifying the conqueror. But Melagor cut off the ear and a tusk, and presented them to Marea, insisting that the girl whose hounds had trapped the boar, and whose arrow had drawn first blood, be awarded the prize. This was the first and final gesture of love. Not a trophy or gift, but simply a gesture of fair due. The other men insisted they would be shown up, despoiled by a mere girl, if she were given the trophy, and an argument ensued. They ripped the tusk from her hands and then began a violent argument among themselves. Marea made a grave mistake here. She laughed. At this a battle in the mud ensued, and Melagor inadvertently killed one of the men. This was the first sin, though some say it came before. The girl who at first had blushed and laughed now tried to pass by, still carrying the pig's ear. With slain warriors at her feet, the girl who was at first indignant, then amused, was now hysterical with grief, and these strange emotions, laughter and tears, so soon upon one another, stopped the men momentarily, and caused them to reconsider that the triumph, inexpert as it was, was somehow to be shared. But soon they were fighting again amongst one another, not for the glory but so the other could not have it, though by now the ear was shredded and of no use to anyone. The god of little faith watched this athletic spectacle in utter boredom. He had not gone through his furious motions to watch such predictable and banal sport, and resolving to begin again, changed all the Telechines into stags, forgetting Marea's hounds, who remain to this day in the marsh as pike, and once the god had exited, other tribes easily caught the stags and destroyed them. Now alone, Marea leapt into the sea and was turned into a star, lit with a low blush . . . ”

Gubik concluded his obmutescent soliloquy, took a long drink of soda water, and waved his hand as if brushing away a fly. The group around the fire fell silent.

"That's all?" the Professor insisted, flabbergasted. "I mean, it's not exactly Goethe."

Gubik crossed his arms and said nothing more.

"They changed their minds," the Professor insisted. "It's the beginning of civilization you're describing. They saw their error."

"Yes," said Gubik, smiling with impromptu gravitas. "But it was too late."

"Ah, yes," Father echoed absently. "Too late. Right from the beginning."

"And no one came to their aid?" the Professor said.

"No one," Gubik said emphatically through a thin smile. "Dogmeat! The aurochs laughed so hard milk came out their noses."

"And the star, the girl who changed into a star," the Professor whined. "What was the name of the star?"

Gubik shook his head slowly. "Just one of the stars," he said laconically.

"Then there's no lesson at all," the Professor said curtly. "It's not very charming. I mean it rather dribbles out, don't you think? You don't make any connections!"

Gubik licked the rim of his bowl. "Thus far and no further."

"There are, Doctor, you must admit, some pertinent if pessimistic observations," Father broke in, as always protective of Gubik. The Professor was growing slightly apoplectic.

"Then what, may I ask," said the Professor, now at the far side of exasperation, "is this story of injustice called?"

Our Astingi Homer squinted and looked up into the sky.

"'The Dog in the Manger,'" he stammered. "There are probably better stories." Then he rolled over and covered himself in sheepskin, and soon we were all asleep, save the Professor and Catspaw, who, with the help of an astronomical atlas, were scanning the heavens for the star of Marea.

"So full of holes, so flat," the Professor was moaning, "no respect for either verisimilitude *or* illusion, and yet," he pounded a fist into the flat of his hand, "everyone is entranced."

"Strange how the ancient bards were so unobservant of nature," Catspaw said consolingly. "Virgil didn't know the Pleiades from Pisces, or whether the moon was rising or setting." And then he uncorked the plum brandy as the Professor produced two Trabuko cigars.

The two men leaned against the wagon wheel, alternating puffs and swigs, until the phosphorescent constellations doubled. And though he had the weaker eyes of the two, it was the Professor who first spied the star sitting directly upon the Eastern horizon, and laid a hand upon Catspaw's thigh.

Catspaw squinted at the low blushed light for some time.

"A shepherd's fire," he dismissed it as, and returned to his oral pleasures in a doze. But ten minutes later, the Professor again squeezed his leg.

"It's getting brighter."

Catspaw took another look, and with surprising agility climbed into the wagon bed. He emerged with an old-fashioned, long-barreled American squirrel rifle and a pair of Zeiss binoculars.

"In all my years in the Marches," he said, "I have never seen a shepherd moving *toward* you." He adjusted the glasses, closing one eye, but could make out nothing but a faint glare, perhaps six miles off. Concluding this was no heavenly body, and that the odds of something benign approaching you in the Marches at three o'clock in the morning were nil, he did not wake his Master, but checked the tether ropes of the horses and oxen in case he had to fire the eardrum-shattering rifle. Resting the weapon on the iron siding of the wagon, he brought the long barrel to bear on the flickering light.

The Professor inquired as to what he should do.

"Mind the dogs," Catspaw said only, as he stuffed his ears with moss. He felt underwater in this new alertness, as vivid remembrances sprang forth: the schoolmaster putting a thermometer in his mouth in a musty classroom, his first fall from a horse, a village church burning down, a corridor of lime trees, his mother's freckled arm encircling his neck, his father's drooping lower lip after his stroke . . . and then he was aware of an intoxicating and unfamiliar perfume—conifers, acacia, lupines? No, none of those, but some combination of human, animal, and herbs. He was about to fire when he took one last look through the glasses. It was Ainoha at furious gallop on a sweat-streaked Moccus, carrying a torch and rising in the stirrups German-style, led by old Sirius, still our best tracker. Her knees were bare, and her flowing skirts were kirtled up about her waist.

As the dazed sleepers roused themselves in confused welcome, Moccus snorted through his vibrating nostrils, then stamped about, foam dripping from his teeth. His musculature seemed hammered metal, his bulging eyes like stone. All the animals, even the oxen, were respectful of his entrance.

Ainoha, just come from a dinner party, was attired in a white empire dress of astonishing boldness, its transparent white muslin leaving her bosom bare. She rode barefoot on a tight pea-yellow English saddle, and rather than a crop, an ivory fan pierced with emeralds hung from the wrist of her long white gloves. She was paler than usual, a trace of childlike obstinacy below her regal coiffure.

Father, uncharacteristically dumbstruck, reached up to swing her down from the saddle. But she simply handed him a violet telegram, like a good adjutant. It had been delivered during dinner by a particularly officious but weary messenger. As it was in Russian, she couldn't decipher it, and thought it urgent to get it to Father. Messages from the East, infrequent as they were, generally were of momentous importance, and she knew his trips into the Marches had a way of stretching into weeks. Father kissed her hand as he tore open the envelope. But it was not even from Petersburg, and far more startling, was addressed to Master Seth Sylvius Gubik. It was an invitation from the rector of the Moscow Conservatory for a scholarship audition. A second-class rail ticket would be awaiting him at the Chorgo Station to be claimed within a fortnight. Father began to translate the telegram for Gubik, but the boy snatched it from his hand, saying, "I can make out Cyrillic." Then he read it aloud to the astounded *manège* gathered in the Marches, opening his bloodless mouth in a terrible smile, revealing carious chipped teeth, his gold fillings sparkling in the firelight.

This harmless missive quite out of the blue, which no one, even Gubik, it seemed, had any inkling of, precipitated the most perfunctory conversation and threw the routines of encampment into disarray. Even the sunrise seemed reluctant and uncoordinated. After sour bread and burned coffee it was decided that the family should return at once to Semper Vero, and it fell to me to accompany the Professor back to the border, and if no Skopje were available, thence to Sare—taking care not to run the horses home.

I had always been instructed not to engage the Professor in conversation unless he initiated it, so that he might have the opportunity to reflect upon the object lessons of the day. He rarely said a word to me in those days, but that was partially due to the fact that the actual landscape, which theretofore had only been a backdrop in the press of canine lore or literary analogy, was gradually becoming visible, even startling to him. I realized that this was the first time he had experienced the landscape of Klavier without a dog in it.

The ancients saw the Marchlands as a "nightland," not properly sea or air, but somehow unromantically concocted from those elements. Their suspension was not easy to walk on, and though well-watered, impossible to navigate by sail, oar, or boathook—only during shallow floods caused by high winds were they accessible. Their only architectural feature were lighthouses, built by the Astingi apparently out of contrariness—for why should only the sea have lighthouses?—though no one could recall seeing one lit. The plain was technically not swamp, steppe, or desert, but, commingling the three, an anomaly of neither volcanic nor oceanic origin, never forested, where no shrub or tree larger than a man would grow. Indeed, nothing taller than a man could exist there; even the fallow deer and wild ponies were of shoulder-height, along with darting, bite-size birds, tiny fingernail butterflies, and dwarf scooting rabbits no bigger than a rat—though a dozen skewered on a spit over an open fire could be the high point of a lifetime. The herds of diminutive and nonthreatening ostriches, llamas, and camels introduced by Grandfather Priam in his Noah phase thrived in the Marchia; a place, in short, where human scale was finally oppressive and where, like heaven, visitors invariably remarked upon the shortness of the grass. This no-man's-land had been subdivided into lots in the seventeenth century on the premise that the velocity of the trade route would create another boomtown. Yet for three hundred years no one had bought so much as a sliver. One could not project a plan upon it. Nor could one imagine improvements upon it, any more than divine its history. It was the lord's own subdivision, the infrastructure intact, your basic shrubbery in a grid of lots and no demand. For a man on the run there was no place to hide, for a man with a plan there was no one to take him up on it. It was a province of the utmost idleness and carelessness, where procreation itself was initiated by a slight nervousness or boredom. Even the railway had skirted the area, preferring through some combination of engineering perversity and convict labor to be built upon cedar pilings.

Always lush with grass and underlain by an enormous aquifer just under the surface, not so much as a trickle of a stream crossed the Marches. Yet water was everywhere, just beneath a network of roofless limestone and coral caverns studded with opals, complicated as a neuron. It had neither hillock nor true swamp, forest copse or declivity of any kind, and for that matter, not even a single rock for miles. The terrain absorbed our common violent storms effortlessly, yet its huge filter was so packed with moisture it would not burn, and thus was abandoned reluctantly even by the prehistorical personality.

Unlike its sister steppe, its soil would grow anything you put into it with absolutely no care, but never at a rate of growth acceptable to modern agriculture. If ploughed it would become cloddy and slick; to fertilizer it was vaguely indifferent. The peculiar lime-green grass was so elastic that it defied the scythe and clogged the mechanical hayrack. It produced no minable minerals, yet the soil was so fully nutrient that it was toxic to domesticated animals. Entire herds perished, falling over with a collective sigh in a heap, poisoned systemically by a sudden overdose of trace elements. Wildlife, however, continued to thrive. It supported more species than any other part of Europe, as their reduced size was disdained by royal hunting parties. Spared the atrocities of agriculture as well as the euphemistic and even more destructive "hunting and gathering," it was a place to picnic and loll, and to carry out one's little experiment; and above all to sharpen one's eye. It had its own ecological integrity, for the Astingi believed that whatever or whoever you killed in the Marches was doing someone else a favor.

In our family album there were photos of ladies in sailor suits and parasols stooping for an extinct wildflower in the Marches; aunts masquerading as young girls with pigtails and flowered aprons seated in a horizonless rectangle of air, a clutch of newborn goslings in their laps; a mysterious woman in a striped double-breasted suit and straw hat, standing with her easel in the scrub with no subject it seemed, conveying only the aura of a stylish woman with time on her hands. There were photos of Grandfather standing in a black fedora and velvet cape, his back always turned to the camera. Every scene with him was exactly two-thirds sky, flecked with enormous glandular cumulus, and one-third muddy ground. A hazy uneven horizon implied the fluvial course of a river in the distance, but was in fact only the road to the ferry, a seam of top-heavy poplars and goiterlike topiary shaped by the absence of any care. My caped grandfather never looked out to the horizon, but always gazed toward the ground, at the faint trace of an old wagon wheel rut, which, creasing the strange wide-bladed grass, soon disappeared from sight. It was kind of a farmer's field, or rather a rough sketch of one, as if a full crop of sweetgrass had been pulled from some edenic meadow, transported to this plain, and carelessly transplanted in irregular tufts, dried and scrofulous.

The main feature of the *Marchia*, besides the itsy-bitsy game, were the wells, a veritable forest constructed of large locust trees lugged from the foothills and topped so that only the main fork remained. After the trunk was wedged in the sod, a hickory log exactly three times the length of the forked tree was laid at the fulcrum, creating a natural lever. The hickory log had been wrapped in burlap and soaked in hot lard at its friction point, and a weight, if possible a Roman millstone, was then lashed to the shorter end for ballast. At the lifting end of the pole a leather thong was noosed and attached to a brass swivel, and from there a rope fell spiraling upon the ground. Only then, where the noose dropped, was the actual well-digging begun, dirt being slung around in great arcs by the diggers, and in no time at all, one meter at the most, the shallow aquifer was exposed, the mud taking on a silken, vulvaic sheen. Then a box of oaken slats was built to keep the bubbling gloss pure from grazing game. Once this reservoir filled, a wooden bucket was attached to the rope, and a good fellow might leap up and grasp the pole just ahead of the stone, and hanging there, his arms clasped about the hickory lever, observe the log rise slowly as a bucket of sweetish, slightly carbolic water would be hauled from the Marchlands—an elemental brew.

The strange thing about these wells was that no man or animal really had need of them. No one had ever gone thirsty in that country, and of the thousands of wells erected on that plain I sincerely doubt if more than a handful ever swung a drink upward to anyone.

Eventually, the "Y" of the locusts sprouted new limbs and shoots, the pivotal architecture of the redundant pump slowly refashioning itself back into a tree. On the hickory fulcrums the bark shredded and fell off, the treegut glistening and hardening to a coarse gray like wet stone. And not a few were carved, whether by the horns of rutting animals or the steel of idle men, it is difficult to say.

In the spring, great irregular seepage pools formed about the rectangular boxes, so that the lifting mechanism was reflected in them, and yet they never even earned a proper noun. There was no name for them. "You know, the ----!" the Astingi would say with a smile and a shrug, holding up two fingers, one less than their usual salute.

Lopsided crosses, shattered capitals, polylifts, inadvertent art, machinery not born of a function but in search of one—it was this woodland of unmanned, unnamed drooping poles, this no-man's land of pointless ionic hydraulics and arrested pumping, this forest of levers with its unsettling religious quality, that the Professor had to traverse to turn homeward, until at the northern border of the Mze the fields suddenly began to whimper and submit to the ambience of dovecotes and lighthouses, as prettiness broke out.

We proceeded with impeded canter and the jingling of curb chains toward the ferry landing. Although the Professor had been given the gentlest of the piebald mares, every time her hoof struck a stone it went directly to his heart. His hands had begun to hurt, and I gave him my riding gloves. He shifted to ride in the burdock beside the road, but I warned him to return to the roadway, as the prickly burrs would accumulate in the joint behind the hoof and cause infection. Finally, he found his seat, and the mare pointed her ears and settled into an affected, dance-like gait. On the ferry, pestered by midges, she became restless and kicked out her hindquarters. I made a low whistle, putting one hand upon the mare's brain, and the other soothingly between her flank and the Professor's knee, and she quieted down. On the far bank not a carriage was to be seen, so I suggested we proceed to Sare by the old military road.

The periphery of the Marchlands was not without its history of bloody stalemates, the Marches themselves being too soft a terrain for a battle proper. Offering no vantage, no cover, and such fragility, only a single man with a good dog leading a good horse might traverse it and not sink into the hidden river. While the wars of the last century had made not a dent in the wildlife, the unburied dead routinely surfaced in the floods, skeletons with their helmets and boots intact, a perfect row of steel buttons between the ribs. Even halberds, swords, spears, and cannonballs were occasionally belched up from furious geysers. This band of warring, serpentine rivers coiling back upon one another, where every property had a water view, was noted on the ancient maps as *Inter Canum et Lupus*. It was open country where the fool for love might gambol, and the loathed ex-lover might lick his wounds. And though many a flag had been hoisted on the horizon, no battle had actually been concluded on that ground. The monotony of the landscape was only superficial, for it was home to an enormous variety of species and held an equal variety of enormous, submerged hatreds. If no actual ruins were to be seen, traces of every form of failed social architecture had survived in a twilight where one might ponder the most astounding things. For between the dog and the wolf, as between their human versions, there are really only two stories—that of the wild being tamed, and the tame reverting to the wild.

We passed through a toll gate at the military border. Constructed in a bad imitation of the wells, its crotch sank lower in the ground, and the lever forming the gate was fir, three times the length of the well standard, with a cargo net full of cannonballs for the counterweight. The fir was squared off and thinned with an ax down to the tip, where the rope, connected by a chain apparatus, fell not to water but to a cogwheel to haul the gate down. It took great strength to crank a gate, which is why they invariably remained open at forty-five degrees perpendicular, an angle high enough that the tallest hayrick might pass beneath. Once beneath a gate, hat in hand, passport in the other, the primitive leverage of the wells seemed benign, big check marks in the sky, as if you had accounted for all the inventory before you left and could now do business without anxiety.

Of course, there were times when distant artillery shook the already tremulous ground in these fields of nothingness. The well levers in the Marches would seem to rise on their own, the locust sprouts shocked into bloom, and the toll gates would be cranked down, at which point no amount of love or money could open them. There existed no document lucid or authoritative enough to get you through that station, but when finally released, the two-ton gate would spring up like some child's toy.

The two armies manning the borders had similar uniforms; only the colors of the epaulets and the weave of their braid differed, and both had a defeated look—puzzled faces and broad, unreferenced gestures, many of them maimed and on crutches, sitting around waiting to be demobbed or disembarked to another front. Occasionally they would form up and fan out in a long column, two abreast, simulating a withdrawal or reconnaissance around an empty field. And semi-occasionally a file of these hangdog men in full battle gear, packs sagging at the small of their backs, rifles slung butt-up over a rounded shoulder, would appear like phantoms out of the fog, but they would never look you in the eye, much less threaten. Another day you might find them all on one knee, service caps crumpled in one fist, at Mass. But their most common and dignified maneuver, it appeared, was squatting on their field latrines, half a dozen at a time, those waiting in line knocking pipes out on their rifle butts, bayonets stuck in the ground, staring out over an embankment or a half-filled trench, writing letters on each other's backs.

On anniversaries of major battles the two adversaries would have a soccer match among the wells, or a boxing competition on a tarpaulin stretched from stump to stump in a patch of woods. But more often than not they would simply lounge around the benches by the gatehouse, holding hands sometimes, lagging the coins of the realm, which depreciated before they even hit the ground. Theoretically, they were locked in primordial and eternal combat, but in fact both were armies in full desultory retreat from politics, ideology, and nationalism, from the cant of every discipline, comical but serene.

Any time I felt, as one increasingly did in those years, that the impersonal forces of history were grabbing hold as the hum of the social machinery started to miss, every time I felt such an anxiety, I would ride out to watch those aimless soldiers guarding the unmarked foggy border, pants crumpled around their boots as they eternally sat on their latrines, and be touched by the moments of tender feelings of men lost in the last outpost—soldiers who in the end had become skeptical of every plan and were protected by nothing but the commonplace delicacy of their own displaced credulity, pondering how to refuse the abstract mission which had befallen them without being traitors. And while I come from a long line of noncombatants, never put a stick to my shoulder as a child, never learned with my tongue how to make the sound of a gun, I loved those crumpled, fragile, degarraloused soldiers as much as a man could love another human being. Parades never did a thing for me, and serried ranks assembled brings up in my gorge only the great graph of Napoleon's four hundred thousand setting out from the Marchlands to Russia, and returning in the cold with less than ten thousand men, marching without fear and hope.

Those guard-stations at the gates were more full of life than any art I ever saw, more beautiful than ballerinas. Common soldiers no longer brave, no longer lads, not prideful yet gay, covered with scabs and lice, pay in arrears, their only amusement half-decks of cards and half-finished letters, soldiers who, silently and collectively, provided the greatest moral example by simply refusing to be killed.

The green steeples of Sare had come into view. We trotted though the empty cobbled streets in the moonlight, and I left my charge at the train station, also deserted save for the little green locomotive, which was being washed.

If any of this made any impression on the Professor, he did not say.

It was two in the morning when I entered the lime-tree avenue of Semper Vero, the horses trotting on their own accord. Everything on that transparent day had given me pleasure. A thunderstorm was coming up, and as the first rainbursts crackled down, the horses' withers glittered like a dung beetle's back. Once in the stable, they swiped at the fragrant hay, then playfully brushed each other's faces, batting their silken lashes and pawing at the stable floor. Saddle and bridle removed, they exhaled and flung themselves onto a small haystack. Kicking out all four legs and running like dogs in their sleep, they petulantly destroyed the fodder racks, knowing that this night's grooming would be up to them, groaning in their stalls.

As I entered the hallway I could hear someone playing scales, as was often the case in our house, any time of day or night, but these were exercises of stunning rapidity and monotony. From the top stair I could make out Gubik's back working robotically on the Bösendorfer, preparing for his audition no doubt. But then I noticed a fat book with scarlet bindings open on the music stand, which he was reading while playing, repeating the scales over and over, as if he were only pretending to practice.

TOPSY AND THE PRINCESS
(Iulus)

An enormous black-lacquered Panhard-Levassor limousine, whose exaggerated aerodynamics, as with so many French designs (which ape the birdlike only to end up reptilian), was the first automobile ever to arrive at Semper Vero, its bonnet still throbbing even when the engine was turned off. I was astonished to see Öscar Ögur at his footman's post, only moderately drunk, and for the first time in memory in full uniform: gray-green jacket with horn buttons, gray riding breeches with scarlet revers, and knee-high polished boots. The car was quickly surrounded by a few shaggy fieldhands and slender, wistful goosegirls. Mother, attuned only to the echoes of quadrupeds, had for once not anticipated this arrival; indeed, she was still abed as I ran to rouse Father from his lair. Only when he emerged, gruff and disoriented, did Öscar open the car door, and there Felix recognized the still beautiful if melancholy face of Princess Zanäia, dressed in a simple muslin dress with a single string of pearls and rubies. And behind her, the stolid chocolate gaze and arch benevolence of the Professor.

That very night the Voo returned, or rather his dog did, a final inane augury demanding divination. Azure flecked his mottled back, dappled golden light set his scales ablaze, and in his heads, left and right, his jaws were clamped about the whitest of femurs, while in his middle muzzle, his lips were pursed ovulate, as if around a vowel. He stood there a long time, straining as if to defecate, offering me the bribe of sleep. But omens no longer impressed me, for what good is foretelling if you cannot prevent the disasters you foresee?

"It must be a quarter of a century since I've visited your . . . *parc*," the Princess announced wistfully. "A wonderful place to discover that childhood is not all asexual, *non? Hélas!*" She turned slightly to the Professor, holding a hand to her breast. "I cannot keep my eyes fixed on any single face or feeling. The immobility of the eyes is forbidden to those who survive." And then she moved serenely, save for her darting glances at each footfall, up the staircase to greet Ainoha, who had just emerged in a hooded capuchin robe to mask her disheveled hair and sleep-filled eyes.

In the car Felix could make out a dog with its face squashed horribly against the windscreen. The rear compartment of the Panhard, with its needlepointed empire jump seats, held a number of crystal decanters, several small portraits, an herbarium full of fern specimens, and great wads of manuscript.

"And we've brought you some sardines," the Professor winked, as if this were a gift to the fishiest tapestry on earth.

Father's first reflex was to move toward the injured animal trapped in the limousine, but sensing his concern, the dog bounced at once through the rolled-down window, exhibiting that it was not maimed at all, but merely an extremely brachiocephalic specimen of a golden chow, its undershot jaw smashed back in its skull like old green potatoes.

"*Now* what *petit toxemia* have you brought me?" Father chuckled beneath his breath.

"You see before you Sophroniska Vom Pouilly-Gepackt," the Professor said proudly. "The Prinzessin calls her 'Topsy.'" Topsy staggered with self-importance out to the oval lawn, and before she knew it Father had slipped the Dresden links upon her.

"An interesting specimen," he murmured. "Full of nothingness, yet oblivious to it." Then his eyes flared on the animal as if to calm her, as one sets a fire line to contain a larger one. "Put on this bow, my little bitch," he said to her. And then, linked by the telephone cord, they walked about the grassy circle, entering for a moment the netherworld of direct apprehension.

"The fair sex, as with asteroids, are either coming toward you or going away from you. That is the first thing we must determine," Felix intoned, "though with *royalty*," he grinned, "we can measure where they have been, if not where they are going."

"She appears *supernormalian* to me," the Professor beamed, though Topsy had begun to stray impertinently as the Dresden circlets imperceptibly swallowed one another, an aimless sluttish gambol, the chief aim of which was apparently to advertise that her every sense was as good as dead, a fact to which Father at first gave a little slack of compassion. Topsy had brought all the self-indulgence of the future Age of Solipsism into Semper Vero with her scraggly arse.

"We have a saying in Cannonia, Professor. 'From a dog, you will never get bacon.'" Then Felix walked on, relaxed and erect, whistling a little Turkish march, mimicking Topsy's minimal alertness like a flaneur in a strange city for the first time who pretends he is lost to see what random reaction that might precipitate. This calculated air of absence caught her attention. He cut a scallop from the circle on the next pass, just a fraction, taking the rind off their route and making it ovoid, the telephone cord gradually straightening, until it was taut as the horizon. And then, with the greatest delicacy, he gave neither a *pop*, a *snap*, a tug, nor a yank, but something at once more forceful and precise—a pulse before the beat—which drew the collar ringlets taut just above the larynx. This caused Topsy to catch her teenage breath, and thus inverting her sense of smell, focused her brain upon her sphincter, and, like sensing a burnt cake taken out of the oven in the next town, take in the faintest whiff of the invariance of life.

Of course, she lunged. But the impersonal mechanism did its job, the simple line of force instructing Topsy that it was *she* who was injuring herself. Then Father spoke.

"Topsy," he said, as if she were the most important person in the world, "so *schtupid*!" And their eyes, blue above and bronze below, met for a moment in a single violet transplant.

Another lunge. This time determined and powerful, as a man walks more deliberately when his hands are tied behind his back, but the line of legitimization, the opposite of breathing, again enforced itself.

"Soooooooooo *schtoopid*!" Topsy's eyes bulged at the judgment, the first virginal sign of focusing, after surviving a few footfalls of fear. And then they walked on together in a little collective shudder, not interested in diminishing the circle any longer, but only in maintaining a proper distance, Topsy watching Father's mouth out of the corner of her eye. Then it happened. She took a single cautious step, not without spring, and perhaps for the first time ever—like a man who has done his first backflip and then never forgets how—it was evident she was paying attention to where she was going, not just following her nose.

"So *schmart*," Felix said softly. "*Sie schmart*, Topsy!"

They took a few more somewhat grandiose turns, feelings without names pulsating along the cord, then Father stopped short without taking up the slack, and Topsy copied *him*. He reached down, and patted her head.

"*Schmart* Topsy," he said, and then removed the collar. "Nunc scio quid sit amor" ("Now we know what love is"), he muttered to himself.

The Professor stared incredulously. "So schtupid? So schmart? That's the whole of it?"

"All for now," Father said cheerfully. "Never work a tired dog." Topsy rolled on her back in the grass, arching her spine, as if to rub away the stain of the experience. "Lest the neurotica become psychopathia."

"And what do we call this . . . methodology?" the Professor sniggered.

"Ah, Professor, try to be serious for a moment. The only true method is this: you try to hear all the notes before you hum the tune."

The Princess had been watching this demonstration attentively through her lorgnette like a drowned man. "She's just like me," she murmured sadly. "A little barbarous, but only on the inside. It won't come out." Topsy had begun to walk backward like a snail trying to fit itself back into its lost shell.

"She seems to have no particular problem," Mother said brightly, wiping something from her eye. "She is beautifully shaped, with perfect little feet, and her nostrils are expanded more than I ever saw in any dog, I think."

The Princess smiled mysteriously. "Her only problem is . . . abdominal."

"If I may say," Father interjected without a trace of irony. "The fair sex, though possessing unbounded and most *proper* influence over *us*, have but little control over their canine favorites. This is because when they take the poor soul for a walk, they constantly call to it, lest it should go astray. Ere long, the dog pays not the slightest attention. There is also a varying in the tone of voice which generally prevents teaching anything beyond the art of begging. 'Beg, beg, beg, sir. Beg!' Am I not correct? And sitting in a begging attitude is not an agreeable position for a dog. One might quite as easily teach her to dance, hold a pipe in her mouth, shut the door, pull a bellrope, leap over a parasol, or drag forth a napkin and spread it as a tablecloth. What would you have, Princess?"

The Princess had once made a show of good will and benevolence to those who, being different from herself, could not imagine her true interests and tastes. But she now made little effort to explain herself, knowing that in most cases this would be futile.

"Your husband, my dear," she turned to Mother, "seems a man very much in contact with his *uck*."

Ainoha reacted as if she had been struck by a bullet, and quickly braced herself by grasping the Princess's forearm, which caused her in turn to blanche. The very mention of that word, and the merest chance that it would set off the causeries of abstract chat of the last visit, threw a fear into her she had not experienced since seeing a dog run over in the road, and watching it scream with pain as it dragged its broken hindquarters off into the woods. She resolved to lock the door forever on this lumber room of discourse.

"Do you enjoy diving, Prinzessin?" she blurted out.

"I beg your pardon!"

"Diving. You know, into water." Her voice trilled back in her throat.

"Well, not since I was a child," the Princess murmured. Her sadness had, if anything, deepened.

"Then it's settled. We must recast the days of your youth here. I'll take care of everything. Then we'll go shoot some arrows." And as she rushed her guest into the house, the men doffed their hats, and even Topsy herself seemed somewhat relieved.

"Another didact, I see," Father said under his breath.

"Her virility and station have caused her a great deal of suffering," the Professor said evenly. "She deserves your every consolation."

"There are, no doubt, griefs and distresses no physician can measure. As for little Topsy, who can say? She is either a little too absent or a little too present, and always a little off center. Beauty with nothing else is worse than shit. You can mix all the raisins you want with turds, but they're still turds. But who knows, we may see a bit of progress yet."

"We are in need of a success," the Professor intoned. "This woman, who can have anything she wants, is desperately alone."

"In my experience, friend, privileges are more difficult to overcome than abuses. I trust you have arranged for the fee. *Avanti!*" And with a wave of his hand, Father gestured across the river. "We will work the high ground first, to see how she behaves when she knows her mistress is not watching after her. We must take care to never use any words she is likely to hear from others. And please remember, Professor, hallooing spoils the sport."

Then he strode off, singing an old Venetian ditty:

Three golden horses
taken from the heathen.
A marvelous fair pair of
gallows made of alabaster.
So the Duke himself
might see the punishment at hand.

The ladies disrobed quickly, like schoolgirls, in the great hall of gray vibrating radiators. As the suits remained wet, they decided to swim in their chemises, and as they galloped down the path to the bathing beach, they could make out Father and the Professor traversing the shallows upstream, with a recalcitrant but unleashed Topsy following them by leaping from one slick stone to another.

"Have no fear of the diving board," Mother announced over her shoulder. "It was left over from the piano lumber, good Cannonian pine used to line the trenches in the Balkan Wars, blasted with shrapnel and blood, and therefore incapable of splitting or further mischief." This was something of an exaggeration, but our board was huge indeed, jutting fourteen feet out into a lagoon entirely concealed by reeds and anchored with a clutch of welded cannon balls. Ainoha sprung immediately to the end of the board, and without hesitation accomplished her patented half-gainer, disappearing into the Mze without so much as a fleck of foam. When she resurfaced and shook her golden mane, she saw the Princess follow her with only slight trepidation, though she held both her nose and mouth when she jumped, producing a fine geyser. They floated on their backs spitting modestly and scrunching their toes. Then, on a shawl, upon the weedy beach, as their crinolines conformed to their wet bodies, they regarded themselves intently as they turbaned their wet locks.

"My husband," the Princess offered as an icebreaker, "is a disgusting fellow."

The swimming hole marked the edge of the first Stone Age settlement in 6000 BC. At that time a riverine ledge extended completely across the Mze, a natural ford and the future site of a Roman bridge. But the attraction here for the mentality of mankind's first predatory age was not the crossing so much as the whirlpools just beneath the ledge, which churned up vast amounts of nutrients and attracted carp, tench, loach, pike-perch, and sturgeon. The votaries discovered in this settlement's burial pits were human heads with fish lips, as well as cave paintings depicting trained dogs diving into the tawny river to retrieve live fish, as they believed the whirlpools to be bottomless. The river and their dogs gave them everything. There was no need to bait a hook, cast a net, or sharpen a spear. The Mze washed away every little miserable existence, and its banks provided water chestnuts, sloes, field pears, rose hips, cornel cherries, wild plum, and crab apple. Yet the site was soon abandoned, and it was this ledge, now exposed at low water for the first time in anyone's memory, that Topsy and her pedagogical duo traversed until they came to the Roman central arch, where the remainder of the ledge had been blasted away in the early nineteenth century for massed boat traffic. From the broken arch, a slatted rope bridge enjoined the far cliffs, and Father carried Topsy this final third.

From my vantage on the chapel promontory, I could see far downstream, across the ledge and bridge, past the bathing beach, and well onto the old mill where the Mze bent double and disappeared. There I was taken aback to spy my Waterman, lying beside the drying riverbed, leaning secretly, silently, invisibly upon his elbow. His hair was matted, and runnels of water ran from the hem of his green overcoat into the disappearing Mze, like muddy tributaries to the sea. In the streaming weeds and waters of his face, he was smoking one of Father's innumerable lost and waterlogged pipes, with an acrobat's smile. And in his lapel, a bright green leaf sprouted from his gray, storm-broken trunk.

The Mze was ebbing away. The Mzeometer, a calibrated Roman well at the old mill, could have confirmed this, but we disdained even this most elemental of scientific measures. The river was doing its best to flood, to no avail. The pastures were no longer striped. Where streamlets, subterranean aquifers, and proud torrential brooks once entered the river, now were only baked gulches, deep and narrow as saber cuts. The effervescent runnels in the banks had quit, and the receding waters revealed tin pots and the carcass of a laced boot, as well as rusty culverts discharging waste from god knows where. The true self-forgetfulness granted by the contemplation of water was no longer possible. There was not enough left to pray to.

High above the ladies, cresting the bluffs on the far side of the river, the two men strode through grass up to their waists. At first submerged, Topsy started to leap up dolphin-like from the sea of lime, until they reached the bald, which had been cut through with gravel allées to an abandoned folly, slippery for men and painful for animals—another French idea. Suddenly a cold breeze had come up.

"The time has come to transfer the lines of force, my friend," Felix said. He slipped the cord and passed it behind his back to the Professor's clumsy hands, and the two figures staggered out upon the bald like a hung-over couple who just met at a New Year's party and cannot decide whether to go to a hotel or a *coffeehaus*. Topsy did not test him out of pity, and the Professor was reluctant to press what seemed an overly tactile advantage, recalling with embarrassment his ineptness at vivisection and even the most cursory minor surgery.

"Stocks and bonds," Father said, "that's how you must learn to think about this. We're the bond boys: we decide when to leave the house and when to return. But once underway, the animal is free to lead or lag. We can move in opposite directions for a while, but we can *never* be decoupled, even if we wanted it. That is what is so hard for human beings to understand. We are tethered not to our own, whom we abandon on a whim, but to animals, as to the market, by an unknown sentiment."

The Professor at first was silent. He did not mind Felix acting like he had an ace up his sleeve, but he did not like him acting like God himself had put it there.

"Can it be that nature is so bourgeois?" he asked.

"Ah, how many times have you invoked that phrase, Herr Doktor? Let us not, if you please, rush to the cupboard of concepts so quickly. Dear friend, the bottled members of the bourgeois are more difficult to grasp than the profoundest of geniuses. It's much easier to deal with a Franz Schubert, than, say, that 'cheese of a man' over there. And what is the essence of bourgeois thinking?" Felix wagged his finger. "Preparing for the eventuality when the romance is over. The dog does not anticipate that he will lose his love. On the other hand, he behaves because the friendship might end. He is aware that it can end at any moment, yet he makes no contingency plans. So with animals, the foolish human cycle of romance, rejection, and reconciliation is collapsed to a workable order. There is no forgiveness after the fact, which is just as bad as punishing after the fact—bad with men and catastrophic where females are concerned. But this is what gives us room for movement and maneuver, and upon which we must now capitalize!"

And with that Father sat down upon a pink granite plinth, his head cocked slightly to one side to watch his charges. The man and dog moved tentatively across the bald.

"Loosen your gait, Professor. *Heftig, wuchtig*, you haven't been drafted, you know. And this is no funeral!"

And indeed, as the Professor allowed his ankles to loosen, his spine to sway, Topsy picked up her feet with a bit more merriment. "*Kraftig, nicht zu schnell!*" They had reached the line where a graveled track crossed the grass. With their backs turned, they stopped and stared across the broken path as if it were a wild Russian river.

But they had stopped together, without so much as a tremor between them, and that was the point. Topsy sat down gently, her golden cape settling about her haunches, and the Professor's shoulders seemed broader for a moment, almost athletic. Father nodded approvingly.

"Anything diagonal across the body relaxes it," he said. Then the Professor's hand dropped tremulously to Topsy's muzzle.

"So schmart," he crooned, "so very *schmart*."

"*Cantabile*, Professor, *non troppo lugubre*, if you please," Father said. "Now turn and take care not to get tangled, *sehr langsam*."

The Professor accomplished a cautious half-circle in front of her nose, and then as the couple headed back toward Felix, Topsy pirouetted on her butt and they moved as one, a perfect arc of affective slackness in the cord— arm in arm, so to speak.

"*Schmart*, sie *schmart*," the Professor chanted softly, but then self-consciously he broke his stride, and the cord suddenly drew taut. Topsy resisted, and the grace note fell away flat. Both master and pupil looked mournfully to Father, who, walking quickly toward them and taking up the cord, took Topsy through a quick series of snappy turns, in order that she finish strongly. Then, as he released her to run, he said over his shoulder:

"Walk the walk, Professor, *then* talk the talk. It's moves that make views, not the other way about."

At the ford, a furtive, boney stag with a broken rack and patchy coat appeared, pawing at the water. But as he pricked up his ears and crossed, there were no splashings, no white-fringed wavelets about his fetlocks. Here was a river that could be stepped in twice and twice and twice again, the Heraclitian riddle broken: no flow, no flux, no exchange—only stasis. Left foot, right foot, still he could not step into the river, even once. I saw that my little aesthetic trick, my devotion to the precious pause and the language of omission, was a flimsy thing, for in this world the basic constant is not change, despite its many apologists. What goes unremarked is that, without any reason, things just stop. For nature loves to hide, and history is mostly stillness.

My Waterman seemed quite content, even louche, out of his element, constantly lighting and relighting his sodden pipe, and pouring a stream out of a figured urn into the blackening marsh. Fish occasionally stuck their heads out of the water to stare at him, as they will sometimes do for sick men.

The ladies had known of each other since childhood, but heretofore had seen one another only from a distance. Through the turn of the century, the Cannonian royal family had left their wooden palace at Umfallo to vacation at Semper Vero for the summer, as the nether-reaches of our acreage were still technically part of the royal hunting grounds. It had been the decision of Zanäia's father, King Peveny, to live as the people do for the best part of the summer, for it was well-known that rough as a peasant's life might be, they invariably looked out upon beauty, even while locked in a starving carnal embrace. Every member of the court changed into peasant clothes for the season, living in elegant Turkish tents and small portable cottages brought in by oxen. Princess Zanäia herself resided in a small gabled treehouse, a portion of whose parlor still remained in the crotch of a huge beech, which could bear the weight of her many surreptitious nightly visitors, though by now the view had lost much of its charm. But the court kept its distance from the gentry, suspicious of any intercourse with the upper middle classes, and as the gentry themselves of course felt morally superior to the aristocrats, they got along quite well. To underline the simplicity of the royal summer, a large scaffolding had been erected between the trees, suggesting some kind of pagan sacrificial platform, and around this stood supercilious servants in frock coats, each standing with a flaming taper by a satin footstool. There were as well some large and rather unconvincing life-sized dolls, impaled on tritons for Scythian effect, as the royalty liked nothing so much as to remind themselves that they, too, had once been classified as barbarians.

This *mise-en-scène* was framed with long wafts of diaphanous silk trailing down from the beeches, making a kind of osmotic proscenium. It was as if they could only accept the view if it were made commonplace while you were looking out and pornographic while you were looking in, creating a kind of allegory, though suggestive of what it was hard to say, except that the traditional invasion route had been turned into a kind of slow-motion *debauche*, particularized by large potted plants, beautiful young city boys, angelic peasant girls, petards, and Vaseline.

King Peveny himself was a strange man, given to visiting exhibitions in Cannonia about foreign lands, then writing speeches giving the impression he had actually traveled there. Once, when bouncing his darling, curly-haired Zanäia on his knee, he had looked at her sideways, saying, "You know my sweet, if you were in a brothel, you are not the one I'd pick." In their most recent hysterical quest for a ruler, the Astingi had sent out feelers to all the royal houses, magnates, and grofs without privilege, even unmarried daughters of the higher nobles. But nothing remotely like a prince would consider them, except one Grof Peveny, "Falconer of the Hereditary lands," who, tired of hunting rats in Poland, was enticed by the promise to take unlimited Cannonian forest pig from horseback. But despite the unprecedented game potential, he reluctantly withheld his candidacy for a time, as he perceived the ancient hermit kingdom to be a troubled place. Yet times were such for the minor nobility that he was finally forced to accept the regency. So in 1875, Grof Peveny moved his loyal retainers, sporting chums, knockneed horses, and scruffy dogs to the wooden castle with no stairway and a leaking roof at Umfallo, where to polite applause, and with only a single assassination threat, he summed up his feelings in his acceptance speech: "My people are neither handsome nor gay, meseems. They are neglected, superstitious, and ignorant. But they are indescribably picturesque, and I have learned to love them." And then they all stood round and sang the new national anthem, a reorchestrated Astingi revel.

Over the creation of thy beauty,
There is a mist of tears
Oh my poor strange land
How long have I kept watch with thee . . .

Princess Zanäia and Count Zich had been heavy petters of a sort since thirteen, and the Count had been credited as her lover, an improbable distinction. Each of them liked nothing better than to take the *Eroica Express* anywhere. That famous train was twice as long as any in Europe, its double-hinged steam engine running wildly as if in terror of itself, hauling its notorious Cannonian first-class sleeping coaches, in which all the bedrooms were adjoined by secret inner doors, and each car in turn bracketed by ornate buffet and smoking carriages. Theirs were intermittent and compensatory attentions in later life, consoling one another with infinite tenderness and solicitude during those intervals when the other had driven away another lover, due to a gross instability and selfishness which they knew better than to practice on each other. It was noted in Father's daybook that had they been joined in matrimony and publicly practiced the management science and cosseting they adopted when the other was most forlorn, they might have shrewdly ruled the Central Empires, and entirely sidestepped the horrific detour of the twentieth century.

The two women regarded each other evenly. It was the first time they had been this close. The Princess was in remarkably good fettle, Mother thought initially. Her skin was ivory with no crowsfeet or créche at the neck, but as her slip settled about her wet body, Mother noticed the Princess was a veritable web of scar tissue, sutured expertly to be sure, as if one had taken a vellum map of Cannonia at its greatest extent in the Middle Ages and superimposed upon it the late-nineteenth-century railway system. There was a much-repaired main spur across the bridge of her nose, crescents beneath each ear and jowl, trunk-lines beneath the breasts, and a strange, serpentine freight-changing yard at an angle to her navel.

They spoke of surgeries, their mutual fear of microbes and loathing of physicians, not to mention the men who you have to teach to comb their hair and eat with a fork, and who then deceive you. "Marriage is an entombment," the Princess whispered hoarsely, carrying out the general line of argument she had begun, "but my husband is the only man who will love me to the death."

Mother refused to be drawn into this. "My husband brought me out of childhood without pain," she said. "He freed me from the gods of the riverbanks. I can never forget that. And in all relationships, everyone enjoys in different ways, and different times, the position of the master."

"But what, my dear, do you *like* about him?"

Ainoha thought this over for some time. "Well, he remembers what he reads."

"You *can't* say so!" the Princess exclaimed.

"And he makes no claim on feelings he doesn't feel."

"*Extrordinaire!*"

"Yes, and there's this: he suffers over *real* things."

The Princess appeared downcast as she studied her faux-tigerish nails, registering the boredom of a triangle player in a symphony.

"But isn't it odd," she blurted, "how resentments start to build even the very first day?"

"My only regret is that there was no one to steal him from," Ainoha averred. "That would have made it perfect! In any event," she went on, depetalizing a daisy, "the problem is neither of the marriage yoke nor one of equality. The issue is how to be superior, or so I've always thought."

"How well you put it," the Princess laughed, her absentminded expression dissolving for a moment.

"And the problem with superiority," Mother mused, "is how to show it without being unfaithful."

"Ah, yes," the Princess cawed. "I may love my country, *mais mon cul est international!*"

The ladies' frank talk was interrupted by coarse shouts across the water. On the towpath on the far bank, thirty pairs of horses, interspersed by an odd brace of water buffalo, were towing a ship upriver, the craft itself still concealed around the bend. Preceding the ship in a dugout canoe rowed by four men, the pilot called out to the driver managing the straining animals on the bank, and while ropes twanged, horses whinnied and zillions of frogs and birds began to scream, he cursed them through a speaking tube: "Heave, you cuntbitten crawdons, you dodipal shit-a-beds, heave on!" Just then, around the bend appeared a small three-masted frigate, Count Zich's *Penelope III*, green sails lashed to her mast, its twenty-four rowers straining furiously at their portholes. At such moments Ainoha loathed the river, a ditch of universal filth and violence beside which sat women deflecting the desperate glances of men looking up from work of which they had little comprehension except its difficulty, and no aim but to escape it in their arms.

"Heave, you ninny lobocks, heave you turdy membertoons!"

As few boats were worth towing on the arduous journey up the Mze, no passengers were ever carried on these return trips upstream, only the most profitable cartage. Generally, the ships were abandoned downstream, broken up at Therapeia, and sold for scrap. Through her opera glasses, which she was never without, even in the water, Ainoha could make out the bulky cargo lashed to the deck between the leering sailors. It was an Astingi theater set. The *Penelope III* carried the sky, the earth, a bower of roses, a dungeon, a town's spires, many swords and spears, as well as the sun, the moon, and a great sheet of winking stars—Astingi props, being towed against all the forces of history and nature.

The horses stepped in the wake of the others like a caravan of camels. The drivers ran among them, keeping the towropes from entanglement, alternating lashings with gifts of oats. The towpath often disappeared and the horses went up to their bellies in the foaming muddy water. The sailors, dressed in Venetian garb, ran to and fro on the deck, bidding sweet farewell, saluting, and finally gesturing obscenely toward the two unblushing, unmoved women on the foggy shore.

In the half-hour it took for the *Penelope III* to pass, the Pilot was the only man on the river whose back was to the women. Ainoha saw the captain on the fo'c's'le, his spyglass trained upon her. She raised her glasses to the bluffs, where Father and the Professor strode back and forth, occasionally waving their arms at each other, totally absorbed in Project Topsy. She could see the hair in their ears and the sweat on their brows.

"It's almost as if they're dancing," the Princess said.

Across the river, below a rocky ledge wetted with streams, Ainoha could also make out an Astingi squadron emerging from a dark wood of unlimbed beeches. They were in ceremonial warrior garb, carrying lances of cornel tipped with iron, and burnished quivers stuffed with blue lead darts. Their glossy golden mounts wore purple saddlecloths and golden snoods with golden bits clamped between their teeth, and both horse and rider wore pliant twisted strands of gold upon their upper chests. But as this vanguard cleared the wood and descended upon a large bald, the Field of Mars, striplings practicing horsemanship appeared on either flank, like birds driven inland from the sea. They rode barechested, their pantaloons held up by suspenders of their mothers' hair, skulls smartly slicked beneath wolfskin caps, one foot roughly booted, the other bare. The commanders cracked their whips as they weaved left and right, and behind each, two files of six boys rode in open columns. The columns cantered left and right, wheeled, and with their lances lowered, charged one another, alternating parades and counter-marches, retreats and skirmishes. The Field of Mars was white with bones, and on its distant reaches one might still come across the skeleton of a horse, its ribs plunged with the skeleton of its rider, surrounded by an iron hedge of spears. Fertilized with blood and ashes, the earth sprouted giant nasturtiums and violets which would make the best dog giddy, even faint. Horses got the bends, cattle bloated and toppled over. Bees locked their feet in clouds over gargantuan lilies; even the butterflies were punch-drunk. But now this field was sere.

This was no patrol but a mimicry of combat, and its seriousness was sealed when Mother saw the Shaman himself, never before present during maneuvers, observing from the edge of the wood astride a huge stallion with white pasterns and a snowy blaze across his forehead. He alone was dressed simply, no military decorations nor an ounce of gold, his white beard flashing down his raspberry tunic into his lap, and armed only with a cello. The Astingi were on the move to enlist new gods.

Topsy was salivating and the Professor was perspiring. Father's hands were moving slowly, doing a bit of detached minor surgery upon the air.

"I believe she is beginning to understand," the Professor said.

"One can understand a great deal and change very little," Father said absently. "You can't change ability, but you can change attitude."

"But she is behaving, no?"

"For the time being, perhaps. You must learn to listen to those who won't answer."

"And then, dear friend?"

"And then you must make sure that *your* silence is perfectly understood. And then to make your cold silence, warm."

"Either you are a genius or the worst charlatan, Councilor."

"Ah, no," Felix said quietly, tugging upon an invisible leash as if he were fly-fishing, "hardly a genius. I just know how things *are*, you see. I don't know why."

"These are certainly all new theories to me," the Professor said brightly, "if you don't mind my saying so."

"Selves don't need theories. I mean, dear friend, where do you think we are? Athens?" Father snapped out scathingly. "What is needed is a new tone, a new tempo. Something beyond irony and hyperbole." He glowered out over the darkening river. "Something *dead-on*."

"Yes, something scientific," the Professor rubbed his hands. "*Eine unsägliche diagnose* (an unspeakable diagnosis)."

"Not quite," Father sighed. "A proper science would be critical and humorous, as slippery and sardonic as art. If there's an idea involved, it's just this: if the nutcase is to be taken off your hands, she must know there will be no *next* physician!"

He had drawn abreast of his students. "Now, remove the cord, but not the collar." And they walked on, Topsy in perfect step, her eyes never leaving their knees.

"Tell me Herr Doktor, what is the longest distance in the world?"

The Professor shrugged, preparing himself for the joke.

"To move a man from his intellect to his brain."

"Surely this is not so difficult as you make it out."

"You still are much too interested in unveiling hypocrisy. The point is to pass on a certain tolerance so that authority becomes affordable. A stern but benevolent ally can *create* courage!"

Topsy had stopped, raised a rear leg, squatted tremulously, and micturated.

"Ah, what a wonderful specimen," the Professor guffawed.

"Sarcasm is fine, if you use it no more often than a polka in a symphony. Now, by yourselves then."

The two moved diagonally in something of a clumsy gambol.

"Much better, comrade. We have made some progress today."

The Professor was flushed, stammering. "And what is down the road, Councilor—the next lesson?"

"It will be a long journey, Professor, and it is still possible that in the future, spoiled and incurious, she will become everything we hate. The next steps, in order, one on each visit, will be the *Col Pugno* (With the Fist), the *Ruhevoll* (Serenity), the *Mordent Coraggio* (Caustic Courage), the *Trotta Sentimento* (Heartfelt Trot), and finally, with luck, the *Adagio Religioso*."

"This last," the Professor snorted dismissively, "is either *schmonzes* (nonsense) or *schrecklich* (frightening)."

"Life is not a 'Society for Obvious or Underlying Jewish Themes,' my dearest friend. But my oath to you is that you will experience it by honorable means, if possible. If not, not."

At this point Topsy wrapped her front legs firmly about Father's knee and began to deliriously hump away upon his be-putteed leg. Father glanced down knowingly, and for the first time I can recall in a training session, fairly shouted, "Phui!"

She slipped to the ground in the idol-like attitude of the sphinx, paws extended, head elevated, thighs pressed close to her body, her bestial eyes narrowing to mere slits.

"Now *there's* a command for you!" the Professor beamed. "Forget the damn music—*that's* the one I want to master."

Father had looked away. "Ah, friend, it takes a great many *phui*s to make a religion or a work or art."

The Professor and Topsy had turned toward the river. The wind had picked up, swirling the grass into viridian pockets. Gray Siberian crows, blown in from the steppe, settled about them unconcerned. A crane walked up and passed them by, looking at them over its shoulder like an old gentleman going to the mailbox.

"Relax. Never an angry gesture. Not so constricted . . . *Nicht eilen* (do not hurry), not so close to the body . . . *Bedächtig* (deliberately) not too quickly, give her time, *feierlich langsam doch nicht schleppen* . . . Come out of your bag. If you are tense to begin with, you'll have nothing left. Stay within yourself. That's better . . . Now, *narrante!*"

The chapel promontory was suddenly cupped with gusts of wind. Squirrels raced hysterically about its mullions as skylarks fell twittering aimlessly in descent, ceasing their song only a few inches from the ground. Inside, Waterlily was warming up, but she was no longer singing to herself, as she often did. This was a performance.

Ma-*la*-mi-*doe*-doe
Ma-*la*-fi-*ta*-do

Waterlily, to her credit, was apparently trying to wrench the Art Song from its culmination of bad history and bad poetry, those recitals solemnly progressing through four centuries and five languages, a trial for all concerned. She was also experimenting with a form of *voix mixte*, at once guttural and falsetto, combining both head and chest registers, so that each vowel had two rates of vibration. It gave quite a special and eerie effect, suitable for the songs which feature children dying in your arms, but seemed a bit overwrought when glowing sunsets, woeful monks, singing larks, overgrown churchyards, or maidens fishing from a bridge were invoked, and all in all it was best that only I could hear her. Sufficiently resonated, she began that afternoon's recital with a strange Cannonian water rhapsody, as if she were standing alone in the bend of the all-time resonant piano which was Semper Vero.

> Over the tops of the westerly wood
> Friendly beckons the reddish gleam,
> Beneath the branches of the easterly wood
> The sweet-flag murmurs in the reddish gleam
> Until upon loftier, radiant wings
> Myself shall flee this changing time.

Eagles were now floating downriver from the upcountry, routing the owls from turrets of the chapel, then walking back and forth on the roof, preening their skulls, their wings folded behind their backs. These heraldic birds—austere, aloof, ill-tempered gentlemen—had little intelligence and no plasticity, their flat heads all inexorable lever, all beak, all pupil. The Astingi abominated the eagle above all things, not only because they carried away their lambs, billykids, and even small foals, but because every empire had adopted them as their symbol of authority. They were the antithesis of the Astingi warrior aesthetic—a beast of prey, aristocracy turned pointless and cruel—which is why every Astingi entourage was brought up in the rear by an eagle trudging on a chain, fed on grub worms and corn gruel, and why Astingi flutes are made from the largest bone of the wing.

The two men breasted the ridge and gazed across the river at the two women sitting, almost classical figures in the light mist. The *Penelope III* was concealed from them by the angle of the cliff.

"Look," the Professor said, "their breasts are shaking."

"Laughing at us, no doubt," Father replied. "Women are more attuned to reality. That's why they get hysterical."

The Professor scowled. Topsy was gazing up at him, blinking nervously like her mistress. "Such beseeching!" he groaned.

"You must put up with this and more," Father intoned. "We may be witnessing the poorest performance ever given by a dog. Everything depends upon the master's glance."

"But she's *so* narcissistic."

"No one can stand unconditional love for long, good friend. Bounce it back to her. Accept her damage. The suffering cannot end prematurely. Your only command to her is this: use your strength. *Molto sentimento d'affeto.* One must be tender even with the women one has lost."

The Professor turned back from the river. The cord had tightened inadvertently.

"Pull on her that way, and the only thing you'd be able to predict is where she won't be."

"You contradict my every move!"

"Don't you see, my friend? It's like playing an instrument. Get the mid-range right, and everything else will follow. *Più tosto presto spiccato.* We walk as between two rivers."

"Very well, Topsy." The Professor swallowed his gruffness. "Let us ply the bloody golden mean," and she waddled through the grass approvingly.

"And stop seeing events as if they were always in a drama," Felix barked.

The frigate was now directly beneath them, its oars tearing at the water like an uncoordinated centipede. Sailors scurried in the rigging and swore amongst the stacked scenery. But on the main hatch, strewn with pebbles and potted palms, a hodgepodge of a play was being rehearsed to no one's apparent notice. The Astingi vowels floated up:

"Si spus-am ochiului meu trist: Imbrâtiseazâ!"

And then the translation, in perfect Oxbridge cadences:

"And then who knows whether it is better to be or not to be? But everyone knows that what does not exist feels no pain, while pains in life are many, pleasures few, to be?"

"Good Lord," the Professor expostulated. "Even the dogs in Cannonia bark in a foreign tongue." And from the kennel, only broken-winded yelps.

The Princess had lost herself in thought. Mother genuinely tried to deflect her from this course.

"What *are* they doing up there?" the Princess queried nervously.

The men were facing each other, apparently doing a kind of calisthenics, though upon closer inspection, it was rather a kind of grave conducting of a silent orchestra.

"My husband has devoted himself to the learning of grace, which he has no instinct for. First, conducting lessons from Gundel, the great closet maestro of Monstifita, then flamenco lessons, Greco-Roman wrestling, and ballet at forty-five. Can you imagine?"

But the Princess did not look up or react to this. She insisted, rather, in dwelling upon the history of each of her scars, from her Roman nose (a piano top had collapsed) to her petite cicatrized feet (the bones were growing in the wrong direction, she had been told.) She had also apparently been convinced by a certain Dr. Halban of Monstifita to move that peculiar female member of wondrous nerves, her *sucre d'orange* as she put it, closer to the urethral passage, a two-step procedure which would allow her to mount more easily ocean's orgiastic wave.

Ainoha stared at Princess Zanäia for some time, watching as she traced her scars with her forefinger, adumbrating their causes and consequences. Then she threw herself into the river. Staying under for an anxiously long interval, she emerged some fifty yards away with a collar of water lilies, and shouted back to shore, "Surely there are worse things than monogamy!" Then she paddled aimlessly about, trying a number of different strokes, none of which relaxed her, until finally she realized she had no choice but to return to the tiny beach. But no sooner had she dried off than her royal confidant asked her if she could be of assistance in gaining entrance to the Silbürsmerze morgue, so that the Princess might make certain measurements of any female corpses there, as it was common knowledge that the Astingi women's *apparat* was the least complicated in the world, and also rumored to run horizontally.

Mother replied that this was certainly a myth, though no doubt a useful one. But she was neither used to exercising self-control nor to asking someone to stop speaking in her presence. And she was also surprised to realize that indignity was as difficult to come by in this situation as compassion.

"Oh, I know you ardent women detest frigid women," the Princess wailed.

Mother replied somewhat helplessly, "But I know no one at the morgue."

The Princess was downcast. All her scars seemed to raise slightly. Tilting her head to one side, lips pursed, her nervous glance finally solidified, it was clear she was contemplating a measurement upon the most prominent live specimen of Astingi-related womanhood.

"You are quite the iconoclast," Mother offered icily.

"Actually, no," the Princess moaned, "just a misfit," and burst into tears.

Ainoha had soiled her chemise.

Searching for the perfect non sequitur, Ainoha was mercifully interrupted by Catspaw, who had sensed his Mistress's distress. He tottered down the steep path in a Russian blouse and white spats, precariously balancing a silver tray with several fruit spritzers and what appeared to be a skull from Father's collections. He was extemporizing even before he stopped before the Princess.

"Here lies the water; good; here stands the man; good: if the man go to this water and drown himself, it is, will he, nill he, he goes—mark you that; but if the water come to him and drown him, he drowns not himself: *argal*, he that is not guilty of his own death shortens not his own life."

"Bravi." The Princess clapped her translucent hands.

"Goodness gracious," the Naiad groaned. "Later, dear Catspaw, *argal*, not now."

Pain crossed his face as he turned on his heel and began to trudge back up the path. At one point, he turned to recite the breathless messenger's speech from *Macbeth*, but Ainoha, drawing her hand across her throat, cut him off.

Topsy was flagging and kept looking longingly across the river.

"In order to compensate for the mind's imperfections," Father was saying, "all the other senses must be put into compensatory concert. Now that we have run out of *session*, we must be quiet."

They stood stock-still for some minutes.

"Do you feel it?" Father queried.

"Yes, indeed, a kind of energy . . ."

"A displaceable energy, in itself neutral, but able to join forces with another impulse. An immanent movement?"

"Blast, now I've lost it!" The Professor snapped his fingers and groaned.

"No matter. The patient takes what she needs. You don't know what it is, but she takes what she needs and leaves the rest. *Semplice ma mysterioso.*"

The Professor gesticulated sardonically to the heavens. "I don't suppose I'll ever be permitted to play my own cadenzas in this concert?"

"Sir, speak sequentially, without ungainly pauses. Where you choose to breathe is where her character is defined."

The Professor sullenly took up the cord and dog, and with quick strides headed for the rope bridge, gradually lengthening the distance between the two men. Father followed, correcting the Professor's various postures and gaits, a repertoire which, to his credit, was expanding:

"Much too correct, *nicht blutwallungen, brutalmente* . . . Now, there we go, that's better . . . There . . . *Allegro maestoso* . . . No, no—fast but not all that fast. There, easy, but not too easy. *Adagio, adagio, adagio, adagio, adagio, adagio!*"

The Professor's Trabuko had fallen from his mouth, leaving a trail of embers and ash down his sweat-stained shirtfront. His gaze was locked on a grove of trees on the far side of the river, and Felix himself was taken aback when he saw the winding file of naked girls, their hair undone, jars on their shoulders, bells on their anklets, garlanded with coins, gold chains, and shards of glass. The Peraperduga had been set in motion, one hundred paranymphs dancing in the wilderness in search of purling streams as yet unknown, praying for rain in three languages on the back road to Silbürsmerze, and shivering for joy. A dry muddy-colored rainbow arched over their wild hymns like a faded provincial opera set.

"What can it mean?" the Professor whispered hoarsely, and Felix intoned sadly:

"For us, it is only the definitive sign of drought. Or worse."

The sun had been cut off quite suddenly by the bluff, as the ladies were startled by a horrific sucking sound.

"Strangely enough," Mother observed evenly, "the river is often ugliest at dusk."

The sucking continued and the Princess gazed out nervously at the Mze, which was busily regurgitating a new island: an ovoid slab of primordial mud flecked with quartz.

"Receiving semen is my greatest ecstasy," pronounced the Princess apropos of nothing.

They returned to the house in a nude monotonous march.

At the peak of floodtime there is absolute silence, as every discord has been harmonized. But now with its strange resorbent sound, the river seemed to be looking to acquire a language at the very moment it had lost its power of metaphor. It was as if the Mze had lost its primal force, had tired of making limpid aesthetic statements and become self-conscious, yearning to be expressed. Its gurgle was rather like actors in a play whose lines are so densely poetic you cannot grasp them or the action; just the opposite of Father reading to me, that tumultuous cataract, those enfilades of dirty soldiers marching through the night. If this were a language its waterfall was now played out, its once curved body flat and meager, the pother as its base, vanished. The surface rapids were no longer visible, curving backward in sulfurous currents. There was no osmosis, no flowing—just a series of little scum-covered puddles, half-suffocated with water lilies and spiked rushes, into which ivory scavenger gulls, no longer able to plunge for fish, gingerly stepped, dreary, sad, and invested with an air of desperate deprivation. Poorly equipped, they carried away mysterious and far-from-appetizing fragments of this language, which in no time at all reappeared on the newly exposed rocks as a squirming white cape of excrement.

As an unwanted encore, Waterlily had launched into a conclusion of Astingi frontier songs, snatches from the decasyllabic "Ballads of Heroes" (*Kange Krajišnice*) of which every Astingi girl had a repertoire of hundreds—short song-cycles formulated in the fifteenth century to conquer the boredom of the men's endless recited epics. I had always thought their artistic value slight, but as she refashioned them in *voix mixte*, her uvula flickering, ad lib with variations as the player pleases, she emptied the landscape of everything save the text, and Semper Vero consisted of only the solitary singer and her page.

Once in the East
A host marched in helmets
A man was with them on horseback
With two dogs.

I pulled him down from his horse
Where he fell I stood up
I put on his clothes, whistled his dogs
Blew into my cupped hands
As the helmets drifted dead in the stream

The ladies were playing desultory tennis in men's whites when the Topsy party returned, a brace of Chetvorah chasing down and retrieving any ball which left the court. The straw target was stuffed black with arrows.

The Professor was red-faced but proud, and Father walked behind, pale but also proud. The Princess waved her racquet, and the Professor, showing off, dropped into a half crouch as Topsy heeled.

"Nervorum atque cerebri mala affecto (don't get creative on me)," Father hissed in camp Latin.

The Chetvorah sat on either side of the net like referees, waiting for a mishit and pointedly ignoring Topsy. The Professor thought they were slyly winking at him.

"And how did my little darling do?" the Princess queried breathlessly, one eye on her pet and another on a ball rolling slowly off the court.

"She takes it all very well," the Professor beamed.

"Not bad at all," Father informed the party, "considering her rational part is defectuous and impeached." Then he went to kiss Mother, whose hair was still wet. "How goeth it?" he whispered in her ear.

"Oh, we do not enjoy seeing one another, but would be unhappy if we didn't," Ainoha mused. "She's not in love with her husband, and what's worse, not in love with anyone else." She had on that fake brave grin which always affected Felix more than her natural smile.

"If I were religious, I would pray for one thing, dear heart," she whispered as Father took her in his arms, "and that is, we ought to leave . . . the retail business."

"My thoughts exactly." He held her close. "The best pet is a pet idea."

They walked back to the Professor and Princess, who were also talking earnestly and intimately. Topsy was calm, golden flecks in her hazel eyes.

"The time has come for the ultimate reinforcement," Felix gastriloquized, and after taking the cord from the Professor's pocket, he ambled out on the lawn away from the court. "You see, training finally becomes four-dimensional, not by aspiring beyond the material, but by humblingly, gruelingly, and systematically working every fine point into the body until it becomes second nature."

First he gently pulled on a fold of Topsy's neck, then released the cord nonchalantly, keeping the flat of his hand on the place the cord had occupied. Turning to his audience, he rasped, "It's the last mile, of course, which is the hardest to hold." Topsy blinked coquettishly.

"Care, take care," Father whispered as he drew away from her with a slow backward tango-tread, tracing out a pause in which his partner could play in and adorn. Then he raised his right arm perpendicularly and gently pressed his left hand against her back.

"Toho," he whispered, and the dog slowly turned her head, eye on his hand, tail flagging, but mute. "Bend," he orated softly, "*bend*," and Topsy slowly arched her back, raised her head, and lifting a forepaw ever so slightly, she turned and twirled.

"Utter transcendence," the Princess swooned.

"A million-dollar move," the Professor ejaculated.

"That will do," Father whispered to Topsy. Then, balancing on one boot, exhaling as the breath was drawn out of the dog as well as the assembly, gradually spreading his hands as if he were pulling apart dough, all movement was suspended. The air itself seemed to disappear, sucked away, and the earth pulled all heads downwards. Then Felix slowly pivoted on one leg, and scarcely giving the sign of a downbeat, he concluded the muted elegy as all the players resumed breathing.

"All we want in this world, all we want," Father whispered hoarsely, "is that the damn dog follow our lead, that she walk calmly by our side with her head high." A tear came to his eye. "But . . . this is all too rare. Not one in a thousand dogs is worth keeping."

"But to move the patient from hysterical inversion to common misery and to forget the self-dramatizing," the Professor comforted him, "*that* is progress!"

Waterlily was reaching a harsh crescendo, a cosmic C-minor, then a roulade of one-and-a-half octaves of stunning rapidity. She hurled out the notes to the sky, neither words nor sounds, but distended spheres, mucoid globules unattached to anything.

From thirteen gods
and fourteen goddesses
I am descended
From my son
I begat myself once again
blinder of hosts.

My name is now Astinge
And by that only I shall be called
As I go to the nations.

She was caterwauling like a bathhouse nymph.

The chatter was animated on the terrace that late afternoon. "Can you imagine how glorious it is," the Princess giggled, "to see *into* a dog, and to tease oneself into her exactly at her center, the place out of which she exists as a dog?"

Felix had turned away from this, but was immediately cornered by the Professor.

"My gratitude is boundless, Councilor, but have you no concern at all that the Pzalmanzar method, this taking of the animal into liberality, is something of a trick?"

"Balderdash," Felix replied in a stage whisper. "We are tricked into being born and tricked into staying alive. Each time we're saved, it's with a different trick."

Öscar Ögur actually served drinks with aplomb, spilling only one tray, which no one mentioned. He had taken over for Catspaw, who could now be seen furiously ferrying Gubik downstream to the *Penelope III*, in the hope of catching a ride to overtake the *Desdemona* at Razacanum on her route to Chorgo, there to pick up the *Valse de Mocsou*. As Catspaw strained at the oars, Gubik stood in the bow of the copper-prowed caique, arms folded like Napoleon, caped and white-gloved, his swineherd's Phrygian cap pulled tightly over his skull. As they drew abreast of the *Penelope III,* a rope net was thrown down from the scuppers and our prodigy scrambled aboard, his white gloves flashing, just as the frigate, with its magical cargo and dispirited crew, disappeared into a fogbank at the mill. Felix and Ainoha toasted him sadly and silently as his pig herd filled the woods with bellows of protest. The Professor noted irritably that he seemed to be carrying one of his custom plaid valises, and I realized that the red sash about his waist was the banner from my sister's tomb.

After much cranking and cursing, the limousine finally started. The golden ponies in the far pasture galloped from corner to corner as the ignition coughed.

As a celebratory gesture, all the kennels, coops, and stables were flung open, and the *menagerie entire* was released for a run. Moccus and Epona thundered up and down the drive at forty miles per hour, packs of Chetvorah dove off into the woods for randy deer, arthritic seventeen-year-old cats tottered through portals, doves alighted on the furniture, chickens and ducks strutted fearlessly about, and the tame gray parrot, Arnulph, whom I hadn't noticed for years, hopped from shoulder to shoulder. Topsy walked like royalty, calm and dignified amongst the miffed, milling Chetvorah.

The Professor thanked Father over and over.

"The Princess is always welcome," Felix lied, "but keep her well clear of the stables. She gives off a scent of fear."

But just as he concluded this, he realized the Princess was standing behind him and had already forgiven him.

"Topsy and I will be forever in your debt," she said modestly.

"Ah, *Prinzessin.*" Felix bowed deeply and kissed her hand. "Now that you have seen a few miracles, perhaps you will begin to appreciate realism."

"The next thing you know, we'll be hunting her!" the Professor beamed.

"This child was not meant for the field, my friends. While she will raise many cocks, I fear you will get few shots."

Topsy had lain down next to them, head between her forelegs. The Princess's eyes began to dart again. "Shouldn't one write all this down?"

"All dog literature is worthless, because it is written either by owners or scientists. Everything you want to know and more you will find in this pamphlet, Prinzessin," Father bowed again as he handed her his private printing, *Breaking Strange Dogs and Vicious Horses*, bound in white satin. "I've inscribed it for you." And she read it out, her voice quivering.

> Who lives to learn, the properties of hounds,
> To breed them first, and then to make them good,
> To teach them to know, both voice and horne, by sounds,
> To cure them too, from all that hurts their blood:
> Let Her but buy this book, so shall she find
> As much as may (for hounds) content her mind.

"I am not desirous of making you unsatisfied with anything you possess, Prinzessin," Felix adumbrated, "but a judicious exertion on your part will add much to Topsy's usefulness, as well as to your own enjoyment. Much may be done through the affections. Do not be contented with a disorderly cur, when a trifling addition to your pains will produce an extravagant companion."

"I am most grateful for the proper commands," the Princess said, a bit choked up.

As the two couples walked to the hissing limousine, Father took her arm. "I must tell you honestly, Prinzessin, such commands mustn't smack of an order. Language is hardly absolute. Words have meaning only in the stream of life. And the world is, I'm afraid, full of independent subjects." He opened the car door and Topsy raced by them, flinging herself into the back seat. The Princess pressed a small bag of uncut garnets into Father's hand. Had she looked down, she could have picked up twenty more from the road.

"My husband often gets carried away with the spirituality of his projects," Mother now confided, fearing a scene, while helping the Princess negotiate her way into the dark petit point interior of the limousine. "Let me send you on your way with some practical observations. First, the little hussy ought not be tied up, even if she wants it. Straining at her collar will throw out her elbows, and she will grow up bandy-legged. Two, if you must administer a powder, mix it with a little butter and smear it on her nose. She will readily lick it down. This is also the best time to pare her nails. Lastly, *never* lend your doggie to anyone, not even a brother. It may seem selfish, but an ignorant sportsman will bring you nothing but grief. I hope you will forgive me for saying so."

The Princess did not reply, but for the first time in her visit did manage to make eye contact.

"And what departing advice have you for me, dearest lady?" the Professor queried, batting his coal-chunk eyes. But before Ainoha could answer, Felix had broken in:

"For you, sir, keep it simple, songful, and slow. And go easy on the melancholy."

"And next time," the Professor sang like a child, "we shall do the *phui, phui, phui!*"

So it was that the *goldenischechow*, Pouilly-Gepacht, was delivered back to her mistress with the silvered words of her commands written in a daybook, to demonstrate that even with the most spoiled of bitches, bloodsport can ultimately be put in the service of civility—that in all of us the urge to pounce can be turned, if not quite to grand effect, nevertheless to leading gestures and illusions of spectral beauty.

Leaving the estate in chastened profile, the Princess lay her hand on the Professor's shoulder as he pulled his bowler ever more tightly on his head, while Topsy, punished but forgiven, could be seen in the front seat in more of a *demi-plié* than a rapt quivering point, but nevertheless scanning the barren fields for signs of life.

She would outlive both the Princess and the Professor, and from that day on, never had a leash upon her.

Master and Mistress walked arm in arm down to the bathing beach in the wolf-light, reflecting upon the bankruptcy of their business venture, smoking their pipes, and regarding their new island, so amphorously regurgitated from the Mze. Only yards from the bank, it already sported a fern.

Felix flung the bag of garnets far out in the stolid waters. Ainoha snapped the pleats out of her skirts, raised them above her sunburnt legs to her golden bee, and beckoned her husband to follow. He removed his boots and trousers, and they waded through the murmuring reed-beds, the face of a virgin saint on the tip of each stalk of underwater grain. And there like Quality and the Muse, Mnemosyne, they had a quiet conversation on an uninhabited island.

"I've never seen the Mze so low," Felix murmured, and for the first time in his life, he saw a streak of fear in his wife's eyes. Realizing that her sorrowing, even for good reason, was the only thing which could frighten him, Ainoha took her husband's hand and resolved to change the subject.

"Dearly beloved, I know you have need of your men friends, but it's *their* friends who have become the issue. What a pair of cold fish, I should say."

"Indeed," Felix concurred, "there is such a thing as too thoughtful a performance—and too singular a person."

"But perhaps the Professor is on to something with his obsession with . . . *bourgeoisiosity*? Darling, what sort of century do we face when aristocratic royalty behave like plebs? Perhaps," she threw back her head and laughed like a horse, "perhaps the time has come for a bit of *anti*-bourgeois thinking?"

Felix stroked her hair as he stroked his beard. His concentration had been broken for a moment, for while pondering the receding waters, he had noticed a dark shape circling the island, a shadow longer than the largest sturgeon. "Well," he murmured absently into her loosened hair, "it's their century, no doubt, but wouldn't it be grand to throw them off-stride for a moment?!"

They embraced as he placed his right hand on the flat of her back. Then Felix began a gliding stride about her, counterclockwise, though he was following more than leading, and once she had thought several moves ahead, sure of her loveliness, Ainoha tempered his figures by placing a bare foot with great care into his pauses, as if the new sand of the island was scorching—and with this counter-proposal, it was he who twirled in the air, a grin in his underwear.

"Oh, Cavalier," she gushed, "one is always making history, isn't one."

"Let us put it all behind us, dear. Live and learn."

"Oh, darling," she punched the heavy air. "Learning or forgetting. Who knows what's worse."

They raced each other back to Semper Vero for an early dinner and bed, but were surprised to find Count Zich's sweat-drenched grays standing at the door. He sat slumped behind his silver-buttoned groom, swathed in a cadmium orange blanket embroidered with his huge monogram, his granite hatchet-face pale and unshaven.

"There's not enough water in this landscape," he greeted them in a bad humor.

From my lookout, I had watched their pretty dance, and knew my place in the Age to Come—the dumb dancer who must keep silent during the dance, acting the part of the clown and cracking a whip to keep away evil spirits. But I was also the flagbearer, the dumber one who will invariably assume the lead.

In the last of the wolf-light, the foothills and answering ranges beyond gleamed like sheetmetal hammered into angles, and the Mze was ablaze with floating shields and helmets. Deep, diurnal shadows rocketed up the peaks and zigzagged down ravines, convex and concave changed from insubstantial radiance into geometric figures—parallelograms, rhomboids, polygons—as drought brought spring and autumn into one. I felt it ludicrous that this landscape would one day be registered in my name.

But suddenly, as if to trump my own self-mockery, thermal hurricanes were charging down the gorge, a cold front turning the sky green and the grass blue. The air was filled with the disordered wingbeats and jargon of birds, lightning was held captive in the incandescent cloudbanks, and when it finally struck without a single drop of moisture, small fires broke out in the cornfields, and the currents paled in sulfurous ravines. White legions of thistledown blanketed the flickering thickets, and the woods were garlanded with snowy wool. Flash after flash of lightning ripped from the burst clouds, and the air was sullied by the chemical smell of fading leaves as the solar winds tore about our house.

A large tulip tree was uprooted in the garden, its soil-clotted roots ripping a hole large enough for a swimming pool, its branches parting just in time to fall to either side of a statue without injuring it. Shutters opened, slammed shut then opened again, shattering their hinges. Rooftiles and chimney cornices spun through the air like ducks with their heads shot off. Stripped of their leaves, empty colonnades of poplar bent double. Hedges were flattened, yews exploded. And from his tower suite, Father's papers fluttered in an endless stream from the open windows, leaves of manuscript littering the grounds like a week-old battlefield of a lost empire.

The last aria had gone sharp and faint at the same time, shuddering bell-notes on our grim scene. Then there was a great beating of wings behind me, and against the gray clouds a flash of white, as dearest Waterlily, a lace-strewn dove in gilded talons, was borne from the cold heights across the lustral waters to the Field of Mars. Her corpse was never found.

The wind and sun went down together. A tongue of flame licked at my hair but did not burn; I was blushing for my sister and myself, Ainoha's Fire Child.

My thoughts were full of singeing old men's beards and burning babies in their cradles, as I heard for the first time in many years the fly buzzing in the buried doll's skull, and every image cried out, "Kill!"

I descended into the spinal fluid of Cannonia to cool off. The shore was no longer a resilient couch but a shingle in a chalk-white sea. The remnants of the Mze seemed to be a series of strings, syrupy, glassy, and clear, like something you could cut with scissors.

Half in unhappy love, I leapt into the slack shallows. The exposed reed-beds issued no love song; their chant had been replaced by cicadas. The young virgin's faces on the stalks of underwater grain now fell flat on the black ooze. I washed my own flushed face as Ainoha once did when she smeared her half-frightened boy with mulberry juice upon his brow and temples, and set prehistoric time to ticking. But I now knew I was well beyond her rule over the limpid, beyond the reproval of her rosy lips. Stripping down, I walked briskly through the Mze to the meadow bank, never once submerged, then back again to the deepest part of the motionless channel, to take the tally of the darkness. The water came up only to my heart. There, beyond my father's athletic instincts, I could ponder his pre-Christian lesson—that while the father can lighten every care and crisis and shape his fall, the father cannot save his son from fate or bring him back to life. For it is the *world* itself which has a tragic flaw.

The water boiled around me and the seething Mze went white with the bellies of dead fish. The percipiencies of the river washed my wounded senses; its susurances tempered something sharper than mere manhood. Rising from the sheen of marble with a penumbra of reeds and poplar leaves, beneath a straying moon, I moved naked through the clichés of shadows, returning to my home and a sleep of iron. Above the river, resting in its course, the stars ran backward.

The Astingi believe that the Mze does not disperse when it enters the ocean, but remains a river within a river, fresh, sweet, and ochre. Taking hidden channels through the sea, it emerges as a fountain on Big Turtle Island, in the courtyard of a castle built upon a swamp at Port Chaonia, a mime of Troy, City of the Tired Ones.

And you, Stars! Pray witness Waterman's return to his remnant element, there to welcome me in yellow depths, and buoyed by my thousand names, proceed downstream toward allies, to resume our life beneath the waves.

IULUS AWAKE
(Rufus)

There were several years, during the sixties, when the whole country was grinning from ear to ear, that I heard nothing from Iulus, and my letters to him went unanswered. If you could have licked my heart it would have poisoned you. The Company was not amused and threatened more than once to cut off his modest stipend. Even Ed Kirby was distinctly uncool. "He's having us off again," he growled. I could have put a tracer on him, but Iulus had his nasty side, and I didn't see the point in sacrificing any of our polite Notre Dame boys.

In any event, in the early seventies, when it became clear that the country had suffered a kind of stroke, our correspondence resumed sporadically. For a time Iulus had worked as a civil engineer in Arizona, a gymnastics teacher at a girls' school in the North Carolina mountains, and as a *répétiteur* with the Pacifica Opera, and while he never responded to any of my queries directly, one could infer from his general observations what he was up to. He apologized, incidentally, for his silence, admitting he had gone a little crazy in the sixties. There had been so many dashing young women, so many wonderful groups to infiltrate—"never have so many had so little to revolt about, but," he chortled, "the worst dancers in history." His autoportraits from this period are particularly compelling; though he was embarrassed only to find that even the strongest drugs had no effect upon him whatsoever, "except a slight ringing in the ears," surprised to find how a fully formed and hardened personality might resist modern chemistry, country music, and sex in public.

And then one fine day, I arrived at work to find the hallway blocked with crates, and on my desk an index of their contents with Company instructions for summary, translation, and vetting. It was the balance of the Semper Vero Archives.

You will appreciate what I discovered that I had to deal with. There were, first of all, several thousand pages of Iulus's family observations written in dense High Cannonian; "the Professor's" unpublished, unreadable, endless novellas; and the secret scientific correspondence of "The Academician," as well as OGPU surveillance records of his activities. Add to this tens of thousands of documents in every European, Slavic, and Turkic language; his mother's letters and diaries, his father's *Chronik*, an elaborate daybook in which his personal reflections were surrounded by daily accounts of Semper Vero, missing only a single day in fifty years; as well as the balance of his *Historae Astingae*, a subject for which no further sources existed, but everything remained to be said—not to mention more than you could ever want to know about our canine friends throughout world history. And there was more. Each box of papers was topped off with a handwritten *precis* which attempted to place his annual autobiographies in the context of the other papers. The sonuvabitch had gone literary on me! Still, I was reenergized by Iulus's calligraphic handwriting and old-fashioned idiom immediately, and set to work with an intensity I had not experienced since the war years, like Petrarch fondling the Homer he could not quite understand. I realized that for good or ill the rest of my life had just been filled up.

In their typically understated and monotonous manner, my colleagues filled me in. It turned out that Iulus had kept a *rezident* house in Connecticut where there has always been a high incidence of abandoned homes whose attics contain some amateur unpublished work, and while this summer home had provided him with decent enough cover, his notes testified that Connecticut was his least favorite state—"an inbred and dilapidated working class servicing an incurious wealthy, whose sole motive, like the gypsy moth, seems to be to escape any troublesome sensibility. . . a political economy canopied with a warren of second-rate boys' and girls' schools, giving a delusive caste of renewal to the entire nonentity of a state."

That said, it was in the imaginatively named New London-on-the-Thames, that an Alcohol, Tobacco, and Firearms unit broke into his unattractive green shingled splitlevel on Polaris Drive, between the malled highway and the river road, and while no incriminating substances were found, there was a complete log of every nuclear submarine which had ever sallied forth from Groton Naval Base or the Electric Boat Company, including those which had been scuttled.

Since his arrival on the *Anti-Drakon,* Iulus had always been fascinated by submarines—their fevered interior discipline, their certain silent grace and competence unknown on shore. At the back of the log, with his usual evenhandedness, there were also the routes and radio frequencies of Russian fishing trawlers, so topheavy with listening gear they often capsized in Newfoundland swells.

Iulus loathed the sea with all the irrationality of his land-locked people. "No book was ever written on a boat," he often said. "The sea means stupidity." And Lord knows how he suffered on his many transatlantic trips aboard that ghostly septuagenarian sub, which had to surface every three hours to expel its diesel fumes, and in which our elegant world traveler had to bunk in a rusty torpedo tube. He often mentioned to me a recurrent dream in which he was disguised as a mysterious woman in a polka-dot dress with large shoulder pads, a wide-brimmed hat, and a cheesecloth veil who flung, with a force that took the officers aback, a christening bottle of champagne against the bulbous glans of a new Trident sub, and then watched her, longer than a football field, slide rearwards into the river. Just before he awoke, the thirty-foot Douglas firs which had braced the hull's scaffolding snapped like matchsticks.

In any event, the Semper Vero Archives which now graced the dim fluorescence of our pea-green halls were found in his backyard, sorted carefully into some one hundred and eighty-five Styrofoam picnic hampers beneath the deck of a large aboveground heated kiddie pool, where, according to neighborly reports, he often sat nude, Russian-style, keeping his log, surrounded by adoring coeds while drinking himself into insensibility. Needless to say, he had moved out a week ahead of our investigatory team. His aged batman, Catspaw, with his shock of white hair and muttonchops, looked on with mild disdain as the orange-vested agents hurtled about— emptying drawers, scattering papers, peering behind pictures and portraits— in the end offering them whiskeys and soda when they were exhausted.

The hampers of manuscript clearly worried my associates more than the log, its odd literary digressions so redolent of deep tactical and strategic deception. Why, for example, did a man who had his fine hand in every momentous event of the post-war years concentrate only on his youthful education, glossing over his considerable coups and generally taking the view that, in any event, everything was on our plate by 1938, and that we have just recycled it since? It is a daunting notion, is it not, that all the cataclysms we have experienced in our several lifetimes are historically aberrant, even insignificant? That in effect we are back to 1901, "back into the future," as the Astingi are fond of saying, where all the threads that were dropped at the turn of the century are being taken up in our soft shaking hands again?

Now, our analysts had been largely trained in the Ivy League humanities, with more degrees than a thermometer, and their readings tended to confirm whatever method they wished to validate. They could not understand a fully contradictory work which apparently had no preconceptions, much less any self-promotion; they could not imagine what it feels like *not* to know. I suppose there will always be people who believe that art comes from ideas, culture from values, and politics from ideology. These are people who are bound to be finally ignored and disappointed, because when such notions are not confirmed by life experience, they don't amount to a hill of beans. But nothing, not the most humiliating rejection, seems to stop them. What I found truly astounding about our analysts is that they never had a strategy in mind in case their interpretation turned out to be totally wrong. Indeed, it was only after many rereadings that I came to understand that there was no symbolic resonance to Iulus's reticence, and that this was the key not only to understanding him, but an insight into how and why books come to be written at all—that it's expediency and exhaustion, not ideals, which inform the edges of all art. For Cannonia, in truth, is like a seal over a seal over a seal, where the symbolic cannot penetrate and only reinforces the forgotten ancient truth that everyone is based on someone else.

My superiors kept after me, rubbing their abstractions together to see if they could make a fire, and I began to glimpse the poor distended privates of that warped modern marriage between artist and recipient. Their interrogations over casual aseptic cafeteria lunches were incessant, and somehow both infantile and patronizing. Why had I not pressed to solidify our relationship? In what percentile did his work rank in the area of its peer expertise? In private, the questioning became even more breathless. I saw that my credibility, not to mention my clearance, was on the line. To save my ass, I would have to give a little seminar.

As to not following up upon our acquaintanceship, I could have simply pled our no-fraternization policy. But in fact I learned a long time ago to avoid meeting those whom you admire. Those whom you look up to ought to be kept under constant but respectful, discreet, and distant surveillance. It's a question of manners, really, though I hesitate to even mention that word nowadays—the truth is that personal encounters are invariably less satisfying than the paper trail which establishes them. And the only thrill of espionage, when you get right down to it, is that it sexualizes the gathering of trivia. When you embrace a document, just as when someone flirts with you, you understand from the first that while the drama is addressed to you, it is also (this is the hardest thing for a young person to understand) aimed at the *not*-you. You are merely the momentary custodian of the transaction, and one must be on guard not to over-interpret it, as well as accept the fact that its author may not be a whole person, or perhaps even a historical person with a fictitious name and feelings. And so to my superiors, I had further to say— here is something which is *not just all for you*, boys—and that acceptance is what separates the men from the boys. Wasn't it tough old Berdyaev who said that all culture rests on the open and voluntary admission of inequality? And one can only observe that a writer who has actually known a number of interesting and remarkable people has a tremendous advantage over his peers, for Iulus, in truth, was sufficiently well-placed to observe the last generation in western society with its psyche intact. What I came to admire most about Iulus was that his was not a tale of personal suffering, though he has proven to be the ultimate survivor in every sense. He did not consider himself a victim, and unlike most immigrants, he didn't lie. He knew that in the modern world it is necessary to turn oneself into a character in a drama if one desires to act at a high level of ethicality. He was determined to contradict experience and emerge stronger from exile.

What the Company was interested in, of course, was not an "appreciation," much less some "interesting interpretation," or even what they euphemistically referred to as "evaluation." What they wanted was *knowledge*. By reconstructing the past, unraveling his operations, they thought they could extrapolate his future behavior. They didn't really want to catch him, any more than they really wanted to read him. What they wanted, desperately, was to demonstrate that as good theoreticians, they were closing the net, reducing his options.

But proper knowledge is in no way proper judgment. The one thing the soldier-life has taught me is a profound suspicion of professionalized knowledge. You can professionalize force. You can professionalize etiquette. You can even professionalize the erotic. But you cannot professionalize intelligence. Intelligence fails when the first shot is fired. Battle plans are everything, but worthless once the battle is joined. Von Clausewitz was right to say that unless you cross the battlefield, no permanent happiness can be yours; but he neglected to add that when you are in the midst of fighting it, the battle does not exist. Espionage is a lot like literature in that it is invariably about loss, and full of folks busily writing away for people who no longer exist. History is driven by failed artists. And the main lesson of the intelligence business is this—it takes a long time to learn just how much intellect to smuggle into any transaction without ruining it, and this is as true in love and art as well. The effortlessness of the smuggling is in direct proportion to the affect of the intelligence, a fact not widely understood by our illustrious higher pedagogy. It's not exactly that the intelligence is mostly wrong. It's that you have the capacity to believe, when the intelligence is right. In our business, strange to say, it is the most radical skepticism which often leads to the gravest errors, our pushing of metropolitan fancies to ridiculous extremes, just like the Russians.

Further, the essential strategy of intelligence has been misunderstood by the earnest moralizers who seem to take to American soil like soybeans. Breaking the code is just the first step. Secrecy, leverage, and momentum are only marginal effects. What you really want enemy intelligence to have is sufficiently accurate information to allay their paranoia and thus hold the more maniacal of their politicians at arm's length. It's easy enough to create disinformation, to mislead, to ensnare, to corrupt, to assassinate. What's difficult is to create the illusion in the worried reader's mind that he is getting the right information in spite of us, rather than with our specific assistance. Naturally, you will need a safe house on occasion to let down your hair and hatch a plot or two, but your real safety resides in the fact that your own agencies are riddled with your opposite number, that you know what they know about what you are doing. Wasn't it Persius who said that knowing really means nothing to you, unless somebody else knows that you know it.

The fact of the matter is that most agents *never* learn anything of consequence in their entire careers and so must continually inflate the significance of their observations—a driving force of history which makes the class struggle look like a game of whist. Young men seeking academic promotion, old men seeking publicity—all of it worthless rot, worthless, worthless. Thus, espionage is mostly the story of some poor fellow being shadowed by another, and who by throwing away his brown paper lunch bag invites a generation of tortured analysis and brilliant speculation. What was remarkable about Iulus is that he never inflated his own significance, never gave undue meaning to his dreary routines. To climb the ladder in this business you must entertain the last conclusion that you would expect your training and temperament to lead you to, and that is this: The world in fact does not depend in the end of the individuality of the speaker, but upon the transmission of *other* voices, which somehow overflow into our world.

Now the intelligence fraternity has taken a great deal of abuse in recent years, and while I can hardly add a laurel to their brow, I ought to point out that they were often ahead of their time. By this I mean that they were among the first to suffer from the affliction primarily responsible for the disintegration of the modern personality—when the ability to collect information greatly outstrips our ability to make any sense of it. I myself must confess that I do not know of a single decision, personal or political, which can be improved by more information. The modern way to keep a secret secret is, after all, to surround it with trivia. Information makes it easier to mask real events and hide meaning. Ours is the age of ultimate, unobtrusive continual surveillance. Never before have so many been overheard and so much written down. Never before has behavior been so closely observed and recorded. And yet never in history was there a vaster contrast between the extraordinary precision of our diagnosis, and the recalcitrance of the data from which nothing could be learned, much less prognosticated. The most difficult thing in history is to ascertain motive, and you will not find me trying to account for it. As the great Dickens has said, "Most people cannot read character, and the greatest of all their mistakes is to mistake shyness for arrogance."

In any event, when I came to make summaries of Iulus's work for my aegis of superiors—the inter-office memo is truly the cruelest art form— pressure began to mount. Various directorates came into conflict. The Office of Damage Assessment dismissed it as magical fantasy. The Office of Imagery Analysis believed it to be enigmatically coded reality. Now you won't catch me pulling that Anaxagorian banality, that the world is a mixture of the real and imagined. It's simply that *all* war reminiscences are exchanges of the fake with the genuine, and it's quite impossible to tell the difference. My final task was to divide it up on a "need-to-know" basis between our specialized warriors, and to elicit their cramped annalistic initials in the proper box. But boxes are boxes precisely because they are meant to convey something besides boxes, and they did not appreciate my reminding them of this.

For my own part, it was difficult to police a project in which I was so thoroughly engrossed. Indeed, intelligence-wise, within Iulus's larger candor, there was no hidden conundrum, enigma, or agenda. The deeper one went into it, there seemed to be nothing but *more* tact and *more* discretion. Even the most worried reading revealed no breaches of faith or security; it resisted utterly any allegorical partiality. The most bizarre matters were related in the most matter-of-fact manner, as if to remind us that it is only the most fantastical tales which have direct historical equivalence, while it is the banal tissue of everyday documentary coherence which is totally fabricated. If you really believe you have made something up, it only means that you haven't looked far enough, in my experience. "Imagination" is simply the relation of another person's memory that can't be exactly retrieved. There was nothing, you will notice, not even a proper name, which might compromise a personality, much less an agent. (In the summaries made by the lady copyists, every human and place name was left blank to be later written in by hand at a higher directorate.) Whatever else it was, this was no crank's fiction or self-serving confessional. It addressed itself to the seniormost level, yet it wore its authority easily and remained accessible to the most peripheral of participants. Its sheer number of heroes and heroines might well overwhelm the dubious and jaded contemporary reader, but Iulus was the only man I knew who lived a truly fascinating life and wasn't a boring writer. His work made you forget the injunction whereby you had come to read it—the highest praise you can give a document.

In all honesty I have forgotten in the press of other duties exactly how it was further processed. What I *never* forgot was the effect of the whole—as when you read too profound a book at too early an age, and all you can recall about it was that it required a new level of concentration, that brief and glorious lost time in everyone's life, when you are watching yourself get smarter. I understand that this will sound of exclusivity to contemporary ears, but at my age I cannot muster a suitable self-effacing apologia. My trembling hand is quite democratic enough. These days, I rather go in for being misunderstood.

There is still no good explanation as to why a man who sprang from a people who loved silence above everything should suddenly come out of his commodious closet and reveal himself. The intelligence community, like the literary, remains divided on the issue; professors and spooks competing as usual for the lowest esteem of their fellow citizens, as they trawl literature for moral fishies.

Devotees of economic man speculated that his cash flow was cut off. The psychological fraternity inferred that he experienced a crise de conscience. The Third Estate believed the book to be a hedge against betrayal by his sources. And literary folk worried about his intentions, only to dismiss them as irrelevant. Their methods leave no leeway for a personality who remains a mystery but who was also unafraid of any ethical test. Some have said he was a greater man than a writer. Well, who isn't?

But certainly he was not giving himself up or away. Only an American could believe in that sort of historical resolution. Pzalmanazar passed messages as most of us mere mortals pass water. And whatever we found of his, we "intercepted" it when he wanted us to.

I believed, in short, that the release of his papers was meant to mark the historical top in the snooze of the all-powerful. If Iulus was now fully awake, would it be long before, at long last, reality would step forward in America, all the contracts redrawn, and incredibility be recognized? It was time to cash out. Cannonia had a tryst with Destiny and her girlfriend Fate. At the stroke of the midnight hour, when the world sleeps and America comes into its tenth generation, Cannonia will wake to life and freedom.

So when the Company asked me to prepare a final digest, reduce his ten-thousand page opus to a bland four-page summary, I saw that any appreciation of Pzalmanazar imperiled simplification as well as my station. The sophistication of his observations simply could not be paraphrased. A memoir without hindsight? A meditation on the inherent wildness of history? A novel for people who hate novels?

It was finally conceded that the only man we could hire capable of tracking him down was himself . . . and his code name was changed to "Lost King." (None could spell or pronounce "Iulus" anyway.) It was as if our two selves were rushing to meet across history, but as I closed the distance and reached out my hand, I saw that he had been walking away from me backward the entire time. The best I could do was put real people into situations that probably did not exist, which after all is what history is all about. And so I reluctantly ran this summary up their flagpole:

> Fellow Colleagues:
> Even our disenchantment has definite limits. The mystery is not that the documents in question offer knowledge which is largely unknown. The mystery is that there is no knowledge to be known about them.

That snake in their lunchbucket cost me plenty. Having been routinely told to forget everything I learned, I resolved now to earn my pay by garrulating elaborately on what I had formerly denied I knew. But Iulus the author, if not the agent, was soon forgotten, and I, supposedly so severe and disinterested, controlled the files.

Don't get the wrong idea, but yes, Traveler, I fell for him.

GENTLEMEN ERRANT
(Iulus)

Much of the next month was spent in expeditions to gather up Father's manuscript. I climbed the tops of trees, Mother slashed her way with a saber through beargrass and thistlesage, platoons of hired hands were sent six abreast across the fields, while Catspaw and Öscar tracked with a pair of Chetvorah. The brambles dripped with our bloody dew.

Some pages were found floating on the stagnant face of the Mze, others plastered on the gnarled boles of great oaks, still others nailed like theses on a nest of thorns. The black velvet curtain in the study had been stripped of its quotes, the neat piles of manuscript scattered, the chess piece paperweights overturned. The vortex had even turned pictures to the wall. Clothesline was strung throughout the den, and every available paperclip and safety pin had been recruited to dangle dry the smeared pages. About a third of the manuscript appeared to be lost. For the first time in history, dogs were barred from his tower suite, and Father was in a low mood.

After one of these expeditions, our disconsolate crew was seated on the front stairs when a shabby closed carriage appeared through the lime trees at the end of the drive, driven by a not-so-excellent specimen of Skopje in a wide-brimmed hat, transporting a man dressed in *tête de nègre* and accompanied by what appeared to be two equally black bear cubs. Thinking it was perhaps a rich gypsy with his road show, Father reached in his pocket for the smallest change, then squinted in disbelief as the Professor and his charges hove into view.

No words were exchanged as the Professor dismounted and the black balls of fluff bounded out and immediately began to tear at each other's throats on the gravel, a fight beyond anything witnessed in our animal world. They couldn't have been more than six months old, their teeth and claws hardly more than cartilage, yet strings of blood and spittle flew in the air, and from a brief glimpse of the set of the jaws, Father recognized a fight to the death among embryos was ensuing, and that no human hand, no matter how courageous, could separate them. The Professor himself seemed paralyzed. Mother mobilized me—luckily enough, the garden hose had been laid out that morning across the drive like a mamba, and the jet of cold water broke the dogs' rage, shocking them into a civilized stupor and leaving them sprawled in the gravel at a third of their former size, the soaked black fur settled about their still-soft skeletons. With almond eyes they regarded the gashes in each other's throats.

"Sisters?" Father asked cheerfully, and the Professor nodded curtly.

"Chows?" Father inquired.

"Chow chows," the Professor adumbrated.

"Yours?"

"The Prinzessin's royal stock—a gift. The very finest. I couldn't be prouder."

Father refused to touch the dogs or try to ingratiate himself in any way. He instructed Öscar to isolate them and dress their wounds.

Both men were still inwardly seething from the Professor's proffer made and refused at the Black Dog, and Father curtly waved his confrere inside, apparently not wishing to lose control in front of the family.

The Count's visit before the storm had, as always, been brief and to the point. Count Zich was the proudest man in Cannonia, his ancestors clan chieftains and margraves when the Hohenzollerns were still goatherds. He was greatly respected throughout the country not for his wealth, station, or political power, but because he was a world-class pianist who only performed for his friends at parties, never in public. He had just come from one performance, apparently, his stiff dress shirt protruding from his lintwhite duster, smelling of rockrose, veal, and lavender water. His still-dark hair was slicked back, but his sidechops were white as his starched shirtcuffs. His soft boots were of the same yellow leather as the fringed harness of his grays. And his malacca cane was topped with the ivory figure of a defecating mountain goat. The Count's immense composure relaxed everyone. He always took his seat facing east, where his ancestors had been kings. Ainoha lay on the chaise lounge in pantaloons *à la turk*, her long clay pipe nested between her breasts. Father was bolt upright in his favorite chair, smoking a straight pipe but letting it droop sideways from his mouth, as if it were curved. And even the dogs, feigning sleep, had their ears cocked for what was to come.

It seemed that the Count's vast network of spies, whose main brief was to keep his friends out of trouble, had alerted him to certain delinquencies in the tax rolls of Semper Vero, and while Zich had covered these with his own funds, he thought it best to personally urge a sober retrenchment upon his *camarade*. As an afterthought, he mentioned the fact that as Europe and Asia had broken the peace, funds for a general mobilization might require some two thousand million imperials. And then as a second afterthought, he opened the monogrammed leather briefcase which never left his side, revealing a gold telegraph key, a small ivory composing keyboard of one and a half octaves, as well as a piano roll, and with incredible nonchalance, his beautiful, beringed hands tapped out a precautionary message in C-minor to the army (Caparison the horses, lower all border toll gates) with a coded variant to the king at Umfallo. Then, swearing everyone to secrecy, he confided the latest coup of his intelligence service, the shocking information that the Americans were about to outlaw drinking! this ominous news producing general incredulity.

The Count was not surprised when his hosts expressed little anxiety about a potential conflict. Indeed, the attitude of everyone he had talked with, including his ministers, seemed to be one of inevitability, even enthusiasm. When he mentioned that the Russians might be drawn into an invasion, Ainoha said only, "Well, let them."

As he took his leave, Count Zich asked Felix to use his influence with the gentry to prevent them from withdrawing funds from the savings banks. Should a war ultimatum be necessary, he would ask him to journey to Malaka and make his independent judgment available to King Peveny.

"This thing could be started by a bird's chirp," he confided. The grays fairly tore down the drive.

That evening, abed in Mother's suite, Felix felt gaseous as lightning struck about his heart. But the thought of summoning Dr. Pür and being in his debt was too much to bear, and indeed, the small stroke he suffered seemed to calm him for the morning's horrific discovery, when he found his white book wound tight about the blackened whale ribs of his estate.

After organizing our battalions of woe to run down his papers, Felix locked himself in the den for a month, admitting only Öscar with victuals, drink, ink, twine, and the daily quota of rescued manuscript. He leafed back through his *Chronik* and did the sums. Count Zich was quite right of course: there was not a liquid farthing to his name, and even after deducting advertising and meals, the training project, begun so innocuously with the advertisement in the Sunday *Tagblatt* a year ago, had through its cash drain forced him into general default. He asked himself what god, what madness had brought him to Cannonia, but did not have the strength to actually write this in the margins.

As one should know by now, blows of fate had the opposite effect upon Father as on most people. His mountains did not blow their tops, but rather fell ruined into themselves. His reaction was a sort of reverse hysteria, a chilling focus and self-control, the eerie calm of the sniper, and his abandoning of projects was most meticulous. He studied the *Chronik* for some days, arriving at a fair value for Semper Vero and all its dependencies, and detailing each asset, put the sheaf in the secret drawer holding the burnt-edged half-scraps of the Professor's partially discarded lucubrations.

He then began a maniacal cleanup, discarding books and journals he would never read again, dusting, scrubbing, polishing, and painting, as if his rooms were a yacht. So when the Professor entered, ducking under the reams of stained and drying manuscript, he beheld a chamber nearly devoid of its old charm and eccentricity. On the large cherry table, once piled high with papers and indescribable objects of every sort, there was now only some perfectly coiled telegraph wire, a green accountant's shade, and a pistol. There were also three large bronze-lipped vessels, one filled with Charbah Negra, one with golden water from the Mze, and a middle one, empty. These limpid, liquid pools flung discs of reflected light about the newly whitewashed ceiling. The black velvet curtain had been drawn together to a fraction of its former breadth, revealing a new set of empty, gilded cubbyholes to memorialize the lost transitions of the manuscript, but in its dark folds I was to discover later the first new quote, I think from *The Aeneid*:

But now commit no verses to the leaves
Or they may be confused, shuffled and whirled

By playing winds: chant them aloud, I pray.

A gleaming bronze telescope and its tripod had been placed on the balcony, the only place now free of the rustle of warped paper. Across the bitter river, a file of Astingi were moving, not en masse but in an endless single column, streaming beautifully as the Mze once did.

"Have a look," Father said, adjusting the telescope so the Professor could glimpse a few of their faces close-up: hollow-cheeked with emerald eyes and unkempt hair, aquiline jawbone, nose and brow decisively but delicately finished, the Ur-Goyim departing. What struck one was neither their military nor sportive rituals, but the ultimate distinction of their manners in looks and bearing, their reckless tempo and lack of fuss, their almost preposterous patrician mien, which made even the most elegant modern courtier seem hopelessly gloomy and plebeian in our spoilt eyes.

"Sometimes," Father mused, "I think they are the last real people left on the face of the earth."

The Professor did not take the bait, and believing he had achieved a kind of trump with ownership of the royal chows, began tentatively, hoping to break the ice.

"Is it a book then . . . that you're working on?"

"I wouldn't call it a book, really." Felix replied evenly, his knuckles white on the balcony railing.

"But through all our talks, you've never once mentioned it!" the Professor, now truly hurt, blurted mournfully. "How can that be?" Then the question authors dread above all others:

"Pray, what's it about?"

Father pointed silently across the river at the column heading East.

"A fine *spektakel,* no doubt, but do not you think it a waste of time to write about barbarians doomed to disappear?"

"Exactly what Marcus Aurelius thought upon this very spot, dear Doktor."

"On the edge of the ancient world, you choose to write about the only people *without* a history?"

"They lost their written language some time ago," Felix said softly without turning. "I aim to give it back to them before they depart."

"But surely this is a project that with . . . fresh capital . . . might best be finished in southern France, or even Italy."

"I moon not for your *vie méditerranée*," Father said without edge. "Oxen and wainwrights could not drag me away from here. I appreciate you playing the fool the other day, but despite your ineffectual gallantry, you're still not ready for a Chetvorah."

"Not ready," the Professor said sarcastically, "or not deserving, Councilor?"

"Ah, always the *justiz* business, eh, Herr Doktor?"

The Professor let this pass with a superior glance, and Felix felt his self-control slipping away.

"I find it passing strange, Herr Doktor, that of all the girls in the world, you would attach yourself to this, this brace of chowlets from the uncircumsized East."

The Professor was unperturbed. "That's quite the point: the Prinzessin traces them back to the eleventh century BC. They are the true ancestors of the basic breed, migrated from the Arctic Circle. They joined us in our time of troubles, the glacial age, when hair was hair."

"I see that the Princess has been reading *Popular Dogs*," Father enjoined. "But how far back must we go, Herr Doktor? Could we just for a moment climb out of prehistory and concentrate, say, on something more admissible? Their parentage, for example?"

"Lun and Jofi," the Professor announced, "are of the Tartoum line." And he handed over the pedigree papers like a military messenger under artillery fire.

"Tartoum?" Father interjected. "British stock!" Then, placing his pale hand on Professor's shoulder, he made preparations for a long, soft soliloquy. "Let us go and do some lineage work," and they passed directly across the library, now shaded by a huge tree of manuscript fluttering in the breeze. Felix offered nothing by way of hospitality, and the Professor's usual martial walk became tentative. He suspected that he was not adventuring that day, but trespassing. The chows' violence had released some unspeakable aura into the air. Father sat him down behind his desk as he scanned the dogs' papers.

"One shouldn't make too much of this, but I can tell you now that these dogs will never get along. There are forces here, a jealousy say, that is well beyond our control, and you are going to have to choose between the two.

But let's defer that. You seem to forget that in this part of the world we have a certain sensitivity to visits from the East, and that your fondness for the Ice Age neglects the somewhat more contemporary fact that it was precisely these dogs, with their black tongues and stiff gait, who accompanied the Tartars on their raids. And so, for hereabouts, they are the veritable symbol of Asiatic carnage. I'm surprised that they weren't shot right out of your carriage. If word got around, I could have my whole kennel poisoned. So I must ask you to remove . . . I forget their names—the girls—by darkfall, and to return without them."

The Professor accepted this with equanimity—indeed, he seemed to take pleasure in what Father told him. He simply said, "I need something, someone strong in my life."

Father pretended not to hear. He had already removed the drying manuscript pinned to the periodical rack where the issues of *Dogdom* for each year had been bound annually in blue cloth with leather spines. He matched the Prinzessin's papers with the subsection on "Chow Life," and found the lineage quickly, whereupon he broke into a devilish grin.

"It seems, Professor, that what we have here is a hegemonic Anglo-American cross."

The Professor's face fell.

"And there seems another burden you must bear, my friend: the pater, Tartoum the Fifth. The chow breed became popular in England when Queen Victoria put one in her kennels. Tartoum won the show at the Crystal Exhibition despite biting the judge and his handler. He was owned by one Marchioness Hurtley, who, after centuries of random breeding, decided to fix, in a fit of *Darwinism*"—Felix spat this word—"the traits she most prized. In this case the project was to deangulate the hindquarters and perfect the perpetual scowl. She was trying for aristocratic aloofness, one must suspect; what she got was bitterness. She strengthened the back legs, no doubt, which is why we now have a leonine body upon pencil legs, like an old whore. In any event, Tartoum continued to win and bite—the more he won, the more he bit—and the English dealt with this in their usual manner, by changing ownership often, so that Tartoum accumulated as many masters as medals, bringing glory to a succession of not-so-old families—always in need of certification—who, having filled their trophy case with his ribbons, passed on his viciousness at a profit to one another. Tartoum did manage,

309

randomly, to produce some notable dogs, mainly daughters: Blue Cobweb and Tam Wong Ton come to mind. I saw the latter drag a child on a sled once at Berlin."

This too did not perturb the Professor. His eyes were black as coal and his jaw was set in a particularly determined line.

"Given this line of development, Councilor," he said calmly, "what would you suggest in the way of reinforcement?"

"It's perhaps too late," Father said, "but chows do not like to let go of things, and for some reason do not like to be touched around their hindquarters. The Tartars' whip, perhaps? Without delay you should let them play with your hand in their mouth and touch them all about their privates. When you can insert a finger under their tongue without being hurt, and a finger in their anus without hurting them—well, that's about as far as you can go with a chow."

The Professor nodded reflectively.

"Of course, we only have half the story."

"Pardon?"

"The American mother, sir, is Arrogant Melody Moonbeam! The credentials, if we can believe them, are impressive: a certificate at Westminster," he read further, "yes, yes, this should interest you. It seems that the great preponderance of American chow exhibitors are doctors. Arrogant Melody is owned, but not handled, by a Dr. Herb Fagen of Staten Island, a proctologist, it seems."

The Professor's hand felt inside his vest for a Trabuko.

"And *her* parents are from the great state of California. Would you care to know their names? Here, write this down: "Sid and Maurey Mintz are the breeders in Sacramento, California. Sid is an oral surgeon, Maurey a 'homemaker'"—what do you suppose *that* is? And the grandparents are here: Bring the Bacon, a four-time champion of Orange County, and Rabbinic Petticoat Lane. Curious names, no? These chow-minded folk."

The cigar was lit but there was no smoke; it was all inside the Doctor. Father gravely turned the pages.

"And two littermates of Moonbeam have eight points toward their championships: Don Li Chowtime and Cotton Candy Chink. So it would seem that we have invigorated the inbred royal line with the hardy middle-class blood of the restless people of Aaron."

"Bourgeois," the Professor snorted. And through the murmurous whispers of manuscript Father cocked one ear like a dozing dog who hears a distant gunshot. Perhaps he was trying to wiggle his ears, but there were no puptricks left in his repertoire. He fixed the Professor with an arctic gaze. He was cool, so cool it burnt.

"You of all people should know," he spoke with icy lucidity, each phrase like a scythe blade, and widening his eyes as if to take in all the room, "that we will always have need of a place outside the bourgeois and beyond capital."

The Professor made a small sheepish gesture. "You have an extraordinary ability to discompose a person," but Felix again did not hear. He repeated his last words to himself as if dazed, then wandered over to another glass vitrine of artifacts and began to strip it of manuscript.

Now, one kind word (or less harsh joke) from either one would have ended this confrontation, and concluded our tale on a still tenuous but more appealing note. But the time had come for their favorite game, the game which spared no feelings, a game which could only be played spontaneously by two powerful men, each believing the one was incapable of hurting the other, a battle of the polymaths.

It was in an exorbitant, hyperbolic mood that Father opened the vitrine and set out the two artifacts of the day: first, a female figure cut from lava, schematic and wide-buttocked, a goddess with elongated neck and stumps for arms, wearing a belt with discs on the pubis and each hip, the shoulders incised with meanders, chevrons, and semi-circles; and next, a veined, rosy, marble male member, half-hooded, with a single incision in its tip, and broken from its torso.

"Of the goddess we know nothing," Father said, "except that pieces like it are invariably found whole, the lack of a head and arms due to the indifference or crudity of the maker. Of the other, we know even less, except that both statues stood on the Via Ocampo in Rome, the goddess within the temple, the naked general without. Here, speak into the radio." He picked up the pink penis of Marcus Aurelius from the table as if it were a tarot discard. "Put it in your mouth," Father said slowly. The Professor gazed across at him quizzically.

"Pretend you're a horse and think of it as just another sort of snaffle," Father continued in a rather uncharacteristic singsong. "Put it in your mouth and I'll tell you a story, better than that little bastard, Gubik. It's called 'The Bourgeois and the Barbarians.'"

The Professor held the piece of marble between his fingers like a cigar. "You must be joking."

"Never more serious in my life. You'd be far better off with that in your mouth than those damn Trabukos. *Saxa loquuntur*! (Stones speak!)"

The Professor knew he was being double-dared, and so, with rather too much exaggeration, replaced his cigar with the stone.

"How is it?" Father asked.

"Is *kalt*."

And with that, Father began to murmur about that admirable man, the last of the good emperors, who on the very spot where they had now taken their stand, had been the first to scan the Astingi across the Mze.

"So, Marcus," Father invoked his name, as if he were seated at the table, "that befuddled and permanently transitional figure, sent to an unattractive region to stem the tides of barbarism, only to end up theoretical and melancholy. The first real westerner, Marcus, weary of life, unable to praise an uneasy peace, denied a climactic victory, waiting for the retreat to sound, avoiding malice but never really sealing the borders, yet never quite overrun, and forgiving the avarice and treachery of those around him only because there was no adequate form of revenge. The first intellectual, Marcus, a man of good intentions who was nevertheless basically a humbug and a prig, a kind of schoolmaster silently condemning everyone, obsessed with self-perfection and the reiteration of moral platitudes, full of precepts and self-exhortations, addressing no one but himself, even though he is king, general, and scribe. In an Age of Hypochondria, he finds his audience distracted. He has a bad marriage and knows the most deplorable of his children will succeed him. He meditates, if that's the word, not upon the empire, but upon death. The Mze is frozen solid, and one moonless night there is a cavalry battle on the frozen ice floes, the horses slipping and sliding amidst showers of sparks, the torches held by the horse handlers. Two mounted regiments clashing head on in a medium where every strategy and virtue is turned into a nightmare of pure chance. And after this, ignoring the most amusing thing that might befall a commander in all his campaigns, Marcus does not even count the bodies in the morning, but returns to his tent to be alone with his 'diary,' his nocturnal, where, after many a midnight lucubration, he

312

submits his body to his mind, the only struggle being between the thinker and his thought—real *pensées* such as 'Virtue is the only good,' 'Time is a torrent,' and 'Put down the bitter cucumber.' And there in his tent, Marcus makes the astounding discovery that serenity is possible only when all things are external to you. While from across the Mze comes the taunt, as it comes still: 'Fight Marcus! Get naked and fight!'"

The Professor's lips around the marble cigar had turned light blue. His eyes were closed.

"Had he been more attentive to detail," Father continued, knees pumping like an adolescent's, "he would have noticed that when his soldiers stripped the bodies on the floes of the frozen river the next day, they found women among the dead, their heads and arms cut off, but clearly women in armor. When you find a woman in armor, the campaign is over, my friend, whatever the results of the battle. It's time to turn around the elephants and go home."

The Professor popped the marble from his mouth, holding it between his first and second fingers.

"Why is it, Councilor," he rejoined, holding his own against the rhetorical onslaught, "that everyone these days thinks they're a Herodotus or Thucydides?"

But the narrative trance was not to be interrupted.

"Ah, Marcus," Father whispered across the table, gripping its edges with his hands, "Marcus, Marcus, *Mar-cus*!" He cupped his lips about his mouth and called across the table as if it were a river. "Marcus Aurelius . . . has a little penius," he giggled. The Professor's face had by now sunk into his beard.

"I'm not at all sure," he said gravely, "that as a general rule I would recommend listening to those shouts from across the river," which of course is the most provocative thing he could have said.

"No greater fear than to be named by those who have no name! And when someone hates you, Professor, one must approach their souls, penetrate inside, and see what sort of people they are! And to do that, one must give up notions of both literary and military fame. One must cross the arbitrary river which divides Cannonia Superiore from Cannonia Inferiore, enter the black room from the white chamber. To discover *our* people, Professor, when we were *all* Jews! There they sit watching across the ancient barrier of the Mze, so often violated and so often restored. Shall they sweep it away, shall they enter Europe by the Mze in a shower of faggots and arrows, so all Europe is a mangled stag? For across the river, they see what soothing relief it is to turn the personal into the intellectual."

The Professor absently took a puff on his surrogate cigar.

At this point Father grew exasperated, and leaping to the south wall, tearing down more manuscript, drew down with a crack like a rifle shot a map which for the rest of the decade covered "The Scale of Being" and "The Tree of Life." It didn't appear to be a spontaneous gesture, but one he had been preparing for some time, with wide reading and a good deal of note-taking. From what I could judge through the closed doors where the dogs and I lay panting, our noses squashed against the keyholes, he'd been rehearsing even the cadences of his delivery, as he often did before his rare jury trials. He was about to give the master speculator himself a complicated history lesson, and hopefully reinvigorate their conspiracy to unite Logos and Eros.

The map was a conventional one of European "Christendom," with the outlines of the Roman Empire superimposed in all its varicose purplescence, cutting improbably through Spain and England, across Middle Gaul to the Rhine, then falling precipitously along the Danube, where the lines veered off to the northeast, to the no-name land of the beech forests where we made our home. On the far left edge of the map was Martha's Vineyard, and on the far right, Ulan Bator, both pink, the former incised by the three diagonal lines indicating marsh, the latter surrounded by scalloped lines denoting desert.

Father addressed himself to the pretensions of those Rome-centered minds who bequeathed nothing but ruins, noise, and organized cheating in merchandising the corpses of their ancestors. As long, he insisted, as the Professor was so interested in regions which could not, as it were, speak for themselves, perhaps he might pay some attention to the 95% of the dehellenized ancient world from which both their ancestors had come by cart (albeit from different directions) and to which they would undoubtedly one day return by similar conveyance. Then he drew an *X* upon the map at the exact location where they now sat. He would speak, he made it clear, not on behalf of the empire and its labored self-conscious chroniclers, but of those who exploded it, those whose lands stretched from northern Ireland to northern India, whose names and languages we do not know. He would speak in brief for all barbarians, celebrate their perpetual playful ambush of the pygmy Romans humping away in their lonely bathhouses on the Mze, all balls and no prick. In his tumultuary acclamation, the Roman cavalry was cut to pieces by an immensely tall and exotically beautiful people, with long penises and tight scrotums, those warriors whom the Professor blamed for the glacial battles in our hippocampus, whose campaigns resurface in wife-beating, pederasty, and all the other gratuitous violences of street and stable.

"Why is it, Professor, that the story is always told in terms of inner collapse, of debauchery in high places, poor leadership, corruption, subversion of the constitution, debased currency, or flawed electoral processes? Why not in terms of the superiority of the invaders, not only tactically, but in the measure of their courage, and the superiority of their nomadic culture?"

Father took up a shooting stick from the umbrella stand and tapped it on the map as if it were a divining rod. "Do we measure a people by its glut of architecture, their impulse to brick over every last inch of green earth on the continent, rivaled in excess only by the Dark Ages, when they built a church for every two-hundred inhabitants in Christendom? Architecture tells us zero. When our people moved they didn't have any idea of where they were going or what they would do when they got there. They failed to seize almost every favorable circumstance. Is this so hard to grasp? All they knew is they had to turn the pressure from their front and rear somehow to their advantage. Now, that's a human heritage to be proud of, Professor. No lyric there, I suspect, just the purest kind of physics. Look!" The shooting stick slapped the map with a sharp report. "In one pass it's all Wagnerian flame and thunder; in another, a miserable group unsure even of its own race, driven by abstract ratios of bears to berries, indifferent to treasure, hair golden and pitch, eyes both bright blue and dark as midnight. Startled fugitives, they look into the cradle of the world and all they see is a vast landscape of categories, and small works of art that you might bury with your mother. And each time they made a breach, inadvertently overrunning another tribe, they would absorb whomever was there, and in so doing only open an inroad at their rear for a tribe even more savage and disconcerted than themselves! *That*, my friend, not Master Gubik's mythotherapy, is the story of civilization, and one which does not lend itself to excavation."

The Professor continued listening courteously, with a quizzical look on his face.

"But look!" Father exclaimed. "In the last millennium before the nailed-up corpse shows up, look."

The pointer flashed to the passes of the Unnamed Mountains, down the great angled rivers and tributaries renamed with every change of government, through the dissipated empires like moist blotting paper smoldering and blackened at the edges.

"Tribes pushed by even more shadowy tribes, falling upon and absorbing other tribes. Nothing but an avalanche of mineral dialects and honest disbelief informs their armies, changing their names each time they cross a river. Bowl-faced and hatchet-faced, long heads and round heads, dark and fair. Once across the river they begin to undress, shed their sodden clothing and leather armor, and take their trousers off. Brandishing their javelins, painted blue with a paste of cedar and cypress, long penises tied up around their waists, not as a show of masculinity but on the contrary, to remind their foes of their own swinging soft vulnerability, the oddness and fragility of that member, the only thing in nature which is beautiful when wrinkled, that moiety which they cut off and stuffed in the corpses' mouths, as that odd *sarmentum* which once produced a scream of pleasure now stoppled one of fear! There was panic in the outposts. Livius speaks of the barbarians moving across the landscape like dancers, their muffled vowels and harsh dactyls piercing through the spruce and poplar, so that frozen lakes with black holes became burned pastures. And what do the Romans make of them? Herr Marcus's *stupor mundi*: 'Men murder and die of remorse. They never get back home. The privileged seem to fail at crucial times.' He retires once again to the dark tent of his nocturnal to ask, 'What is evil?' And there under the heading, 'To Himself,' he begins those self-sodomizing speculations on why we are here. It's not success in ventures that counts, he concludes, but the moral attitude with which they are undertaken. Phui! In the forest," he whispered hoarsely, "in the reed-beds, our people wait for the hour to strike. And we wait with the superior knowledge that everything is going to vanish!"

Suddenly the pointer twitched all over the map from the Jutland Peninsula and southern Sweden to the Bay of Kent, swiping across Gaul to the Pyrenees, and then with a flash across Spain and the Mediterranean Sea, on to Carthage and Sicily.

"All this in a single generation! An undeveloped, swinish people? A rude, forest hatchet people who had somehow acquired a naval fleet? Well, there you have it! Thus speaks the stone."

Father's shirt was soaked with sweat.

"But surely there was a motive, an idea," the Professor calmly interjected, "a dream, a fantasy, a belief that welded such disparate folk?"

Father cut him short. "Nothing of the sort. Ideas have their origin in explaining to your family why you have to move again. They simply took aim at the only coherent target, those peacock strutters on their pathetic walls, wrapped in their pastel winding sheets affixed with unattractive brooches."

The Professor paused with infinite sarcasm. "Every dog will have its day, I suppose. And yet," he continued more softly, "there were ancient wonders."

"Ah, the old German dreaming of the sunken empire," Felix rasped.

"No," the Professor protested gently. "I was thinking of the Egyptians."

"Fifteen centuries to determine that the dog is more venerable than the cat? A plodding people."

"You are too hard on Aurelius," the Professor went on, adopting a plaintive tone. "Have you no pity for one who prayed and worried for his men, who in turn only wished him gone? He was not superstitious; he was lenient. He was . . . a gentleman."

"He was only the first of men," Father huffed, "who would force us to be intellectuals and take away our pastimes and pleasures!"

The Professor had spat out the marble, and it lay on the table in a small glistening pool of saliva. Father took no notice. He was scribbling down what he just said *in furiant*. And then I realized that this harangue was not rehearsed or calculated at all, but a desperate attempt, through the pretext of a debate, to recover the lost pages of his manuscript, not unlike Gubik deciphering his narratives from his mute mother's sign language. Thus ended my aristocratic education. I had learned everything I needed to know for my career. For life with friends and lovers is essentially this: that we assist each other in recovering and rewriting the book which is always blowing away, when the words don't mean what you say. If one is attentive to this in another, you may be idealized or hated, but you will never have to spy. If you are unlucky enough not to find such an accomplice, or sufficiently torpid to refuse to be one, we go to war. We go to war not only to save face, but because we are deliriously happy and relieved to set aside the incredibly demanding project of rewriting the lost book which is always being written. In our hyperacute consciousness we will seek the help of the barbarian, will urge him to come and deliver us from our final agony of revision, and burn the bloody library. Only Count Zich, it seems, was aware that we were in such a moment.

The Professor, putting his feet upon the table, resorted to the one name which he knew would get a response.

"I believe you neglected the bourgeois part of the story," he said without a trace of conviction.

This slight remonstrance indeed gave Father second wind, allowing him to play his trump, literally, and the dogs and I shuddered as he approached the huge instrument which took up the end of the library, half-tank, half-lyre. He saw that he had the Professor half-persuaded, and knew that to bring the old dog finally around, to fix the new trick in the netherfolds of his cortex, he would have to demonstrate that his own diagnostic powers were yoked to compassion—this by reinforcing his subject's *weakest* sense, in this case, the Professor's lack of an ear, his natural tone deafness, worsened no doubt by years of fake listening. He managed one of those compact turns, spinning on his boot heel, always the prelude to putting his nose through the facts, and with this he seated himself at the instrument of black Cannonian pine, nine feet tall, built as a right pyramid, with a single unblinking Masonic eye carved at the garlanded apex, the keyboards held up by twin little negroid figures, one carrying bells and the other a sort of drum.

His little finger rose and struck a single note—*boing, boink*—and the Professor's face lifted up as if an invisible training whistle had sounded.

"*This* is what Marcus heard, Professor, beyond the voices and the taunts: *boink.* This is when he knew there was some magic boisterousness going on in those transalpine bastions which had to be constrained. *Boink* came the monotone, a note with his name on it, floating across the misty swamps and reedy islands of our melancholy region, the sound of reality, Professor, which Marcus mistook for the sound of attack."

Father's hands rose up to strike a chord from the huge furnace.

"Most prized of all, Professor, our people had in their wagons a rude wooden box or gourd across which was stretched a single string. Crude by Marcus's melodious standards, perhaps, but let us never forget what stupefaction must have resulted from several millennia of the harp, relieved only by an occasional blast of the royal guards' marine trombones—much less their callow attempts at choral harmony, which could be nearly pleasing only if chanted very slowly and with the utmost gravity. Against this officious flatulence, our tribes advanced with their crude dulcimers, their monochords, holding in their heads certain passages, something in E-flat perhaps, without a slightest notion of how they might be performed. But they knew one thing, which had not occurred to the routinized wizards of Rome, a discovery equivalent to fire and undoubtedly just as inadvert . . . That great day when a javelin toppled over upon a gourd, and our predecessors realized that a note might be struck as well as plucked, plonked and plinked as well as bowed and swiped, smited more than strummed, iron on the wire of history . . . Yes, Professor, our people, the percussionists! Strike the string and turn Marcus white sitting in his dark tent. Watch carefully as those clear-eyed, clean toga'd men with their souls floating like little balloons above their head, will turn . . . When from across the Mze they heard the first modern sound—*boing*—throwing fear into the slender ghostly voices of the homogeneous lyre, calling into question all constitutional guarantees, natural rights, and the niceties of law—*boing*! And as they advanced, they learned quickly through victorious campaign after campaign, and not a few strategic retreats, that the other hand on the string might alter the tones. Wielding the spear through the Cannonian countryside, it was above Razacanum as forty-three churches were consumed in flames, that it was first announced that the thumb was no longer an apologetic pivot, a subordinate, but equal to the other four fingers, and there assumed a lead over the other fingers it would never relinquish. By expert force, we could diminish the sound, hold the note, fictitiously enlarge the span of the hand, while you went on with the next area of business. All great musical cultures are military, Professor, and as the great Robert E. Lee once said, 'You can't have an army without music.'"

Father raised his hands once again, though he had not yet struck a chord.

As Father detailed the wholesome reforms of our Astingi predecessors, admittedly transmitted forcibly for a time, I could not but reflect on their long march to the true imperium of the piano, and the brief time of my youth when all experience, technical and emotional, had been transcribed for it.

The original instrument in question had been purchased from a Turkish pasha by my grandfather Priam as a focal point for his sad, overstuffed furniture, which had nothing to do but face the fire. It served for a brief time as the national instrument of Cannonia, constructed as it was into two small pianos severed from their keyboards, so that they might be slung over donkeys and transported to concerts in the mountains. They were strung so they could be played inside with sticks by peasants, or outside if connected with the keyboard for those whose brain hemispheres happened to work together. Eventually the two halves were wedded with an innovative iron frame which insured consistently unequal tension, allowing the instrument, by separating wood from metal, to come as close as possible to the timbre of the singing voice, the illusion of the vocal.

By the time Grandfather had finished with his tinkering, the instrument was two pianos in a single case, coupled together by a lever, one tuned an octave above the other, for four-hand music for those without a partner, once again increasing one's fictitious reach. The evolution of the instrument had followed the revolutions of the arms industry in the border fortifications, for Priam's theory was that if you couldn't have a battleship or a locomotive, you could have a piano and make your women play it. Grandmother Eriphyle had perused it in the half-hour before retiring, but as she refused to allow him to smoke while she played, he refused to attend her concerts. And so it sat for a year or so in complete desuetude, and while Grandfather never played a note, he carefully polished it, purchasing by mail order from Breslau a cushioned, inclined stool in black walnut, a telescopic lamp in bronze, and an automatic music desk to store the sheets. From Dresden he procured an obsidian finger-guard and pocket hand exerciser, as well as a correspondence course on how to play, to which he devoted the remainder of his life. He progressed rapidly in his music-reading ability, specializing in pieces which were impossible to play with two hands alone. But when he reached a certain level of proficiency, he noted that as hard as he struck the keys, there remained a certain dynamic inflexibility, and when he tried to sneak from one key to the next with the same finger, the notes disappeared abruptly like a stone in mud. When he smote the keyboard with a balled fist, the sound was delightfully smooth, but without vitality, and the damping pedal only increased the ghostliness of the tone. He found that he could string the chords together only with a kind of pointless ornamentation of each phrase. Arabesques, which he loved in wallpaper and dressing gowns for reasons he did not wish to explore, he loathed in melody. He had the curious unpleasant feeling that something was acting as an unnatural check upon his tone. And so he wrote straightaway to Württemberg for a steam-activated, hydraulic booster mechanism, a large and beautifully crafted copper dome called the *wohltemperer*, which connected the keyboard to the coal furnace, and when properly stoked by a servant, filled the house to the turrets with the organlike resonance of a hearty baritone voice. Thereafter, the same firm supplied him with a gearbox, designed from a secret alloy which allowed him to tighten the strings equally and test the tension of even the iron frame. And in a specialist magazine he came across a third pedal, the *spiccato*, for forty Louis d'or. "Low as a bassoon yet high as a flute," it advertised, which allowed him to pass from major to minor without modulation, and disguised his weak left hand, which tended to lope after his right like a wounded deer. Then, successively, from the same company he added a fourth pedal, a *chordata*, which somehow strew a silk curtain upon the strings, and a year later a fifth offering arrived unsolicited by express post, a *pedal d'expression*, which sustained any chord and virtually redefined the notion of forever. Finally, a *sixth* pedal for Janissary music was attached, the only accessory manufactured in his homeland, which added an accompaniment of triangle and drum at random intervals. He christened this endlessly modified *attroupement* the "Archicemblelomachord," and its renown gathered many prominent people and distinguished visitors to Semper Vero, including suitors for his daughter, as well as famous composer/virtuosos, who on their way to concert tours of Russia made a point to stop by and try out their repertoires of Kalkbrenner, Hummel, Herz, and Moscheles. (Mozart was then considered too old-fashioned, his piano music mere sketches for quartets, while Beethoven's sonatas were ignored as monstrous abortions of German idealism.) These guests often admitted the instrument was superior to the piano, but they did not wish to learn their art over, much less rely upon a *klaviergeschichte* which was by now virtually impossible to transport.

Over the years Priam refined his own tremulous tone, which he called *vibrando*. In the evenings he played for his wife what he called "keyboard conversations," and she occasionally accompanied these rondos with a half-hearted tambourine. His favorite program consisted of several new pieces, such as "To a Dying Poet," "Easy Sonata Spanish Dances Manqué," Lefeburewely's "Monastery Bells," and his favorite of all, the *fantasia effusio*, "Battle Fog," commissioned especially to incorporate all his modifications, and to this day the only piece ever played upon it not written for other instruments. So it was that this clavicytherium consisting of three keyboards (fretted and unfretted) and six codimentary pedals, driven by a steam turbine large enough to power a small factory, passed on to my father's hands in the first years of our blind century.

Felix was in his thirties before he felt comfortable with the prerogatives of heirs and began his own modifications, according to preferences he himself only vaguely understood. His childhood memory of musical soirees consisted of excruciatingly boring evenings on hard chairs without conversation, the crossing and uncrossing of legs, suppressed coughing, stale sweets, unventilated rooms, a grossly extended family which expressed itself by brief programmatic bursts of applause, and an audience applauding itself for enduring a trial for all concerned—the tyranny of the human.

He felt that things had gone too far in the direction of taste and touch, too far toward emulating the overrated human voice, which was not there in the first place. Somewhere in that instrument lay delicious secrets which had nothing to do with singing, but rather the Assyrian ratios of wood against metal. It cried out to be shorn of its language props, its symphonic rhetoric, and above all the endless technical compromise to improve trumpetish compositions.

There came a day when Ainoha declared her own disinterest, one too many whiskeys being set down upon the instrument, each leaving a pale white ring, and a small army of locals was hired to move the relic to Father's den. During the move, an inadvertent brush on the keyboard suggested to Felix that it sounded better when played upon men's backs, and when finally set down in the library, he ordered it placed upon two worn tractor tires.

The acoustics were muffled by the rubber base as well as the room's books. Disconnected from the steam turbine, as well as its social function, the gothic lettering across the instrument's brow was changed to serrified Roman capitals. Its tone was confused, as if unsure of its place in the history of technology. Yet if there was little it allowed, there was nothing it violated, either. When he played, say, the bravura "Capriccio for the Departure of His Dead Brother," it was no longer music from another better world, but music which did not require a world. And now alone with his instrument, he began a movement toward a feeling he could not name, although he knew it was away from originality and personal expression, while still extremely novel and highly private. First he replaced the French action, which was always a trifle sloppy, with the tinny but more lifelike American castings. Then he replaced the English cabinetry, which had begun to split and check, with pine salvaged from the lining of trenches during the early Balkan Wars, which thus weathered, warped, gassed, and blasted by every inhuman invention, was incapable of further mischief, insuring an even resonance throughout the sharply changing seasons. He also installed a curved maple bottom to disperse the harmonics, and along the trebles added a fourth silent string to pick up any lost vibrations. And finally he replaced the all-leather hammers with those of rabbit skin, a single capercailzie sewn in the tuft.

Throughout this my mother and I occupied ourselves without the slightest guilt with the used Bösendorfer of infinite nostalgia and a gramophone of His Master's future voice. But as we whiled away the hours in the music room, in his study Father had became increasingly aware of the slight error which centuries of technical subterfuge has distributed throughout the twelve fifths of the keyboard, in order to make the remotest tonalities undistressing to the ear—and this began to annoy him as much as the fulsome, too wholesome tone color of Priam's heritage.

One day when Father attended an afternoon concert in the Silbürsmerze park, he saw a composer—dressed more like a mechanic than an artist—get up from his stool and crawl inside the grand piano, where he continued to play. He loved the offense it gave to the office-heroes in the audience, but once inside the instrument, Father knew that they were at no cutting edge but back to the stringed gourd which had so unhinged Marcus. As much as he enjoyed for a few moments the mutilation of the classic, he found that his delight in the discomfort of the audience was gradually evaporated by the tonal dice games, an artform constructed almost entirely of hurt feelings, and he had his first premonition that there might come a day when Klavierland would exist no more.

It was not long afterward that he sniffed out a retired professor at the Monstifita Conservatory, one Dr. Janko, who before arthritis had curled his fingers like so much burned paper, had been at work on a massive keyboard in which all auxiliary vibrations had been preserved—four keyboards of thirty-two keys each, so that each semitone succeeded another, each sharpened sharp, each double-sharpened flat, were preserved in all their purity to their remotest diatonic regions, yet all these faraway places were still staunchly related to the key of C, so that the notes could not be made to disappear until the vibration of each string came naturally to an end.

The Janko keyboard was invincibly difficult to play, but it fully suited Father, who had perfect pitch but no formal training to forget. Of all Grandfather's accessories, he found only the pocket hand exerciser from Dresden useful, though he still found occasion to use all the pedals, like all fortunate men whose antecedents have their place in every piece they undertake.

He knew then that if he would not play for a public, neither would he play for himself. He would play it for *it*self, allow the instrument to be the judge of him, frozen in a history that no one could locate. No performer, no composer, he would devise an instrument which only he could play, and so he performed without embarrassment a kind of random, dodecaphonic, dysphoric nonsense which gave him enormous satisfaction, in which no one in the entire countryside, much less our house, could share, nor was meant to.

There would be no evenings, merry or sober, spent round this instrument. No suitor would come to beguile his nieces. No strange hirsute visitor would call on him and ask him to sponsor a recital. No reviewer would get caught up in the finer points of explaining the intention of his composition. And he was grateful above all to realize that he would attract no pupils. He came to see that the Janko keyboard did not lend itself to those ineffable inner states which must elude the poor written word. However, as a weapon against artpiousness it had no equal. It was, indeed, the only way he could relax after training sessions and contact with the general public.

He began to see that this eclectic machine could be turned against the very class it captivated, and had he been interested in making such a thing as an aesthetic, he might return music to its military origins, and march against the sentimentality, stuffiness, and weepyeyed pale virtuosity by which the weak could make overstimulated women weep, a weapon which could be brought to bear against the cult of family values and civil society in general. It was shameful, no doubt, to work such idiots over, yet he couldn't help indulging himself in this anti-bourgeois music par excellence.

His hands were about to fall.

"And now for some *chow*music, Herr Professor!"

And thus he began, like the mechanic, with a few sweeps of sentimental C-majorness, to gradually disconnect the phrases from their harmonic center, willfully losing its heartbeat in chattering thickets of sound. In this many-layered but non-propulsive music, the notes were no longer played singly, but looked forward and backward at once, sub-harmonic resonances separated by fifty-second pauses, rappelling into the lost world of the future. Then he opened the pipes of the old *wohltemperer*, solo to swell, transposing the *heckelphone* onto the *quinte tromba*, the *tuba mirabilis* onto the *flûte à cheminée*, the *bois celeste* onto the *muted viole* and *corno d'amore*, and finally launched into the double counterfugue, *A Confutatis Tremendae*.

"Enough, *dayenu*, enough!" cried the Professor, clapping his hands over his ears, but too stunned to move.

Father responded only by dropping the flats of his hands onto the lowest and highest octaves of Janko's keyboard. The chords enveloped the tone-deaf Professor, on whom it produced goosebumps of a strange, indeterminate hue, and the dogs curled about me at the door—who had merely cocked their ears in semaphores of puerile curiosity at the sound of the Bösendorfer— now suddenly rose as one, totally alert. Sitting on their haunches in deep reverential respect, like a pair of tawny sphinxes, they took the notes into their bodies, those chords flying out to the east, a sound like that of walking on birds, away from the singing voice into the soul of the percussion people, dividing the hemispheres of the brain with Time's Arrow. This reverberation seemed to go on forever, back to the original timbre, with no separation between wood and metal, past Marcus's smoking braziers to the campfires across the river, which the barbarians could only extinguish by wounding themselves and dousing the embers with their blood. It was as if he had canceled out all those echoes buzzing in the soft dilettante's sleep of ages and approached the Heraclitan ideal—registering the overtones of the original historical note. The style of styles did not rise or fall—it was neither calming nor exciting. Only the Chetvorah seemed to recognize it as the sound of primeval men breaking camp without a goal, a well-known accompaniment to a task with unforeseen consequences, a rasp of wood on metal, the real prelude before the etude, the sound of changing your mind. And when it finally seemed unendurable and the air itself was smeared with notes that would never die on their own, Father kicked out the damper as well as the sixth pedal, and as the tone began to subside, the two tiny negroes swung out from each side of the instrument, ringing in a little postlude of triangle, bells, and trapdrum—to remind us that the task of the barbarian is to civilize the men of science.

The afternoon disappeared into a mournful, barely audible triple *pianissimo*, at once sardonic and ethereal, a solitude which was itself almost art.

The Professor had drawn himself up in a perspiring, quivering glower, his tone hyperboreal.

"I believe, sir, our business is concluded."

Father seemed taken aback.

"You're going away, then?"

"Yes, I must see about the horses."

"Very well, very well. Why must you . . . Do you find it dull here?"

"You *will* excuse me."

"Very well, then. I thought you would stay with us a little longer. A few hours . . . It's rather little, Berganza, rather little."

"Sir," the Professor stammered, his jaw jutting and rattling, "you ridicule me, sir, and have insulted the only comfort of my old age. And if there's one thing I've learned, it's this: people do not love you for what you know!"

Flinging open the study door, he barged past us spies down the stairs, as Father gave a start and clutched at his chest.

The horses were at the door. The Skopje in high felt boots sat listlessly in the box, his soft, fleshy torso and smooth, puffy face bloodless in the twilight, while his white scarf and shirttail blazed purity. In one hand he held the reins within a white cloth, in the other a popular illustrated magazine. His face had the yellow cast of a burning manuscript. Lun and Jofi sat chained on either side of him, white dressings stained with gore about their necks, and muzzled with bows of white satin ribbon. The dogs stared impassively to the east with reddened, slanted eyes, their faces reminiscent of those hirsute teenage fanatics whose passport photos hung in every postal guild, with eyes which neither see nor mirror, just places to take hold of the skull like a bowling ball. As the wind turned the poplar leaves silver, Father continued his efforts at repair, as he assisted the Professor in mounting the carriage step.

"You have taken on a complicated history, my friend. These dogs, you must understand, are the only hunting dogs native to China. There's mastiff in them, and Samoyed, no doubt. But they were never used for guarding their honorary patrons. They pointed and retrieved, if you can believe it: a lion stalking a golden quail—now there's a mandarin bit for you," he said with a false laugh. "And then as the civil wars ceased they were used for herding. Thousands of years denied their natural function, and only later, when the Tartars took them, did they become natural assassins. So you see there's some confliction here, which no doubt appeals to you. Their very lack of balance might be turned to an advantage, who can say? No one ever knows how a dog might assist a man."

Then he reached up to shake his hand, but the Professor refused to acknowledge him.

"One final thing you ought to bear in mind as far as upbringing goes," Father went on, grasping the coattail of his only male friend in Klavierland, "is the westernizing that these dogs have suffered." He reached up and ruffled Lun's fur to show the straightened rear leg. "Shortened thigh bone, yes?" And then he squeezed the roll of fat behind her neck. "This we owe to our British fanciers. If this were a human fetus, Professor, what would be your *diagnoze*?"

The Professor said nothing.

"Professor," my father said, his untaken hand almost shaking, "an interpretation, please! Here's a hint: an ugly synonym for certain Asiatics . . ."

There was a long harsh pause, then through the Professor's silence, the word appeared crisply in my father's throat:

"Mongoloid."

Then he nodded and stepped back, waving to the Skopje to be off.

"One last thing, Herr Doktor." He grinned mischievously, "The chow carries its tail over its back. As long as it's up the weather's fine. But if it ever drops, even a centimeter, run like a lunatic."

Then he offered his hand again. But the Skopje cracked his whip, bellowing out in a high falsetto:

"Stand clear, ye warmints!"

The wheels spun gravel and the kennels issued a baleful, incandescent roar. As the carriage door slammed on Felix's hand, from within the cab there came only a hiss:

"I walk out of your heart!"

My father ran alongside the carriage for perhaps a mile, only his apologetic white thumb visible in the black doorframe. He felt lonely as that little finger when, at a sharp turning of the road, he was flung into a ditch.

The village clock did not sound but showed such a time as perhaps never comes.

HISTORAE ASTINGAE: *Sport*
(Aufidius)

No country offers as much variety in hunting as the great pied-à-terre of Cannonia. An hour's drive in any direction will give the Sportsman an unlimited extent of moor and forest where he can range at will, whilst taking all manner of bodily relaxation in jorrocks, jaunts, and jollities. The visitor who is able to ride cross country, drop birds, take the tiller of a yacht, play rackets with skill, lure a great salmon to an artificial fly, keeping it in play for hours on the trace of a single gut, will have little difficulty in securing an invitation to a shooting party.

It is nevertheless advisable to put yourself under the expert guidance of one of the peasant nimrods of your district. They are capital walkers, generally amusing companions, and by no means despicable shots. Seek a good cragsman, untiring and dependable, clammy of brow with good lungs and heart, and a hand which when called into play, shows no tremor.

The shooting season commences on the fifteenth of July at the intersection of our sixteen migratory routes, which comprise the complete trajectory, song line, and career of every bird alive. First come the willow grouse, hazel grouse, woodcock, grate, single, and jack snipe, golden plover, curlew, corn crake, *et alia*. The double snipe arrive about the twelfth of August, but a night's frost will drive them southwards. Then come the incantations of Asia: duck, teal, thrush, titmouse, swallow, sparrow, swan, fieldfair, wildgoose, nightingale, plover, raven, lark, lubber, goldfinch, seagull, and merganser. (Also cranes and white pelican, though these are not considered at the head of the game list.)

The foreign minister of the country, Count Moritz Achilles Zich, founder of the famous antlers collections in Munich, often leaves his estate at eleven at night, shoots his birds high in the mountains, and is back for his daily duties at seven. At Scipsi, in 1895, he shot eleven hundred and twenty pheasants in one day, dispensing twenty-five thousand Purdey cartridges, and near Chorgo he had the good fortune to bag thirty-two duck with a single discharge of his gun. His estate at Malaka includes eagles, vultures, and flamingoes on the jealously preserved game list, though in middle age his most esteemed sport is the killing of skylarks with golf balls.

The ibex was reintroduced to Cannonia by Victor Emmanuel and was carefully preserved there by his son, King Humbert, until his assassination. The golden pheasant was provided to several forests by a former Marquis of Breadalbane, and the mouflon is from an unknown donor in Hungary. The American rainbow trout and turkey were imported in the 1890s, as were the great gray wolf from Iskalisia; oryx and coubain hail from the Grand Duke Serge's estate in the Caucasus. One can replicate here the equivalent of Turkish sea fishing, a goose shoot at Seville, the ibex stalking of Novgorod, an otter drive in the Pontine Marshes, or the dolphin shooting off Cattegat.

In July, when raspberries come, the bear turns vegetarian; then mulberries and wild apples in the month of September; then acorns in October and November. By the end of September, *Black Game* have retired to the thickest woods. The willow grouse are so packed in the turnip fields as to defy the wariest dog; the rest have left for warmer climes. It is now that the bateau and boat shooting commences. Punts contain boatmen only. In coot-drives the etiquette is to complete the line and keep it closed, driving from one end of the lake to the other, pressing the game ashore. If the birds should fly overhead and settle on the other side of the line, the punts are put about and the drive repeated from the other side.

In bustard-stalking, the sportsman goes to the other extreme, making no attempt to hide, but on the contrary, showing himself carelessly, as if unaware of the birds' presence. In a native cart with a thatched roof he drives slowly beside the plowed fields like some farmer inspecting his land, then brings them down with a knout.

Rabbits are met with in most places, even in the dunes, and are not protected. Ferrets are used to thin them out. There are red and white hares in the woods that may be enticed by imitating a doe's bleat, which may also produce the bonus of an amorous, twenty-six point red buck.

The winter season comprises the following: vulpecibism is not here considered a crime, and many a gallant fox has fallen from a deadly barrel behind a bateau. As the country is mostly unrideable, foxes are nevertheless contingent and are trapped adrag, or hunted with clubs near Phamaphy.

The forest pig should be approached from behind, leaping upon it and gripping it with your knees. While grasping with one hand the thick mane of the creature's shine, plunge the knife into the body behind the right shoulder blade, between the first and second ribs.

With bear, the Sportsman is generally provided with two guns and a spear as a *dernier ressort*. When ringing a bear, as it is termed, should the peasant guide again cross the track of a bear he knows is out of the circle when making his ring, rather than returning to his starting point, he will accordingly follow the fresh track. Many Sportsmen will pursue only when the animal has settled himself for the winter. When the peasant has discovered the spot where he has made his den, the Sportsman thus informed goes to the place alone, generally taking with him three or four rough dogs, to rouse the bear from his lair; and thus he has only himself to blame if he returns empty-handed (or does not return).

Wolves are very wary, difficult to drive from their lurking place. (Tether a young pig as bait and pinch its ear to make him squeak.)

On the inaccessible little island of Reil, once featured on coins (unapproachable and fog-bound most of the year), one may stalk a group of ibex which have been carried there by volcanic disruption. Patriarchal rams have dark yellow fleece. The parti-colored hybrids are bigger and more powerful with superb ebony black horns which curve backward, saberlike, almost to the spine, like the bow of Pandarus. No dog can keep up with them.

The coveted lynx, our European tiger, are here considered vermin. In the Marches, miniature antelope sleep like dogs near the railway tracks. As for Belgian wolves and white blackbirds, more people talk of them than see them.

The Mze, as Thucydides tells us, is the "fishiest" river in Europe, "comprised of two-thirds fish and one-third water." To this unaddicted observer, the fish seem quite unsophisticated, picking at almost any fly in the book at random, though the gaudier ones are preferred. The tributaries are run with trout of microscopic size, as well as salmon (the only piscivorous animals which profit by abundance.) A new American method to catch pike involves a short line, a strong hook, and a big worm. The great sturgeon must be shot in the head, for if wounded, they go off at great speed or sink immediately, only to reappear inflated by decomposition. They are best retrieved by two large men in a rowboat, though recently a Russian prince retrieved thirteen in five days by swimming. Ponds should be avoided as the natives often net the narrow places and dynamite the deeper pools.

Among our most intrepid guests are, of course, those English counts and American physicians who court landrails, the king of quails, returning home with barrels of them preserved by cooks, and generally setting off a great migration of dead birds by steam launch to the poulterer's. Often they use lighted torches to attract exhausted quails, net larks at night, surprise wild bustards with their wings frozen (driving them in this helpless state straight to market) and gather wild ducks after the frost, starved to death on the golf links. Their weapon of choice is a .303 sporting Lee-Metford or Mannlicher.

But true sport in Cannonia is for neither show nor pot. You will find no downy tailfeathers of the golden eagle in our hats. Only the Capercailzie Chase, our national sport, retains its original characteristics, which the invasion of the Western hunters have banished from so much of our cultural life.

The male of the species capercailzie is in splendid condition in April, when the valley corn is still short, his beak ornamented with a pair of bristling mustachios which he will soon lose to his rivals. When the cock and hen are seeking each other at first light (or twilight) they make low deep notes of love somewhat resembling a woodcutter's saw, notes that cannot be imitated in words or music, and it is only in April or possibly early May, when his lovesong betrays him, that the Sportsman can locate this wild and timid bird, and then only his silhouette on the driest limb of the tallest tree.

Leave the three or four hours before dawn, astonishing the poultry. Flop the old horse behind the ears with a pig-driving whip. Load your dog in the fantail of the gig. Set out chuckling silently and at the very best pace, on the lane leading to the steepest mountains, for the capercailzie lives only where the water rushes dangerously down from the hills. The standard uniform for such a hunt is a loose gray Tyrolese coat with buckthorn buttons, trousers garnished with green braid, mouse-gray felt boots fit loosely at the ankle, and a Phrygian cap. The dog should be cleansed the night before with a douche of rhubarb, aloe, syrup of buckthorn, and Castile soap.

If nothing can be done in Cannonia without a count, in Klavierland nothing can be accomplished without a dog, and of its many species, only the Chetvorah is capable of dealing with the capercailzie.

Full-blooded, sanguine, up and apt, the Chetvorah are bred to leave their point and return to the Sportsman, showing by their movements that they have found game, an invaluable quality in thick cover. They must point and retrieve alike; in summer act as bloodhound on the trail of a wounded roe; in winter retrieve ducks from water; and in spring act as a spaniel for snipe. In September they must take no notice whatsoever of hares, but two months later they must hunt them down without noticing partridges, as well as retrieve teal from ice-floes. (Occasionally, with large game, they will adopt the expedient of Ulysses and squat upon the ground.)

The capercailzie is the oldest, largest, wariest, and proudest member of the *Black Game* genus, as well as the finest table bird in history. He has been with us since before the Ice Age and will, no doubt, survive us as a species. While his crowing and rearing grounds occupy the wildest areas of the world, where his chicks survive chiefly on bilberries, the adult bird prefers the edge of man's destructiveness, diligently following the axe, the plough, and his fist of fire. In ancient times, they were salted and exported to China, and while small families of distant relatives survive in the Italian Undine (*Valsavaranici pharatrope*), the Black Forest (*Kaltebrooner bastobarbus*), the Scanian Forest (*Fjall ripa*), and in Siberia (*Glukar naryank*), they were extinct in Britain by 1760, the only one left is stuffed in the Earl of Surrey's manse (the Earl being the first man to teach a dog to stand before the gun), and they thrive today only in the Unnamed Mountains of Cannonia.

As a semi-historical bird of Jove in a semi-natural habitat, the capercailzie live a strange and most fascinating life. Never a corsair of reckless daring, he is a woodland sage of unusually perceptive faculties, a wisdom which profits by past experience, and he becomes wild only as an essential to his existence. (Since the children of Israel slew nine thousand at Kobroth-Hataaven in 1350 BC, the modern record is held by Count Zich, who killed eighteen sitting on a rail fence atop a stone dyke while they were looking in different directions.)

With his bristling beautiful plumage—brownish-black speckled with light gray and tan, emerald-breasted with red and yellow spots and feathered to the toes—he would do credit to an ancient eastern potentate. (The Astingi will use no other feathers on their arrows.) His voice—*tack, tack, tackatack a tack*—will tell you when a female of any race is in close proximity.

As you squat beneath a dripping tree, listening for the first clucks of the invisible fowl perched in the countless branches around you, all social distinctions dissolve as you await the lovelorn bird. The call is not only meant to bewilder and fluster his foes, but also to entertain them with the odd, ridiculous mockery of a professional clown. But the peculiarity of the bird is that at the end of his call, he will close his eyes, spin around, and become oblivious to everything. In this trance is the only time you can advance.

As you scramble up the mountains in the dark, it may be necessary to hang a tiny lantern from the tail of your Chetvorah so that he might repeat his lessons *en miniature*. Once on the weird plateaus of Exiliadesertas, where in April violets and buttercups burst from the earth the instant the snow melts, the stalk commences as soon as it's light enough to see the end of the gun barrel.

Now we enter the ancient space, between the prey's apprehension and the predator's alertness, for during his call the bird cannot hear and the dog cannot see. The dog creeps a few feet, from tree to tree, then stops and waits for the hunter to draw alongside. Then the man takes the lead, creeping a few feet on all fours, and the dog, between stanzas, gauging his steps carefully, reciprocates his crabwise movement, which is not random though it may appear so. We are not between ideas (as those parasitic priests and peripateticizing professors who pass themselves off as the friends and disciples of those whose sufferings they live off, would have it) but between two sets of *instincts*—which is a finer way of looking at the world, as reason is not a force but only one weapon of the warring instincts.

Nor is this the place for bourgeois hunter lads, for woe to those who are limited to being happy only in the style of their times. Mad with the untold misery of those who hunt regularly but do not like it, they seek honor where none is to be found and pleasure in places where no pleasure lies for them. As the stalk draws nigh, such poor fellows' delights become vague and still more vague, emptying their flasks before noon, and yet they talk of nothing but their runs, worse than the barrister who talks of nothing but his briefs; most tedious and heavy in hand, such toy histories. For sport requires something more than a Sportsman, as one must see whole the stages by which the hunter becomes the hunted.

This war of two instincts must be mediated by a third, for contrary to conventional wisdom, the instincts of men go to far greater extremes than those of animals, especially when acting en masse. *Tack, tack, tackatack a tack.* Now the Chetvorah's time has come, where all models, methodologies, paradigms, and parameters have been abolished, and one must rely upon a love quite distinct from the love one feels for oneself. Man is *une bête d'aveu* (a confessing animal) and man requires the Chetvorah's classic firmness and *scrupulosité* to mitigate our most recent mannered tendernesses.

Presently you will discover how much your dog is like you in action and temperament. For during the short time the bird is in a trance it is possible to take three long steps toward it, then quickly come to a halt before the next stanza, behind a tree large enough to hide. When making this stalk, it is the Chetvorah who picks the next tree, often standing straight up on his hinder legs to conceal himself and beckoning you with a single vibrating ear. (Whilst waiting, take care to neither whistle, whittle, nor munch on bilberries, but occupy yourself only with the plaiting of grasses.)

Prompted by the occasion, we are summoned to the final stage of education, and the hardest. For the dog has, after all, been trained to point, retrieve, and track—yet the bird is too high to give a scent, strong enough to carry away any ball or shot, and is in any case too large to retrieve. To go the final mile, it is necessary to roust out the errors which come from undivided attention. For to succeed in Sport, forgetfulness is the precondition for all action; one must disrecollect the last thing one has learned.

The bird's antics permit us to advance another three steps into a stand-off, where the dog dares not to move and the bird dares not to call. In the gray dawn, the envelope of the real, in a world without premises and presuming, where our duo knows only that they do not know what is going to happen, they must slip the wraiths of reason, fantasy, memory, and education, and lay down the gauntlet of the heart. Submerged in this atrocious confluence of nothingness, wrapped in their solitude, both must exercise a *counter-instinct*; the Chetvorah realizing that the time has come for the dumber of the two parties to take the lead, straight upstream against the current of their training time together, an *impromptu extempore.*

For your part, *Chasseur*, do not allow your sport to consume you. One must not be reluctant to abandon what it has cost so many hours to learn—that is to say, one must give up the role of Master, and in directing movement, do so in a way which does not invite a particular response. No written lesson, no spoken words, no lectures, be they too often repeated, can teach a dog or man to finish the capercailzie chase with a flourish. If there's an ultimate command, 'tis this: "Don't look at me; I'll follow you."

So if you would not break the hunter's heart, let the hound be your mark. In all the packs of hounds and herds of hunters that you see, only one is really hunting, the others are just doing what the others do. It is for you to follow the real guide in view, not behind your hound but drawing alongside, keeping your distance but losing no yard, whilst not reminding him of your presence. It should be your honor and glory to so place yourself, and *si inter eos ita vives, te vertens sicut se vertuant, sed numquam inter eos verteus* ("If thus you live with them, turning as they turn, but never turning among them") you will have mastered, with the help of your wide-awake wiseacre, the noble artifice of *venere*, the aim of which is no affected piety, but a sentient society without sanctimony, where the estimable is esteemed and the mediocre ignored, the style of styles. For an alert respect is the highest mood a man can hope for, and the most difficult of all to sustain.

Then that liminal figure who sings and dances suddenly flies up, rising as always with his breast upwind, not from fright but in laughing sadness, to settle on a rock, soft with lichen, where he may better copulate. And one feels that miraculous exhilaration which hunters have experienced from the beginning of time. The world ceases to exist, and nothing else matters but this perpetually alert encounter on the bulge of the horizon—a *delectatio nervosa*. Thus the sunken world arises.

Black Game forever foresees the hunter and lives forever in the hunter's eyes. We hunt each other's favors, but keep score by different rules. And the truth is, man promiscuously hunts whatever crosses his path, so why not devote ourselves to a first-rate quarry? Life is a grandiose torment and something of a joke, but we together, fellow hedonists and fellow victims, may for a moment outwit existence.

As the day wears on and you fail to hold your sights even on a haystack, the sundry violent hisses are repeated as two knives whetting against one another, until further acceleration seems impossible. Finally, often between five and six P.M., the male closes with a distinct *smack*. (Before the amorous ditty ceases, all must be still as the grave, as the twilight reveals the hunter, his dog calmly backing him, balancing on one leg in the final approach: the *anspringen*.)

When he emits his *smack*, the bird is entirely deaf for a moment and his eyes shut for three or four seconds, just time enough for a man to make a large jump toward him. Even the greatest Sportsman will turn away his head as he pulls the trigger in partial disgrace.

CHARLES NEWMAN (1938–2006) was born in St. Louis and grew up in the Chicago area. In 1964 he became editor of *TriQuarterly*, which he nurtured into a journal with an international reputation. Newman's own novels have been compared to the work of both Thomas Pynchon and J. D. Salinger, and his two works of nonfiction are both classics of the form. Newman was a professor at Washington University in St. Louis from 1985 until his death.

SELECTED DALKEY ARCHIVE TITLES

HENRY GREEN, *Back.*
Blindness.
Concluding.
Doting.
Nothing.
JACK GREEN, *Fire the Bastards!*
JIŘÍ GRUŠA, *The Questionnaire.*
MELA HARTWIG, *Am I a Redundant Human Being?*
JOHN HAWKES, *The Passion Artist.*
Whistlejacket.
ELIZABETH HEIGHWAY, ED., *Contemporary Georgian Fiction.*
ALEKSANDAR HEMON, ED., *Best European Fiction.*
AIDAN HIGGINS, *Balcony of Europe.*
Blind Man's Bluff
Bornholm Night-Ferry.
Flotsam and Jetsam.
Langrishe, Go Down.
Scenes from a Receding Past.
KEIZO HINO, *Isle of Dreams.*
KAZUSHI HOSAKA, *Plainsong.*
ALDOUS HUXLEY, *Antic Hay.*
Crome Yellow.
Point Counter Point.
Those Barren Leaves.
Time Must Have a Stop.
NAOYUKI II, *The Shadow of a Blue Cat.*
GERT JONKE, *The Distant Sound.*
Geometric Regional Novel.
Homage to Czerny.
The System of Vienna.
JACQUES JOUET, *Mountain R.*
Savage.
Upstaged.
MIEKO KANAI, *The Word Book.*
YORAM KANIUK, *Life on Sandpaper.*
HUGH KENNER, *Flaubert.*
Joyce and Beckett: The Stoic Comedians.
Joyce's Voices.
DANILO KIŠ, *The Attic.*
Garden, Ashes.
The Lute and the Scars
Psalm 44.
A Tomb for Boris Davidovich.
ANITA KONKKA, *A Fool's Paradise.*
GEORGE KONRÁD, *The City Builder.*
TADEUSZ KONWICKI, *A Minor Apocalypse.*
The Polish Complex.
MENIS KOUMANDAREAS, *Koula.*
ELAINE KRAF, *The Princess of 72nd Street.*
JIM KRUSOE, *Iceland.*
AYŞE KULIN, *Farewell: A Mansion in Occupied Istanbul.*
EMILIO LASCANO TEGUI, *On Elegance While Sleeping.*
ERIC LAURRENT, *Do Not Touch.*
VIOLETTE LEDUC, *La Bâtarde.*
EDOUARD LEVÉ, *Autoportrait.*
Suicide.
MARIO LEVI, *Istanbul Was a Fairy Tale.*
DEBORAH LEVY, *Billy and Girl.*
JOSÉ LEZAMA LIMA, *Paradiso.*
ROSA LIKSOM, *Dark Paradise.*
OSMAN LINS, *Avalovara.*
The Queen of the Prisons of Greece.
ALF MAC LOCHLAINN,
The Corpus in the Library.
Out of Focus.
RON LOEWINSOHN, *Magnetic Field(s).*
MINA LOY, *Stories and Essays of Mina Loy.*

D. KEITH MANO, *Take Five.*
MICHELINE AHARONIAN MARCOM,
The Mirror in the Well.
BEN MARCUS,
The Age of Wire and String.
WALLACE MARKFIELD,
Teitlebaum's Window.
To an Early Grave.
DAVID MARKSON, *Reader's Block.*
Wittgenstein's Mistress.
CAROLE MASO, *AVA.*
LADISLAV MATEJKA AND KRYSTYNA POMORSKA, EDS.,
Readings in Russian Poetics: Formalist and Structuralist Views.
HARRY MATHEWS, *Cigarettes.*
The Conversions.
The Human Country: New and Collected Stories.
The Journalist.
My Life in CIA.
Singular Pleasures.
The Sinking of the Odradek Stadium.
Tlooth.
JOSEPH MCELROY,
Night Soul and Other Stories.
ABDELWAHAB MEDDEB, *Talismano.*
GERHARD MEIER, *Isle of the Dead.*
HERMAN MELVILLE, *The Confidence-Man.*
AMANDA MICHALOPOULOU, *I'd Like.*
STEVEN MILLHAUSER, *The Barnum Museum.*
In the Penny Arcade.
RALPH J. MILLS, JR., *Essays on Poetry.*
MOMUS, *The Book of Jokes.*
CHRISTINE MONTALBETTI, *The Origin of Man.*
Western.
OLIVE MOORE, *Spleen.*
NICHOLAS MOSLEY, *Accident.*
Assassins.
Catastrophe Practice.
Experience and Religion.
A Garden of Trees.
Hopeful Monsters.
Imago Bird.
Impossible Object.
Inventing God.
Judith.
Look at the Dark.
Natalie Natalia.
Serpent.
Time at War.
WARREN MOTTE,
Fables of the Novel: French Fiction since 1990.
Fiction Now: The French Novel in the 21st Century.
Oulipo: A Primer of Potential Literature.
GERALD MURNANE, *Barley Patch.*
Inland.
YVES NAVARRE, *Our Share of Time.*
Sweet Tooth.
DOROTHY NELSON, *In Night's City.*
Tar and Feathers.
ESHKOL NEVO, *Homesick.*
WILFRIDO D. NOLLEDO, *But for the Lovers.*
FLANN O'BRIEN, *At Swim-Two-Birds.*
The Best of Myles.
The Dalkey Archive.
The Hard Life.
The Poor Mouth.

FOR A FULL LIST OF PUBLICATIONS, VISIT:
www.dalkeyarchive.com

SELECTED DALKEY ARCHIVE TITLES

FOR A FULL LIST OF PUBLICATIONS, VISIT:
www.dalkeyarchive.com

SELECTED DALKEY ARCHIVE TITLES

DUMITRU TSEPENEAG, *Hotel Europa.*
   The Necessary Marriage.
   Pigeon Post.
   Vain Art of the Fugue.
ESTHER TUSQUETS, *Stranded.*
DUBRAVKA UGRESIC, *Lend Me Your Character.*
   Thank You for Not Reading.
TOR ULVEN, *Replacement.*
MATI UNT, *Brecht at Night.*
   Diary of a Blood Donor.
   Things in the Night.
ÁLVARO URIBE AND OLIVIA SEARS, EDS.,
   Best of Contemporary Mexican Fiction.
ELOY URROZ, *Friction.*
   The Obstacles.
LUISA VALENZUELA, *Dark Desires and*
   the Others.
   He Who Searches.
PAUL VERHAEGHEN, *Omega Minor.*
AGLAJA VETERANYI, *Why the Child Is*
   Cooking in the Polenta.
BORIS VIAN, *Heartsnatcher.*
LLORENÇ VILLALONGA, *The Dolls' Room.*
TOOMAS VINT, *An Unending Landscape.*
ORNELA VORPSI, *The Country Where No*
   One Ever Dies.
AUSTRYN WAINHOUSE, *Hedyphagetica.*
CURTIS WHITE, *America's Magic Mountain.*
   The Idea of Home.
   Memories of My Father Watching TV.
   Requiem.

DIANE WILLIAMS, *Excitability:*
   Selected Stories.
   Romancer Erector.
DOUGLAS WOOLF, *Wall to Wall.*
   Ya! & John-Juan.
JAY WRIGHT, *Polynomials and Pollen.*
   The Presentable Art of Reading
   Absence.
PHILIP WYLIE, *Generation of Vipers.*
MARGUERITE YOUNG, *Angel in the Forest.*
   Miss MacIntosh, My Darling.
REYOUNG, *Unbabbling.*
VLADO ŽABOT, *The Succubus.*
ZORAN ŽIVKOVIĆ, *Hidden Camera.*
LOUIS ZUKOFSKY, *Collected Fiction.*
VITOMIL ZUPAN, *Minuet for Guitar.*
SCOTT ZWIREN, *God Head.*

FOR A FULL LIST OF PUBLICATIONS, VISIT:
www.dalkeyarchive.com